THE EXECUTIONER'S REBELLION

THE EXECUTIONER'S SONG BOOK 4

D.K. HOLMBERG

ASH PUBLISHING

CHAPTER ONE

The iron master guarding the debtors' prison was a dark-haired man with a sour expression, and the sunlight coming through the windows reflected off of his receding hairline. He'd been at the job for many years and had survived the purge of iron masters when Finn and Meyer had gone looking for rot.

"Wilbur. How are you today?"

The iron master cocked his head, frowning at Finn. "Didn't expect to see the Hunter."

Finn snorted. He still didn't care for his nickname any more than he cared for the first one he'd been given. He supposed it *was* better than just being called Hangman.

"I'm here to see Reginald."

"You mean the bastard they brought in last night?" Wilbur asked. "Can't believe he'd make a mistake like that. Swindling his way in that section? Gods, you've got to be stupid to pull something like that."

In that part of Verendal, too many had money, the kind of real money that easily recognized somebody who didn't *really* have it. When Reginald had decided to try not to pay someone he owed, they had quickly reported him to the Archers. It didn't take long before he ended up in the debtors' prison and drew Finn's attention.

Even without having met with Reginald yet, Finn had an idea why he *had* caught his attention. There was a sense of pride in a man's station, and if he felt his station was threatened, he would do whatever it took to maintain it. Sometimes, that meant going to extreme lengths.

"Can you bring him to the closet?" Finn asked Wilbur.

He nodded at Finn.

Finn headed into the prison. The air had a fragrance to it, a hint of rose or perhaps tulip. The distinction between the two was not so easy for him, despite his training with apothecary medicine. The walls were smooth stone, and windows high overhead allowed plenty of sunlight into the room. He hurried along, the steady clopping of his boots over the stone the only sound that carried.

The closet was similar to the chapel in Declan, though there wasn't the same feeling of violence. It was almost comfortable.

He looked over to the cupboard. The closet didn't even have any of the same implements for questioning. There simply wasn't the need.

He didn't have to wait long before Reginald was brought in.

Reginald had a neatly trimmed beard, a thick mustache with a bit of oil curling the ends, and close-cropped hair.

He was dressed in prison gray. There was something almost dignified about him, as if regardless of where he was and how he was dressed, it didn't really matter to him. It was as if he were the questioner, not the prisoner.

Wilbur put him into a seat. The chair was small and smooth, and it didn't have the same straps as those in Declan. He didn't expect Reginald to react with the same sort of violence that he often encountered in the chapel, either.

Finn nodded to Wilbur. "I can take it from here."

"I can wait with you if you think he's going to be a handful."

"Are you going to be a handful?" Finn asked Reginald.

Reginald cocked one brow, glaring at Finn. "I'm here, aren't I?"

"You're here now, but do you intend to cause trouble?"

Reginald leaned back, still glaring, and crossed his arms over his chest, a gesture that made it seem as if he were in control of the situation. It was an effective strategy, especially considering how he had pulled off his swindle. Give the appearance of wealth and make it easier for others to believe he was exactly what he claimed.

Wilbur stepped out, closing the door.

Finn pulled a stool over, setting it down in front of Reginald, and leaned forward, resting his elbows on his knees. "Tell me what happened."

"What's there to say? I'm here. So, obviously, I owe someone money."

"Obviously."

"As I'm sure you're aware, anyone can make that claim. That doesn't mean it's justified."

Finn chuckled slightly. That was the angle he was going to take?

It might even work. At least, it might have worked had he pulled that on Finn earlier in his career. Finn had been an executioner for the better part of seven years now, and with that experience came a certain understanding of the kind of men he dealt with; he knew what to expect from them, especially when they were guilty.

"Perhaps the claim on you has more merit to it than you believe." Finn leaned toward him, aware of the menace in the gesture.

"Why?"

"Because I'm here," Finn said.

"They called you *Hunter*. You some kind of debt chaser?"

"You can call me executioner," he said. It had the desired reaction. Reginald leaned back again, his eyes widening slightly.

"I didn't do anything to bring the executioner here."

"You did something." He left it unsaid that he was here as inquisitor.

"Nothing I need to hang for."

Finn shrugged. "It's possible your stature would get you the sword, not the rope."

Reginald watched Finn and crossed his arms over his chest again. His sleeve pulled as he moved his arm, revealing a tattoo of a black rose. "What am I accused of doing?"

Finn studied him. Given Reginald's current predicament, he should be more concerned. "We're going to start again. I don't have any problem with having you brought to a different prison. Maybe you'd prefer to spend your days in Declan."

He tensed but his expression didn't change. "I haven't done anything to be placed there."

"At this point, I can't say with any certainty what you have or have not done, especially as you've decided not to share any information with me. You can tell me everything, and when you do..."

Finn preferred to let the fear of what might happen be the reason Reginald decided to share, and whether he chose to elaborate was up to him.

Reginald looked past Finn, glancing at the door. "They would've told you."

"They would have, but I find it better to uncover the answers myself."

"Why? So you can let me hang myself?"

Finn chuckled, shaking his head. "Again with the hanging. As I told you, you wouldn't hang. You might see the sharp edge of the sword, though, which many think is better." That was assuming he deserved that status and hadn't simply scammed his way to it.

"Many wouldn't be facing the blade."

"You might be surprised."

"How many have you hanged?"

"More than you care to know," Finn said softly.

"How many?"

Finn looked up, holding Reginald's gaze. "This isn't

going to go the way you think it is. You aren't in control of the situation. I am."

Reginald glared at Finn again. Something in his demeanor shifted, and there was a flicker of the confidence he displayed when he'd first been brought back. "You have no right to hold me here."

"The king would say otherwise." He turned casually, looking toward the door. "And I'm thinking the accusations about you are accurate. In that case, you *would* get the rope." He looked back at him. "Maybe you *will* do better in Declan. I have access to better tools there, and with someone like you, someone who's been so belligerent so early on, I'm starting to wonder if perhaps I need those tools. Maybe it would serve both of us better if I had even more control of the situation."

He started to get up when Reginald raised his hand. "Stop."

"I told you. I'm in control here."

"I know," he said hurriedly. "I'm not trying to take control." Reginald looked toward the door, then behind him, seemingly seeing the cabinets for the first time. Maybe that would be enough for him to realize that Finn had some items here he could use to interrogate. Not nearly as many as he had in Declan, though enough to intimidate him. "What do you want to know?" Reginald asked, his voice losing some of its hard edge.

"Let's start with where you live."

"What does that have to do with anything?"

"I'm trying to determine how much you're going to tell me, and how much of it's the truth. If you decide to keep the truth from me..." Finn looked over to the cabinets. There really wasn't much there for him to use, but the threat of something more, the threat of the possibility of a more enhanced type of questioning, had its value.

"I live on the edge of the Hamel section. Is that what you wanted to know?"

Finn smiled tightly. The Hamel section was one of the wealthier parts of the city, home to merchants and other people with money—many of them *old* money, the kind of place Finn and his crew once would have targeted.

But that wasn't where Reginald really lived.

The *edge* of the section was different—home to new money, and those who wanted to play at having money. That was where Reginald lived.

"That's a start. Now, for what reason are you here?"

"I'm here because somebody turned on me," he said softly.

"You don't think you're guilty?"

Reginald snorted. "Guilt. What did I do that hurt anyone?"

Finn had moved past arguing with people like him. There was a time when he would've explained the consequences, when he would have shared with somebody like Reginald how his actions *had* hurt someone else, but Finn no longer found it worth it.

If he didn't see how what he did hurt someone, and if he couldn't see how stealing from someone who couldn't afford to lose what they took was wrong, then Finn wasn't going to be able to change his mind. All Finn could do was acquire the details of the crime. Then, hopefully, the jurors would see fit to sentence him in a way that would help him grasp the severity of his actions.

"Again," Finn said, "we can do this any way you like. If you want to make this complicated, that's your prerogative."

Finn waited a moment, watching Reginald.

Every so often, Reginald seemed as if he wanted to flash the same arrogance he'd had when he first came in, though the longer he was here, the longer that arrogance started to fade, disappearing to the point where Finn started to think Reginald might actually talk.

"What do you think I did that hurt anyone?"

Finn leaned back, his gaze lingering on Reginald. This was a man who didn't even see what he had done, didn't recognize the way his actions had hurt somebody else. This was somebody who felt as if he were above the law. Here Finn had started to think Reginald was some sort of a swindler, but maybe that wasn't the case. Maybe Reginald was simply not smart enough to do that.

Arrogance. That was his crime.

Finn had been around plenty of people like that over the years, and while he didn't like them, as a general rule, he at least understood them.

"Like I said, we're going to go through this carefully, and you're going to reveal to me what you did."

"I didn't do anything other than..."

Finn got to his feet. "I see. Normally when I come to the debtors' prison, I find the people here are a little more accommodating, but occasionally I find someone like yourself—someone who thinks they're beyond the rule of law." Finn just shrugged. "I do have ways of handling men like that."

He pulled open the door. Wilbur stood outside, resting his back against the stone, and he hurriedly stood up straighter. "Did you get what you needed, Hunter?"

Finn cast a glance over her shoulder. "Unfortunately, no."

"Well, you know how those highborn folks can be."

"Do I?"

"Seeing as how you're highborn yourself, that is."

Finn resisted the urge to laugh. "See him to Declan. I intend to question him more there."

Wilbur's eyes widened a little bit. "Declan? You sure about that?"

"Is there a problem with that?"

Wilbur blinked, turning to Finn, and he shook his head quickly. "Of course not, Hunter—I mean, Mr. Jagger. I can get him transferred this morning."

Finn glanced back at Reginald. He didn't take much joy in the idea of transferring a man like him to Declan, but he wasn't about to have a man like him continue to challenge his authority, nor was he about to let him escape the arm of the law.

Finn turned, prepared to head out of the debtors' prison, but changed his mind and made his way toward the warden's office.

He hadn't visited the warden that often. Ever since Declan's previous warden had been involved with witchcraft, Finn had taken a very different approach to addressing the wardens. It was a lesson Master Meyer had wanted him to learn anyway, though he suspected Master Meyer would've preferred it be a lesson that Finn would have mastered in some other manner—through time and experience, not through the near destruction of the prison system.

There were paintings along the wall, most of them depicting the king and his predecessors, but there were a few of the previous wardens—serious men stylized to look regal. It reminded him of what he'd seen in the Heshian Palace when he had visited King Porman. There was no real malicious intent here, he didn't think, but these portraits celebrated the wardens rather than the kings.

He stared at one of them. The man was older, with a balding head and piercing blue eyes that gazed out at him. A small silver badge along the bottom of the portrait revealed his name: Idathon Bruster.

Likely he was important, or had been, but was he so important that he should be immortalized within the prison? Finn doubted that he or Master Meyer would ever have a portrait of themselves hanging anywhere within the kingdom—not that he necessarily wanted one. He wasn't sure how he wanted to be remembered, if at all.

"Can I help… Mr. Jagger?"

Finn looked down the hallway. Warden Arlington was an older man with graying hair, ruddy cheeks, and a thin nose. He had been stationed within the debtors' prison for the better part of ten years, and as far as Finn had been able to tell, he still served well, despite the upheaval within Declan.

"Warden Arlington. I was admiring the artwork."

Arlington joined him, keeping a few feet between them. "We have a long tradition of remembering our predecessors here at the debtors' prison."

"Only a few of the king and his family," Finn said.

"The king has his own decorations throughout the city. He doesn't need them here," Arlington said.

Finn glanced over. "We serve the king's justice here. In all things."

Arlington opened his mouth before closing it again. He just nodded. "Perhaps a modification in our decoration is in order," he mused.

"Perhaps."

"Did you come to admire the artwork, or was there another reason for your visit?"

Finn smiled to himself. The warden supervised the prison, but the executioner supervised *the wardens* and the prisons. It had taken Finn a long time in his service as an executioner to feel confident in that role. Even now that he was a journeyman, Finn wasn't always comfortable in that role.

"*Should* I have another reason for my visit?" Finn asked, turning to glance at Warden Arlington. He cocked a brow at him, regarding him with as much intensity as he could muster. Finn didn't necessarily know Warden Arlington well, though he had taken the time to become more than passingly acquainted with him. It was what Master Meyer had asked of him. "Supervising the prisons is just one aspect of the assignment the king has given me in Verendal."

"The king himself?"

Finn tipped his head in a nod. "Indeed. Does that surprise you?"

"I'm only surprised that the king has any interest in the prisons at all," Warden Arlington said. "For years, he's left us to our own devices. We *are* isolated, as you know."

"Perhaps too much," Finn said. "Though not nearly as isolated as some might think. We still must adhere to the rule of the law. And the king does make his presence known from time to time." Lately, he'd made his presence known more often than Finn would've expected.

Some of that had to do with the events that had transpired during the time Finn had served as an executioner, though some of it predated that. The role of the Alainsith certainly did. The treaty with them had required constant attention.

"As you can see, the debtors' prison runs quite smoothly. I have ensured that we follow the king's rule of law in all things," Warden Arlington said.

Finn glanced over. "In all things?"

Arlington clenched his fists. "In all things, Mr. Jagger. We have a measure of pride here you don't see in all prisons."

Finn smiled, trying to reassure him. He didn't need Arlington on the defensive.

"I think all wardens pride themselves on how they run their prison," Finn said.

"Maybe, but not all do it nearly as effectively as I do." Arlington smiled tightly, turning to Finn. "That is one advantage of us having this wall of previous wardens on display. We can see where we've come from and we have an obligation to fulfill the requirements of office in a way that would make our predecessors proud."

If that was the case, then maybe Arlington served the way he claimed. He was willing to give him the benefit of the doubt.

"I came to visit with Reginald Smith. He was not the most forthcoming."

"He's an arrogant man," Arlington said, shaking his head. "As I'm sure you have determined. We can continue questioning him for you."

"There will be no need," Finn said, waving his hand. "I've taken the liberty to have him moved to Declan."

"Declan? For that crime? You have no need to..." He trailed off as Finn shot him a hard look. "We can obtain the confession," Warden Arlington said carefully.

"What if it's more than just a confession I'm after?" Finn asked.

"What more would you be after?"

Finn just shrugged. "That will be for me to determine. In Declan." He glanced at the wall of portraits again. He noticed a heavyset man with beady eyes and a pointed beard, Arlington's immediate predecessor. "How well did you know him?"

"Warden Loran?" Arlington shook his head. "I served under him for a few years, but I didn't know him well. He was like all of the wardens in the debtors' prison. He wanted nothing more than to ensure we served the king in everything that we did."

"I should hope so," Finn said softly.

"If you would prefer to keep Reginald Smith here, we could convert the closet into a more conventional questioning chamber."

Finn looked over. "Is that what you think I want?"

"I just assumed that was the reason you wanted to bring him to Declan."

Finn regarded the warden for a moment. He knew he had to choose his next words carefully, not wanting to anger him too much, but at the same time, he needed to squash any potential rumors that might have started to spread about him.

Finn was acutely aware of how rumors could spread, and he was acutely aware of his role in those rumors. He had been a part of many of them over the years. From the moment he was first claimed by Master Meyer with his executioner right, Finn had been subjected to rumors. Some were fascinating—such as how Finn had survived his execution, which was the reason Master Meyer had to claim his right—while others were tawdrier, accusing Finn and Master Meyer of some relationship, and that being the reason. Some rumors, like how he had acquired his nickname the Hunter, were fitting. Finn did have a stubbornness to him, and it was through that stubbornness, and the desire for a mixture of justice and vengeance, that he'd uncovered the plot against the city, thwarting it before all of Verendal burned.

Then there was the plot to try to drive a wedge between the Alainsith and the king. That was one Finn had unintentionally discovered, though he was prouder of it. It had revealed the depths of danger within the prison system, the depths of wardens' involvement, at least within Declan and the iron masters, and Finn still struggled with it.

Were there rumors that had started to spread about his interest in interrogations?

He could understand how they might start. They would be tied to his progression as journeyman executioner. Meyer had permitted him to progress, grow, and to take on increasing responsibilities, which involved him handling most of the interrogations. That alone might draw the kind of attention that would lead people to accuse him of an interest in torture.

"There are many reasons I would want him moved to Declan," Finn said carefully. "First and foremost, it would ensure he was secured as well as he needs to be." The warden stiffened. "Then there is the matter of Reginald Smith himself. Declan provides enough of a terrifying environment that a man such as him might be persuaded to share more openly."

"I see."

"Do you?"

The warden frowned at him. "I do. I must say I didn't realize Master Meyer was so near to retirement."

"I didn't make that claim."

"If we are to cater to your needs, Mr. Jagger, then one must assume Master Meyer is nearing his retirement." Warden Arlington cocked his head to the side. "Unless that isn't the case, and he doesn't know you've come here making these demands."

Arlington was pushing back. There was a part of Finn

that actually relished that. He understood, and he thought perhaps it was for the best. Having a strong warden, somebody with a bit of a spine, was beneficial when dealing with prisoners. There was a danger in it, though. Some wardens might see themselves as above the supervision of the executioners—or worse, the law itself.

"Perhaps you would prefer to ask Master Meyer. I can have him stop by, if that would appease you."

Warden Arlington held his gaze. "Why don't you."

Finn turned back to the portraits. "Interesting that these are all here."

"Why is that interesting to you, Mr. Jagger?"

"Well, they have served here and moved on." Finn glanced over to Warden Arlington. "Where will you be moving on to when your time to serve is done?"

Arlington looked straight at Finn, then turned to the portraits, biting back anything more he might say.

CHAPTER TWO

The summons to the prison had come in the middle of the night. Finn got up, the knocking at the door alerting him, and rubbed the sleep from his eyes. His room was small, and the lantern had dimmed to a faint glowing, casting just enough light for him to see the outline of the door.

He stumbled out of bed, heading toward the door, and grabbed a cloak from the closet to cover himself. As he pulled the door open, he frowned.

"What is it?" Finn asked.

A tall, slender Archer stood in the doorway. He had his helm tipped slightly to the side, and his face was lined with wrinkles, his inky eyes making them seem little more than hollows.

"Are you the hangman?"

"Finn Jagger. Did you need the master executioner?" The man looked past Finn for a moment before shrugging and handing him a piece of paper, which Finn took and unfolded. He scanned the page before looking up at the Archer. "When was this sent?"

"Just now."

"Thank you. You may go."

The man's gaze narrowed for a moment, but Finn ignored it as he closed the door. He turned to see Master Meyer standing at the bottom of the stairs, dressed neatly in his pants and jacket, his gray hair combed. "What is it?" he asked.

"It seems my prisoner at the debtors' prison has killed himself."

Meyer frowned. "At the debtors' prison?"

Finn nodded, explaining how Reginald stood accused of stealing from dozens of people in the city. "He didn't strike me as somebody who'd kill himself." And he was *supposed* to have been transferred to Declan for questioning. Finn hadn't been around too many criminals who had killed themselves. Some had tried, but Declan, in particular, made it difficult for anybody to choose their own exit. Most were forced to take the king's justice, and for that, Finn felt a measure of pride. They had secured the prison, along with the clothing, and made sure there was no place men could hang themselves effectively. Master Meyer had done the same in the time before Finn had come, and Finn had worked with him to ensure he secured everything as much as possible.

"You should go," Meyer said. He was steeped in the shadows, only the faint light from Finn's lantern giving off any visibility. Meyer was tall, though his shoulders were a little hunched, as if the weight of the lateness of night weighed upon him. Finn couldn't see the deep wrinkles surrounding his pale-blue eyes, but he imagined the expression Master Meyer looked at him with. He'd seen it far too many times.

"I plan on it," Finn said. "You can get your rest."

Master Meyer chuckled softly. "I'd planned on it." He started toward the stairs. "One of the benefits of being the master executioner."

He trudged up the stairs, his footsteps heavy with a steady thudding. Finn turned back to his room where he quickly got dressed, slipping on a shirt, jacket, pants, and boots. He pulled the cloak back over his shoulders and headed out into the night.

He had no idea how late it was, but he could imagine the hour from how tired he felt. The air was cool, and a hint of a breeze carried the smells of the city, the sound of the water rushing along the Vinlen River, and even an occasional whistle that seemed to come from the forest on the edge of the kingdom.

He made his way along the street. Most within the city had a curfew, primarily to prevent criminals like Finn had once been from having free rein over the city—though there were plenty of criminals who still operated within the city despite the curfew. Finn certainly had. The curfew slowed their work a bit, but didn't stop it altogether—just made it more difficult.

He hurried through the streets, passing a couple of patrolling Archers, nodding to them rather than slowing down and worrying about them. By the time he reached the debtors' prison, he'd finally woken up. A faint sheen of sweat covered his brow. He pulled the keys from his pocket and tested them in the lock, pleased that the warden had found it fitting to lock the door.

Once inside, lanterns glowed softly. The paintings on the walls were darkened, and Finn couldn't tell whether the warden had removed the offending paintings Finn had called out earlier.

He hurried to the row of cells and found the prison humming with activity. A half-dozen lanterns glowed within the area, far more than usual at this time of day. One of the iron masters turned toward Finn, but then relief swept over him.

"Hunter," he said. "We found him like this. We'd been watching, but we don't know how this could have even happened."

"What could have happened?" Finn asked, striding forward.

He didn't need to ask, though.

As he reached the cell, he realized just what had taken place.

He found Reginald wearing only his pants, his shirt somehow tied to the top row of the bars, which weren't nearly as thick here as they were in Declan, though they were thick enough to keep anybody from leaving. They ran from the floor to the ceiling, with the support bars high enough to the stone that nobody could slip anything between them to anchor to. It was equally difficult to do that where the bars met the floor. The cells were designed to make it impossible for anyone to do what Reginald had somehow managed to do. His shirt had bound up along the top of the bar, and he hung from it, his face contorted, eyes bulging, mouth slightly ajar.

"Don't know. Like I said, we found him like this," the iron master said. Finn didn't recognize the man, though he didn't recognize many of them in the debtors' prison. They recognized him, though. "He worked himself up there. Don't even know how such a thing was possible."

Finn reached for the shirt and pulled on it. The cloth slid easily on the crossbar.

Had he ended up in Declan, this wouldn't have happened.

"Let me in," Finn said.

The iron master hurriedly grabbed his keys. Finn could have let himself in, but he wanted to keep an eye on the prisoner. It was possible that Reginald had somehow made it *look* as if he'd died, though Finn had been around plenty of men who'd hanged over the years, and he recognized a distinct bulging of his eyes and an expression of death on his face that couldn't be faked.

The iron master pulled the door open and Finn stepped inside, watching Reginald as he did. He checked him for a heartbeat, for breathing, for anything that might indicate he could be saved, but he was gone.

"I'm going to need to see all of his belongings that the Archers confiscated."

"We'll have to wait until the warden gets in."

Finn looked over to the iron master.

The man's eyes widened, then he nodded hurriedly. "We will get them for you, Hunter."

As Finn prepared to leave Meyer's home the next morning, the old executioner appeared at the bottom of the stairs, frowning at him. He was dressed in his formal clothing, as he often was early in the morning. Finn rarely saw Meyer poorly dressed. The old executioner felt they needed to maintain appearances.

"You're leaving early."

Finn nodded slowly. "Unfortunately, I need to look into what happened to my prisoner. I'm not sure why he would've killed himself."

"That's the working assumption?"

Finn smiled. "I don't think anyone else at the prison did it. At least, not yet." Meyer didn't smile along with him. "I don't want to jump to conclusions, but the most logical explanation is that, yes, he killed himself," Finn said again. The alternative was that someone had managed to sneak into the prison to kill him, and though the prison wasn't as secure as Declan, it would be difficult to do that without attracting notice. "I don't know why. He was a swindler, but he didn't strike me as the kind of man to sacrifice himself."

Meyer nodded, making his way toward the kitchen.

Finn yearned to join him and have breakfast, but that would come later.

"Warden Arlington wants to speak with you."

Meyer paused. "About?"

"About your retirement plans."

Meyer cast him a sideways glance. "Am I retiring?"

"I didn't think so, but I had a few things to say about the portraits in the hall of the debtors' prison. I suggested that they didn't need to honor all of the old wardens."

Meyer's brow furrowed. "I will visit with him."

Finn hesitated. He hadn't been sure what Meyer might do or say, and didn't know if Meyer might be angry with him. He was often difficult to read. "Was I wrong?"

Meyer breathed out slowly. "You have an opinion about how things should be done. That is all I can ask of you."

He started back in the kitchen, and Finn frowned.

That was all?

He expected Meyer to say more, but he found it increasingly difficult to get much out of him these days.

He stepped outside, closing the door behind him, and set off at a quick pace toward Reginald's home. He knew the section, and he had taken time to check the maps Master Meyer had in his home to ensure he knew where to go. It shouldn't be difficult to reach. At this time of day, there wouldn't be too many people up and out, which meant he would be less likely to encounter any stray eyes watching him, questioning why an executioner was in a merchant section of the city.

In the distance, one of the church bells tolled softly. It was a steady ringing, a gentle sound, and he paused long enough to look up and see the Shisen bell tower. From this part of the city, it was usually faint, but maybe in the early morning air it was easier to hear.

As he passed through one section on the outer part of the city, before crossing the Vinlen River, a poster on a tavern caught his attention; it was small, at chest level and slightly off-center.

Finn stopped in front of it. Had there been more people out, he might not even have noticed it. It featured a painting of what looked to be a black rose on a white background. He had seen posters like that around the city quite a few times lately.

He had no idea what their purpose was. Then there was the tattoo on Reginald's arm, which looked very similar. It was something else to look into when he had time.

Finn approached Reginald's home and looked at the houses on either side of it. They were all nice and well-maintained. None of them were terribly large, which wasn't altogether surprising—it was probably expensive to maintain property in this part of the city—and none had walls around them like some of the even nicer houses nearby did. Still, it was more than he would've expected from a man like Reginald.

Now he had to get inside.

There were some skills that still hadn't faded from his days on the thieving crew. He knocked, but he didn't expect anybody to answer. He slipped a lock pick set out of his pocket, having brought it for this specific purpose, and quickly pried open the door.

He paused in the doorway.

The air was musty. Reginald hadn't been imprisoned that long, had he?

He looked around the home and found it to be sparse: two chairs, a table, the trunk in one corner, and a layer of dust over everything.

Finn popped open the windows, letting light in.

He rummaged through the trunk, finding nothing other than a stack of blank papers. When he looked in the kitchen, the cupboards were empty, which was even more unusual. He didn't have any food or utensils—nothing to suggest he even lived here.

Only a bed and a table with a drawer furnished the back room.

Finn pulled open the drawer, finding a small wooden object. It was smooth with a strange symbol on the surface. He'd been exposed to quite a bit of magic lately and knew to treat symbols like that carefully. He traced his finger along it but didn't recognize it. He tucked it into his pocket.

He checked the wardrobe, but it was empty other than a change of clothes that looked like they would fit Reginald, then he pulled back the sheets before lifting up the mattress and finding a black leather-bound book and a wooden marker.

Finn grabbed them and headed back to the other room, taking a seat at the table and flipping open the book. It was a ledger.

He had started to think that maybe this wasn't even Reginald's home. The debtors' prison hadn't had many belongings for him, so anything he learned about him would be found here.

His gaze skimmed across the ledger. He had grown accustomed to reading ledgers like this, and as he looked through it, he found a list of names and businesses.

What reason would Reginald have for keeping a book

like this? Finn would be busy going through this whole list of names, but all he had was the book and the wooden marker.

Finn had to believe that both had been important to Reginald, considering the sparseness of his home.

Now it was up to the Hunter to figure out why.

CHAPTER THREE

F inn stopped at the outside of the small shop on the edge of the river in the Yanish section. The storefront was simple. Judging from the scent of sap and metal, and the wood shavings scattered on the porch, it likely belonged to a carpenter. It was on a narrow street in one of the southern parts of this section. The shops all around were quiet at this early evening hour, and as the cool breeze gusted along the street coming out of the north, Finn pulled his cloak around him. Thankfully, the wind alleviated the city's stench.

Finn had spent the last two days visiting the men from Reginald's ledger. None were helpful. Reginald had owed money to each of them, but not so much that it would have been worth sending him to the debtors' prison for. This was the last place on the list, and Finn wasn't even sure it was the right place.

He knocked, then stepped back. He didn't want to

intimidate or antagonize anybody. This was to be a cordial visit.

The door opened a crack, and a golden-haired young woman peered out through it. "May I help you?" she asked, her voice soft and tinted with a bit of an accent that Finn couldn't quite place.

"I'm looking for a Master Harry James."

"That's my father," the woman said, a question in her piercing blue eyes.

"Is he available to speak with?"

She glanced behind her for a moment before looking back, then nodded slowly. "May I ask what this is about?"

"I just need to speak with him about a business transaction he had been a part of."

The woman's face fell. "What did he do?" she whispered.

"He didn't do anything," Finn said.

She frowned. "He didn't? Then why are you here?"

Finn forced a smile. "I just have a question for him. Nothing more than that."

"My father is a good man. He wouldn't do anything to harm anyone."

"I'm quite sure," Finn said.

She stepped aside and waved for Finn to come in.

He stepped into the shop. The smell of sawdust hung over everything and a layer of it covered the floor.

The young woman closed the door. "Let me go fetch my father. He's just upstairs."

She hurried off, her footsteps light across the sawdust-covered floor, barely kicking up any dust. When she was gone, Finn looked around the inside of the shop. A long table occupied the center, and tools were placed neatly along the table's surface: several saws, a couple hammers, pliers, and other tools Finn didn't recognize.

Stacks of lumber rested in one corner. Most of it was of uniform length and width, though there were some irregular pieces with a rougher bark texture on their exterior.

He turned to the back wall. A row of glass-encased shelving ran along the wall, parallel to the table. Finn headed toward it, hunching over as he peered inside. Most of the work here was intricately done. He saw a bowl with detailed inlay, different diamond patterns of wood set together creating an interlocking weave along with the symbol for Heleth. It was done with as much skill as Finn had ever seen from any woodworker. There was a collection of small circular items too, all of them equally inlaid with a diamond pattern, the wood species seemingly different from each other. As Finn crouched to look at the next shelf down, a voice behind him caught his attention.

"Can I help you?"

Finn straightened, and he turned to see an older man with slumped shoulders and drawn eyes, though they had a hint of a sparkle within them. His hair was short, a fading yellow color, and it was obvious to Finn that he was the young woman's father.

"Are you Master James?"

"I am. And who are you?"

"My name is Finn Jagger." The man's eyes narrowed,

and Finn pressed forward. "I have come to you to speak about a Mr. Reginald Smith."

"Why?" Master James asked.

Finn hadn't been sure that Master James would even recognize the name, but the slight rigidity to his posture suggested he did. "He stands accused of stealing. I'm investigating those who have reportedly lost something from him. Your name was on the list."

"He does owe me," Master James said. "I wouldn't have made a claim against him, though. It's been long enough that I don't even think of it."

"Yours would not be the only claim made against him." At least, not now that Reginald was dead. The others had all put in their claims during the investigation, hoping for reimbursement from the crown for the crimes. It was rare, but occasionally those with enough of a claim were able to recover some of their money from the king, who would then have the claim against the debtor.

"It's not?" Master James asked, his gaze drifting to the ground before looking up at Finn.

Finn shook his head. "Unfortunately, no. I have been looking into the various claims against him, and I came to yours."

"I'm not so sure it makes any difference," Master James said.

"What can you tell me about him?"

He shrugged. "What am I supposed to tell you? He hired me to do some work for him a few months back—which I did—then he disappeared without paying me for it."

"Only he didn't disappear," Finn said. "Can you tell me the value of what you made for him?"

"With everything I had invested with time and labor, it would be about three branna."

Three gold branna. Not a windfall, but more than what someone would normally spend on a carpenter. What exactly had Master James done for Reginald?

"Is that typical for your work?" Finn asked.

Master James made his way over to the corner. "I would have charged more, but he stopped paying…" He shrugged. "The cost mostly comes from supplies." He looked down, nodding at the stack of wood. "The forest provides for access to simple stock. Pine. Oak. Elm." He glanced over at Finn. "Those are useful in the right situation, but the kind of work I've become known for is a bit different. It requires species of lumber not easily found within the confines of the forest. That, and those who hire me often request something a little more exotic. Some of them bring me to the capital itself."

Finn looked down at the stack of wood. "So you're importing it?"

"Most of the time," Master James said. He scratched at his shoulders, and a bit of sawdust drifted off of him. It surprised Finn that he would leave his shop as dusty and messy as he had. "There are times when I need to travel out of the city myself. I try not to do it quite as much these days, though I did it often when I was younger."

"I didn't realize carpenters traveled to acquire lumber."

"As I said, Mr. Jagger, the type of work I do is valued."

He turned, clasping his hands in front of him. "May I ask how Reginald Smith was captured?"

Finn shrugged. "He tried to avoid paying a general store owner. A rather well-known one."

That was the reason he'd attracted attention. He could have swindled any number of poorer merchants and managed to escape notice, but not Master Ihliar, who tended to cater to a wealthier clientele.

"I see," Master James said. "I imagine he doesn't have the funds for the job he hired me for."

"I doubt he does," Finn agreed. And he certainly wouldn't have them now.

"Such a waste of time," he whispered.

"What exactly did you make?"

"Not my usual. Just a few small boxes."

"What do you usually make?" Finn asked. He hadn't seen any boxes.

"My specialty are inlays," he said. "There is something quite delicate about them. I use different species of wood to create patterns. In this case, I used a wood so dark it could be black, and it creates a very particular appearance."

He thought of the circular wooden item he'd found in Reginald's home, but it didn't sound like James had made it for him. "Just that?"

"I haven't seen him in quite a few months. I would have declined additional jobs, Mr. Jagger, unless he paid upfront. Given the infrequency of my work these days, perhaps I would have still taken any job he offered…" The carpenter sighed. "I have to provide for my daughter," he said, looking toward the back of the shop. "Jamie has tolerated my work over the years, though she has encouraged me to move where the work may be more plentiful."

"You don't want to move?"

"If I move, I lose the business I have. It takes time to establish yourself, and as you no doubt ascertained on your time coming to the shop, we aren't the wealthiest of merchants. Others in nicer sections can charge much more."

"Even if their work isn't as skilled as yours?"

"There are few who can distinguish the difference between my work and another's," Master James said. "And when it comes down to cost, that often is the deciding factor. Some think only of how much coin it will be and want the best value. What that leaves out of the equation is the training and skill involved." He nodded to the coin. "Something like that cannot be created by many within the city," he said.

"Not many outside of the city, either," a soft voice said from the doorway.

Finn looked over to see Master James's daughter standing there, her arms crossed over her chest. She looked at her father with adoration in her eyes.

"What my father doesn't want to say is that there aren't many men who can do his work."

"Jamie—"

Jamie shook her head. "You don't have to be modest, Father. I know what you can do. I know what your work is worth."

He chuckled. "If only others would see it."

Jamie looked over to Finn. "That's the hard part of this kind of work, you know. Getting attention. There are others who come from the high-class sections where they're given access to those with money we simply cannot obtain." She glanced over to her father. "All he needs is an opportunity."

"It's more than just an opportunity," her father said. "It's the chance to gain consistent work."

"If you could prove yourself..."

Her father chuckled. "If I could prove myself to the king, perhaps that would make a difference, but unfortunately, the king isn't hiring a man like me." Master James looked over to Finn.

Finn understood some of the pressures Master James experienced. He had to prove himself in the same way. "I'm sorry that Reginald Smith took advantage of you," Finn said.

"I wish he hadn't. Each of these takes me about three days to make."

"How long were you working on his project?" Finn asked.

"On and off for the better part of three months," he said.

"I will get to the bottom of it," Finn said, though he doubted there would be much that could be done about it. Reginald had taken the money, leaving them with nothing. "There might be several other claims coming to the king," Finn said, turning to the door. "I will put in my report that you should be compensated along with other claims upon him." Now that he was gone, it was possible they'd be able to sell whatever property he owned and compensate his debtors.

"That would be appreciated," Master James said.

He'd learned nothing useful.

Just another mystery about Reginald—something that never sat well with Finn. He liked answers. He *was* the Hunter, after all.

"Have a good evening. I'm sorry I disturbed your time," Finn said.

"It is not a problem, Mr. Jagger. I'm just thankful you had no reason to bring me in."

Finn nodded again, turning to the door, and stepped outside. Jamie watched him for a moment in the doorway before closing the door behind him.

The day was still early, though at this point, Finn didn't really have much else he needed to do other than taking care of some tasks in the city. Perhaps it was time to return to Master Meyer, maybe offer his healing services for the night, or perhaps even sit with his sister and study.

Lena might like that. With Helda not coming around as often, she lacked companionship. He took a deep breath. There was one place he could go.

He suspected Oscar would welcome him to the Wenderwolf tavern, but it was a little early for that. He stood in the street, and for a moment, he thought he felt movement near him, but then it was gone.

Perhaps it was only imagined.

It was times like these when Finn wished he had others he could socialize with. He'd tried befriending iron masters, had been friendly with the wardens, and even found a few willing women over the last few years, but nobody really wanted to socialize with an executioner. It left him with Master Meyer and his sister.

It was times like these when Finn felt lost, despite knowing exactly what he needed to do. Perhaps he shouldn't feel lost. He had an assignment, and he was comfortable with it—at least, as comfortable as anyone could be with the type of work he'd been asked to do. Without meaning to, Finn found himself near the outer wall of the city, looking through the Teller Gate.

It had been too long since he'd gone searching for an understanding of the Alainsith outside the gate. He had taken several journeyman assignments—that wasn't his issue—but after having saved the Alainsith man from certain death, Finn felt he would have gained a greater understanding of the culture. Except that hadn't come.

Perhaps that was what he needed to do. Get outside the city, look around, and see if he could uncover anything that would provide him with answers about the Alainsith. After his experience with them, he'd wanted answers.

If nothing else, he could go to Esmerelda and the hegen, but he suspected she would warn him away. Finn tore his gaze away from the gate and headed back into the city, back toward his usual responsibilities.

Now the light was fading quickly, and with his errands done and a full day of work behind him, Finn was tempted to return back to Master Meyer's home and settle in for the night. It wasn't that he had nothing to do. There was always something new to learn, something more he should be experiencing, even after serving all this time.

What he really wanted was to settle in at a tavern and enjoy a mug of ale.

He found himself drifting toward the Olin section, toward the Wenderwolf, knowing it was a mistake. He shouldn't be heading there. Not at this point. Oscar wouldn't refuse him entry, and he doubted that Annie would either, but it still felt odd returning. Maybe it shouldn't. Oscar was his oldest friend, and these days, he often felt like his *only* friend.

Finn reached the street that would take him to the Wenderwolf tavern before heading away. He passed a poster with a black rose on a white background, pausing for a moment and looking at it, then moved onward.

There were other taverns he could stop in, and he crossed over the bridge leading toward the center of the city. The Veiled Thistle was an old tavern just on the other side of the river. Finn had started frequenting it over the last few months when he needed a place to go, though he had always done so on his own.

It was quiet inside, not nearly as boisterous as the Wenderwolf. No minstrels played as they did at other taverns, though there was a steady murmuring of voices. A few people looked up when he entered, but then looked away. Finn doubted that any recognized him. He fit in here, especially with the way he dressed now.

He nodded to one of the servers and took a seat at a table along the wall, resting his hands on its polished oak surface. When the server brought him a mug of ale, he handed over a few coppers, more than he ever would've spent when he was younger, and they were scooped off the table.

Finn leaned back, sipping at the ale.

It was too bad he couldn't go to the Wenderwolf, but it didn't fit him anymore. He wasn't part of the crew any longer. Though, if he was honest with himself, that wasn't the only issue. Finn had grown more serious. It was because of the risk of the job, he knew, but he didn't want to end up like Master Meyer, which was the reason he still came out at all.

He pulled out the journal he'd found in Reginald's home and flipped through the pages. Meyer had made it clear that allowing himself to get distracted by pointless leads was only a waste of time. And Finn knew it was true. He hadn't been able to make sense of Reginald's notes.

Loud voices at the table nearby caught his attention, and Finn looked up for a moment, watching the men wagering at cards before turning his attention back to the journal. He took another sip of his ale, feeling there had to be something here. He just had to find it.

CHAPTER FOUR

The journey to the paper mill outside the city had been a waste.

Reginald's journal had mentioned the mill several times, but the manager hadn't known Reginald, and hadn't cared that he'd died. He had been too busy to even care that he was talking to the executioner. Finn wasn't accustomed to that, but hadn't any real reason to push.

And he'd wasted too much time. Getting to the mill took an hour by foot, so he'd borrowed a horse and now had to return it. The stable was on the edge of the Durn section. Most of the sections on the edge of the city were rundown, and Durn was no exception, though it had the advantage of catering specifically to city newcomers. Since the Durn section was close to Teller Gate, it had many of the same shops and suppliers that could be found farther inside the city, but they were cheaper, allowing visitors the option of avoiding travel into Verendal, even though there were plenty who viewed the city as a necessary evil.

A butcher and a farrier were on either side of the stable, something Finn found unsettling. At least he never purchased from this butcher, though they weren't all *that* far from the slaughterhouse, so perhaps he didn't need to think that way. Another poster of the black rose was on the butcher's store front.

He would need to look into that too. Reginald had a similar marking.

What did it mean though?

He pulled on the bell on the side of the stable and a stableboy came running out of the back.

"You weren't gone long," he said. The boy looked to be fourteen. He was dirty, and his shirt was a bit tattered and stitched, but working in manure was still more honorable than the kind of work Finn had done when he was this boy's age.

"Just a short errand," Finn said, patting the horse's side. He'd found that when he rode, his legs ached for the better part of a day afterward. They always managed to find him the fattest horse.

"Will you be back again tomorrow?"

Finn had gotten a reputation for traveling out of the city. They thought him a merchant, and he'd done nothing to clear them of that notion. It was easier that way. If they had known who and what he *really* was, he'd probably have a harder time with them. They'd likely still rent the horse to him, but they wouldn't be pleased about it.

"I haven't decided." He looked around the inside of the

stable. Most of the stalls were empty. They were typically full in the mornings. He tried to get his pick of the horses, but they guided him instead, telling him that a man his size needed the right horse—as if he were that large. He'd grown more solid over the years, but he still wasn't large enough to scare anyone, and he'd certainly never be confused with a bruiser. "I'd like something less stout the next time."

"Not much choice in that, I'm afraid," the boy said. "They don't all get the same activity. Some of them are better on longer trips, but those shorter rides you've been taking..."

"Then I'll just have to take a longer trip," Finn said.

Even when he'd been gone for a few days at a time, taking trips to some of the surrounding towns to serve as their executioner, he hadn't found a horse he could really enjoy. How did some people love riding?

"Of course. I can let Master Ungar know you're thinking of doing so."

Finn sniffed. Ungar had been the one to give him the worst horse he'd ever ridden. It was a wonder that Finn had even bothered coming back to this stable, but it *was* the closest to the gate, and they hadn't tried to overcharge him the way others in the city had.

Finn started to turn when a shout outside of the stable caught his attention.

He frowned, and the boy just shook his head. "Don't mind them. They've been hollering like that all morning."

"Who has?" Finn asked, turning back to him.

"Those fools who think to protest the Archers. Said they're mad that Ole Junker got pinched."

Finn hadn't known about any protest of the Archers. They hadn't been protesting when he'd left, so for them to do so now seemed odd. But he knew about what happened to Junker. He'd been caught during a robbery and had died accidentally as the Archers tried to bring him to one of the prisons for questioning.

"What sort of protest is there?"

"I don't know. I try to stay out of it. I've got enough going on in here, you know."

Finn smiled slightly. The boy was smarter than he gave him credit for. It was better to keep out of trouble, especially if it involved something that might land him in prison. Protesters in the city were typically dealt with quickly. The king always wanted to ensure that he maintained his grip on the action in the city, and if the protesters decided to cause trouble, the king would deal with them.

It was a problem for Finn, though.

If the protesters were dealt with, as he expected they would be, it meant that he would likely get pulled into questioning them.

He sighed and started forward.

"Here," he said, pausing and grabbing a couple coppers from his pocket, then flipping them to the boy. "Thanks for your help."

The boy caught the coins out of the air and nodded to Finn.

Maybe that would help him get a better ride next time,

though Finn didn't put a whole lot of stock in that possibility. More likely than not, the kid would come to expect it.

He stepped out into the street.

There had been a crowd as he had come through the Teller Gate, though Finn hadn't paid that much attention to it.

Perhaps that was a mistake.

A crowd had a purpose, and now that he knew there was a protest, he followed the crowd's movement, wandering along the street, looking for signs of where they were going and anything else he could discover. If he was going to be tasked with dealing with these protesters anyway—and Finn was increasingly certain that he would —then he might as well follow them now and learn what they were doing and planning.

He caught up to them and heard their shouting and chanting.

Finn looked over to the man nearest him and frowned. The man had long, dark hair and was a little bit lanky. He was dressed in a heavy cloak with a twisted symbol embroidered along the lapels. Finn doubted he was even from Verendal.

That was odd.

"What's going on here?" Finn asked him.

The man glanced over, a tight smile on his face. "Heard about the Archers and how quick they are to gather up innocents," he said. "We're making our voices known."

"We?"

"Us. The crowd." The man tapped his chest. "The king is going to hear us this time."

"I don't know if the king cares so much about protesters," Finn said, frowning again as he looked over to the man before turning his attention to the crowd. As the man said, the crowd was getting thicker, and a crowd like this could quickly become unruly.

"He's going to care about this."

The man whistled, and there came a series of loud whistles throughout the crowd in response. It rang up along the line, then somebody threw something at one of the buildings.

A bottle, and flames began to creep along the building once it struck.

Finn looked over but the man was gone.

He'd slipped off into the crowd, and it was difficult to see anything. Finn stumbled forward, knowing he needed to help put the fire out before it spread—and it would spread rapidly in the wooden buildings in one of these outer sections. He'd seen it happen in the Jorend section once before, and an entire part of the city had practically burned up.

The shouting in front of him grew louder.

Finn hurried to the side of the street. The crowd continued chanting around him, and he knew he would get crushed here if he couldn't get farther forward.

More than that, there was a real danger in the section burning.

Another bottle shattered and Finn looked behind him.

They had thrown it at another building.

Finn tried to push forward, but the crowd was too thick.

Gods, this was a mess.

Someone needed to get word to the fire brigade.

Not that way.

He'd get stuck.

He could try a different way though.

Finn backed away, moving in the opposite direction of the crowd. It was increasingly difficult to go anywhere. As the crowd pressed around him, it made it hard for him to do much of anything.

He shoved his way through. Another bottle exploded.

Fires rushed along the street, and Finn pushed ahead, trying to get out of the crowd. Somebody shoved him and he stumbled, slamming into a man. He was large, dark-skinned with dark hair, and dressed in a tattered cloak.

He took one look at Finn and punched him.

Finn twisted out of the way but collided with a mass of mottled gray and black hair. The owner, a woman in a particularly dirty brown dress, pushed him back and shrieked, "How dare you!"

Finn realized that he not only didn't belong here, but he *looked* like he didn't belong here. He had grown up in a poor section of the city, poverty-stricken himself, and had never truly felt like an outsider in these outer sections. But for the first time, he did.

It was not only his clothes, but the rage he heard from the voices around him, the anger. A flicker of panic worked through him that he quickly tamped down.

He murmured a quick apology, but the woman pushed him.

Finn twisted with it, sliding back, and forced his way through the crowd, moving against the flow of traffic.

He needed to get out of here. Find the fire brigade. Get the Archers coordinated.

Finn stumbled backward in his attempt to get away from the crowd and get to the side of the street.

Somebody shouted in the distance.

Finn looked over, no longer trying to force his way back.

The crowd screamed, and it seemed to have more to do with something that happened rather than the fires that were now raging along the buildings. It wasn't only the fire that was too much, but the crowd pressing around him.

Finn fought through and finally managed to reach the side of the street. From there, he slipped along an alley.

His heart hammered.

It was a strange thing for him to be afraid in this city, given the role he had taken on.

The people continued to stream along the street. Smoke billowed up, filling the air, and Finn just watched.

There was no way the fire brigade would be able to make its way here to put out the fires. Not with so many people creating chaos.

The Archers wouldn't be able to handle this, either.

They would have to wait until the others cleared out, until the protest died down—if it ever would.

Finn started along the alley when he heard a shout

behind him. He turned to see two men coming toward him.

"Where you think you're going? Some highborn bastard in our section of the city thinks he can watch? Well, we'll show you what we do with your kind."

Finn shifted his gaze from one man to the other, trying to decide how to react.

He could try to fight. Neither of them looked all that large. One of them was only a little larger than the stable boy, though the other did appear a bit muscular. Both were dirty and had a strange desperation in their eyes.

Neither appeared armed, which would normally make him feel he had the upper hand, but in this case…

Finn knew it was better—and safer—for him to just get out of here.

He turned, heading along the alley. Thankfully, though he had forgotten quite a bit in his days working the crews in the street, he had not forgotten how to navigate through the alleys.

He knew how to intersect with the streets nearby, and he figured that if he could just get ahead of the crowd, just keep ahead of the protests, then he could avoid confrontation.

Finn reached the intersecting street.

The two men were still behind him, but now that Finn had emerged on the street—thankful there was no crowd here—he jogged forward.

He glanced back to see the two men watching him from the shadows of the alley.

Maybe he would take a bit more of a roundabout way back to Master Meyer's home.

Finn slowed to a walk. There were no signs of the protesters, though they were still in the same section. Smoke drifted nearby, and he could see the flames starting to crackle along the rooftops of the buildings, drifting above him, making it difficult to see much of anything else.

Finn darted off to the side of the street and turned to see the crowd squeezing its way along the street he had just come down.

The protestors were moving faster, louder, and more buildings were burning.

What did they think to accomplish by burning these buildings?

Finn took another alleyway, ignoring its stench and the standing water from the rain the night before, then emerged back in the Olin section. From there, it was easier for him to make his way to Master Meyer's home.

A line of Archers had started moving toward that section. The fire brigade, pulling one of their leather hoses, followed.

He had nothing more he could do.

Finn listened to the crowd, noting the noise, the chaos, the violence, and the smell of smoke that continued rising all around him, permeating everything.

When he finally reached Meyer's home, he stepped past the stone wall and breathed out a sigh of relief.

There was a part of him that felt ashamed of his reaction—ashamed that he would feel concerned by the attack and feel the need to run—but he had seen the look in the people's eyes and heard the violence in their cries.

He had been around violent people enough during his service as the executioner that he recognized that violence, and he recognized that there wasn't anything he would be able to do to stop it. If it persisted, the king *would* get involved. Was that what these people wanted?

He headed inside, only to find that the house was empty.

Lena wasn't here. Meyer wasn't here.

Which meant they were out in the city.

CHAPTER FIVE

Finn had been pacing for the past ten minutes, and had just made up his mind to check Helda's, when he caught a glimpse of Lena's brown braids bobbing down the path.

Finn breathed out a sigh of relief when his sister came home, clutching her cloak around her. Some of the strands from her braids had pulled loose and a bead of sweat worked across her brow. Lena quickly wiped it away without saying anything then hurried down the hallway. Finn jumped up from where he'd been sitting at the table and stopped her in the hallway before she started up the stairs to her room.

"You're back," he said.

"Finn? What are you doing here in the middle of the day?"

"I just wanted to make sure you and Meyer were safe."

He didn't need her to know he was just as concerned for himself.

"You mean with the fire?" She glanced toward the door, shaking her head. "It seems like Verendal has had quite a few more of those these days."

"I was there when they started it," Finn said. "The protesters were responsible."

"*They* started it?"

"Where were you?" he asked, noting that she had a pack clutched under one arm. Her braids were pulled back with blue ribbons, and the satchel under the other arm looked to be filled with books. "You didn't see the protest?"

"Protests?" She shook her head. "I smelled something burning, but I couldn't see much of anything. It was coming from the Inar section."

"What were you doing?"

She looked away from him, a hint of color coming to her cheeks. "I had certain supplies I needed to acquire, Finn." She headed to Meyer's office, pushing the door open and dropping the satchel on his desk. "You're not the only one in this household who has responsibilities."

It was almost enough to make Finn laugh. "I know I'm not, Lena. I just wanted to make sure you were safe."

"The city has dealt with protests before."

Finn took a deep breath, letting it out slowly, and looked toward the doorway. "Not like this one. I don't know if we've ever seen anything quite like it."

"Was it really that bad?" Lena frowned as she pulled

the books out of her pack and set those on the desk as well.

"It was bad," he said.

She looked up at him, meeting his gaze. "I see. Do you know where Henry went?"

He shook his head. "I don't. That's what I'm concerned about."

"Then you should go see if you can find him. You know the places he visits," she said.

Lena was always so matter-of-fact, and always seemed as if she knew exactly what she should be doing, though Finn wasn't sure if chasing after Meyer in the streets was really what *he* needed to be doing.

"I'll wait here for him."

He went back to the kitchen, standing there for a moment, before turning to the hall.

Finn needed to be here to ensure that nothing worse took place. He wasn't one of the Archers. He wasn't even a soldier. But he *was* an executioner.

That meant more than just carrying out sentencing. That meant knowing the crimes, investigating them, and uncovering what was taking place.

In this case, Finn thought perhaps he did need to get back out to observe the protests, especially since he was increasingly certain he would be responsible for investigating what had taken place.

He started back to the door before pausing.

There was a part of him that wanted nothing more than to take his sword with him, but that would be a mistake. The sword was a representation of the king's justice. Carrying it would only make him a target. Finn shook his head and stepped back out the door, nearly colliding with Master Meyer.

"Good. You're here," Meyer said.

"Tell me you saw the protest."

Meyer's wrinkled face frowned. "I saw it. We need to go watch."

"Because we might get called in?"

"Very good," Meyer said. "With everything that's taking place, we'll likely be drawn into the investigation." Meyer motioned for him to follow and Finn joined him.

These days, most of the time, Finn investigated on his own. That Meyer would come him with him now suggested this was an even worse situation than Finn had known.

"Where are we starting?" he asked Meyer.

"They were targeting the outer sections first."

It wasn't long before Finn started to see the flames in the distance begin to grow fainter.

"I overheard a few comments when I got caught in the crowd. They seemed angry with the Archers over Junker's death."

Meyer glanced over, shaking his head. "Anger can lead a man to do many things."

"I've seen," Finn said.

Meyer smiled tightly. "Yes. You have. Unfortunately, in the time we've been working together, you have seen much more than I would've expected. My own apprenticeship, and time as a journeyman, did not have quite as much excitement as yours."

Finn grunted. "I don't know if I'd call it excitement."

"Perhaps not. I would never have expected Verendal to be the forefront of such activity, but perhaps it is a sign of something more to come."

Meyer knew all about the magical attack on the city and he knew about the Alainsith, even if he didn't want to acknowledge that there had been something going on there. Meyer had never wanted to be involved in magic, as far as Finn knew. He recognized the benefits of the hegen, acknowledged that there was a role for them within the city, and had even encouraged them to take their place and to have a level of influence, but he had done nothing more than that.

"You were out of the city," Meyer said as they passed over the river, heading into one of the more central sections of the city.

"I was," Finn said.

Meyer looked over. "You've been going out of the city quite a bit these days."

Finn caught Master Meyer's gaze and nodded. There was no point in denying it. Finn suspected that Meyer still kept tabs on him, watching to ensure that he either stayed in the city or fulfilled his obligations, though he was a bit surprised that Meyer would admit it so openly.

"I have."

"Is this about you chasing the hegen?"

Finn flushed. He didn't want Meyer thinking that. "I wouldn't need a horse to do that, would I?"

Meyer frowned at him. "You've been borrowing a horse?"

So much for the extent of Meyer's knowledge.

They passed by a row of houses. The houses began to get increasingly larger the farther they went into the city. The closer they got to the palace itself, the houses started to tower over them, and the street widened. Smoke in the distance drifted over the outskirts of the city, a fog rising up, the smell of it filling the air. That smell might be pleasing in the outer sections of the city, but most of the houses had gardens here in the more central sections, and it was unfortunate to have the smoke overwhelm the floral fragrance.

"Borrowing. Renting. Trying to ride." Finn shook his head. "They like to give me the fat ones."

"You're getting taller," Meyer said.

Finn chuckled. "I'm not getting any taller."

"Fine. You're getting bigger. Time spent working as you do tends to build a man."

"I wouldn't say the work I do is all that physical," Finn said.

"Not the day-to-day work, but there *are* aspects of your work that require certain physicality, and your practice has put muscle on your frame."

Finn shrugged. "I suppose so."

"What have you been doing?" Meyer asked it softly, carefully; nothing in his voice suggested irritation, but rather curiosity.

More and more these days, Meyer had been granting him leeway with his work. Trust had evolved in the time he'd been working with him.

"Ever since the attack the last time, I've been interested in trying to better understand the Alainsith."

"You won't find any Alainsith outside of the city," Meyer said.

"Esmerelda says the same thing."

"You *have* been spending time with her." Meyer chuckled. "She's an interesting woman. No one could fault you."

"I have a feeling she's partial to those who are of her people," Finn said.

"Partial to them, but it is not a requirement, I suspect."

"You only suspect? You don't know?"

Meyer grunted. "I'm not an expert in all things hegen, contrary to what you might believe."

"I just figured you might know things."

He chuckled. "I do know things, but I also know there are things I should not be involved in."

"Such as me with the hegen?"

Meyer tipped his head, nodding, but then something caught his attention. He turned, looking off into the distance, back toward the edge of the city. "All I would suggest is that you're careful with that one. She is unique in her situation."

"As hegen?"

"As one of the hegen elders," Meyer said softly.

Finn frowned. "You're going to have to explain that to me. How is Esmerelda one of the hegen elders?"

"They don't rely upon age," Meyer said. "They rely upon knowledge, and knowledge can be gained by anyone, regardless of age."

"I see." He debated whether he should tell Meyer about

what he had uncovered of the Alainsith building, as Meyer didn't share Finn's curiosity about them, but a sudden shout caught Finn's attention, and he never had the opportunity.

Meyer nodded and waited for Finn to step off to the side of the road.

"What's going on?"

"The response," Meyer said softly.

Finn looked over to see a line of Archers marching along the street. He'd seen them from a distance, but they felt different up close. All were dressed in leather, with their metal helms gleaming in the sunlight, and all were armed with short swords. A few even carried crossbows. That was a new development. Mixed among the city Archers were a dozen palace Archers. Far more deadly than the city Archers, they were dressed in bright silver armor and their boots thundered on the stones.

"That's it?" Finn asked.

"Did you think the king would need to send more?"

"I saw the crowd, Master Meyer. I saw the violence in their eyes. They're going to need more than just fifty city Archers and a dozen or so palace Archers."

"You'd be surprised," Meyer said. "You have an unarmed population, and though they might think they want to engage the Archers, they will change their mind as soon as they confront them."

Finn hoped that was the case.

There was the possibility the instigators would engage, trying to battle with them, and if that happened...

"I think the attack was coordinated," Finn said. "They whistled to communicate. Like the Archers."

Meyer frowned. "That would pose a problem."

The Archers moved past them, casting a look in their direction, and Finn just nodded. He recognized a couple of them, though he didn't know them well. Ever since he had come to realize that his role as executioner isolated him, he had avoided spending time socially with the Archers and the iron masters.

"Anything else about them?" Meyer looked around. "The kind of thing we've seen a little too much of over the last few years?"

Finn cocked a brow. "By that, you mean magical?" He shook his head. "Not that I saw."

"Unfortunately, given our recent events, I wasn't sure."

Finn chuckled. "I hope we don't face another magical attack so soon. Or ever again."

"I should hope not," Meyer said.

"I could talk to Esmerelda about it, if you're concerned."

Meyer smiled slightly. "You may talk to her all you want."

"Not like that," Finn said.

"You mean you have no interest in a beautiful woman?"

"Not one that dangerous."

"The best women are dangerous," Meyer said softly.

When the Archers moved past, Meyer motioned for Finn to follow. They began to trail after the Archers, taking up a position behind them, which surprised Finn.

"Are you sure you want to follow them?"

"We need to observe. We haven't had anything quite like this in a while," Meyer said. "Civil unrest like this is not common, though it does happen. Typically, it's not quite so coordinated."

"So you agree it's coordinated?"

"For the protests to happen at this time, yes. That's what it suggests."

"What do you mean, 'at this time'?"

Meyer frowned, glancing over to Finn. "I thought you knew. The king is in the city."

The number of palace Archers suddenly took on a different meaning for Finn.

The king coming to the city would mean that there would be far more of their presence here than usual. Typically, the palace Archers were only tasked with protecting the crown jewels within the palace, but for this many soldiers to be marching along the street...

The king came to the city often enough, though Finn wasn't typically privy to the timing. The only time he'd been alerted to when King Porman had come to the city was when Finn had sentenced the magister, and only then because there had been a need to keep a measure of peace.

"Are the protests because he's here?" Finn asked.

"There shouldn't have been any way for anyone to know the king was coming to the city. He came under the cover of night, and his soldiers came later."

Finn looked over. "What do you mean, 'his soldiers'?" When Porman had come before, there had been a regiment that traveled with him, but they typically remained stationed outside of the city. Only the officers traveled into the city, presumably because the king wanted to keep Verendal from getting too militarized.

"The Realmsguard are in the city," Meyer stated.

Finn looked along the street. The Realmsguard were the best trained soldiers in the kingdom. "Then he should send them to keep the peace."

"I suspect he might," Meyer said.

They trailed after the soldiers, heading along the street and toward the chaos. The sound of shouting persisted, though Finn couldn't figure out why the people were so angry from listening to them. Maybe they didn't even know.

They rounded a curve in the street and found the bridge across the river blocked. On one side were the Archers, most of them armed with crossbows, and many of them holding their crossbows out, and on the other side were protestors. Those in the front line of the protestors shouted the loudest, and some of them even threw items toward the Archers. That surprised Finn. Targeting the Archers was a sure way of getting on the wrong side of a crossbow bolt.

"The damn fools," Meyer muttered.

That was a considerable amount of emotion from him. Meyer was usually far more reserved, and for him to make a comment like that...

"This isn't going to end well," Finn said.

"Never does."

"You've been around things like this before?"

Meyer nodded slowly. "Not quite like this, but I've

seen men challenge authority. Happens from time to time, and they're never prepared as they need to be."

"You think the people should challenge the authority of the king?"

Meyer looked over to Finn as if he were mad. "I didn't say anything like that. All I'm saying is they're never prepared. If they wanted to accomplish whatever goal they have for themselves, they would need to be ready for the fight. Unfortunately, I can't say I've ever seen—or heard—of men who are truly prepared for that fight."

"We almost had one man that was prepared."

Meyer nodded slowly. "That was similar, but different. When you have outside forces pushing on the city, you're going to get a different level of preparation. I don't think this is Yelind, though."

"They wouldn't have abandoned their push on the city." Verendal was close enough to be the natural target for Yelind if they were interested in attacking the city. There were other places within the kingdom they could target, but none that would be as impressive if they succeeded in bringing it down.

"I doubt they've abandoned anything, but they drew the king's attention. He's positioned soldiers to the south, keeping them at bay."

Meyer had been better connected than him when it came to knowing the workings of the kingdom, but it sounded almost as if he'd been kept informed of the king's actions. Maybe he had.

"What of the Alainsith?"

"They have maintained peace with the Alainsith," Meyer said.

The shouting intensified. Someone threw a flaming bottle at the Archers that exploded where it landed. It was quickly stomped out as the Archers stormed forward.

Crossbow bolts flew.

Men in the front of the protest fell screaming.

Finn wanted to turn away, but he needed to watch.

The Archers pressed forward, moving with a march. The palace Archers guided the city Archers, and together they pushed the protestors back. As they fell deeper into the city, Finn found his attention drawn to the men lying bleeding, dying, on the street.

"Should we help them?"

"Not much that can be done for them," Meyer said softly.

That comment surprised Finn. "We should do something." He started forward when Meyer grabbed his wrist, holding him in place.

"Not with this, Finn. We serve the king, and they attacked the king. That's how he would see it."

"But we might be able to question survivors."

Meyer took a deep breath, letting it out in a frustrated sigh. "You're going to get me killed." Still, he nodded.

Finn and Meyer reached the bridge. On the far side of the bridge, four Archers remained, all armed with crossbows. As they approached, one of the Archers spun toward them, holding his crossbow out, but Meyer just raised his hand, trying to calm him.

"Turn back," the Archer said.

Smoke swirled in the distance behind the Archer, rising up and over the city in a pale cloud. The air hung with the smell of it, mixing with the smoke and the heat, but also carrying something else. A different sort of stench that Finn couldn't quite place.

"We need to question those men," Meyer said.

"Question? They're dead," one of the other Archers said.

Meyer continued forward, moving with a confident step. Finn followed him.

"In order for us to know who organized this plot against Verendal, we're going to need to question these men," Meyer said.

"There's no organization," the Archer said. "Bastards just decided to attack."

"I was there. I saw what happened when they decided to attack," Finn said, stepping forward. He could feel Meyer's heated gaze but ignored it. He thought he could do this. He could be helpful. Even if Master Meyer didn't want to help these men, Finn wanted to. And it wasn't just because they could question them, though that was a part of it. "This was not some simple protest. They had organizers. We need to question them."

Finn looked past the Archers to the men lying on the street. Several of them weren't moving at all, and Finn doubted there would be much that could be done for them, but there were three who still moaned and they would likely be useful.

"Let them pass," the other Archer said. "That's the hangman and the Hunter."

"I don't care who it is," the other Archer said. Finn noted the stripes of rank on his shoulder. A palace Archer. "We're under orders."

"Orders from the king, I presume," Meyer said. "I am under the same orders."

The Archer eyed up Master Meyer before stepping off to the side, turning his attention to the other side of the bridge.

Meyer motioned for Finn to go. "You wanted this. Let's get moving."

Finn slipped past the Archers, tensing slightly as he felt them shifting their attention toward him. Crossbows aimed in his direction left him uncomfortable.

As soon as they crossed the bridge, he got to work.

Meyer had trained him in many things: interrogation, questioning, sentencing, and healing and wound care.

They had no supplies, but they could stabilize any wounds that could be stabilized. Anything that wasn't fatal could be treated.

Meyer stopped in front of one of the men, and Finn moved on, kneeling down next to a man with a puncture wound to his side. He been stabbed. The man moaned, writhing in place.

Finn grabbed his belt knife and carved through the man's dirty brown shirt, cutting a strip off and placing it in the man's hands. He had shaggy brown hair and pale-blue eyes that were already starting to fade as he looked up at Finn.

"Hold this here," Finn said to the man.

"Bastards stabbed me," he managed to get out.

"You attacked them," Finn said.

"Bastards…"

The man moaned and his head rolled off to the side.

Finn pulled the strip of fabric up, looking down at the wound.

It was deep, all the way into his belly, but looked as if it angled upward. There was more blood than Finn would've expected for a belly wound like that.

He wasn't going to be able to save this man.

He got to his feet, moving on to the next wounded man. This one had a crossbow bolt sticking out of his chest, but it was off to the right side.

The man took a deep, gasping breath.

Finn pressed his hands onto the man's shoulders. He had a weathered, suntanned face with wrinkles around the corners of his eyes. He could be any man from Verendal. Dirt stained his fingers, streaking up his arms, and he had on a simple brown jacket and pants.

"Easy," Finn said.

The man opened his eyes, looking over to Finn, and cried out.

"Easy," Finn said again.

He cut the fabric away from the man's wound, separating it from the crossbow bolt, and evaluated the skin around the puncture site.

It would've been from close proximity, and the crossbow had penetrated fairly deeply, but the fact that the man was still alive gave Finn at least a measure of hope.

Had Esmerelda been here, the hegen might've been

able to do something to save some of these men, but would she have?

"I need to remove this bolt," Finn said.

"What are you doing?" the man asked, his voice breathy. "Are you going to kill me?"

"I'm trying to help you, so stop resisting," Finn said.

The man looked up at him. "I know you," he said.

"Do you?"

"You're him. The Hunter."

Finn held the man's brown-eyed gaze. "That's me."

"You're here to sentence me."

"I'm here to question you, but only if I can save you."

He used his belt knife. It wasn't ideal. It wasn't even clean. But he needed to get the crossbow bolt out, then he could investigate whether there was anything more he could do. The wound wasn't stable, and without supplies, Finn didn't know if he could do anything to help the man.

At the same time, he didn't even know if he *wanted* to help the man. He didn't know if he should be helping these men at all.

As he looked over to Master Meyer, he had a feeling the executioner felt the same way.

Maybe Finn was making a mistake here. Helping men who had attacked the king…

No. Finn was right in seeing if there was anything he might be able to do to save them.

Not only because doing so would provide him with answers, but also because it was the right thing to do.

That mattered. That had to matter.

Finn dug at the crossbow bolt.

The man cried out, but he ignored it as he shoved the knife down into the wound, working the bolt out, prying the barbs free as he pulled them out of the man's chest. As soon as it was out, he pressed his hand down on the wound. The man took a gasping breath, then started coughing.

"Easy," Finn said again.

"I…"

He tried to sit up then coughed again, and a bubble of blood-covered phlegm came to his lips. He leaned back, the blood pooling down his cheek.

Finn cursed under his breath.

Maybe he wasn't going to be able to save this man after all.

He grabbed a strip of cloth from the man's shirt, shoving it down on the wound, then leaned his head forward, listening.

His lungs sounded relatively clear, and he still had a heartbeat.

He was alive.

A wound like he had sustained could be fatal. It could puncture a lung. The heart. Any major vessel. Somehow, the man had gotten lucky. Though he had seemingly passed out, he was still alive.

Finn looked up to see Master Meyer making his way through the fallen and injured men. Others from along the street had come out and they were watching. Most of them were from this section of the city and had dirty clothes, dirty skin, and haunted expressions in their eyes.

The Archers had the crossbows aimed at them, as if they were concerned any of these people might attack.

"This man should pull through," Finn said.

"Good," Meyer said. "I have two others who should make it too."

Finn grabbed another strip of fabric off of the man, which he wound around his chest, binding it tightly, then shuffled off to one of the other injured men. He was beyond Finn's help.

He moved on to one more, a man who was moaning, holding on to his head.

Not a man. A boy.

He couldn't be much older than fourteen or fifteen, and he clutched his face. A long gash had stripped part of his cheek away, and he was bawling. Blood pooled around his hand, spilling out onto the cobblestones.

"Let me help you," Finn said.

The boy started to pull away, but Finn grabbed his shoulder. He didn't look to be injured in any other way, so if he could bind this wound…

He would have a scar. He might even lose a chunk of his face. He might get an infection, but the wound itself was something he could survive.

"You aren't going to die from this," Finn said.

"I'm… not?"

"Not if you let me help you."

The boy stopped crying out, and Finn cut off a strip of fabric, tearing it free then using it to put pressure on the wound. He could tell the blood loss was significant, but the more he put pressure on the boy's face, the more he started to see the blood easing, not spilling out around him quite as much as it had at first.

"I'm going to have to wrap this around your cheek. You're not going to be able to talk, and we are going to have to get you to a surgeon who can stitch this up."

"Not a cutter," the boy said.

"You're going to need a surgeon if you want to live."

The boy started wailing, but he let Finn tear the fabric free and begin to bind his face. The wound was deep, and it cut through the muscle of his cheek, leaving his jaw hanging slightly open and a little bit askew.

Maybe he'd been wrong in his initial assessment. It was possible a wound like his wouldn't be survivable.

Finn wasn't going to tell the boy that, though.

He finished binding it then got to his feet, looking around.

A crowd had gathered around them but didn't press inward.

"Meyer?" Finn said.

"I see it," Meyer said.

"What do we do?"

"We take the injured with us," Meyer scolded.

"And if they don't let us?"

"Then the injured will die," Meyer said with his voice raised a bit, loud enough to be heard over the din of the crowd.

Meyer grabbed one of the men he'd helped and pulled him.

Finn looked over to the boy. If any of the injured were going to be able to answer questions, it would be somebody who had only lost part of their face, but a boy like him might not know all that much about what had happened.

Besides, the other man needed Finn more. Finn scurried over to him, grabbing him under the arms, and started to pull.

Faces in the crowd turned toward him, watching, but Finn ignored them. All it would take would be for the crowd to grab for the injured people, and to push Finn and Meyer back, and they could be overwhelmed. Given that he and Meyer had forced their way across, he doubted the Archers would offer them much help. Still, Finn knew he needed to do something now.

The Archers weren't helping, but they were more concerned about the protesters.

He dragged the man. They reached the cobblestone bridge, and the crowd still hadn't pressed toward them, but as he pulled the man onto the bridge, the crowd headed forward, getting closer to the injured and the dying.

"Get that one," Meyer said to one of the city Archers while pointing at another man across the bridge. "He can provide answers."

"He can stay there and rot," the Archer said.

"Grab that man, or I will tell the king myself that you did not."

The Archer's eyes widened and he nodded quickly. He hurried over the bridge, holding on to the crossbow, swinging it toward others in the crowd as he aimed it away from him, then grabbed for the man Meyer had indicated. Finn couldn't see what was wrong with him, but he had a bandage around one side, and another along his shoulder, both soaked in blood. The man moaned a bit as the Archer grabbed him by one arm and began to drag him.

"Go get the boy," Finn said to one of the other Archers.

"You go get the boy," the Archer said.

Finn straightened, looking at him, and jabbed a bloody hand at him. "Go get the boy, or I will tell the king that you refused."

The Archer glowered at Finn, but he turned, storming off, holding onto the crossbow. Several people from the crowd started to converge upon the Archer, and he swung the crossbow, pointing at each of them, hurrying through the fallen bodies until he reached the boy, where he grabbed him by the arm and started pulling him.

The boy wasn't nearly as injured as some of the others, and he came willingly, babbling the entire time. By the time the Archer reached the bridge, the crowd had swelled to even more people, and they surrounded the fallen.

None of them were shouting the way they had before, and none of them were as violent either.

"What now?" Finn asked, whispering the question to Meyer.

"Now we see if any of them pull through. Then we question."

CHAPTER SIX

The room stunk of medicine, but it was more than that—a mixture of rot, filth, urine and feces. The cut flowers Lena had brought to the room did little to improve the smell, though Finn appreciated the effort. He sat on a chair next to one of the beds. The four men they had saved, dragged from the dying, all lay on beds near him. There were others from the fighting—nearly a dozen, all told, in various states of injury—who also lay on the beds, waiting for their turn at healing.

Meyer and Finn had been busy. Lena had joined them, offering what help she could, and it had been she who had stitched up the boy's face, doing a far more skillful job than any surgeon Finn had ever seen.

Each time he thought he understood how skilled his sister was becoming, he found himself marveling at the increase in her abilities. He supposed that, at this point, he should just accept the fact that she was going to be a far superior healer than he was.

Lanterns blazed on tables, casting the entire room in warm light. The walls of stone were a bit confining, and carried a bit of dampness that Finn had found common in most of the prisons within the city.

"We could have taken them to a nicer facility," Lena said, making her way between several of the injured, pausing to look at one, then peeling back the sheet of another to gaze at his wound. "And not some repurposed old prison."

"Meyer wanted some place the protesters wouldn't know about, and I don't think the city's used this as a prison in many years," Finn said. Declan *should* be secure, but he trusted Meyer in this.

"Nearly a hundred," Lena said, looking over to him. Her hair had pulled free of the band, leaving strands dangling down in front of her face. She had an ink stain on one cheek, and what looked to be dirt on her hands, along with flecks of dried blood. Sweat glistened on her brow.

She'd been here ever since they had pulled the men free, working diligently and trying to save as many as she could.

"I didn't realize it had been that long," Finn said.

"Henry told me that when we first came to the old Noreg prison," she said. "I think he felt guilty about asking me to help."

"I doubt it," Finn said.

"Why?" Lena asked, shooting him a look.

"Not that I doubt Meyer would want your help," Finn said hurriedly, raising his hands to try to cut off any irritation his sister might have with him. "But I doubt he felt guilty asking you to help. He knows you would be useful."

Lena moved forward, pausing at another bed—the one with the boy. He'd been sedated and no longer moaned quite as much as he had when he was first brought in. The babbling, too, had thankfully eased, so he wasn't crying as much either.

"There are times I don't feel quite as useful as I would like," Lena admitted, looking over to Finn after replacing the dressing on the boy's face. "There are only so many people willing to accept healing from me."

"Because you trained under Meyer?"

"Because I'm something different," she said, shaking her head. "I'm not quite an apothecary, but I'm not a surgeon, and I'm certainly not a physician."

Finn sat up, rubbing his hands on his thighs. He was tired. It was a strange sort of weariness. Not physical, but more of a mental fatigue that had come from the time he had spent working with Meyer and Lena and even Wella trying to save as many as they could. They were the only ones Meyer had trusted. There were others in the city who had skill, but it was telling that Meyer had only trusted a few people to heal the wounded.

Of course, these wounded men were the ones he would ultimately end up questioning, so perhaps that had something to do with it.

"Well, you are smarter than any apothecary I know. Maybe not Wella," Finn said, looking to the far side of the room where the old apothecary woman hunched over a table, mixing more medicinals. She had carried her supplies with her, and had been busy mixing medicines, ointments, and different treatments that could be used to ensure infection didn't take hold, the men's wounds clotted appropriately, and they didn't suffer too much. "But smarter than any *other* apothecary I know. And I don't know any surgeon who could stitch up that boy quite as well as you did."

"I'm sure any of them could have done that," Lena said.

"I don't know. He had bone exposed. You stitched the muscle and then replaced the cheek." Finn had marveled at that. She had told him that she had to repair the muscle beneath the skin in order for the boy to have function in his jaw again. It made anatomical sense to Finn, but it wasn't something he would have thought of doing.

His training revolved around ensuring that men were physically capable to stand trial, then physically capable to withstand sentencing.

Though he did train to help heal others, and he could use that training the way Meyer did in order to supplement his income, Finn didn't have the breadth and depth of knowledge Meyer had obtained, nor did he have the information Lena already possessed, even though she'd been studying for about the same time as Finn.

"And what does it matter if you aren't a physician?"

"It matters to some," Lena said. "In some of the central sections of the city, most think that if you're not a physician, then there's no point in getting healing from you."

"Maybe," Finn said.

He shifted on the chair, looking around the room. They were in the lower level of the old Noreg prison, a place that had been abandoned as the needs of the city had changed. Newer and more secure places had been built, but as far as Finn knew, it had once housed prisoners, much like Declan currently did.

"There's no maybe about it," Lena said. "That's what so many people believe."

"And do you care?"

Lena looked over. "What?"

Finn shrugged. "Do you care what others believe?"

"If I am to heal them, shouldn't I care what they believe?"

"Of course you *can* care, but does it matter?" Finn looked at the men lining the beds. "How many of these wouldn't have survived had you not intervened?"

"I don't know."

Finn smiled at his sister, getting to his feet. "I do. There are at least three here who wouldn't have pulled through if not for you."

"Henry would've been able to help," she said softly.

"I'm not so sure," Finn said. "Meyer is incredibly skilled, but I think you've gotten to the point where you're starting to surpass even his skill."

"Don't say that," she said to him.

"Why not? Because it's true? I have little doubt Meyer would feel the same."

She took a deep breath, wiping her hands on her apron, and looked over to Finn. "You don't have to do this," she said.

"Do what?"

"Try to make me feel better."

"Do you remember when we were younger?"

"I remember a lot about when we were younger," she said.

"Do you remember how you used to follow Mother around the house? I used to tease you about it at the time."

"At the time?"

"Fine. I teased you even after we got older, but I think I was always a little bit jealous."

"Why?" Lena asked.

"Because you were always so assured of what you could do with Mother."

"You had no reason to be jealous of that," she said.

"I did. Father didn't want me involved in what he was doing. Not serving as a cartwright, but—"

"For good reason," Lena said, pausing at one of the beds and pulling back a dressing to check it before nodding to herself.

"For good reason, yes, but I never really had the same opportunity as you."

"You had every opportunity I had," Lena said.

Why was he going into this with her? It wasn't that he regretted anything that had happened. He had found his place. Finn had long ago given up the idea that he would ever serve on a crew, and he didn't even want to run the streets the way he once had, no longer wanting the dangers they presented. He was content with his role—content with knowing he served the king and was a valuable part of the city.

"I remember one time when Mother chased you out of the kitchen. Father had come back from a job." Finn closed his eyes, thinking back to that time. His father had staggered into the home, and Finn remembered the way he had clutched his hand up against his side, remembered the blood that had spilled out, staining his shirt. His father had forced a smile at Finn, as if trying to protect him from seeing what had happened, but Finn was not stupid, even then. He had known something had gone wrong.

When he had gone to the door, he found Oscar standing there, looking into the house, concern etched upon his face. When Oscar had seen Finn watching, he'd snuck off, disappearing down a nearby alleyway, leaving Finn alone.

"Mother took him to a back room. She was peeling away his dressings, and she looked as if she didn't know what to do."

"Mother wasn't a healer," Lena said.

"But you seemed to be, even then," Finn said. That had been a time when Finn had also thought he had an interest in healing, but hadn't reacted as well as Lena. "You told him to hold his hand up against his side, then you took his other hand and spoke to him."

"I didn't want to lose him," Lena said.

It was the first time Finn had been aware of the fact that their father's line of work might lead to his death. While Finn had known that his work had its dangers, he had always considered them theoretical dangers, not real ones. It had appealed to Finn up until that point. He thought chasing after his father and following in his footsteps was some grand adventure.

It had all changed for Finn that day.

Then it had changed again when their father had gotten pinched, tossed in the prison, and banished from the city.

"Finn?"

"I'm sorry," Finn said. "I don't know what got into me."

"Thank you," Lena said, turning back to him and taking his hand, forcing him to look up at her. "I don't know if I've ever thanked you."

"For what?"

"For caring." She started checking the man in front of her. "Even when it was dangerous for you, you still cared."

"That's just it," Finn said. "After a while, I started to forget how dangerous it might be."

"I never forgot," Lena said softly. "I tried to ignore it, and I tried in my own way to get you to stop, but I realize now it didn't do anything but drive you away from me."

"And that was never my intention," Finn said.

"I know."

He took a deep breath and looked around the room. "I have other things I need to be doing. Will you be okay here?"

"Of course," Lena said.

"Will you send word when anyone comes around?"

"I'm not sure I will even need to. I suspect Henry will continue to stop by."

"Probably," Finn said.

Even though Meyer would come by here, Finn still felt

as if he needed to be involved in the questioning. Meyer would want that.

Finn was the reason they had risked themselves coming here. He was the reason they had saved these men. And he was the reason they had somebody to question. Hopefully they would get answers that would provide them with information about who had precipitated the protests.

Finn nodded to Lena, but she had already turned away, continuing her work as she weaved through the beds.

As he neared the door, Wella looked over to him. "Leaving so soon?" She held out a jar of pale-white powder, twisting it in her hand. Her gray dress flowed down, brushing along the floor, and her stooped back seemed even more hunched than usual.

"I have other things I need to be doing," Finn said.

Wella cackled. "An executioner's duty is never done, is it?"

"I suppose not," Finn said.

"And what does Henry have you doing today?"

Finn shrugged. "It's not so much what he has me doing as it is what I'm choosing to do."

"I see," she said, giving him a knowing look.

It reminded Finn of Arlington's irritation when he'd asked for modifications to the prison. Meyer hadn't gone to him yet. Finn wondered how Meyer would get along with the warden after he did.

Finn shook his head. "I'm no master executioner."

"Not yet," Wella said.

"What do you have there?"

"Seeing as how you brought in so many injured, I thought it might be best if I mix up a little more sedative. These men are going to suffer if I don't."

"There are some who think they deserve to suffer."

"As I'm sure there are some who thought they should have been left to die," Wella said. She held Finn's gaze, and he wondered if she knew what had happened, and whether she knew that Meyer had suggested they leave the men behind.

If she did, why was she looking at Finn that way?

"They have answers that might help explain what's taking place in the city."

"Is that the only reason they deserve to live?"

Finn sighed. She knew how he felt. "Not the only reason."

"The hangman who heals. It's a shame so few see that side of your profession."

"There are enough who know," Finn said.

"But only those who need to. The ones who don't know probably should."

Finn grunted. "Now you're speaking in riddles."

"Maybe," she said, cackling again. "Your sister has proven herself yet again."

"She doesn't always feel that way," Finn said, turning and looking over to Lena, who was hunched over one of the injured. She was moving bandages again—peeling them away, applying ointment, then dressing the wounds once more. "She doesn't feel like she has her place."

"Then she must make one for herself."

He regarded Wella for a moment, an idea coming to him. "Can you help her?"

"Can anyone help a person make their way in the world?"

"Yes," Finn said.

"If they were helped along the journey, they wouldn't reach their destination."

"And if they weren't helped, they may never reach it."

Wella laughed and turned away, mixing another series of powders. "Go and do what you must, Finn Jagger."

"Thank you for helping," Finn said as he reached the door.

Wella nodded and began to hum to herself, whistling under her breath as she shifted from one foot to another, as if dancing in place.

Finn didn't how to react to Wella anymore. She had been his first instructor in apothecary medicine, teaching him about mixing various powders, medicines, lotions, and ointments. It was because of her that he had developed the nose he had for the various compounds involved in creating healing balms. If not for her, Finn didn't know if he would have the same depth of knowledge he had acquired. Lena had thanked him for caring, but maybe Finn needed to do a better job of thanking those who'd worked with him.

He paused at the door, and seeing her dancing in place, he decided perhaps he should do so another time. She seemed busy and distracted, the same way Finn was distracted.

He headed out the door and up the stairs. From there,

he made his way to the main level of the old prison, which reminded him of Declan. The walls were plain stone, the halls were dark and narrow, and there was a sort of oppressive feel to everything around him.

When he reached the door leading to the outside, he pulled it open and stepped into the cool daylight. The northern breeze still gusted, carrying the crisp, almost biting cold he'd been feeling for the last few weeks. Finn pulled his cloak around his shoulders, wishing he had dressed better for the weather.

They needed to question the injured, but first the injured had to come around enough for him to have the opportunity to do so. Until they did, Finn wasn't going to learn anything from them.

Even after they did, would it make a difference?

Nearly a hundred citizens had died in the protests—trampled, burned, or beaten by Archers. Several Archers had died too, most of them burned or trampled, but even a single Archer dying had raised the ire of the king in the past. Finn wondered how the king would react to the news this time.

He found his gaze drawn toward the Heshian palace in the distance. The protesters must have known the king was in the city. Somehow. That knowledge posed a danger to the city, to the kingdom, and to the king himself.

Finn typically didn't worry about the king, but if the protesters had come out because they had known the king had come to Verendal...

Finn would end up even more involved than he was now.

He took another deep breath.

He had to get back to his regular tasks.

While questioning those involved in the protests was a *part* of his regular tasks, it wasn't all he needed to do. One of the things Finn had learned in the time he'd been working with Master Meyer was that he had to ensure he didn't ignore any aspects of the job; he couldn't sacrifice one thing for the sake of another. He had done that before, and had allowed one disruption in the city to blind him to others.

What he needed was information.

Finn hurried through the streets, making his way past familiar shops. Many of them were left with shattered windows from the protests, forcing store owners to keep their shops boarded up or risk having them looted. Only those who had the means to do so were able to get their shops restored quickly.

When he passed a few people, they veered across the road, staying as far away from him as possible, and even the men cast nervous glances all around them, as if Finn might attack. He was dressed better than most within this section of the city, but was not expecting a response like this. Every so often, shouts rang out behind him or in the distance, and once he heard a shout that seemed to come from an alley nearby.

All of it left him tense and uneasy. He could easily understand how it would make those who had to live in this section feel much the same way. At least Finn could get out and go elsewhere. Others who lived here, like the child who scurried past him now, were stuck. Several of the buildings he passed had the marking of the black rose —some had it on posters like he'd seen before, but one looked as if it had been burned into the side.

As Finn was making his way through the street, he caught sight of a familiar face. Her golden hair was recognizable from where he stood, and as Jamie made her way toward him, he stopped until she looked up and noticed him.

"Mr. Jagger," she said. "My father spoke highly of you after you left. He was surprised that the king would care so much about his debt."

Finn tipped his head politely, looking around him. It seemed more dangerous in the streets of Verendal these days, which made him worry for her being out here on her own. "We try to resolve all debts," he said. "I'm just doing what the king asks of me."

She frowned, her brow furrowing, and it seemed as if a shadowy look crossed her face. "I can't imagine that's easy for someone like you."

"Someone like me?"

She waved a hand, motioning up and down his body. "Someone who comes from a place of... well, wealth, I suppose."

Finn started to smile. It was now the second time someone had thought that about him. Meyer wanted him to dress the part of the executioner, but he also wanted him to be able to blend in. There was a benefit in doing so.

"I come from the Brinder section. I didn't have much when I was growing up." He shrugged. "I've had to work for everything."

She nodded. "That might explain why my father liked you, then."

"Is that right?" He wanted to ask whether *she* liked him, but that didn't feel proper.

"Are you on the job?"

"Unfortunately." He realized what she was asking. "I should have an update for your father soon, I hope." It wasn't entirely true, but it felt better than telling her that they might not ever see compensation for Reginald's theft from him.

She twisted the fabric of her cloak and smiled tightly. "I have somewhere I need to be going, Mr. Jagger. I hope you understand?"

He nodded, watching her go for a moment before tearing his attention away.

By the time he reached the Wenderwolf tavern, Finn had counted dozens of shops that had needed to be boarded up. There was a strange suspicion in the streets, people glancing in every direction as others passed them, many of them darting off to the side of the street to avoid anyone getting too close. The entire city was on edge.

It saddened Finn to see the city get to this point, that there would be so much upheaval here, but at the same time, he understood. Everyone had their breaking point. Eventually, even the city itself had its breaking point. And the fact that an Archer had killed another man in one of the poor sections of the city—even if he'd been guilty of stealing—had tipped them over the edge.

The Wenderwolf tavern was situated in one of those poorer sections, though the Olin section wasn't quite as rundown as some of the others were. The tavern itself was well-kept, though Finn was a bit disappointed to see one of the windows had been shattered and boarded over, but the others were intact. Paint had been thrown on the side of the tavern, leaving a red splotch that looked like blood. For a moment, Finn thought it *was* blood, but the pattern was off and the color a bit too pale.

Music drifted out of the tavern, and he pushed open the door, stepping inside and pausing for a moment for his eyes to adjust. It was still early, so Finn didn't expect to find much activity there, but he hoped he could find Oscar, mostly so he could see if he knew anything about the protests. It was the only way he knew how to get in touch with him. If Oscar were to stop coming to the Wenderwolf, Finn wondered if he'd lose touch with him completely.

He didn't recognize any of the waitresses working today, though they were dressed in the way Annie preferred: always a bit revealing, with considerable cleavage showing—a way of drawing people in and keeping them there.

Finn took a seat. A young, blonde-haired woman sidled up to the table, leaning forward and winking at him. She offered him a full-lipped smile. "What can I get for you?"

"I'll take a mug of ale, and let Annie know that Finn Jagger is here to see her."

The woman straightened immediately and crossed her arms over her chest. "What are you here to see Annie about?"

"Just one friend wanting to talk to another," Finn said.

She regarded Finn for a long moment, and looked as if she wanted to argue, but then she spun around, heading toward the kitchen.

Though he had been back to the Wenderwolf many times over the years, he still had an uneasy feeling coming here. Annie treated him about as well as he expected her to, but the tension between them lingered, despite how she'd helped him.

So much had changed for him since he had become the executioner.

Now he was a journeyman, which meant he had a place within the kingdom, regardless of whether it was in Verendal. No longer was he a thief on a crew.

But it wasn't just Annie with whom he had felt some tension. Finn had drifted apart from Oscar as well.

There were times when he missed Oscar and wished he could know his old friend better than he did, but he felt that way about many things these days.

"I hear you came asking for me."

Finn looked up to see Annie sliding into the booth opposite him. She was two decades his senior, though her hair was still dark and her eyes bright, if lined with wrinkles. She had on a pale-yellow dress underneath a white, flour-stained apron.

"Annie."

"Finn Jagger," Annie said. "I haven't seen you in the tavern in a few months."

Finn frowned, looking around. The Wenderwolf still had a comfortable familiarity, despite the fact that he hadn't been here in a while. Could it really have been a few months though? It seemed like only a week had passed since his last visit, but his assignments often pulled him away, and between errands, questioning, and journeys outside of the city, Finn often found himself distracted. That said nothing about the studying he did, trying to master healing and apothecary medicine.

"I didn't realize it had been that long," he said.

"I'm not the only person who's noticed how rarely you visit these days."

"That's why I'm here."

Annie cocked her head at him. "You came to apologize to the Hand? I'm sure he'll be pleased to hear that."

"I'm sure."

Annie laughed softly. "Not apologize, then. And now all of this," she said, spreading her hands off to the side.

"This isn't my fault," he said.

"Who ever cast blame?" Annie said. "I was just remarking on the fact that we now have this." She leaned forward, and the waitress who had first greeted Finn came over to the table, sliding a mug of ale in front of him and looking over to Annie briefly before turning and heading back to the kitchen.

Finn frowned, looking from the waitress then back to Annie. "An interesting new hire you have."

"Who said she was new?"

"I might not have been around her quite as much as I used to be, Annie, but I recognize your kind of girls." It finally occurred to Finn what had felt off about that woman. She had been similar to the kind of girls Annie preferred, but not the same. "Guards?"

"Careful, Finn," Annie said, lowering her voice.

"You don't want others knowing?"

"You don't know what you're talking about."

"I think I do." He looked around the inside of the tavern and realized it wasn't just that one woman who had seemed a little strange. Most of them were buxom, lovely, and could easily have worked for Annie before, but all of them had something a little peculiar about them. Perhaps it was the edge to them, but regardless, Annie was worried. Her protections would be effective though. Guards disguised as servers would certainly provide a measure of security that others wouldn't expect.

"Do you care to tell me why I have the pleasure of your visit?" Annie asked.

Finn pulled the mug toward him and took a long sip, then set it back on the table. Annie's ale was always some of the best in the city. Maybe it was just the familiarity of it, more than anything else, but Finn had always appreciated it.

"Did you hire them before the attack or after?" Finn asked.

"Which attack?"

"The one on the city."

Annie leaned back, crossing her arms. "That's why you're here."

"I'm looking into what happened."

"Some stupid bastards got a bug in their ass that they deserved more from the king." Annie shrugged. "It happens from time to time, so I'm not terribly surprised it would happen now."

"It happens that protests are organized to the point where men decide to attack Archers?"

"After all that the Archers have done lately? Why does that bother you?"

They *had* been more violent during their arrests. Junker had been the catalyst, but he wasn't the only one who'd suffered.

"What bothers me is that a hundred men died because of those attacks," Finn said.

"How many else have died throughout the city for other reasons?" she asked.

"I don't know. Probably just as many."

"And who are the murderers?"

"You're going to say it's the king."

Annie shook her head slightly. "I would never make that claim. I know better than to make the mistake of speaking against the king."

"I didn't say you were speaking against the king."

"Making comments like that certainly suggests that I am," Annie said. "Besides, all I was getting at is that we face other threats in the city."

"It depends on your line of work," Finn said.

"And what about in *your* line of work?" Annie asked.

"I serve the king," Finn said.

"Of course you do, Finn," Annie said. "I wouldn't assume anything else."

Finn leaned forward. "I'm not trying to cause trouble with you, Annie."

"I know you're not."

"I'm just trying to do the right thing."

"And what do you think that is?"

Finn shook his head. "I don't know. I've got men who nearly died who I'm waiting to question so I can understand what's taking place in the city—because I can assure you that what is happening here is certainly coordinated in some way."

"What makes you think anyone would intend to coordinate a protest in the city?"

"Just what I've seen," Finn said. "What can you tell me about the black rose posters hung around the city?"

Annie fell silent, leaning back, keeping her arms crossed over her chest while Finn sipped at his ale. "I can let Oscar know you came looking for him."

She knew something. Why not tell him?

"Annie?"

"I can't say much about it. Just a part of the Black Rose movement." The way she said it suggested a name behind the movement. "There was a time when you wouldn't have needed to ask."

"Does it have anything to do with the protests?"

"Probably not, but you'll have to figure that out on your own."

Finn considered pressing her more before deciding against it. "Thank you."

"I don't know if Oscar wants to get involved," Annie said.

"He doesn't *want* to or he *won't*?"

Annie took a deep breath, letting it out slowly as she

looked around the tavern. "I never wanted anything to happen to the Wenderwolf. I had a place my girls could be safe, but..." She shook her head, turning her attention back to Finn. "When I was targeted, I didn't know what to do, or how to protect everyone else. I tried, but it seemed like there wasn't any way for me to ensure everyone was safe."

"No one blamed you for what happened," Finn said. She'd never gone into that with him before. She preferred to keep what happened with Gina and the witchcraft to herself. Finn understood.

"I know what happened. I know I could have done more, could have dug into who I hired more." She looked around the tavern again before her gaze settled once more on Finn. "So you ask about these new girls. I'm trying to ensure everyone here is safe: the girls I have working for me, my patrons, and the tavern itself."

Finn just nodded. "I think everybody appreciates what you do for them."

"I'm just trying to do what's needed," she said. "I wish it weren't necessary, but unfortunately, somebody has to intervene." She watched Finn for a moment, then got to her feet. "Don't get Oscar involved in something that's going to get him killed."

"I don't intend to."

"Even if you don't intend to do it, he would do anything for you, Finn. That's what I'm afraid of."

"I would do anything for Oscar," he said.

Annie tipped her head to the side, regarding him. "Would you?"

It was a loaded question and Finn knew it.

He and Oscar had this same discussion several times before, and each time they did, Finn understood the direction of the conversation, knowing that Oscar wondered whether Finn *would* be willing to sacrifice on behalf of his old friend. And each time they had that conversation, Finn questioned whether he could do what Oscar wanted.

If it came down to it, what would Finn choose?

Would it be his friend, or would it be his duty?

It seemed like it should be an easy answer.

But it was something that had always left Finn worried.

He didn't want to have to choose, and he certainly didn't want to be put into a position where he'd be forced to make a decision like that, especially not one that would place Oscar's life in his hands. But Oscar had also promised Finn that he would never put him in such a position. Finn counted on him to live up to that promise.

"Can you let him know I came by?"

"He'll know," Annie said, "and when he does, I'm going to tell him he should stay out of it."

"I understand."

"We have a good thing going here now. He's gotten out of some of the troublesome habits he had before and he's finally found a bit of stability. I think he deserves it, don't you?"

Finn nodded again. "Oscar is one of my oldest friends."

"If he's your friend, then you'll leave him out of this."

"I'm worried he's going to get pulled into it one way or another."

Annie regarded Finn, shaking her head. "I know you want to help him. Gods, Finn, I know you care about Oscar. And he certainly cares about you. The two of you have always thought you could take care of each other. He sees you as a son, and you see him as an older brother. But both of you think you can protect the other."

"And?"

"And I fear the more you grow and develop, the less likely it is you're going to be able to offer him anything he needs."

Finn sighed. Maybe she was right.

"I'll do my best to keep him out of it."

"Well, then you wouldn't have come here in the first place. All I'm asking now is for you to not involve him too deeply. And I'm asking you do everything you can to protect him if you *do* have to pull him in." Annie backed away and nodded to Finn. "Enjoy your ale."

Finn drank his ale, though he didn't feel any joy in it. It was disappointing to have a mug of ale in front of him and not savor its taste.

He made his way back to Master Meyer's home and met him in the small garden in front. Meyer was arranging flowers and looked up as Finn approached. These days, Meyer spent more time in his garden than he did anywhere else.

Finn would rather be looking into Reginald and why he'd died, but he had so many other errands to run in order to keep the office of executioner running smoothly.

Meyer could at least *look* like he was trying to help.

"Have you had an opportunity to talk to Warden Arlington?" Finn asked.

Meyer looked over to him, an unreadable expression in his eyes. "Not yet."

Finn opened his mouth to say something before clamping it down.

"I see that upset you," Meyer said.

"He doesn't respect me, Master Meyer. When I challenged him on the decorations in the prison—"

"Was it necessary for you to do that?"

"I don't know." He knew there was a lesson Meyer was trying to get across, but Finn wasn't exactly sure what it was. "It's not only Arlington. The Archers have started questioning my authority as well."

"Does that matter?"

"They need to follow where we lead."

"They follow where I lead," Master Meyer said. "Will they follow where you lead?"

"That's my point," Finn said, suppressing the irritation starting to creep in.

"How long do you think it took for me to develop my authority?"

Finn frowned. "I don't know. I assumed they have always followed your direction."

Meyer sniffed. "There is an aura about our title. I know you focus on the negative aspects of that aura, but when it comes to what we do and the way we serve the king, there are times when that aura benefits us. It took me years to build. And now you think to throw your weight around and force yourself into the chain of command while others know exactly where you stand?"

Meyer rarely became this forceful with Finn.

"If you do things the way you are supposed to, serve the way the king asks of you, your authority will build from there. You don't need to demand respect. It will be given." He seemed to hesitate a moment, then reached into his pocket and pulled out a letter, which Finn took.

"Where?" he asked, immediately knowing what it was. They got requests like this fairly often. Communities surrounding Verendal needed an executioner.

"This one's not far; otherwise, I don't think the court would have asked it of us. A village nearby called Weverth. Should only take you a day or two."

"What about the protests?"

"The Archers have it under control." His voice was firm.

"And Reginald?" When Meyer frowned at him, Finn sighed. Maybe it was something only *he* was concerned about. "The man who killed himself in the debtors' prison."

"If there's anything that comes up, I'll let you know when you return."

Finn knew better than to argue.

Instead, he headed into the house to begin his preparations to leave.

CHAPTER SEVEN

Traveling out of the city didn't bother Finn the way it used to. Needing to ride a horse did, however. He looked over to his companion, patting the fat gray mare on the side, and wondering if the stable had intentionally provided him with another overweight horse for this journey. Finn hadn't been able to endure riding for very long without needing to get out of the saddle, unable to tolerate the stretch of his legs and thighs making his knees bend at an uncomfortable angle.

He'd pushed the horse for speed, though, and she'd responded. She might be fat, but she could be fast when necessary. The forest towered over him on either side of the Kings Road, and Finn found himself looking over to the trees from time to time, mostly out of curiosity, though occasionally because he heard a sound that made him question whether there was anything moving in the forest. With everything that had been going on in the city,

Finn wouldn't be terribly surprised if he was being followed.

It was the fact that there was so much going on in the city that troubled him. How much was the Black Rose movement tied into the protests? Annie hadn't said, but Finn had a feeling she knew more than she was letting on. The city had been quiet when he'd left, but how long would it stay that way? Eventually, things would explode again.

It always seemed like Meyer sent him off on these journeys when Finn felt as if he needed to be in the city. Maybe that was Meyer's way of proving to Finn he wasn't nearly as important as Finn thought himself to be, or perhaps it had more to do with how Finn had progressed in his training.

This time, Finn left after having the feeling that he'd somehow upset Meyer.

Which was even more of a reason for him to rush his return.

It had been a few weeks since he'd been called out of the city. Long enough that the trees had started to take on different colors, the leaves turning from deep, vibrant green to the oranges, reds, and browns of the change of seasons. The air had shifted as well, taking on a bit of a damp quality, and it left Finn feeling as if the cold of winter would be here far sooner than he wished. He had tolerated winters much better lately, ever since taking on his role as an executioner, but that still didn't mean he enjoyed them. In Verendal, winters could be harsh, and he had come to dislike needing to run through the city on all of his errands while it was that cold.

He thumbed through Reginald's journal while he rode, but still didn't find anything helpful within it. He couldn't shake the feeling that there was something there he'd missed. There was a list of shop owners here, including several general stores, a luthier, a bookseller, a silversmith, and a couple Finn didn't recognize.

The horse stirred.

Finn looked over, trying to get a sense of why the mare would be bucking now. She was unsettled, though he didn't know if it was because of him—and it certainly could be, especially as Finn was a little unsettled himself—or whether it was something the horse detected.

"What has you spooked?"

The horse swung her head toward him, whinnying softly, then jerked on the reins, as if trying to get free of Finn.

He held on to them tightly. If she bolted, not only would it take him quite a long time to return to the city, but he would end up walking to Weverth.

"You just need to settle down," Finn said, patting the horse on his side.

Not that he expected that to make much of a difference. The horse probably knew how irritated he was and realized she didn't want to be here either.

They made their way a little farther along the road, and Finn frowned as he looked into the distance. The road curled around a bend. He shifted the pack strapped to his back, including the sword he had there. He wanted to keep one hand on the reins.

A rustling through the leaves caught his attention, and Finn turned toward it.

He muttered to himself, climbing back into the horse's saddle. He nudged the horse on her flank, getting her to speed along the road. Finn's legs screamed at the movement, already pinched from the time he'd spent in the saddle throughout the day, but given the unrest around Verendal, Finn wasn't going to be caught flat-footed.

It was times like these when he wished he had some fighting skills. He might have a sword, and could use it in a pinch, but he wasn't particularly gifted with the blade, which left him at a disadvantage if highwaymen came upon him. Still, carrying a sword had a certain advantage. It made him look more intimidating, even if he didn't necessarily feel that way.

He rounded the curve in the road and expected to come across what had spooked the horse, but there was nothing other than the empty expanse of the road.

Finn kept the horse moving at a trot. The fat mare was difficult for him to stay seated on, and he felt as if he continued to slide around in the saddle, very nearly tipping off the side of the horse. He was thankful that he had been riding for a while, even if it had been on short journeys outside of the city, but at least he wasn't nearly as saddle sore as he would've been otherwise. His backside still hurt, and every jostling step left his thighs aching, but he would survive it.

And he couldn't wait until they reached the destination.

It was near dusk when he reached Weverth.

The village was like so many others in the countryside around Verendal. In this case, it was more forested than some. The last time he'd left the city, he'd headed across the plains that led him to the village of Tell, which he had found well-equipped for what he had needed to do. It had been an easy stop. They had a rapist there, a man who had violated two women before they had a chance to stop him, and he had willingly admitted to his crime. That had made Finn's job that much easier, and he had carried out the sentencing quickly before returning to Verendal. These days, Finn didn't like being gone from the city any longer than necessary. He felt as if he were needed in Verendal, especially as Master Meyer had him doing more and more tasks on his own.

Of course, to hear Master Meyer speak of it, Finn should want to spend more time on his own out in the surrounding countryside. It was a way to augment his income, and Finn certainly appreciated that opportunity, especially as he hoped to one day afford a place of his own.

Weverth was nestled in the forest, just off the side of the King's Road, with towering pine trees surrounding it. A few trees with larger leaves were interspersed among the pines, most of them already having changed color. As the wind tugged on their upper branches, the trees swayed in the breeze, carrying the energy of the wind—but also something else.

The air smelled crisp, earthy, but there was a coppery undertone to it, along with a hint of rot. Death.

Finn slowed the horse, heading toward the village more carefully, noting only a few people milling in the streets. Maybe there was nothing for him to be concerned about, but he had grown cautious in his time working with Master Meyer, and had learned to trust instinct when it flashed in him.

As he neared the village, he climbed down out of the saddle and approached the closest of the buildings.

They were farms, though small, and most of them had fenced-in yards to contain livestock. Several cattle grazed in the yards, and he caught sight of a couple of pigs wallowing in the muck.

Finn passed through, making his way along the main thoroughfare into the village itself. He looked along the street, taking in the sight of the houses and a few shops. All the buildings in this village were two or three stories tall, with steep, sloped roofs, and were situated along the narrow cobblestone streets. With only a few people moving along the streets, there was an empty, albeit cozy, appearance to them. The houses were painted in browns and whites, with an occasional splash of color on shutters opened to the day. His gaze drifted to the massive church that rose up in the distance. As he approached, he realized the church had both the markings of Heleth and the Church of Fell.

The Church of Fell was a newer sect, having cropped up over the last decade or so. Finn didn't have much experience with them, but the priests of Fell had a different attitude toward sentencing than the priests of Heleth, who offered comfort and forgiveness to those who came before them in their final hours. It was almost as if the priests of Fell, however, wanted to torment the condemned, berating them in their final moments, castigating them and telling them how they would suffer in the afterlife.

Finn didn't put a lot of stock into any of the different gods, not nearly as much as what he suspected he should given his profession, but he found the particular ideology of the followers of most of the gods to be unpleasant. Most of the people who were sentenced to die had good reason for it, and while all of them had caused suffering and anguish to others for them to be sentenced in such a way, Finn still felt as if they deserved a humane approach.

He had never been to Weverth for a sentencing. Many of the small towns and villages dotting the landscape around Verendal were like that. They were self-sufficient, and rarely did Finn ever spend much time in them—rarely did he *need* to spend much time in them. The only time he had been back to a village more than once had been when he had needed to obtain additional information.

He paused along the road, noting the happenings around him.

A child running down the street was dragged away by his mother, scolded for being out.

A bell tolled softly, a steady ringing that carried to Finn's ears from the massive temple in front of him. Heleth.

Or, it might not be Heleth. It might be celebrants of Fell.

Finn frowned, turning and looking all around him before heading forward again.

He didn't know where he was to go. That wasn't uncommon when he took these journeys out of the city. Oftentimes, he was simply to come to the village, find out what they wanted from him, then figure out what the condemned was guilty of.

He patted the horse on her side.

He didn't have to wait long.

Another bell tolled, this one a little more urgently than the last. There was a hint of energy to its sound along with something else—a vibrant, trembling pulling that seemed to carry deep within Finn. He felt as if there was a message hidden in it.

He pushed those thoughts away. That had to be his imagination, nothing else.

The tolling continued.

Each time it rang, there came another jolt from some place deep within him.

Finn had been around magic enough times over the last few years to have a passing familiarity with it. Not only hegen magic, but now witchcraft—and even Alain-sith magic, though that was something he didn't have quite as much experience with.

The door to the church opened. A dark-robed priest stepped forward. Finn recognized the robes, as the priests were common enough in Verendal, even if he'd never celebrated at one of their churches. One of the priests of Fell. Was Heleth not celebrated here anymore?

The priest frowned as he took a look at Finn. He was thin, his wiry frame hidden by his robe, and had close-cropped brown hair, leaving him with an almost angry appearance. He studied Finn for a moment, then the parishioners started to pour out of the church, making their way quickly beyond, out into the streets, dispersing back to houses, businesses, and their evening activities.

He made his way over to the priest, tipping his head politely. If he was a priest of Fell, Finn needed to be respectful, even if he didn't celebrate Fell.

"My name is Finn Jagger, and I am—"

"I am aware of who you are, Mr. Jagger. We had word that you would be coming."

Finn looked around the village, his gaze settling on one person then another, before turning his attention back to the priest. "Are you my contact here?"

"The village of Weverth is a faithful servant of Fell," the priest said.

Finn smiled tightly, squeezing the reins of the horse. "And what does it mean to be a faithful servant of Fell?"

The priest tipped his head to the side, frowning at Finn. "I would have figured that an executioner, especially one from the city of Verendal, would be familiar with the expectations of Fell."

Finn shrugged. "I serve the king, not the church."

"And the king serves the church," the priest said.

Finn glanced over to the church. "Does this church still celebrate Heleth?"

Finn had given some thought to Fell over the years, but he was an unusual god, and one whom he had struggled with while in Verendal. Presumably, he was the god of wealth and abundance, which might be the reason that the people of this village celebrated him. He could see a desire to celebrate the harvest by honoring Fell.

Part of it bothered him though.

"Heleth and Fell both lead toward the same purpose," the priest said. "And the people within the village of Weverth recognize that. They recognize how they must serve all the gods."

He would never have imagined that anyone would describe the church of Fell as being somehow correlated with that of Heleth. Heleth was the mother who oversaw everything within the church. It would be unusual for anyone to make that claim, though Finn hadn't spent much time with any priests of Fell.

"Perhaps if you have not had a chance to fully understand the way that we all serve Fell, you and I should spend some time together," the priest continued.

Within Verendal, an invitation to celebrate Fell was rare. They wanted only the wealthy, and Finn was far from wealthy.

"Perhaps when my assignment here is complete."

"You might find you need to visit Fell in order for you to understand what is asked of you here."

"I didn't realize I would need to coordinate with any of the priests to accomplish my task," Finn said.

"Certainly not to accomplish it, but you must understand you have quite an interesting position to those within Weverth," he said.

Finn wasn't about to argue with a priest, especially one who he didn't fully understand; he hadn't come here to get into a religious debate.

"Who do I speak to about my fee?"

The priest frowned, and for a moment, Finn wondered if he'd guessed wrong about him. Maybe he wasn't the one to ask.

"You serve the king."

"In Verendal. My standard rate is five drebs plus housing for the night."

He'd learned to ask for room to be included; otherwise, he ended up paying for it.

The priest was silent.

"I will take your silence as an agreement to my terms. I would like to see the accused, if I may."

"Accused? I'm afraid, Mr. Jagger, that you were summoned here because he is the condemned."

Finn nodded. "I understand, but I question everyone who calls one of my guild to the city. We must ensure we satisfy the king's justice and not merely the whims of those in the city."

"I see," the priest said.

"Do you?" Finn asked, arching a brow. "Because it is important that you understand I am here to serve on behalf of King Porman."

"Yes," the priest said. "I do see that, and I understand your predicament."

THE EXECUTIONER'S REBELLION | 109

Finn just chuckled softly. "It's no predicament. I am here to ensure I'm meeting the obligations of the king. Now, if you don't mind, I would like to visit with your *accused*." He made a point of emphasizing that word, and earned another hard look from the priest of Fell, who motioned for Finn to follow.

He headed through the village, leading him along the road. He hadn't even offered to take Finn's horse, nor had he offered to see if Finn had any needs.

"Is there a village council?" Finn asked.

The priest glanced over to him, shaking his head. "Not for many years, I'm afraid."

"No elders?"

The priest shook his head again.

Finn frowned again. "Then the church leads here?"

"Why, the church leads everywhere, Finn Jagger."

The priest continued leading him along the street and Finn followed. They reached a place near the back of the village, and from there, Finn noticed a row of small houses that were different from many of the others— smaller than those he'd found on the outskirts of the city, mostly a single story, and though they were made of wood, they looked to be more hurriedly built and somehow stouter. It was strange.

"We don't have any of the prisons you have in Verendal. We use what we have, and the people are understanding. It is as Fell has commanded."

The priest guided him toward one of the houses. It was small, all wooden, with a thatched roof. The priest pulled a keychain out of his pocket, turned the key in the handle, and pulled the door open. Darkness seemed to stream out, almost as if it were a thing alive.

Finn looked over to the priest. "What is his name?"

"We would have included that in the summons, Mr. Jagger."

"Master Meyer told me only the village, not his name." The priest tensed slightly at the mention of Meyer.

"His name is Lyle Martin. A blasphemer if I have ever seen one before."

"That is his crime?"

The priest looked over to Finn and shot him an unreadable look. "If his only crime was blaspheming against Fell, then you would not have been summoned here, Mr. Jagger. The church can handle blasphemers. This, unfortunately, is something else. He serves a darkness, and he has foul urges he found himself succumbing to."

"What urges are those?" Finn asked, a feeling of dread starting to build within him.

"Why, he desecrated the dead."

Finn waited for the priest to expand on that, but he did not.

Finn stepped inside the room. It stank of the smell he had detected when he had first come to the village. Maybe it was tied to what this Lyle Martin had been doing with the dead.

"I would like a lantern," Finn said.

"Is that necessary?" the priest asked.

"I need to question him."

"I'm afraid that questioning him is not needed. As I told you—"

"And I told *you* that I am here serving the king's justice. The king demands that all in my role would look into the claims against the accused. In this case, I must ensure your accusations are founded, and then..."

He had no idea what the priest meant by Lyle Martin desecrating the dead, but considering some of the things Finn had seen over the years, he had far too many ideas of what Lyle might have done, and it left him unsettled.

He had no interest in learning more about it, but he had to. For him to know everything he needed to do, and for him to know the details of what this man was accused of, Finn wasn't sure that he had much choice but to question him thoroughly.

"I will send someone with a lantern for you, Mr. Jagger."

He stepped away, closing the door, and sealed Finn in the darkness.

He tensed, looking around the room, waiting for his eyes to adjust, but they didn't.

Then the sound of scraping movement came scurrying toward him.

CHAPTER EIGHT

Finn braced himself for an attack.

As the movement came toward him, all of a sudden there was a jerk of metal, the sound of chains clanging, and a grunt.

They hadn't left him here untethered.

Finn breathed out a sigh of relief and cursed himself. For a moment, he'd thought the priest had wanted him placed in danger. It was foolish feeling nervous here, but at the same time, there was something unpleasant about this village.

He should take the priest up on the offer of spending time with him. He did want to know more about the church of Fell.

"Lyle Martin?"

His eyes had started to adjust to the darkness.

There was a dark shadow in the room and the air had a foulness to it. More than urine and feces, it was the stench he knew from his time in the prisons—something rotting, as if the man himself were decaying.

"My name is Finn Jagger. I'm the king's executioner. I'm here to question you."

There was another jerk on the chains, a rattling that came from farther away in the darkness. While he couldn't see much, Finn *felt* the sound. It was unpleasant, and it left him worried about what this man might do. He was careful not to react too much.

"I need you to tell me what you are responsible for having done."

He wished the priest would've shared a little bit more with him.

"Unfortunately, if you don't speak on your own behalf, I will have to take the word of the priest—"

There was a louder rattle this time, the sound of chains jerking and clanking mixed with something else.

Something feral.

Perhaps this was a mistake, pushing in here without knowing quite what he was doing.

"If your name is Lyle Martin, I need for you to step forward."

Finn tensed. Waiting.

"It's my understanding that you are accused of desecrating the dead."

"No desecration," a harsh voice said from the darkness, far closer to Finn than he had expected.

"If you didn't desecrate the dead, then why have they accused you of it?"

"No desecration."

Finn glanced back at the door.

That harsh voice, the animal-like growl, and the possibility that this man was involved in witchcraft all made Finn wonder whether he would be able to break free of the chains.

"All I'm trying to understand is what you were accused of doing. If you can share that with me, then we can work together, and—"

"No desecration," he said yet again.

"Then what did you do?"

"Cleanse," he said, his voice low, as if it had been burned.

"How did you cleanse them?" Finn asked.

"Cleanse," he said again.

Finn shivered.

He knew he shouldn't be bothered by this, but there was something strange and terrifying about this man.

Finn suspected that the priest knew more than he was letting on. He had intentionally left him here in the dark, either to scare him or to coax him into reacting in a specific way. If the priest had an agenda, then Finn was obligated to understand what that was, as well.

It wouldn't be the first time he'd found that people in a village had an agenda. He had never found any priests involved in things like that, though.

"Why did you have to cleanse them?" Finn asked carefully.

"They have been tainted," he said.

"How are they tainted?" Finn asked.

"Tainted."

Finn shook his head. He wasn't going to get anywhere like this.

"I'm afraid that if you can't reveal anything more, then the testimony of the others will weigh more heavily. Unfortunately, given the accusation against you, I would have no choice but to exert the king's justice."

He didn't even know what sentence would be appropriate in this case.

"I would like you to come as far forward as you can. Slowly, but enough for me to see you."

Finn turned to the door and thrust it open, letting a bit of daylight spill in. He was thankful the priest of Fell hadn't locked him in here, though he wouldn't have been terribly surprised to learn he had.

"Come forward," Finn said again.

There was a bit of movement. The sound of chains dragging across the wooden floor, and a soft, breathy sound, a wheezing that told him Lyle Martin was approaching.

Finn waited, then looked over to see a thin, older man with gray hair and wide eyes—a wildness in them that Finn had seen in people who were a bit touched.

This might be a religious matter more than anything else. Maybe that was the reason the priest of Fell was irritated with Finn's presence. Maybe they didn't really want Finn here.

"What did you do?" Finn asked softly.

The man jerked on the chains again and glared at Finn, the wildness still present in his eyes.

"Cleanse," the man said.

Finn approached him slowly. He took a deep breath, trying to figure out what the smell was.

"What have they given you?"

"Medicine," he said.

"For what purpose?"

"Medicine," he said again.

Finn still felt like he was getting nowhere with this man.

And until he had somebody here to help him, Finn wasn't about to move any closer, even though the man was bound up in chains and shouldn't be able to escape. Still, he felt he had an obligation to Lyle Martin—one that would only be satisfied by trying to dig into what he had truly done. Finn wasn't convinced that desecrating the dead was enough of a crime to deserve the sentencing that he had been summoned to the city to provide.

"Why don't you tell me about yourself?" Finn shook his head. "I understand you felt like you needed to cleanse the dead. I also understand the priest feels you did not. I don't know who is right and who is wrong, only that I am obligated to—"

The man darted forward, jerking on the chains again, and his eyes got wide. "You. Cleanse."

Finn stared at him.

"He has been like that since we captured him," a voice said.

Finn looked over to see a brown-haired man with a medium build in the doorway, his arms crossed over his chest. At first, Finn thought he might be another priest, but he wasn't wearing a robe like the first priest did. What he did have on was a marker for Heleth, a slender band of silver around his neck that surprised Finn given what he'd seen in the village so far.

"What can you tell me about him?" Finn asked.

"You must be the hangman we brought in." He held out his hand, waiting for Finn to take it. "Name is Olanth Roaln."

Finn briefly shook the man's hand, thinking it was more of the greeting he had expected to get when he'd come to Weverth—not the type he'd gotten from the priest.

"Finn Jagger."

"You don't look much like a hangman," Olanth said and shrugged, his gaze taking in the sword. "Other than that. Though to be honest, can't say I know much about what a hangman might look like."

"You'd be surprised."

"Really? I'm sure you've got a few stories. Maybe when all this business is over, we can sit in the tavern—we only have the one—and share a pint."

There had been a time in Finn's life when such a request would have been welcomed. There was still a part of him that wanted to have friendships, but the job made that difficult. Relationships even more so. Finn had stopped trying to find someone willing to spend their time with an executioner.

"Maybe," Finn said, forcing a smile. If Olanth would know something about what happened with this man, then perhaps he could be of some use. "Can you tell me about Lyle?"

"Not much. He's lived outside of the village for the better part of my life. Comes in from time to time, makes his trades, buys supplies, then disappears. We don't see much of him for months at a time. Sometimes seasons."

"Where does he live?"

Olanth waved toward the trees. "Out there. Figure a man lives alone that long, it's going to drive him a little mad, you know? Can't say anyone was altogether surprised when he was caught."

"Caught doing what?" Finn asked.

Olanth looked over to Finn. "They didn't tell you?"

"I get a summons asking for an executioner in the village. That's about the extent of what I know. It's not usually detailed enough for me to know why I've been called out of the city."

"That don't bother you?"

There was the sound of chains inside the home again, a steady rattle that suggested Lyle was attempting to break free once more. If he *were* using some sort of witchcraft—and that was the only thing Finn could think of to explain what he'd been doing with the bodies—he wouldn't have that hard of a time breaking free.

"That's the job. I serve in Verendal, but as a journeyman, I have to help in places outside of the city when needed. Like Weverth here."

"We don't have much need for executioners normally." He looked behind him, and it took Finn a moment to realize that he'd turned his attention to the church rising up in the background. "The priests have helped with that."

"You celebrate Fell and Heleth?" He nodded to the

necklace Olanth wore before looking over to the man inside.

"We celebrate all the gods in Weverth. Not just the ones that are easy."

Finn smiled tightly. "Easy?"

"The priests teach us that some of the gods are easier to follow than others, but that if we follow all of them, and if we can find a way to appease them, we don't have to fear their wrath."

That hadn't been Finn's experience with the gods *or* with the priests. In Verendal, the priests had a very different view of the gods, though there were plenty of people who thought the way to honor the gods was to fear them. It just wasn't what Finn would have wanted to be a part of how he honored any god.

"I suppose we have to take any protection we can get outside of what Verendal offers," Olanth said. "I doubt it's like that in Verendal."

"Have you ever visited?"

"That's too far away for me to reach."

"It's only a few days." Not even that. One by a fast horse. Maybe two or three by foot.

"By horse. There aren't many of us in Weverth who have one," Olanth said.

Finn looked over to the mare tied to the post outside the house. She'd stood quietly since he'd gone into the home, so if there was one thing he could take from all of this, it was that she had a more stoic nature than he would have expected based on his experience coming through the forest with her. He had thought she would be more skittish and expected her to jump more based on what Finn had encountered inside the home, especially considering how Lyle had jerked on the chains to try to rattle Finn.

"I don't think most people in Verendal have horses either. This isn't mine."

"You borrowed it?"

"Something like that." Finn looked to the house again. "Would you be willing to show me to Lyle's home?"

"I don't know," Olanth started, looking toward the forest. "It's getting late and that's not really the place you want to travel in the dark."

Finn nodded toward the house. Now Lyle had started growling again, his voice taking on a throaty, raw sound. "A man's life depends on me knowing what he did. For me to do my job..." He looked over to Olanth, wondering if that might be the way to get through to him before realizing that wasn't going to be enough. "If you lead me to his home, I would have time to share stories with you."

"I'd rather do that over a pint of ale, but I suppose..." He looked behind him. "Let me get a lantern. I was supposed to do that anyway but forgot on my way here." He shrugged. "Besides, don't want to go traipsing through the forest in the dark and end up lost." He regarded the mare. "We could ride. That might be faster."

"I doubt it." When the man frowned, Finn just shrugged. "The trees would make it difficult to navigate. She's not going to go that much faster than we'd be able to travel on foot."

"That's too bad. I haven't ridden before."

Finn almost smiled at the idea of giving Olanth a chance to ride the mare. With her round body, it was a wonder the saddle even stayed on. "Maybe when we return I'll let you take her out."

"It's a deal."

He hurried off, leaving Finn alone in front of the home. They were on the outskirts of Weverth, the quickly darkening forest nearby. It was mostly filled with pine trees, and the scent of their needles drifted to his nostrils. The earthy, damp odor of the forest lingered in the air as well, though it carried the same strange, almost foul stench he'd noticed when he first came into Weverth. That had faded a little, enough that he didn't notice it quite as much as he had when he'd first come, but not entirely.

He sorted through the saddlebags of the mare and grabbed a few strips of dried meat and cheese, then ate while waiting for Olanth to return. He didn't love the idea of heading out into the forest in the darkness, but he *did* need to see where Lyle lived, if only so he could get a sense of the man. Finn wanted to know what kind of a person he might be to try to understand why he would have done what he'd been accused of doing. As he stood there, he realized he still didn't even know what it was that Lyle had done.

Olanth returned carrying a lantern and a pack slung over his shoulder.

"Do you think we're going to be gone overnight?" Finn asked.

"I can't say that I know. I just figure it was better for us to be prepared for any possibility." Olanth shifted his pack and held out the lantern. "You want to carry it?"

Finn glanced over to the house. The chains had gone silent, almost as if Lyle realized that Finn and Olanth intended to visit his home and wanted to hear what else Finn might be up to. "I don't know the way, so maybe it makes more sense for you to guide us."

Olanth shrugged. "Maybe you should unsheathe that sword of yours."

"It's not that kind of a sword."

"What kind of a… oh. I see. I suppose you wouldn't have that kind of a sword."

Finn just nodded.

"Have you ever used it? Wait, what kind of question is that?" Olanth said, shaking his head and smacking himself on the side. "Of course you've used it. You're an executioner. And you come to Weverth carrying a blade like that, so of course you would've had some experience using it."

Finn chuckled softly. "Why don't you lead the way, and I'll tell you anything you want to know."

"Good enough," Olanth said.

He started off, heading back through the village, not quite the way Finn would've expected.

When they had traveled through a few streets, he veered off, heading north. They reached the outskirts of the village, and the houses lining the forest there were made of stone—the same kind of dark gray stone that he'd seen used by the Alainsith, as if the houses had once been some sort of Alainsith settlement.

"How old is Weverth?" Finn asked as he caught up to Olanth.

"The village itself is centuries old. Some say it was founded by the priests themselves. Honestly, though, I don't really know. Nobody really does." He nodded toward the stone building that Finn had passed. "We see things like that, and those of us who have lived here a long time figure our ancestors built those buildings. It's impressive how long they've stood the test of time, if you ask me."

He continued off, heading toward the trees. Finn watched where he went before he followed him. It was more than just impressive. It was surprising to Finn that they wouldn't realize it was Alainsith who built the village, though maybe there were people who lived in these villages who didn't really understand the influence of the Alainsith and the role they played in the surrounding community.

"How far is the house?" Finn asked.

"It won't be too far," Olanth said. "Far enough that it's going to be dark by the time we get there, but even old Lyle didn't want to live too far from the village. But, like I said, he would stay away for weeks or months at a time before coming in for supplies."

"What exactly did he do?"

"That's right. You asked me that before." Olanth paused and turned back toward the village. "I don't know what your people do in Verendal, but we bury the dead in Weverth."

"We burn them," Finn said.

"I always knew that the people in the bigger cities burned their dead, but never really understood it. Maybe that's because we follow all of the priests, and we don't tie into just one of them like you do."

Finn shrugged. He would've thought it was the opposite. In Verendal, there were churches for each of the different sects of priests, and he would've thought those in Verendal had a stronger connection to all of the gods than those in Weverth had. "It's a big city, and we follow the teachings of Heleth, which instructs us to return the people to the mother. Their ashes become new life."

Finn felt as if he were simply speaking the words without any belief in them. He often felt that way about the priests and the lessons they taught, but he had learned long ago that there was a certain expectation placed upon executioners, and he needed to at least present himself as devout, even if he wasn't.

"You see the village?"

They had moved into the trees, but not so far that Finn couldn't make out the outline of the village.

"I see it," he said.

"If you look just to the east, you might see a small clearing. That's the graveyard. That's where we bury our dead. We done it for generations. Ever since Weverth was founded."

Finn glanced from the clearing back to the village, noting the stone, and doubted that they had done it ever since this village was founded. "And?"

"And old Lyle started digging up the dead. Defiling them, you know."

"How did he defile them?"

"I'm not exactly sure. They tried to keep that from most of us."

"Why?"

"We all knew something had happened. The smell… They don't like to talk about it. But the priests came upon him. They had to stop him, but old Lyle was determined."

"Determined how?"

"You're going to have to ask the priests about that," he said, shrugging.

Finn nodded. "Why don't you lead me to his home?"

"I'll do that, but you need to start regaling me with stories of what it's like to be an executioner. How did you even get into such a thing?"

There was the question Finn had anticipated.

Not that he hid from his past, because he didn't, but he didn't necessarily enjoy sharing the details of what he'd gone through and what had brought him into contact with the master executioner. It was shame, more than anything else.

"I was found by my mentor, and he brought me into the job," Finn said, picking his words carefully.

"Your mentor?"

"The executioners have a guild. I work with a man named Henry Meyer, master executioner in Verendal."

"And are *you* a master executioner?"

"Not yet."

"What's involved in that?"

Finn shrugged. "To be honest, I haven't really given it much thought." The lantern cast enough of a warm orange glow into the trees to push back the growing darkness, but every so often, Finn thought he caught sight of movement beyond the lantern's glow, shadows that seemed to press upon them. Maybe it would've been better for them to have come in the daylight. "I have enough work as it is. I try not to think about what it's going to take for me to get more work."

"Are there really so many killings in Verendal?"

"It's not just about the killings," Finn said. "It's about learning the truth. Digging into the crimes, searching for answers so we can ensure the king's justice is carried out."

"I thought the Archers did that in Verendal."

Finn shrugged. "Most people don't really know the truth of the matter. The role of the executioner is not just to carry out sentencing. We're involved in all the aspects of the crime itself. We're tasked with trying to understand whether somebody is truly guilty or not."

"There's no doubt that old Lyle did this," he said.

"Why do you say that?"

"Only because of how he was found."

"In the village?"

"We found him in the village, but he… well, he stank. There's no other way to say it, and I know they had to drag him out to the stream and force men to scrub him so they could get some of the filth off of him."

He had stunk quite a bit when he'd been in the prison. Finn couldn't imagine how much worse he would've smelled then.

"How much farther do we have to go?"

"Are you already bored with sharing your stories with me?"

Finn shook his head. "I told you I would regale you with tales of what it's like to be an executioner, but I'm trying to figure out how far you're going to be leading me outside of the village."

"It's only about an hour," Olanth said.

An hour.

That would mean a lot of stories.

As he looked over at Olanth, he saw a burning curiosity in his eyes.

Finn should share with him.

And, if he was being honest with himself, he couldn't deny that there were stories to be told. He certainly did have enough experiences, and he understood why somebody like Olanth would want to hear about them. It was probably part of the reason why Meyer documented everything he did. Finn hadn't taken up the habit of journaling the way Meyer had, but if he were to do so, he wondered if it would help him process what he went through in the same way it helped Meyer.

"Why don't I tell you a little bit about some of the more interesting things I've investigated?"

Olanth looked over, grinning.

As they made their way through the forest, Finn shared stories of crimes he'd investigated, focusing mostly on the investigation and less on the sentencing. It was his way of conveying that his role was more than just that of the hangman. As they traveled, Finn found himself looking toward the trees, looking at the shadows, the darkness, and searching for any sign of something else. Every so often, he thought he caught sight of something in the trees, but then it drifted away, fading, leaving him feeling as if perhaps he had imagined it.

They traveled quickly. The path was narrow, but Olanth seemed to know it pretty well. When Finn asked him about that at one point, he merely shrugged, saying that most people knew the way to old Lyle's house, partly because there were other houses in the area, and partly because they had all been tasked with running supplies out to him when they were younger. That seemed a little surprising to Finn, but he ignored it as he continued telling his stories.

The darkness fell in full, and the bright moon started to rise, casting silver beams through the trees. The lantern pushed back the remainder of the darkness and the shadows faded as they headed through the forest. The sounds of the night began to appear: insects chirped, an owl hooted, and somewhere distantly there was the mournful cry of a wolf.

All of it was almost comforting.

Almost.

There was still something a bit off-putting about coming out into the forest, especially in the middle of the night.

It wasn't even the *middle* of the night, but Finn didn't like it. He was a city person at heart, yet in the time he had been working with Master Meyer as an executioner, he had found himself outside of the city far more often than he had ever preferred. Many of his more challenging investigations had taken place outside of the city.

"It's not far now," Olanth said.

He started to slow, and Finn realized that the trees opened up in the distance.

"Is that it?"

"It is. I…"

Finn looked over and realized there was a foul stench in the air. The forest itself had seemed to conceal it before, keeping the odor from him, but as they neared the home, the forest could no longer keep it hidden. He found himself wrinkling his nose at first, then pulling up his shirt to cover it.

"I don't think I can go any farther," Olanth said.

"I need to investigate," Finn said.

Olanth looked at him, holding his gaze for a moment then shaking his head. "We can come back in the morning. I can bring you back here."

"I'm here now," Finn said.

Olanth looked up at the trees. There was something haunted in his eyes. "If you go, I…"

Finn just nodded. "I understand. You need to return."

"No," Olanth said, straightening. "I told you I would lead you here, and I'm going to finish leading you here. You lived up to your end of the bargain, telling me stories about what it's like for you to be an executioner, so I'm going to do what I told you I'd do."

He took a deep breath, then shook his head, as if immediately regretting what he had done. He brought his arm up over his face, covering his nose and mouth, then continued forward, shifting the pack on his back and holding the lantern up.

Finn followed, though he stayed closer to Olanth now.

He tried to keep his mind engaged with what he saw.

There could be dangerous and supernatural things out in the forest. He wouldn't be surprised if there was some Alainsith presence out here, especially considering how far into the forest they were, but he also worried about the possibility of witchcraft. Given what had been described, what he knew about the power of death, Finn thought that more likely.

And if there was witchcraft out here…

He continued forward, moving quickly, carefully, and looking all around him.

The trees occasionally swayed, as if the breeze picked up then died back down. Finn looked over to Olanth, who looked uncomfortable, but continued to head forward, his jaw clenched as if he was trying to prove he was confident enough to do this.

It took everything in Finn to resist the urge to reach for the sword.

There was power in the blade. It had been used more than a few times now, and would have the power of death within it so that it could be used against witchcraft, but he also didn't want to give into the fear. That was its own kind of power.

They reached the clearing.

For a moment, Finn stood there, tensed, looking everywhere around him.

His gaze tried to take in everything. There was a stone

home, small, compact, similar to abandoned Alainsith structures Finn had seen outside of the city. If it was Alainsith, the home itself might have a power of its own. A low, stacked stone wall surrounded the yard and looked to be newer than the home. As the lantern light reflected off of the stone, he saw that some of the sections of the wall had crumbled and started to tilt.

Something else caught Finn's attention.

Shadowy figures were spread all around the clearing.

At first, Finn didn't know what it was that he was seeing.

Even as he stared, he still struggled to make it out.

"What is that?" Olanth asked.

Finn took the lantern from him and started forward. He had to step up over the wall, almost tripping as one section of it crumbled and the stone crashed down.

Olanth jumped, and Finn looked over to him, trying to smile reassuringly, but he wasn't quite sure if he did a good job of that.

He held out the lantern.

Finn crept toward the nearest shadowy form.

He had seen scarecrows in the fields he passed. Finn remembered the very first time he'd seen one, trying to make sense of what it was. He'd never spent time out of the city before he had started working with Meyer. It had been unsettling, partly because of how lifelike some of the scarecrows were. Some farmers took great pains to make it look as if there was a person out in the field.

As he approached one of the shadows here, there was something about it that reminded him of a scarecrow—

legs sprawled out, arms splayed, a propped-up body. Something about it seemed off.

The smell struck Finn the most.

The shadows began to resolve as he neared, but the farther he went, the more unsettled he felt. Not just any scarecrow, but one made from corpses.

What reason would Lyle Martin have in something like this?

"Finn?" Olanth called.

"You might want to stay there," Finn said.

"What is it?"

Finn shook his head. "I'm not exactly sure."

"The smell is awful," Olanth said. He took a step up over the wall, and when he came down, another section of the stone crumbled, spilling inward the same way it had when Finn stepped over it. "Did old Lyle really leave carcasses lying around here?"

The bodies of the dead.

He started forward, holding out the lantern, and knew immediately what he was going to find.

"Is that—"

"Don't," Finn said, raising his hand toward him.

Finn swept his gaze along the inside of the wall. There had to be a dozen bodies, all propped up against the stone wall, all angled toward the home.

Why would Lyle Martin have dug up bodies and brought them back here?

It had to be witchcraft, but for what purpose?

CHAPTER NINE

They came across thirteen bodies.

The number suggested something important, but he didn't know if he'd understand what without going to someone like Esmerelda for answers. Finn didn't know if he could get word to her quickly enough.

They stopped at the wall he and Olanth had come across.

"Did you find everything you need?" Olanth asked. "This has to be enough for you to carry out the sentencing."

Finn just stared. Was it though?

"I need to go into the house."

"Inside? After what we found out here? What do you think you'll find in his home? More like that?"

Finn just shook his head. Maybe there would be more bodies inside, and if there were, then he definitely needed to see them, even if he didn't understand why they were there. "You don't have to come with me. Why don't you wait out here until I finish looking?"

Olanth watched Finn for a moment, then he shook his head. "I can't let you go in there on your own."

"You don't need to do this," Finn said.

"I'm just going to stay with you. If there's anything there..."

Finn didn't want to tell him he suspected there *would* be something inside, even though he didn't have any idea what it might be, or why Lyle would have brought the bodies out here.

They needed to be cleansed.

That was what Lyle had claimed.

Finn didn't know what that meant, nor did he know why he would have wanted to do something to cleanse the bodies—or if there was anything he *could* do to cleanse them. But Finn knew he needed to understand, and he had to go inside to gain that understanding.

He crossed the lawn leading to the house.

The air had taken on a bit of a chill—faint, barely more than a slight gusting of the wind—but it left goosebumps on his arms.

He approached the door to the house slowly. "Did he live with anyone else?" Given what he'd seen, Finn wouldn't have expected it, but he also didn't want to be surprised by anything.

"Old Lyle? Nah. He was alone out here. I used to come here from time to time when I was younger. He always paid us pretty well to run supplies, so most of the kids from the village were happy to take them to him. He could be strange, mind you, but not *this* kind of strange."

"When was the last time you came out here?"

"Probably when I got my apprenticeship."

Finn hadn't even asked Olanth what kind of work he did. "I'm sorry I never asked about that."

"It's quite all right. I'm the brewer."

Finn looked over. "That's why you wanted me to come share ale with you. It's *your* ale."

"Best ale you can find. Well, outside of Verendal, that is. I'm sure there are others in the big city that are better, but I've studied as many of them as I can. Want to make sure I'm brewing the best."

"When we get back, I'll take you up on your offer."

"You're going to owe me more stories," Olanth said.

Finn nodded. "Of course."

He pushed the door open, thinking that if there was some sort of witchcraft involved, then he would need to be careful, maybe even use the sword to carve through it, but he didn't see any symbols suggesting witchcraft. The door had no markings.

But as the door came open, he realized it was only the door that didn't have markings. The markings were on the stone around the door. He stared at them for a moment, his hand resting on the door, and frowned. The markings could signify witchcraft, but he suspected they were even more of a sign of Alainsith.

"What is it?" Olanth asked, looking behind him.

"Nothing," Finn said, starting inside.

He held out the lantern, sweeping it around, and frowned.

Given what he'd seen in the yard, Finn expected to find more bodies and more of a foul stench, something that would tell him what was going on here. He expected to find some other sign that Lyle had brought bodies into the home, using them in whatever witchcraft he intended, but he found nothing.

It was clean and tidy, no sign of anything amiss.

There was a stone fireplace at one end of the single room and a table and chairs, along with a small bookcase filled with books on one wall. Finn approached a row of cabinets next to the table, pulling them open carefully, not sure what he was going to find, but there were only dried meats, jars of canned goods, and some vegetables inside.

Supplies.

He closed the cabinets, looking around the inside of the home before his gaze settled back on Olanth.

"What do you see here?"

"Nothing that tells me what happened," Finn said.

And that was the hardest part of all of this.

Finn sorted through the books, looking for some answers in what Lyle had been reading about. He wondered if maybe he'd find something on witchcraft, some sort of spellbook that would guide him through the practical use of how to create dark magic, but Finn didn't find anything like that.

One had recipes. As he glanced over to the cabinet, the supplies he'd seen, he thought he understood why he had that. Another was a book of maps. Still another looked to be a journal, much like the kind of journal Meyer used. Nothing here would suggest the kind of crimes Lyle had committed, nor would it explain the strangeness in the yard outside.

Finn continued working his way through the room. Meyer had taught him how to be diligent in his search. As far as he could tell, the person who lived inside this home was a very different person from the one who had set up the bodies stationed outside in the yard.

Finn paused in front of the hearth.

It didn't look as if it had been lit in quite some time. It was clean, no logs there, though Lyle had stacked them up next to the hearth—yet another example of how everything about this home was neat and tidy.

Finn rested his hand on the hearth.

The stone started to crumble.

He jerked his hand back.

"What was that?" Olanth asked.

Finn frowned to himself. He held the lantern out and saw the debris piled up in the hearth itself.

He gently touched the stone again. As before, it crumbled, dropping into the hearth.

What is going on here?

"We need to get out of here," Finn said.

Olanth watched Finn. "What is it?"

"I don't know, but we don't want to be here," Finn said.

He backed away, careful.

He looked down, only now realizing that each stone he stepped upon had started to crumble beneath his boots. He hadn't noticed it when he had first come in, but now that he was aware of it, he could hear the faint sound of a soft cracking with each step.

He reached the door.

The ground started to tremble.

"Come on," Finn urged.

Olanth still stood in the middle of the home and didn't seem to notice any trembling. "I never really came inside of old Lyle's home. It was sort of off-limits. He never let us inside when we dropped off his supplies." He glanced over to Finn. "It's nice. A little bit outside of the village, but if you can get past that... Maybe when he's gone, somebody else might take it up."

"We need to get going," Finn urged.

He was at the door, and the trembling he'd felt before continued to press up through his boots, as if it were radiating through the stone. He looked over to see stone cracking and crumbling, debris starting to spill out from inside of the hearth.

The whole structure was going to come down.

Finn darted forward, grabbing Olanth and throwing him toward the door. Finn raced after him, shoving Olanth as he tumbled through the open doorway and out into the yard. The stench struck him immediately, and as Finn rolled back to his feet, he looked over to see the entire structure starting to tremble then collapse. Debris filled the air, dust and dirt mixing together.

Olanth covered his nose and started coughing.

Finn held his shirt up over his nose so he didn't have to breathe it in quite as much either.

As the dust started to settle, Olanth dusted his hands

on his pants, looking over to the remains of the home. "What was that?"

Finn looked around before his gaze settled on the bodies arranged along the fence.

Decay.

It wasn't just the bodies that had decayed. It was the building.

What was this about?

When he got back to Verendal, he'd have to ask Esmerelda. She would need to know what he'd seen. She might have answers.

"We should get back to Weverth," Finn said.

"You don't even want to explain what just happened there?"

"I can't explain it," Finn said. "The building collapsed. I figured that was obvious."

"Does that happen very often to you?" Olanth eyed him. "It seemed like you expected that."

"I recognized that something was happening," Finn said and looked over to the bodies.

Could that be the purpose of them? Finn could imagine that with the right use of witchcraft, along with the corpses themselves, they could cause the Alainsith stonework to crumble. It would be an unusual use of power, but not so far removed from hegen magic that Finn couldn't see the connection.

He made his way over to where one of the bodies rested up against the wall and pressed on the stone.

It didn't budge.

He climbed over and kicked the wall where the body

lay, and found, surprisingly, that it remained intact.

Olanth joined him. "What are you doing?"

"Testing," Finn said.

"By kicking the dead?"

Finn looked over to him, shaking his head. "I'm not kicking the dead. I'm kicking where they're lying."

It was a subtle difference, but it was enough of one that Finn didn't feel as if he were somehow betraying the dead.

He made his way around the wall, testing other sections of it. Strangely, the wall was strong where the dead were positioned, but crumbled a bit where they were not. By the time Finn had made a full circuit around the home, there were sections of wall that were caved in, while the places where the bodies had been propped up remained standing.

He started off toward the darkened path.

"Where are you going?" Olanth called after him.

"I'm going to question Lyle."

"At this time of night?"

Finn swung the lantern back around, looking at him. "I need to make sure I fulfill the obligations to your village," Finn said.

They walked in relative silence. Every so often, sounds from the forest would draw Finn's attention, and he would spin to the side, holding the lantern out, but he didn't see anything in the darkness. After a while, Finn stopped reacting. There was the buzzing of insects, the occasional sound of movement in the trees, and a sighing breath of wind every so often, but nothing else.

It seemed to take longer to return to the village than it

had to reach Lyle's home. That might be Finn's imagination—perhaps tied to everything he'd seen since leaving the home—but he felt as if the forest itself wanted to keep him from traveling with any speed.

When they finally stepped free of the trees, Olanth looked over, his eyes haunted. "I think I should get back to the tavern. Do you still want to grab a mug of ale?" The tone in his voice suggested he would be just as content if Finn chose to decline his invitation.

"I still need to visit with Lyle again. I appreciate the offer though."

Olanth nodded, then hurried off, leaving Finn at the edge of the village.

He didn't rush back to the house where the villagers kept Lyle. He passed by other houses with fires crackling in hearths and smoke drifting from chimneys, leaving Finn wishing he had the warmth of a flame to sit next to as well. Many had candles or lanterns glowing in windows. The air still held the memory of rot, but the smells of smoke and baking food mixed in, taking away some of the awfulness he'd encountered.

When he returned to where Lyle was kept, he paused at the door and listened. There was no sound inside—no rattle of chains like he'd heard when he'd been here before, nor any of the strange sounds Lyle had made.

He tested the door, wondering if maybe he'd find it locked, but it wasn't.

Finn stepped inside.

He still had the lantern. With the soft, glowing light, he could make out details in the room that he couldn't before. It was a simple, empty room. Like he'd seen before, there was a stone hearth at one end, along with a stout table and chairs, though they'd been moved forward and out of the way. Otherwise, the home was empty.

Lyle looked up at him when he stepped inside. The lantern reflected from his eyes, giving him a terrible look.

"Lyle Martin," he said softly.

Lyle sat up. He'd been keeping his arms and chained wrists curled in toward his body. Having now seen how easily the stone had crumbled in his home, Finn wondered even more if the chains would hold. Could whatever witchcraft he used allow him to tear through them?

"I visited your home."

Lyle jerked forward.

Finn was ready, bracing himself.

He figured the chains *would* hold, but either way, he held out the lantern, daring Lyle to reach him.

Lyle stopped short, just a few paces away from Finn.

He stank. That much was obvious from up close. Olanth had said they'd cleaned him, but Finn wouldn't have known that had Olanth not said it. There were plenty of people who stank in the prisons in Verendal, though typically it came from uncleanliness due to their captivity, not from something fouler. It was almost as if Lyle had wallowed in the graves of the bodies he'd exhumed.

"Why did you remove the bodies from the graves?"

Finn didn't really expect an answer. Given what he'd seen from him so far, he thought Lyle wouldn't even care to answer. Still, he had to know. If it was witchcraft, the village was in far more danger than he'd known before. Finn wasn't sure what he would be able to do about it, but maybe the first thing would be sending Esmerelda and the other hegen like her out here to investigate.

"They were unclean."

Lyle's voice sounded hoarse, as if he'd been screaming.

"Why did you place them around your fence that way? What did you intend for the bodies?"

Lyle jerked on the chains again. "You should not have gone." He took a deep breath, leaning in toward Finn as he did, leaving him with a feeling that Lyle was trying to breathe in Finn's smell. "You're unclean." He jerked on the chains again, rattling them violently as he tried to pull free.

"Why am I unclean?"

There weren't many times when Finn had come to outside villages to investigate and carry out a sentencing that he wished he had a place like Declan to interrogate the accused, but this time he did. It would make it easier for him to feel as if he could get the answers he needed. And he wouldn't have to worry about what Lyle might do. As strange as it was for Finn to consider, he still worried that Lyle might find a way to pull the chains free from the wall.

"You are unclean," Lyle repeated.

Finn watched him and noticed he was fidgeting, his fingers twitching as he tried to maneuver the chains around his wrist.

There was a pattern to the way he moved his fingers,

and Finn studied it, realizing he had seen a similar pattern before—when he had stopped the witchcraft attack on Verendal. There was no doubt in his mind that this *was* witchcraft.

Why now?

And why *here*?

He looked up to Lyle, holding his gaze. "What were you trying to accomplish?"

Lyle jerked on the chains again. "Unclean," he said again.

Finn just breathed out slowly.

As before, he knew he wasn't going to get anywhere with him—and as he stood there, looking at Lyle, he started to wonder if he *needed* to get anywhere. At this point, Finn had already seen what he had attempted to do, had seen the effect of him placing the bodies around his home and yard, so he knew that whatever Lyle intended was tied to witchcraft, and it was certainly dangerous enough to warrant sentencing.

The only question was why.

There had to be some reason he had placed the bodies up around the fence, so close to what had to have been an Alainsith building.

"Your home is destroyed," Finn said. "Whatever witchcraft you were attempting accomplished its goal. The stone crumbled. The building is gone."

Lyle tipped his head to the side, and something in his eyes that reflected the lantern light left Finn unsettled again.

"Were you trying to destroy the Alainsith settlement?"

Lyle's fingers started to twitch even more, twisting, working, and tapping around the metal.

Finn took an involuntary step backward, moving away from him, but caught himself.

He didn't need to back away from him entirely. He needed to stay here. He needed answers.

"If you tell me what you are trying to do, I can ensure you…"

What would he ensure him?

Was it death? He wasn't even sure if Lyle deserved to die. Given what he'd seen, Finn certainly couldn't argue that he had done anything other than defile the dead. Was that a crime worthy of execution?

Even if it was, did he deserve to hang, or should he be offered an honorable death?

Out here beyond the confines of Verendal, Finn had that luxury of the latter option. Within the city, he wouldn't be able to offer anybody an honorable death. He was at the mercy of the jurors, and though Finn could make suggestions, he was not able to request specific sentencing the way he could here. Out in the surrounding villages, he was essentially the juror *and* the executioner.

"What was unclean?" He increasingly felt like he wouldn't get anywhere with Lyle, regardless of how hard he questioned him. The man was mad.

"House unclean. You unclean. Village unclean."

Finn blinked.

Could he have set up bodies around the village in the same way he had around the house?

"Why are they unclean?"

Lyle cried out, his voice a painful shriek, and he jerked on the chains again, pulling on them as he tried to tear the chains free of the stone.

His eyes widened, a wild expression in them, and he screamed as he darted toward Finn, trying to kick, trying to pull on his chains, trying to do anything to get himself free.

Finn took a deep breath. "Under the authority of King Porman, I am here to find the truth."

Lyle glared at him, shaking the chains, and Finn knew there would be no way for him to find any truth.

Maybe there *was* no truth when it came to Lyle. Only more questions, more mystery. He stepped backward, leaving the home and closing the door to the sound of the chains still rattling inside.

Finn stared at it for a long time, unable to tear his gaze away.

"I heard you in there."

Finn turned slowly to see the priest of Fell watching him. "What did you hear?"

"You were asking him what he tried to accomplish."

Finn nodded. "I wanted to know what his intention was by exhuming the bodies."

"Why must he have any intention other than depravity?"

"Depravity alone is often not the reason men commit crimes like that."

The priest took a step forward. The lantern light seemed to shift, sliding past him. "I can tell you what we saw. I understand that you left the village with Olanth Roaln."

Finn nodded. "He guided me to Lyle's home."

"That was necessary to see?"

"It was."

"Why?"

Finn turned toward the door, still hearing the rattling of chains inside, the steady jerking on the metal, and wanted to know if the stone was going to start crumbling in the same way it had in Lyle's home. "You said you'd heard about me."

"I have heard about you. When we requested somebody to come, and received word out of Verendal that you were answering the summons, I thought to inquire more about you."

"And what have you heard?" Finn asked, looking over.

"There are more rumors about you than I would've expected," the priest said. "I don't know how many of them are true, but I imagine there must be nuggets of truth in all of them."

"Probably," Finn said.

"Now, there are some I find difficult to believe. I think it would be hard for me to say that you were executed and survived." The priest smiled tightly, cocking his head to the side. "Much like I think it would be difficult to believe that you have been sent by the king himself, assigned with some magic he has gifted you, to ensure the safety of the kingdom here at the edge of his land."

"I have nothing magical," Finn said.

"There are other stories that are easier to believe: you

are diligent and detailed, and you are relentless when you feel you have the information you need."

"Those are the rumors about me?"

"Perhaps not so blunt," the priest said. "But from those rumors, one can infer some elements of your personality. Are they true?"

"It depends on your measure of truth." Finn turned toward him, lowering the lantern. In his nervousness, he realized he'd been keeping it held out. "I have trained to follow the king's justice. I do so with a determination to find the truth. There are times when others have an agenda, and it is up to me to dig beneath the surface, to find whatever agenda might exist."

"And do you fear a hidden agenda here?"

Finn looked around the village. It was dark enough that he couldn't see anything other than the shape of the houses, the candles and lanterns inside the windows, and a soft swirling of smoke drifting above them.

How much was he to reveal to a priest of Fell?

If there was witchcraft taking place in the village, then he didn't know if the priests would need to be involved. He didn't know if the priests *should* be involved.

"I don't know if there's a hidden agenda here so much as there's always something hiding," Finn said. "In the case of Lyle Martin, there's more to what he was doing than meets the eye."

"He was with the dead," the priest said.

"You keep saying that, but I saw dead arranged around the fence surrounding his home."

"And you assume he had some purpose in that? This is the hidden agenda you think you might find, Mr. Jagger?"

"I'm trying to uncover whatever reason he had for arranging those bodies."

"What if there's not a reason?" The priest glanced toward the home. "I can tell you what Mr. Martin was doing in the graveside at the edge of the village." The priest looked over to Finn. "He was caught at a time not unlike this—late, dark. A new moon, so darker than most nights. The air smelled of pine, not of this filth you smell now." The priest wrinkled his nose. "Ever since he began defiling the gravesites, we have all suffered from the stench it has left on the city."

Unclean.

He kept thinking about the way Lyle Martin had said that word. He described his home as unclean, the bodies as unclean, Finn as unclean, and even the village itself.

Why would he consider them unclean?

And how did the exhumation of the bodies help him remedy that?

It had to be witchcraft.

Finn felt confident about that, even if he didn't know what purpose he might have in using it.

"It was worse near his home," Finn said.

The priest nodded slowly. "A few of us made our way up there," he said, his voice dropping to a near whisper. "Only two of us managed to get all the way to his home. And only I managed to see it."

Finn frowned. "You saw it?"

The priest looked back at Finn. "A terrible thing. I have

never seen anything quite like that in my days of serving Fell." He shook his head. "Such depravity."

"Did you go inside his home?"

"I did not dare. I had no idea what purpose he had in placing those bodies around his yard the way he did, but it was such depravity."

Finn looked over to the door. Every so often, the chain rattled again, and he could hear Lyle crying out, as if he wanted nothing more than to break free of the chains, to pull free of the room that now held him.

"Can you show me where you found him?"

"You would not care to see it."

"I'm afraid I must."

The priest inhaled slowly before nodding. "I could show you in the morning."

"In the morning, I intend to carry out his sentence."

"So you agree with a need to sentence him?"

"I agree that despite whatever he had intended"—and likely witchcraft though he didn't know if it was something else—"he has earned sentencing. At this point, I have decided to leave it up to the will of the village."

"The village has already decided, Mr. Jagger."

"I know."

"You seem... displeased."

Finn shook his head. "It's not a matter of pleasure or displeasure. I serve the way I must serve."

"You're upset that you don't choose."

"I can choose whether or not to carry out his sentence," Finn said.

"I see," the priest said. "You've made it clear that you're

not beholden to us in Weverth. And I cannot disagree with that." He shrugged. "You wanted to see the location of the depravity, so I will show you. I must warn you, if you have struggled with the smells so far, this is worse. Far worse."

He guided Finn through the village and Finn followed, holding onto the lantern. When they crossed beyond the outskirts at the eastern edge, they headed toward a small clearing set far enough away that Finn couldn't even see the lights. A small, stacked stone wall surrounded it, and a single tower stood in the middle of the graveyard—a marker of Heleth, something that surprised Finn, especially as Heleth didn't require the burial of her subjects. The farther they went, the more the air took on the stench of death—a foul, terrible odor that continued to build.

Strangely, the word that came to Finn's mind was unclean.

Maybe that was Lyle's influence. Maybe it all had to do with the way he kept muttering the same word over and over again, as if to sway Finn in some way.

Unless that was some sort of spell.

Finn continued following the priest, and when he stopped near disrupted ground, the priest looked down.

"As you can see, the entirety of the gravesite has been disturbed."

Finn swung the lantern around, noting heaped up earth where the ground had been unsettled then covered once again. Markers made of stone looked as if they had been recently reset, many of them partially tipped over, and a stack of them off to his left had still not been restored.

"He dug all of them up?" Finn asked.

"Most," the priest said. "Though to be honest, we should have noticed it sooner than we did. I think it was just so unexpected." He shook his head. "It was by chance that we encountered him out here."

"What was he doing?" Finn asked.

He still hadn't gotten a full picture of what Lyle Martin had been up to, and Finn thought he needed it. He needed to know just what Lyle had been doing and why, though he had no idea whether it would make a difference. At this point, he knew what the village wanted done, and it was going to be on him to decide whether he would carry out the sentencing.

He was a servant to the king, and served at his will, but at the same time, Finn also needed to help ensure stability.

Unfortunately, there were times when the life of one person caused so much upheaval and disruption around the villagers that removing that person was the safest option.

In this case, maybe that was Lyle.

"I found him lying next to the deceased remains of a Mrs. Wedlow. She had passed only a week before, and the sight of what he was doing..." The priest looked down at the ground, shaking his head.

Finn forced back a wave of nausea.

He had seen depravity in his days, but that would be beyond anything he'd seen.

"What's worse, she wasn't the first one. Only the most

recent. You ask what he was doing, and I tell you that what he was doing is unnatural. It goes against the laws of men and gods."

"You would see him hanged."

"Hanged. Quartered. Burned. Whatever method you feel is appropriate. You are the expert and the king's representative. We are your servants in this case. But he must be removed from this world for his crimes against men and gods," the priest said. "So you see, you might believe he had some agenda, but all he was after was wickedness."

The priest made a steady circuit of the gravesite, keeping his gaze lowered as he walked around it, and murmured something softly to himself.

Finn had been looking for something to help him understand what had taken place in Weverth, but maybe there was no explanation.

He wondered if perhaps Meyer had known.

The old executioner still tried to teach him, even after all the time they'd been working together. Perhaps this was really just one more lesson.

Finn may never learn Lyle Martin's reasons for consorting with the dead and arranging the bodies around his home. Maybe it had to do with the Alainsith, or maybe that was only chance. That didn't mean Finn couldn't carry out the sentencing asked of him.

By the time the priest had finished his circuit around the gravesite, he looked over to Finn, watching him, a question lingering in his eyes.

"Do you need to see anything more?"

Finn took a deep breath and immediately wished he hadn't.

The air was awful, and it troubled Finn that it smelled worse than normal death and decay. There was something else here, though perhaps Finn wasn't to find out what.

He looked over to the small tower representing Heleth, and he wondered what the Mother would want of him. Perhaps nothing more than what he'd already done.

The priest was right, though.

What Lyle Martin had done was an affront to gods and men.

"Mr. Jagger?" the priest asked.

"All I need is a place to sleep for the night. Then in the morning, I will carry out his sentencing as you request."

CHAPTER TEN

Finn had never slept inside a church. He was typically given accommodations in a local tavern or inn, or occasionally in someone's home when he went to perform his duties, but never had his duties brought him to one of the churches in the town. He sat up, rubbing sleep from his eyes as he looked around. The room was small—little more than a closet with a small bed—but it had been a clean, dry place to sleep. More than that, with the traces of incense burning in the church, it had not stunk nearly as much as other places in the village.

A bit of sunlight streamed in through the small stained glass window, and he studied it for a moment, looking at the pattern. The design was meant to signify Heleth, but now must signify something else given that the church had been taken over by the priests of Fell. He saw Heleth, her golden hair streaming down, the circlet on her head marking her as the Mother, her hands outstretched on either side. The intricacy of the design was far more skillful than Finn would ever have imagined.

After changing into his executioner leathers, he slipped his boots on as he sat on the edge of the small cot, glancing to his pack. He had a change of clothes and some food supplies, though nothing else with him. The sword rested at an unusual angle next to the pack, which Finn thought was strange since he was usually so careful with the sword. He took care of it the same way he'd taken care of Justice, though his blade didn't have a name the way Justice did. Perhaps it would over time, if Finn kept using that blade in carrying out the sentences outside the city. Unlike Justice, which had supposedly been used in the war against the Alainsith centuries ago, his blade was newer and didn't have the same history to it.

Finn slipped the pack over his shoulder, held onto the sword, and stepped out of the room. It was near the main worship area of the church, and the steady chanting from the service drew his attention. Finn headed to the worship hall and stopped near the back wall to watch. He'd never seen a service for Fell before, though he had a feeling this priest was a bit unusual for one of the priests of Fell. For one, he wore a band signifying Heleth as well, which meant he served both gods. Either that, or he felt as if he needed to honor Heleth since the priests of Fell had taken over the church. There was also his irritable demeanor, though Finn didn't know if that was unusual for one of the priests of Fell or not.

The worship hall was packed. The villagers apparently

had an unusual level of devotion for their gods in Weverth.

"As we look to the heavens, we must all ask the gods to watch over us, especially in these dark times," the priest was saying. "Fell, sitting alongside the Mother, will guide us. We must observe and listen, waiting for our time to serve the gods as we are asked." He bowed his head and began chanting, though Finn didn't recognize the words. When he finally stopped the chant, his gaze fell on Finn. "And today, as we prepare to move beyond the darkness that has befallen our beloved Weverth, we must ask Fell and the Mother to guide Mr. Jagger as he carries out the gods' will. Blessed be their mercy."

"Blessed be their mercy," the others in the church intoned.

The priest turned his back.

It was a signal to the others. They all rose from their seats around the worship hall and turned toward Finn, looking at him briefly, before they started out of the church. When they had all departed, the priest turned back, making his way over to Finn.

"I noticed you didn't say the words along with us," the priest said.

"I don't follow Fell."

"Do you follow the Mother?"

Finn glanced up to the stained glass window circling the entirety of the worship hall. The light spilling through the windows illuminated the hall, giving off a warmth that didn't fit with what he felt, though that wasn't unique. When it came to Finn's experience with the gods, especially Heleth, as he carried out the sentences, there was rarely a time when he felt their warmth. What he did was necessary, but the longer Finn served, the more he started to question whether he did what the gods wanted, or if it was only the king's justice.

"At times," Finn answered.

The priest smiled slightly. "An honest answer." He looked toward the door where the congregation had departed. "Do you know that most would claim they serve the gods with complete devotion?"

"Many do," Finn said.

"Yes, but I've seen that only the priests can truly claim they serve the gods with complete devotion. Everyone else finds that their devotion is much like yours, Mr. Jagger, despite what they say. It comes with their needs. There are times when the needs of the people are great and they turn to the gods, praying for their favor. Other times, the people are less receptive."

Finn wondered if now would be such a time in Verendal.

Those in the poorer sections of the city had often followed the gods closely.

What would they have done now?

"I imagine you've had times when you needed the gods and found a devotion to them that you didn't otherwise have."

Finn nodded slowly. "I think most would make that claim."

"Or would most simply feel as if they needed to say

what they believe the priests and the gods would ask of them, regardless?"

Finn knew the answer to that. He'd seen it often enough in his time questioning men. Oftentimes, men feigned piousness and devotion to the gods, anything that would hopefully exonerate them. Finn had learned how to suss that out, how to pick apart men who were merely making claims of their religiosity, and uncover the truth.

"I suppose many would claim otherwise," Finn said.

"Unfortunately," the priest told him. "Many men find the gods only in times of need. I've been working with the people of Weverth to help them find the gods as a way to celebrate their daily life. All men need to have a better understanding of the gods, and if they have the opportunity to do so in their day-to-day activities, then they can fully understand just what the gods ask of them." He smiled tightly, looking over to Finn then back to the door leading into the church. "I trust your rest was adequate?"

"Adequate," Finn said. He glanced down to the sword. "Did somebody move my blade?"

The sword hadn't been resting in the same way he had left it. Finn was particular about it, having learned that lesson very early on in his work with Master Meyer. The sword was well cared for, and he made certain to keep it oiled, sharpened, and prepared for anything he might need it for.

"I'm afraid that was me," the priest said, smiling slightly. "I went in to check on you before the service and I tripped." He shook his head. "A wonder you didn't hear the commotion. I tried to replace it so it would be where you left it, but…" He spread his hands off to the side and shook his head. "Unfortunately, I must not have set it quite as you would have."

Finn nodded. "I must've been sleeping too soundly."

"Obviously," the priest said. "The noise made when I tripped on it was incredible." He looked up at Finn. "Are you ready to carry out the sentencing?"

"Only if it is what the village still wants."

"I think the village recognizes that Mr. Martin has disrupted life within the village enough that we see the need to remove him before he violates the will of the gods and men again."

Finn nodded.

As they started out of the church, the priest looked over to him. "Do you think he deserves otherwise?"

"I think he could be imprisoned, if that is your desire, or perhaps even exiled from the village itself."

"Would that satisfy the needs of the gods?"

Finn paused at the entrance into the church, looking out over the village. A small crowd had gathered around the outside of the church, seemingly waiting for him and the priest to depart. A light fog hung over the village, drifting through the streets, giving a dampness to the air.

"I'm not concerned about satisfying the needs of the gods," Finn said. "As I told you, I am responsible for enacting the king's justice, not that of the gods. The gods can manage well enough on their own."

"We're on the edge of the kingdom out here, Mr. Jagger. The king does not come to Weverth, and you are the first servant of his to have visited—and for this reason." He made a motion toward his chest, signaling to Fell. "The gods look over all—even here, where the king does not look upon us." He glanced over to Finn again, then his gaze drifted to the sword. "If it is easier, perhaps you can use the blade. As I said last night, the village doesn't have a preference for what manner of execution you choose."

That was unusual enough to make Finn hesitate.

Most of the time when he came to places like this, the villagers already had a sentencing in mind. They viewed themselves as similar to Verendal, casting their judgment and declaring the sentencing; they often felt as if they should be the ones to decide how and where it was carried out.

They made their way through the streets, heading toward the small home at the outskirts of the city, and the crowd followed behind them. Finn kept his gaze locked straight ahead of him, focused on the task at hand.

Normally when he carried out an execution, he wanted to have a breakfast to settle his stomach, to have the time to steel himself for what must come, but today, given what he needed to do, Finn wanted nothing more than to just finish this task and leave Weverth.

The longer he was here, the more he felt as if he would rather be anywhere else.

When they reached the home, the priest barely paused before pushing open the door, guiding Finn to it, and stepping inside, where the stench struck Finn again.

He found Lyle Martin lying curled up on the ground near the wall, the chains wrapped around him, as if he was using them to protect himself. If he did have any sort of witchcraft abilities, it wouldn't surprise Finn that he had the chains wrapped around him as a way of somehow freeing himself from them. Then again, if Lyle Martin had some way of breaking free of the chains, Finn would've expected he would've done it by now.

"Get up," the priest said.

Finn glanced over. "I will take it from here."

The priest pressed his lips together, frowning. "I thought I could help."

Finn just shook his head, staring straight ahead. "Now that you've passed your judgment and decided sentencing, I will take it from here." He nodded slightly to the priest. "There should be five men escorting him to where the sentence will be carried out. And, of course, you may accompany him to say whatever words are appropriate."

"You wouldn't do it here?"

Finn shot him a look, unable to conceal the surprise in his eyes. "Here?"

"I just thought... I'm sorry. I don't know the intricacies of the nature of your work, Mr. Jagger."

"It should not be here."

"We have a place that is not far from the village. Perhaps that would be better."

Finn shook his head slightly. It wasn't uncommon for him to deal with people ignorant of his process, but he would've expected some sort of preparation. Why would they have ever wanted him to execute Lyle in this place?

"Have them prepare to escort him away."

The priest slipped away.

Finn stepped forward. "Lyle Martin. I, Finn Jagger, executioner to King Porman, have come to carry out sentencing. The citizens and leaders of the village of Weverth have convicted you of crimes against the dead. In accordance with their customs, you have been sentenced to die."

Lyle turned his head slightly and stretched, straining his neck just a little bit and working his arms, before he regarded Finn with darkness burning in his gaze. "Unclean."

"If that is all you have to say for yourself, then I am afraid I cannot intervene any further."

Finn wasn't convinced this was the right sentence. Not yet. Still, he wasn't convinced it was the wrong sentence. It was strange to feel that way, and stranger still that he didn't know whether he should get more involved or less.

Several men stepped into the home, coming up behind Finn, who moved off to the side.

"Bring him to the site of the execution," Finn said.

One of the men was large and muscular with long dark hair. He had a tattoo along his neck and wore a deep-gray shirt. "You want us to grab him? He stinks," the man said, frowning. "They said the bastard was found fucking Gill's dead wife."

"Like I said, grab him and remove him from here."

Finn stepped back outside.

A bigger crowd had formed. He swept his gaze around and started to think that perhaps it was everybody from the village. That wasn't terribly uncommon. When he came to villages like this, most of the time, they treated

Finn's work like a spectacle, though it was less of a festival than it was in Verendal. There the city streets were littered with hawkers selling food, crafts, and other items, a spirited excitement in the air—and the longer he carried out executions, the more it felt off for Finn.

The priest stepped up next to him. "You still aren't convinced."

Finn looked over. "What makes you say that?"

The priest shrugged. "I can see it in your eyes. You aren't sure you are doing what you need to do. I know men," the priest said. "And I know the hearts of men."

Finn turned away, moving his attention back to the door where the villagers had started to drag Lyle out. Two of them carried the chains, which were still attached to him, while three of them stood around Lyle, escorting him out of the home. As soon as he stepped out, the crowd began to cry out—loud, angry shouts threatening violence against him.

"You know the hearts of men so well that you know mine?"

"I suspect you have a surprising softness to you, Mr. Jagger. I expected a bit more darkness within you."

"Because I'm an executioner?"

"Because of the nature of your work." He shrugged. "I wouldn't be able to blame you for that though. I suspect that anyone in your position, surrounded by the darkness you find yourself surrounded by at all times, would find themselves hardened to it. Much like healers find themselves hardened to the smells and sights of their work, or midwives to the experience of birthing."

"What about priests?"

"Why, priests have a proximity to the gods that others do not. That gives us a familiarity with them that most cannot claim." He nodded to Lyle. "And it helps us to know when some men have been twisted beyond redemption." The priest nodded. "Come, Mr. Jagger. If you have hardened your heart enough for you to carry out the sentencing, then let us be on with it."

They marched off, making their way through the streets, then out and to the north. From there, they headed along a narrow, wooded path between the trees, then to a small clearing filled with broken stone, tall grasses, and pale-yellow flowers with a pungent aroma.

The men guided Lyle to the center of the pile of rock and stood around him. The two men holding on to the chains carried them behind the rock, hooking them onto a metal stake Finn hadn't seen. So much for them not having prepared for this. They obviously had something more in mind than they had let on from the beginning.

Finn focused on Lyle, ignoring the crowd growing around him. He approached the man, now once again chained to a structure, and regarded him out in the daylight. There was something eccentric about him, though Finn couldn't quite place what it was—but he knew it was more than just his foul odor. Perhaps it was the way he looked at Finn, an almost knowing look in his eyes, something that suggested he understood what was going on far more than he had revealed.

Finn turned to the others. "You may go," he said to the men surrounding Lyle.

The larger man spat at Lyle before shooting a dark glare at Finn then taking his place with the rest of the crowd.

The others looked as if they, too, wanted to spit at Lyle before taking their place.

Finn looked over to Lyle. "Do you have anything to say for yourself?"

He watched Finn, then his gaze drifted past him, before finally turning to the crowd. "Unclean," he said.

At this point, he just wanted to get this over with, but at the same time, he felt as if he had an obligation to ensure he was carrying out the king's justice in the way he had been trained to do. He didn't want to simply carry out the sentencing without ensuring he had all of the information he needed, but Finn didn't know if he had.

He took a deep breath. "Do you intend to say anything more?" Finn asked the priest softly.

"There is nothing more that can be said for him. He has defiled the gods through his actions, and the gods will not welcome him."

Finn turned. "All men are given an opportunity to return to the gods," he said.

"Perhaps all men, but not this man. As I said, he has defiled the gods through his actions. They will not welcome him back."

Did that make it harder or easier? Perhaps knowing what the man had done, and knowing he had intended to perform some dark ceremony, should be enough for Finn. Still, he couldn't help but feel as if he wanted to know more—as if he *needed* to know more. The man had done something so unusual, and so unnatural, that Finn was almost morbidly curious as to the reason behind it.

He turned to Lyle. It was time this ended.

"May the gods have mercy on you," Finn said.

The priest laughed bitterly. "The gods will not be offering this one mercy."

Finn motioned with the sword.

Lyle didn't move.

"Have him kneel," Finn said to the priest.

"You are the executioner. Why would I need to have him kneel?"

"Have your people have him kneel," Finn said.

"Again, you are the executioner."

Finn glared at him for a moment.

He approached Lyle, standing in front of him. "I intend to offer you an honorable death."

There was something knowing in the man's eyes.

"All you need to do is kneel. Leave this world with honor."

If there was one thing Finn did believe in, it was the opportunity for an honorable death. For whatever reason, that mattered to him. His time in the city, time spent with Master Meyer, had made him have an appreciation for giving men that option. Too many were given the rope, and too many left the world without an option for honor.

Maybe that came from what Finn had gone through; when he was nearly hanged, he had felt as if there was no real honor in it. Or maybe it simply stemmed from his belief that most men deserved to have a quick, relatively painless death.

Lyle looked over to him, then he looked at the sword Finn held, as if seeing it for the first time.

What he did next surprised Finn.

He dropped to his knees, looked up at Finn, and held his gaze.

Finn brought the sword up, stood behind Lyle, and paused for a moment, looking at the people gathered around him.

"May the gods have mercy," Finn said softly.

He brought the blade down in a quick strike.

CHAPTER ELEVEN

After the priest paid him—reluctantly, Finn noticed —he started toward the edge of the village, walking the horse. His pack was attached to the saddle, his sword slipped through it, now cleaned and oiled.

"You intend to go already?"

Finn looked back at Olanth. He had followed Finn to the edge of the town and carried with him a canister. He stood there watching Finn.

"There's no reason for me to stay," Finn said, looking back at the village. The streets had more activity now than they'd had earlier. Now that Lyle had been executed, they could go about their day once again, as if for some reason, whatever Lyle had been doing had been holding them up from living their lives.

"I thought you would have an opportunity to share more stories with me."

Finn just shook his head, holding on to the reins of the

horse. "I have no intention of staying here any longer than needed. Besides, your people need to grieve."

"I doubt many people are going to grieve him," Olanth said.

"All men should be grieved," Finn said.

"Even when they did what he did?"

Finn shook his head. "Even then. Perhaps even especially then. One of the things I've learned in my time as executioner is that even the most awful person has somebody who cares for them and will miss them, regardless of the crimes they've committed." Maybe not Lyle. He'd seen where and how he'd lived.

"He didn't have any family," Olanth said. "He lived out there for as long as anyone's remembered."

"Is that right?"

"Never wanted to leave that strange building, which was odd, if you ask me."

"There are some people who have a predilection to Alainsith items," Finn said.

"Alainsith?" Olanth looked over to him. "Why would you say that?"

"Because his home was Alainsith." Finn shrugged. "There are quite a few like that scattered throughout the kingdom. Especially in these lands. You get out into the forest, and you can find buildings like that. Some of them are larger or older than others, but all are Alainsith."

"I never would've guessed," Olanth said.

"I'm not so sure that it makes a difference."

"Maybe he stayed out there because he had some ties to those people."

Finn shook his head. "The Alainsith left these lands a long time ago."

"You sound almost as if you have some experience with them."

Finn just shrugged. "Some, though I can't say I know them."

Olanth looked over to the horse. "You said you were going to give me a ride."

"And I would have, but unfortunately, I need to be getting back."

"Are you sure you can't stay another night?"

He frowned. "Very few people are eager to have an executioner stay with them any longer than necessary."

"I don't know. You might find Weverth is a little bit more open and understanding than other places."

Finn doubted that. He didn't know Weverth all that well, but his opinion of it was that it certainly wasn't more welcoming than other places he had been—and with the way it was guided by the priest of Fell, it seemed almost *less* welcoming than some.

"Like I said. I need to be going."

"Would you return if we had need of your services again?"

Finn frowned at him. "Why would you have need of an executioner again? Do you think your people intend to do something that would require me to return?"

He shrugged. "I can't say I have the answer to that."

Finn regarded him for a moment, and there was something in his gaze that left Finn troubled.

Maybe he had misread Olanth. Here he had thought he

was a nervous person, somebody who had been unsettled by everything that had taken place, but perhaps that wasn't it at all.

What if he was eager rather than nervous?

Finn had seen eagerness like that before and recognized the danger of somebody who wanted to see death. He should have noticed earlier. It had come from the way Olanth had wanted Finn to regale him with tales of serving as an executioner. Finn should have known.

He shifted the sword and smiled tightly. "It's really long past time that I return," Finn said.

"If I ever make it to the city, can I find you?"

"Any of the city Archers would know how to find me."

He studied him for a moment, but decided he didn't want or need to explain that any further.

"That would be great."

Finn looked behind him one more time before heading out of Weverth.

He'd been here longer than he intended—and longer than he wanted.

He climbed into the saddle and nudged the mare on her side, getting her moving. She whinnied, turning back to look at him, a flicker of annoyance in her eyes. Finn ignored it. *He* was the one who felt annoyed.

"We've been here long enough," he murmured.

An overnight. That was enough for him to feel like he had spent too much time in this village—enough for him to feel as if he needed to be somewhere else.

Thankfully, there was only this one assignment

outside of the city, but even if there had been another, Finn wasn't sure that he would've decided to take it.

The mare took off and they hurried along the path.

He glanced back at one point, thinking that somebody followed him, but realized that was just a rustling of leaves in the trees.

Finn shook those thoughts away, focusing on the road in front of him.

They had quite a ways to go still today, long enough of a ride that Finn wondered if he'd be able to make it back before it got too dark.

He would either have to ride in the darkness—and Finn was reluctant to do so, considering the upheaval that had been taking place around Verendal—or he would have to camp. That was equally unpleasant.

As the day stretched onward, the sun shifted in the sky, falling toward the treetops, then drifting beyond, sending shadows crawling along the King's Road. He had pulled out Reginald's journal again, turning the pages and feeling as if he just needed to find some secret that remained hidden from him.

The horse had slowed to a trot. Finn had stopped a few times, mostly to drink, relieve himself, or give the horse a break, but none of his stops had been long. He worried that if he lingered too long, he would end up stuck out overnight. He hoped that by prodding the horse to go a little faster, they could get back before it got too dark, though Finn started to doubt it the farther they went. Whatever speed the horse had the day before had been lost.

By the time darkness had fallen, Finn started looking for places to camp. He would get off of the road and back into the trees, maybe near a stream. When he had camped out overnight before, he had always preferred to do so off of the King's Road, for a little measure of safety. There were enough highwaymen wandering along the road that Finn knew he needed to be careful. The sword would scare most away, but not all.

He was about to veer off the road when a steady rustling began to build behind him in the forest.

Finn twisted in the saddle, turning to look behind, but the pale moonlight didn't provide enough light along the King's Road. If he could have gotten a little farther, he would've escaped from the forest and would've been able to see much better than he could now, but the forest itself stretched around him.

Worse, the road wasn't a straight shot through the forest, which was partly intentional. The king could use the contours of the forest if were they attacked from the west, but it also made it difficult for anyone to know if somebody followed. Larger caravans would have scouts that wouldn't have the same difficulty as Finn did, but smaller caravans would struggle.

Finn debated whether he should turn back or keep going, or even whether he should consider darting off into the trees to see if there were any pursuers.

He kept going.

It got darker, the moonlight no longer enough for him to see much of anything.

The horse pulled on the reins a bit more than she had

before, struggling against him. Finn nudged her faster, trying to urge her to greater speed, but she didn't respond as quickly as he had hoped.

The rustling grew louder.

Not rustling. Thudding.

Now there was no doubt there was somebody behind him.

Or something.

Finn had seen other things in the forest before. Berahn. Alainsith. Witchcraft.

He didn't know what was out here now, but wondered if it might be one of them.

Finn kicked the horse to go faster and they galloped along the road.

It was dangerous doing so in the darkness, but Finn didn't want to be caught by whoever followed him. Try as he might, he didn't manage to outrun the sounds behind him; the steady thudding continued. He couldn't force the horse any faster.

Finn slowed the horse, then guided her off the road. He climbed down from the saddle and unsheathed the long, blunted executioner sword. If there was something out here in the forest with him, Finn wasn't about to be surprised by it.

It didn't take long before he heard the sound of voices.

Not berahn, then. Not Alainsith, either. The accents were local.

Finn ducked farther back into the trees. He remained as quiet as he could, but then the horse whinnied again.

Finn cursed under his breath and hurriedly wrapped

the reins around a nearby tree, sliding off to the side and putting his back up against it.

Shadowy figures came through the trees.

"Told you he can't have gone far," a voice said. "Just move your horse…"

It was familiar, though Finn wasn't exactly sure why.

He clutched the sword and moved carefully forward, out into the open.

"Can I help you with anything?" Finn asked.

Two darkened figures turned toward him and slipped off the horses they were riding.

"Grab him," a voice said.

"I'm Finn Jagger, executioner for King Porman. Any action you take upon me will be taken upon the king himself."

One of the men laughed—a dark, familiar sound.

A shuffling built behind him, the same sound that had prompted him at first, and Finn spun, holding the sword out.

Another figure jumped back.

He turned again, holding the blade out from him.

"You're no swordsman. You might be quick with that blade, but I told them you wouldn't be able to use it in combat."

That voice.

Finn recognized it—but from where?

Finn swung the sword, and the shadows stayed just beyond its reach. He didn't know how long he could keep it up. He wanted to keep spinning, but it was difficult to see anything in the darkness, and he couldn't figure out where he needed to go with the blade.

"Lyle Martin. Are you with him?" Finn asked.

"The old fool. Got himself caught up in something he shouldn't have, he did."

Finn couldn't tell if that meant they were a part of what Lyle had been doing or not.

"Were you involved in the witchcraft that was used on the Alainsith building?" Finn asked.

"I told you he said it was an Alainsith building," another voice said. This one was quieter.

"Just do it. You'll get your reward."

Finn finally realized why he recognized one of the voices. "Olanth?" he said.

He still held out the sword. He wanted to know what was going on and why Olanth, of all people, would have come at him.

"Warned you to be more careful," Olanth said.

"The Alainsith abandoned everything around here long ago," the first one said.

"None of that matters. We're supposed to grab him."

Finn spun, swinging the sword, trying to put some space between him and the others.

"You don't need to do this," he said to Olanth.

"I don't need to do what? You have something they need. Paid me good money for information too."

"What do I have? The horse?"

Finn glanced toward the trees.

He had just looked away for a moment, little more

than that, but they surged toward him, as if they could see in the darkness.

Somebody reached for him, and Finn spun away, driving an elbow through their chest.

He spun around again, holding on to the sword, but somebody reached for it, trying to wrest it free from his hands. Finn squeezed it tightly, knowing he would be at a disadvantage if the sword left his hands. It was a wonder they hadn't attacked him with any other weapons yet.

So far, he hadn't seen any signs of other swords, but he couldn't see much of anything. All it would take to meet his end would be a dagger in the darkness.

Something hit him in the side.

It was hot, painful, and he cried out.

There it is.

Somebody chuckled, a dark sound that filled the small space around him.

He tried to turn, but the pain shot up his back, through his arms, and he couldn't fully move. He had been stabbed. Either that, or he'd been hit by a crossbow bolt.

But up close like this likely meant a sword, a knife, or a dagger.

Any of them were deadly in the dark.

He sunk forward.

"Grab it."

Shadows moved near him, and Finn tried to strike, but could barely get his arms moving. They grabbed for the sword, ripping it free from his grip.

The sword? That's what they're after?

The answer came to him easily, even injured and with

his mind now working as it should. He had seen it before and knew the truth.

Witchcraft. The sword carves through witchcraft.

Finn stumbled forward, trying to get it back.

"That's for the king's justice," Finn said.

"That's where you're wrong."

It was Olanth. He was close enough that Finn could smell his ale-infused breath. Finn tried to get up, but he sank down. He grabbed for his side, feeling for the injury, but the pain was intense and likely fatal.

This is how I'll go out? In the dark, along the road, serving the king's justice. At the hands of men who were committing violence against the king.

Whatever reason there was for it, Finn didn't know.

He scrambled forward, reaching out, but he knew he wasn't going to be able to grab for anything. The pain in his side was too much.

He lay flat on the ground, clutching his side.

There was a rustling of leaves, then a low, strange sound.

Somebody cried out.

Finn tried to look up, but could not.

Another cry, then it was silenced.

Something was here.

He tried to get moving, to crawl forward, but there wasn't anything he could do. He sank to the ground again and tried to twist so that he could look up into the darkness, but he couldn't see anything—just more darkness.

The pain took him and his eyes fluttered shut.

Sunlight streamed in around Finn and he jolted up, wincing immediately.

Pain shot through his side and he remembered the injury, how he had succumbed to it, and was surprised he was still alive.

He licked his lips. His mouth was dry—almost painfully so—and he could see nothing around him other than the bright light. At first, Finn thought it was a surge of brightness that came from the trees and the daylight spilling around him, but the longer he stared, the more he started to question whether that was it at all, or whether it was something else.

Finn tried crawling forward, moving somewhere, but his body didn't react the way he knew it should. Everything hurt, though it was his side most of all—it throbbed, coursing with pain that filled him and stayed with him as he tried to move.

He couldn't get up.

The noticed that the air had a strange odor to it. At first, Finn thought maybe it was him, but the longer he lay there, the less likely he thought that.

They'd left him here.

Most likely, they thought he'd died—and as Finn lay on the ground, he couldn't help but feel surprised himself that he had survived the night.

He had to move though. Making it through the night was but one step.

Get up.

He suspected they'd taken the horse.

Strangely, the thought that struck him was that he would have to pay for the damn thing. More than just the horse was missing though.

He remembered them grabbing the sword from his hands.

He felt a sense of ownership of it. It was a gift Meyer had given him when he'd reached his journeyman status, and he felt pride in possessing it. It was a quality blade. Not only that, but he felt comfortable using it. Finn could wield Justice, and had done so in Verendal when he was permitted to carry out executions with the blade, but there was something about his own sword that left him feeling far more comfortable.

He groaned, fighting back the pain within him and sitting up. He held on to his side, clamping his hand down to keep the agony at bay.

A wave of nausea rolled through him for a moment before passing. Finn barely tolerated it, but he sat in place for a while, letting the nausea and weakness wash over him so he could move past it. When it finally cleared, he breathed out slowly and steadily, then gritted his teeth as he got to his feet.

That was far more difficult than it should have been. Still, he managed to get to a standing position, wobbling for a moment and staggering toward one of the nearby trees, which he used to rest upon.

A glint of metal caught his attention.

Had he dropped something?

Better yet, had his attackers dropped something?

Stumbling toward it, Finn dropped to his knees, grabbing the item on the ground. It was his sword.

His wounded mind took a moment to process this discovery.

They left my sword behind?

No. They wouldn't have done that. They had wanted his sword.

Something had happened.

He remembered the cry he'd heard.

That had mattered. Something had happened to his attackers.

He stumbled forward, making his way along the road when he saw a leg.

It wasn't attached to anything.

Finn leaned on the sword, using it like a crutch, suppressing the pain within him as he stared.

He stumbled even farther forward, and the stench began to fill his nostrils, that of death, of bowels having been spilled, and he found a body—that of the man who'd spit on Lyle—lying with his hands gripping his belly, his eyes wide even in death, and a massive gash on one arm. A dark circular tattoo on the inside of his wrist caught Finn's attention.

It was a black rose.

Like he'd seen on the posters in the city. The Black Rose movement.

They're all the way out here?

The man had been attacked by some creature.

As Finn staggered ahead a bit more, he came upon the remains of Olanth.

He was missing an arm, along with the leg that Finn had found, and part of his face had been cut off, but it was definitely him.

Berahn.

That was what this had to be.

Esmerelda had warned him that they were the silent killer—that they would spring upon somebody without the victim even knowing they were there—but Finn wouldn't have expected to see anything quite like *this*.

He didn't see any pawprints, nothing to indicate the creatures had passed through here—nothing other than the evidence of violence that left his attackers dead.

What of the horse?

Finn forced himself to stay awake long enough to look through the trees, staring at where he thought he might've left the mare, though he couldn't remember. He had wandered off the road to get away from his attackers and hadn't paid any attention to where he was going or where it would bring him.

He leaned on the sword, wobbling for a moment, and when he managed to stabilize himself, he listened. There was a soft shuffling sound every so often that came off to his left.

Finn limped toward it, clutching his side as he went. When he reached the space in between the trees, he hurried forward as quickly as he could and reached the horse.

She was unharmed.

He laughed to himself. "The damn thing didn't bother

to attack you?" Finn shook his head. "Must not like horse meat."

The mare turned toward him as if knowing exactly what he was saying. Finn guided the horse back to the road and leaned on her flank for a moment. He wasn't going to be able to walk, though he had no idea how he would tolerate the ride either.

To get back to the city, Finn would have to find a way.

After taking a deep breath, Finn grabbed his flank and threw one leg into the stirrup, climbing up and into the saddle. He slumped forward.

The horse took that as an indication to get moving, and though Finn tried to grab for the reins, she trotted off. Each step she took sent new pain surging into his side. He tried to fight against the pain, but could barely withstand it. At one point, he leaned over the side of the horse, retching, the contents of his stomach spilling out onto the King's Road. Somehow, Finn managed to hold onto his pack and the sword, but everything else moved past him in a blur.

He felt every movement of the horse, leaving him trembling with pain. He continued to struggle and strain against it, to ignore the agony coming through him, but could not. He threw up again, then slumped forward, gripping the horse as tightly as he could, afraid to let go.

The moment he let go would be the moment he fell off the horse.

Finn drifted in and out of consciousness as he stayed atop the horse, barely able to stay mounted. Pain was a constant companion, blurring everything around him and leaving him slipping into a stupor. His mind struggled to work through the various injuries. Distantly, he thought he could feel a broken rib and perhaps something else internal, considering how much pain shot through his belly, though Finn didn't know for sure. Broken ribs would heal in time, but internal injuries would not. Even Master Meyer and his skilled healing would not save him.

He had been injured far too many times while working with Master Meyer. It hadn't slipped past him that he had been injured more times while working with Meyer than he ever had while serving the crew.

He needed to keep going.

Just a little longer.

He had to fight—somehow.

He clung to the horse, struggling to hold on, straining for alertness.

Finn could barely keep his eyes open.

Then he felt something touching him. Grabbing him.

He tried to fight, to argue, but the hands upon him were strong, and they pulled, prying him free of the horse, dragging him down. He clutched the sword, squeezing on the hilt, refusing to let go of it, but the darkness claimed him regardless.

CHAPTER TWELVE

When Finn woke again, sunlight streamed in through a window. The air smelled of a familiar aroma—mint and a mixture of medicines. He tried to sit up, but his head felt heavy. His side still ached, though not nearly as much as it had before. His hands were stiff, throbbing, and it took a moment to realize why. He was still holding onto the sword.

Finn rolled over, anticipating another wave of nausea, but thankfully it didn't come.

"How do you feel?"

Finn turned his head over and wasn't surprised to see Esmerelda sitting in a chair, leaning forward and watching him. Her raven-dark hair hung down to the middle of her back, and her full lips were pressed together in a concerned frown. She carried a metal object that looked something like a spoon, but she tapped it rhythmically.

"I suppose I owe you again," he said.

She smiled slightly. "Only if you want to."

Finn took a deep breath, letting it out slowly as he swung his legs over the side of the table. He had been in this room before. It had been awhile since he had been this injured, though perhaps he wasn't nearly as injured as he had believed. Had he suffered a more fatal injury, he would not have expected to have survived the ride back to the city.

"How did you know I was coming?"

"The people saw you heading to the city."

"And that's how you knew to come for me?"

"We recognized that something was off. The horse was a little erratic."

"I think she's always a little erratic," Finn said.

Esmerelda laughed, getting to her feet and standing alongside the table. She took one of his hands, squeezing it for a moment before tracing her fingers along his wrist. The action seemed clinical, but there was something sensual in her touch. "That's right. I sometimes forget how little you care for riding."

"I do it out of necessity, not out of enjoyment."

"Sometimes it's a matter of perspective, Finn. Perhaps if you would take more time to enjoy the necessity, you would find that it isn't nearly as intolerable as you make it out to be."

"I don't think that will change much of anything," he said.

She held her hand on his wrist. "Do you remember what happened?"

"I was jumped."

"Do you remember why?"

"The sword, I think. I'm not sure why. They were villagers from Weverth, but one of them had a mark for the Black Rose movement, which I've seen on posters around the city."

She frowned when he mentioned the sword as the target.

"I imagine you intend to bring Archers with you to carry out the king's justice?"

Finn released his side. It still ached a bit, though it wasn't nearly as tender as it would have been had Esmeralda not intervened. The hegen magic worked quickly, and it was incredibly effective. "There is no need. Justice has already been served."

Esmerelda's gaze drifted to the sword. "That is not how it is to be used," she said softly.

"Not that," Finn said. "They took it from me, and I fought, but…" He looked up, holding her dark-eyed gaze. "I think it was a berahn."

"As I've told you before, they would not have been in the forest," she said.

"I don't know what else would have done it. One of the men had an arm and leg ripped off, another was disemboweled, and I didn't see the third." He thought that was the extent of the attack. Three attackers—all of them dead.

And he had been left alive.

Then again, he'd *barely* been alive. At that point, it was a wonder Finn was still breathing.

"The berahn would not be around the city," she said softly.

"Unless there are Alainsith here."

"They would not be here," she said.

"Why not? If they're concerned about their structures getting damaged, then it seems there is plenty of reason for them to be present."

"They abandoned those structures long ago, Finn. They would not care if they were destroyed. Not anymore."

Finn closed his eyes. "I didn't hear anything. Other than the men calling out. Screaming." He looked over to her. "And then I blacked out. When I came around, I found them like that."

"Perhaps it is Alainsith, then," Esmerelda said and released his hand. Finn felt a moment of regret when she did. "First you have seen one, then one has protected you?"

"I'm not so sure that it protected me as much as it didn't attack me."

She looked over to him, holding onto a card, flipping it back and forth. Every time she turned the card, the ink slithered across its surface, shifting the picture of a mountain to a lake, to a tree, to a noose, then to a sword. Each time she flipped the card, the image changed.

"If the berahn was aware of you, it chose to leave you."

"Why?"

Esmerelda shook her head. "I don't know."

Finn nodded to the cards in her hand. "You saw something. It's in the way you're holding onto those cards. There's something off."

"Perhaps," she said.

"Have you found anything more?" Finn asked.

"More?"

Esmerelda looked over to him, holding a small metal object in her hand, though Finn couldn't make out any of its details.

"I saw an Alainsith structure collapse. The man I went to sentence used witchcraft against it." Pain flared in his side, and he winced as he tried to adjust himself.

She turned slowly, gripping the metal object in her hand a bit too tightly, her knuckles turning white. "What do you mean you saw one?"

"That ultimately was what brought me out of the city." Finn sighed, wincing softly as a bit of pain worked through him. "There was a man accused of digging up the dead. They tell me that he had been consorting with them. Apparently, he was found with a recently deceased woman, having dug up her body, and..." Finn shook his head. "The idea of it is difficult to fathom."

"There is power in decay," she said softly.

"Witchcraft?"

"Possibly," Esmerelda said, frowning as she took a deep breath.

"He didn't deny it. He kept saying we were unclean."

"We?"

"At first, he accused the dead of being unclean, but the more I questioned him, the more he said others were unclean. It was the *only* thing he said."

"Where was this?"

"The village of Weverth. The man lived outside of the village, in what I suspect was an old Alainsith structure, though I didn't have much of an opportunity to investigate."

"Because it fell apart?"

"It was intact when I arrived, but it collapsed as soon as I started to go through it, looking for answers."

Esmerelda set the card aside. There was a sword on it again.

"Interesting that it would collapse the moment you got inside," she said, pressing the tips of her fingers together. "Did you do anything?"

"I didn't."

"Did anyone else with you do anything?"

Finn shook his head. "Not that I know of... Well, one of the men who attacked me was with me. At the time, I didn't really know who he was." At this point, Finn still didn't know who he was, other than dead. "He came along because he wanted to learn more about me."

Esmerelda smiled slightly. "Your profession is an interesting topic of conversation."

"You don't have to make fun."

"I was not."

"I told him a few stories and he told me he was a brewer. He kept offering me ale." At least with Olanth, he'd thought he *could* tell stories. There were some whom he didn't want to tell his stories to.

"Something you likely would have appreciated."

"I don't mind a mug of ale," Finn said.

"And you should not." She smiled slightly, but it didn't remove the edge of worry in her eyes. That remained a constant. When Esmerelda worried, *he* worried.

"Once we were inside, I noticed that the stone started to collapse."

"Were both of you inside, or was it just you?"

"I don't know. Both, I think."

"Is that the only strangeness you encountered?"

"You mean other than the ring of dead bodies surrounding the home?"

"There were a ring of bodies?"

"They were situated all around the wall around the home." Finn shook his head. "It was quite disturbing—even for someone like myself, who has experience around the dead."

"That is... unusual," she said. Esmerelda stopped, pressing her hands together, and turned back to look down at the card she'd set on the table next to her. "I've been looking, but answers have not come."

Finn slipped off the edge of the table. A bit of pain surged in his side, leaving him cramping slightly, but not so much that he couldn't stay standing. "What are you going on about?"

"Something is taking place with these Alainsith structures," she said. "Whatever it is might be dangerous."

"To the Alainsith?"

"Yes."

"The kingdom?"

"Yes."

"To you?" Finn asked, leaning slightly toward her.

"Possibly," she said, turning away. She scooped the cards off the table, flipped them again, then turned them back into her palm and set them in her pocket.

He'd been warned that something more might happen.

When he'd sentenced Elizabeth Jarvis, she'd promised it was only the beginning.

What if *this* was the beginning?

First protests, now witchcraft attacking Alainsith structures?

What was going on?

"I could help. The men who attacked me might be involved in what is going on." Olanth had been a part of him traveling to that Alainsith building, and it was only after he and Olanth had gone into the building that it had corrupted, collapsing. Whatever else had happened, Olanth must have triggered it with his connection to witchcraft. "They were with Olanth, I'm certain."

Esmerelda looked over to him, smiling slightly. It seemed to him that she struggled with a decision, before nodding to herself. "Then there is something I should show you."

Finn wobbled for a moment, catching himself on the table. "Now?"

He really should return to Meyer. There was too much that needed doing, and he'd been away for what felt like an eternity.

But after what he'd seen in the village, he *needed* to know.

"If you are able."

"I don't know that I can walk, not that I want to ride. Wait. What did you do with the horse?"

"What was that?"

Finn shrugged. "The horse. What did you do with it? I have to return it to the stable; otherwise, I have to pay for the entire creature."

Esmerelda started to laugh, breaking some of the tension in the room. It wasn't so much tension between *them* as it was tension about their topic of conversation. "I imagine you would be most displeased to have to pay for a horse."

"Maybe if I liked the horse, I wouldn't have such an issue with it, but this one..." He shook his head. "The damn thing was so fat I could barely stay on it."

"I suspect it was the girth of the creature that kept you atop her when you collapsed." Esmerelda reached forward, touching his side. Finn felt a faint tremble, a bit of excitement at her touch, but pushed that down. "Otherwise, you might have been much worse off than you were."

"So I should be thankful they gave me a fat horse?"

"Yes, and perhaps also appreciative of the mare getting you back to the city safely." Esmerelda tipped her head to the side slightly and her smile faded.

"If I see her again, I will have to tell her that."

"She's tied up outside, so you can tell her yourself."

Finn snorted. "You could've just told me that."

"I did."

He looked around the inside of the room. "What about my shirt?"

"What about it?"

"Do you want me to walk back to the city shirtless?"

"It would be quite the sight," she said.

"I'm sure. And I would likely draw the wrong kind of attention from the Archers. I have a hard enough time with them as it is these days."

"Leading is not so much about dictating what happens," Esmerelda said, "as it is about influence. If you have enough influence, then you can lead more effectively."

"Is that how it is with you?"

"I am one of the youngest of my position among the people," Esmerelda said, glancing down to the table before looking up at him again. "And in my position, I have found it is often easier to influence them than to direct them. Perhaps it would be the same for you with both the Archers and the iron masters."

"It's not just them," Finn said. Esmerelda offered him his shirt, and he noticed it had been stitched up. Not only had she repaired him, but she'd repaired his shirt as well. He slipped it on, wincing again as he stretched the injury. "It's also the wardens. They tend to chafe at having to follow an executioner."

"Perhaps it's not the executioner they chafe at, but the age of the executioner."

"Am I too young?" He had no idea what the typical age was for an executioner to take on increasing responsibilities. The only one he'd ever seen was Master Meyer and the Lion, along with the court. Most of them were older.

"Perhaps not. You're certainly experienced. You have

proven yourself in a way I think others of your age have not."

"Is that a good thing?"

"What do you think?"

Finn chuckled. "I think there are times Master Meyer grows frustrated with me."

"Because you push him?"

"I think he would find it easier if I were to just take directions and follow what he wants me to do."

"Perhaps easier, but not better."

She motioned for him to follow, and after gathering the horse, they walked through the hegen section, taking a different route than they had before. At one intersection, Finn saw an impressive mural painted on a home. It looked to be of a mountain range with snow-capped peaks, sunlight streaming down and reflecting off of it. With the cool breeze gusting along the street, Finn could almost imagine being high in the mountains, even though he had never seen them in person.

"The skill is impressive."

She looked over, chuckling at him. "If you spent more time among the people, you'd recognize that the skill, such as you say, is impressive throughout all the people. Most of the people find joy in their calling."

"Even if their calling doesn't lead to wealth."

Esmerelda stopped in front of another mural painted on a home. This one looked to be of a vast garden, flowers sweeping across the vista, and it spread from one house to another, to another, as if he were looking into the distant horizon. The hegen section was a maze of narrow streets and alleys, and he'd never fully explored them.

"What is wealth but a mindset? What is valuable to you may not be valuable to others." She turned and looked at him. "What is it that you want more than anything in the world?"

Finn's side ached, and his mind hopped through everything that he'd seen and what he needed to do, but the question stayed with him. What *did* he want more than anything else in the world?

At one point, he would've said that he wanted to have stability, but he'd gained that. Another time, he would've said that he wanted wealth, but he had seen the risks and dangers that others had gone through to chase it.

What did he want?

He wanted his friends and family to be safe, but even that had stabilized over time.

These days, Finn wasn't even sure what he wanted.

Esmerelda watched him, a knowing look in her eyes.

"Why are you looking at me like that?" Finn asked.

"How am I looking at you?"

"Like you know the secret to some puzzle."

"Perhaps that's all it is. Perhaps it's the answer to a puzzle, or perhaps it's *you* who has struggled to find the answer to the puzzle."

"There is no puzzle," Finn said.

"Perhaps not," Esmerelda said, shaking her head and shrugging. "Maybe it's nothing more than knowing that even though you look for answers, they might be right before you."

198 | D.K. HOLMBERG

She started along the street again and stopped at a building that was wider than the others. She took the reins of the horse, tied them to a post outside, then pushed open the door.

"We have time for a brief stop," she said. "And this is on the way to what you need to see."

Laughter greeted him as soon as the door opened. Light streamed through the windows and skylights, letting in the daylight, and lanterns, too, blazed brightly. Everything about the space felt cozy and warm.

It was much larger than it had appeared from the outside and filled with the voices of children laughing and adults trying to talk over them; he even heard an occasional bark from a dog scurrying around the room.

"What is this?" Finn asked.

"It's a school, Finn."

"A school?"

"You have schools in Verendal."

"Nothing like this," he said.

"This is how we help the people find what will bring them passion. Without an opportunity to experience other aspects of life, how can one be expected to know what will bring them joy?"

"How do the teachers keep from going insane with the sound?"

Esmerelda looked over and laughed softly. "Why, because it brings them joy."

Finn looked over to one of the instructors. He was an older man wearing a baggy brown jacket, loose-fitting breeches, and thin spectacles that hung off his nose. He leaned over one table where three children sat stacking clay, forming it into shapes, and grinning the entire time.

Another woman, one who was barely older than Esmerelda, had children seated all around her. She was reading from a book as the children shouted.

"What's she doing?"

"She's telling them stories and encouraging them to tell *her* stories."

"Doesn't that get in the way?"

"In the way of what, Finn?"

"In the way of her trying to teach."

"The only thing that would get in the way is if she did not let the children share."

At another station, Finn saw older children, all seated with strands of yarn stretching around them, and they were weaving. The patterns were complicated, though brightly colored, like everything the hegen did. There was another station where the children had small nubs of chalk and were coloring on a small board.

"I check in here from time to time," Esmerelda said.

"Why?"

"Because it is my obligation to teach."

An understanding dawned on Finn. "Are there others who can learn what you can do?"

Was that her point?

Maybe Lyle Martin had some hegen magic. Could that be why she showed him this now? If not, then he didn't know what it was that she wanted to show him.

"There are always others who can learn, but the question is whether they want to learn." Esmerelda smiled slightly. "Not all choose to learn the same things, Finn, and we encourage our young to find what motivates them. Those who chase their passion will pursue it with much more vigor than those who are forced along their path."

Finn grunted. "I'm not sure how to take that."

"Because you were forced along your path?"

"Yes."

"Yet you have embraced it. Is that because you enjoy it, or because you are forced to do it?"

"I don't know how you can enjoy anything when it comes to the kind of work I do."

"You enjoy aspects of it," she said.

"I do."

"Which aspects bring you the most joy?"

Finn shrugged. "Finding the truth."

Esmerelda smiled at him, looking over. "See? That wasn't so difficult."

"I didn't say it was difficult."

"But you didn't want to answer, either." She turned, motioning for Finn to follow. "You will find unpleasant elements in everything you do. Even these instructors, men and women who find such joy in teaching the next generation, find that some parts of their days are not as pleasurable as others. Perhaps it's a child who soils himself. Perhaps it's crying that bothers them one day when it didn't on another. Perhaps they are unwell, and the joyous sounds from the children grate on them." She closed the door, and the sounds within became muted again. "Or perhaps it is someone who takes a different path. One who attempts to use her talents to help her people, but is forced to bargain with outsiders, knowing that what they ask for is not always something that can be attained."

"You don't have to take the jobs," Finn said.

"We must all find our own path." Esmerelda gathered the reins of the horse and led him to the edge of the hegen section. In the distance, Finn could see the Raven Stone and its gleaming white structure, the gallows having been rebuilt over the last few months, though no rope hung from it—a sign that there would be no hanging in the immediate future. Instead, it was a marker of a sentencing to come. Beyond that was the Teller Gate, the massive doors open, allowing people in and out of the city. And then beyond *that*, Finn could make out the edge of the city and some of the people who were there.

"You must find your path, Finn. In all things."

Finn looked over to Esmerelda. "I didn't realize I had lost my path. I just want to find the truth."

"Sometimes the truth is within ourselves, and we must learn to trust it." She smiled. "Now, there is something you must see." She studied him, her dark eyes practically swallowing him. "And I cannot say what it means, but I fear that it will force all of us down a dangerous path before all is done."

CHAPTER THIRTEEN

They followed the road around the city, Finn still leading the horse, and there was a silence that stretched between them for a time. It wasn't uncomfortable or awkward. For her part, she didn't seem to mind that he was an executioner. He found that comforting in a way. Too many people in Verendal despised his line of work, even as they saw it as necessary.

From here, the spires of the different churches rose high above the rest of the city. The church of Heleth rose most prominently, though it wasn't alone. Even the Church of Fell was visible from here, the almost-black stone tower rising against the backdrop of the city, giving off shadows that swept toward Heleth, as if Fell wanted to demonstrate his power to the Mother.

They had been quiet on their journey and away from the hegen section. Finn ached, the injury in his side still burning with a nagging pain, leaving him to wonder just how badly he'd been hurt. He needed to get back to the city, but he feared that if he were to do so, he would lose this opportunity. Right now, Finn felt as if he needed to know what had happened to the Alainsith structure in Weverth.

"You seem troubled," Esmerelda said.

"I'm just thinking about everything I have to do once I return." The city loomed in the distance, and Finn could feel the weight of it near him. "There is almost too much for me to do once I get back. And I don't know how I'm going to find the time to understand what happened in Weverth." It wasn't just understanding Weverth, though. It was understanding the Alainsith, something that he had put aside for far too long.

Esmerelda looked at him with a knowing expression in her eyes.

"I suspect that you will find the time you need," Esmerelda said.

She wasn't wrong. Even if he had several different people he needed to question, Finn likely would have found a way to sequester time to come out here and look. He hadn't ventured into the trees. It was easy to get lost if he wandered too far from the path, and as he was no woodsman, Finn didn't dare do so without someone to guide him. Esmerelda, on the other hand, had no such fear. She had wandered through the forest often, and he suspected she had some magical means of returning.

"I know so little about them. Everything in the city is

rumors and conjecture. The only one who *really* knows anything is the king, and he doesn't talk about what he knows." At least, not to people like Finn.

Worse, the rumors that existed in the city were wrong. His experience told him the Alainsith had power, but they weren't violent. At least, they hadn't been to him. That didn't mean they couldn't be violent toward others. And they *were* powerful with magic.

In spite of Meyer's wealth of knowledge, there were no books on the Alainsith. The closest Finn got to seeing them again was two months ago while retrieving an herb from the forest as a favour to Wella when she claimed her bones hurt. Finn had stumbled across what he thought to be an old Alainsith shrine. He'd circled around to the back of the city, the western edge that abutted the forest and the Alainsith lands, looking for more hints of their presence. Verendal was a large city situated at the edge of the kingdom, in a place that had maintained peace with the mysterious Alainsith through the efforts of the king and had managed to avoid attack by Yelind along the southern border.

Esmerelda swept her hand along the horse's side before dropping it off and clasping both hands together. "People have long tried to understand the Alainsith."

"The king has a treaty with them."

"And you think you could work with him?"

"I'm not trying to work with the king. It's more a matter of trying to understand what has been done."

"It has been my experience that the Alainsith are cautious people. Proud. They once knew these lands in ways that your people and mine do not. They have no interest in fighting, though."

"Even though they wouldn't have any difficulty fighting?"

"Having the ability to fight and having the desire to fight are vastly different things, Finn."

She was probably right. Finn's experience with the Alainsith suggested that they essentially chose who saw them. "Why do you think the berahn helped?"

She was quiet for a few moments as they made their way along the road. "That is surprising." She looked over to Finn. "Not that I don't believe you. You have a unique experience with them, only that it is unusual for them to be seen so often."

Finn started to smile, before the memory of what had been done to his attackers came back to him. "I didn't see it. I just felt it."

"Sometimes that is all it takes," she said.

Finn regarded her for a moment. It seemed as if she were trying to tell him something more but didn't say it.

Esmerelda's comment about understanding his place struck him out here more than in the city. He should be content with his place. He knew better than to try to involve himself in aspects of the world that were beyond him, and trying to understand the Alainsith, and these berahn, was definitely beyond him. He had seen magic in the world, and he had come to know power, but he had also come to recognize that the kind of magic and power he had seen was far greater than he could be a part of.

He was an executioner.

He needed to avoid thinking he was more important than he was. He found Esmerelda watching him, an unreadable expression in her eyes.

"You wanted me to see something with the Alainsith, but what brought you out in the forest in the first place?"

Esmerelda glanced to the trees. "Harvesting."

He frowned for a moment before realizing what she meant. "I didn't realize that you harvested your own supplies."

"How am I to know that they are effective if I don't gather them myself?"

Finn shrugged. "I suppose you wouldn't." Wella, the apothecary who worked with him and Meyer, felt much the same as Esmerelda, and likely for the same reasons, though he knew Wella was willing to purchase her supplies from others who brought them to the city. She always tested them for purity and to ensure that they were what she intended to buy. "What did you find?"

"This time of year is useful in gathering many different items." She patted her side, but Finn only saw her cloak. He suspected she had a pouch for a satchel underneath where she placed the items she'd gathered. "Though the storage of them is difficult."

"You sound like an apothecary."

"The nature of the work I do and the nature of what an apothecary does is not so different."

"I suspect the apothecaries would feel differently about that."

"Where they see medicinals and liniments and concoctions that are drawn from the power of the natural world, I see potential." She shrugged, looking off toward the trees. "You and I have spoken about the power that exists within the world."

"You told me about the power of death."

"Of death. Of life. Of everything that exists in nature. It is a matter of finding that potential, mastering it, and using it in a way that will serve your intention. In that way, it is not so different from apothecary medicine. The goals might be different, but beyond that…" She shrugged again.

"Except there aren't too many people who can learn to be a hegen, whereas there are quite a few people who can learn to be an apothecary."

"It is like many things, Finn. Think of your knowledge of apothecary medicine before you went to work with Henry Meyer."

"I didn't have any knowledge of apothecary medicine before I went to work with Master Meyer."

"Exactly. You came in ignorant, and now I suspect you would rival most of the apothecaries in Verendal."

"I doubt that," Finn said. They had looped around the outskirts of the city, and from here he could make out the palace. Strangely, the palace rested near the back of the city, as if it used the entirety of the city as a layer of protection, only it didn't have the same protection from the forest. "I have some knowledge, but I certainly don't have as much as most within the city."

"Only because you haven't the opportunity to demonstrate it. If there's one thing Henry Meyer has done well, it is encouraging you to learn."

They took a few more steps before Finn looked over to her. "He's only done one thing well?"

"I said *if there was* one thing. I didn't say it was the *only* thing."

Finn laughed. "I'm sure he would appreciate your views of his education."

"Henry Meyer and I have an understanding," Esmerelda said. "He recognizes that we can have a mutually beneficial relationship."

"And you would keep that relationship with me?"

"If you think that is the only reason I choose to speak with you, Finn, then—"

A cry came from within the forest, a mournful sort of sound.

Esmerelda stiffened. "That is my fear," she said softly, starting forward.

Finn followed her. He still guided the horse, and when he reached the tree line, the horse pulled on the reins, jerking his head for a moment. Finn tied off the horse, and then followed Esmerelda.

"What is this?" he asked.

Esmerelda continued to move quickly, winding through the trees, though cast a glance back over her shoulder to him. "You may want to move quietly."

Finn laughed softly. "I can move quietly enough."

"It's a wonder you were ever a thief, Finn."

He snorted, then realized how loud he was. He had to be quiet.

There weren't too many times in his current profession where he had to draw upon the lessons he learned in his previous life. Most of the time, he traveled the streets openly, not trying to conceal his presence or his passing, and he didn't fear going from one section of the city to another.

Occasionally, Finn had to draw upon those old lessons, mostly to keep himself safe. There were times when he worried somebody might trail after him, though that had become increasingly rare these days.

He stepped over a root that tried to trip him, then got caught by a small shrub that did trip him. Esmerelda caught his arm, keeping him from stumbling and sprawling forward. She raised a finger to her lips, ducking low and darting forward.

She moved quietly, quickly, and with a grace he could not even mimic.

The cry had not returned, though Esmerelda didn't seem troubled by that. She navigated through the forest as if she knew exactly where it had come from. He didn't like coming unarmed. He had a belt knife, but nothing else. Normally when he traveled outside of the city, he carried the sword Master Meyer had given him for sentencing, and that at least gave him a measure of comfort and protection—though he hadn't ever tried to use the sword as a weapon.

"What do you think it was?" he whispered.

"This is what I wanted you to see. Perhaps not this, but…" She frowned as she stared into the darkened forest. "I came across something while harvesting, and was troubled by it, but your story about Weverth makes me think that perhaps it was not an isolated incident. Come. I will show you."

She pressed her lips together in a tight frown as she moved forward.

They continued creeping forward. He heard an occasional insect hum, and somewhere up above was a squirrel chattering, though as they approached, the squirrel fell silent. The air was heavy and damp, the rain having saturated the ground, and his boots quickly became covered in mud.

Esmerelda waved her hand, motioning for him to slow.

She slipped forward and Finn followed, deciding to grab for his belt knife. It felt better having something in hand. If there was some creature out here, he wanted to be prepared for it.

Not that he expected to see the berahn. Esmerelda had described them as silent killers—creatures that would sneak up on someone before they had a chance to even react.

In the distance, a stream burbled softly.

Esmerelda veered away from it, though.

He leaned closer to her. "Which way should we go?"

She smelled of roses and a hint of spice. Maybe helthir, though Finn would need to take more time to know for certain.

Esmerelda looked over her shoulder at him. "There will be an Alainsith home up ahead. I fear the cry leads us to it."

"What caused it?"

"The stone, Finn."

They moved a little bit farther along the forest floor when a small clearing opened in front of them. Strangely, the clearing looked old, and collapsed stone formed a ring around it, vines growing up within it. There was something ancient and powerful about it, something that struck him as vaguely familiar, though Finn wasn't sure why. There was nothing else here, though. Certainly no reason for them to have heard a cry out in the forest.

Esmerelda moved into the clearing and stopped in the middle, holding her hands off to either side of her. Her lips moved soundlessly and she began to turn slowly.

Finn had been around her when she had used her hegen magic before, though rarely when it was so openly used. He wondered if he might get in the way of whatever she was trying to do. Would his presence impede her magic?

If it would, Esmerelda would've told him to move.

He wandered to the nearest stone and crouched down in front of it to get a better look. There were strange markings on it in a language he couldn't read, but he didn't need to be able to read it to know what it was.

Esmerelda stopped turning.

"This is Alainsith," Finn said. He traced his hand along the stone, moving it slightly.

Esmerelda nodded. "There are places like this scattered throughout the forest. Most are intact. Alainsith stonework is generally quite stout," she said. "The Alainsith poured much of themselves into their stone, into everything that they built. It should not fail so easily."

Finn crouched down next to another pile of stone rubble and debris. He pressed his hand upon it and felt something warm, but also slick and unpleasant.

"This was once all their land," Esmerelda said. "Even within Verendal, you will find evidence of that."

"I've seen it," he said. "The City Hall itself is an old Alainsith building."

"There are others like it, as well. And there are some who think the Alainsith magic remains within their buildings."

Finn got to his feet and looked around the small clearing. "If the Alainsith magic remains in the buildings, then how would this have crumbled?"

"I don't know."

She hunkered down, her hands pressed out, and surprisingly, he noticed a hint of light coming off of her, as if she were glowing with power. It was as if she were trying to call upon power in a way that would penetrate the Alainsith stonework.

It reminded him of what happened in Weverth, and the way that Lyle Martin had situated corpses around the Alainsith stone. The only places that remained intact were where the corpses had been set, otherwise the rest of the structure had crumbled into nothingness.

He watched Esmerelda, though didn't have any great insight about what she did.

Finn joined her, crouching down alongside her, and thought maybe there was something in the stonework that he might feel, though perhaps that was only his imagination. Having been around magic, he wondered if he would even be able to detect it used near him. He had certainly used the sword Justice before, demonstrating power as he had carved through dark magic, though that had been witchcraft. His own sword, the blade that Master Meyer had gifted him for his journeyman work, had taken on a bit of power too: the power of death, of taking a life. It was that power that had permitted him the ability to overwhelm witchcraft.

As he looked at the stone, he couldn't tell anything else from it. Maybe it was a mistake for him to stay here, a mistake for him to have come here in the first place.

"This structure was intact when I was through the forest the last time," Esmerelda said. She made her way around it, moving quietly. "And if there is something here..."

She didn't continue, other than to move carefully, her hands pressed out from her, though Finn didn't know if she was drawing upon her hegen magic or if she were simply searching for answers.

"This is now three Alainsith structures," she said, her voice soft. "How many others?" It was a question mostly to herself, Finn could tell, but he wanted to try to help her.

She started off and Finn hurried after her. They hadn't gone very far in the forest before they came upon another clearing. It was another crumbled building. Esmerelda paced around it for a few moments, before hurrying off, deeper into the forest. When they came across another clearing, there was an increased tension within her.

Finally, she straightened. "I think we need to return," she said.

"What could cause this?" Finn had seen what he believed to be witchcraft in Weverth. If that were the cause of this, then there might not be anything he could do.

But his attackers had wanted his sword.

Was it to prevent him from intervening?

Reginald's death. The attack outside of the city. Witch-craft. Protests. And now the Alainsith structures.

Finn didn't know where to focus, leaving him questioning even where to begin.

Esmerelda touched him on the arm. "I can see that you are troubled."

"It just feels like there are too many strings for me to pull at, and I don't know where to even start."

"Then let me pull on this one, Finn. The people will look into what is happening with the Alainsith, but you must focus on what is happening in the city."

It should offer him some relief. She was taking something off of his plate, offering him an opportunity to focus on something that he might actually be able to do something about. But having been attacked outside of Weverth, it felt like this was something he needed to be involved in as well.

There was too much, though.

Esmerelda guided him through the forest, back to his horse, and when the city came into view, Finn knew that her suggestion was probably for the best. He needed to focus on his responsibilities, on what Master Meyer would want from him. On what the king would want from him. That was his path.

Still, as they headed back toward the hegen section, Finn found his focus drawn back toward the forest, toward the crumbled Alainsith structures, and couldn't help but feel as if that were important somehow.

CHAPTER FOURTEEN

The return to Esmerelda's home had them both somber. It was fitting. The pain in his side persisted, and he feared that it would linger and impede his duties, but she *had* healed him with hegen magic, so he doubted the pain would persist too long.

When they stopped at Esmerelda's home, she stepped into the doorway. From here, Finn could see that her kitchen was a bit of a mess, different powders and medicines all resting on the counter, the aromas drifting to his nose. It was unusual for her to have such a chaotic home. The other times he'd been here, he'd found it clean and tidy. "You should return to Henry Meyer and share with him what you experienced. You can share with him what we've seen of the Alainsith if you choose, though I do not know what to make of it."

Finn nodded. "I don't know how concerned he'll be

about the Alainsith, but he *will* be disappointed I was attacked during my time outside of the city."

"I think he'll feel more than disappointed." She reached into her pocket and pulled out the stack of cards she had put in there before. Esmerelda flipped through them, moving from card to card before seeming to settle on one that she held outward, flipping it from finger to finger, then turning it over.

"The cards have you worried," Finn said.

Esmerelda looked up. Her normally intense gaze had something of an urgency to it now. "The cards often have me worried, Finn, but this is more than the cards. I do not know what it means that the Alainsith structures are failing, but there is something there, Finn."

Finn looked down. Once again, there was a sword on the card. "These more so than usual for you. Why is that?"

Esmerelda flipped it over. "The cards are markers of what might be and what should be. We don't always understand what the cards intend to show us, only that if we are diligent, we can come to know our purpose." She looked up. "I am trying to find my purpose."

"The cards aren't helping?"

"Unfortunately, the cards can only help so much when it comes to understanding one's purpose."

"I thought these were tied to your magic."

She smiled slightly. "If only it were so simple." She sorted through the stack of cards again before offering one to Finn. "Would you care to find yours?"

Finn looked at them. When he'd been given a hegen

card in the past, it had always come with the requirement that he help the hegen. At least, that had been Finn's belief in the purpose behind Esmerelda having given the cards to him in the past. They had always come from her, though he suspected there were other hegen who had similar abilities and could dispense cards just as well as she could.

This was the first time he'd been offered a card with no strings attached. Somehow, this felt like a test—one he thought he needed to pass.

"What purpose do you need for me to find?" Finn asked.

He hesitated with his hand outstretched, reaching for one of the cards. It would only take him grabbing one of them to see what the hegen magic asked of him.

"It's not what I want you to find, Finn. We both know there is something else out there."

She was not wrong. After they had stopped Holden, and Elizabeth Jarvis, he had been warned that there was another threat, but in his time serving as executioner, Finn had not been able to go looking for it. How could he if needed to remain in Verendal?

The other threat, the one Elizabeth had alluded to before her execution, had not yet come to the city. Unless it had.

"What else is out there?"

She smiled tightly. "It's what you need to find."

Finn met her gaze. "What do you *think* I need to find?"

She tipped her head to the side, smiling slightly at him. "As we spoke about earlier, I think you need to find your purpose, as all of us must."

Finn took a deep breath. There had been times when the hegen cards had guided him in surprising ways. Maybe this would be the same. He could imagine the cards giving him an answer now, perhaps leading him to know why he'd been attacked on his way back from Weverth. Perhaps the cards would explain what had happened when he'd been at the Alainsith structure, or why the stone had seemed to decay so quickly again.

Or perhaps taking a card would bind him to Esmerelda. He found that he didn't mind that as much as he once would have. That was typically the purpose of the cards. They were meant to bridge a person to the hegen so they would serve as the hegen demanded. Or so he'd long thought.

When it came to Esmerelda, Finn wasn't even sure if that mattered anymore.

He'd worked with the hegen—and Esmerelda, in particular—enough times now that he didn't feel the same fear about going to her for help as he once did.

Perhaps that was what mattered.

He no longer thought that Esmerelda simply wanted to use him.

Finn took a card, and Esmerelda turned away from him.

Looking at the card, he found the surface blank. At first.

Then the ink began to shift.

He'd seen it happen with Esmerelda's personal cards, but rarely had it happened for him. It was as if the ink had to register something from within him in order for the card to know what to reveal. As the ink slid and shifted along the card's surface, Finn wondered what the hegen magic would decide for him. How would he be asked to serve next?

The ink started to shimmer... then stopped.

"What does this mean?"

Esmerelda didn't look back at him. "I cannot explain to you what the cards ask of you."

"The card doesn't look like it's asking me anything."

She turned slowly and leaned close enough to look down at it, the frown on her face deepening. "That should not be." She reached for the card but hesitated and looked up at Finn. "You said the man you sentenced called you something. What was it?"

Finn swallowed. "He said I was unclean."

It wasn't only Finn who he'd claimed was unclean. There had been others. The entire village had been unclean, but then that accusation had come from a man who had used the dead for... what? Finn wasn't even sure he knew any longer.

But he knew Esmerelda looked at the card with a different suspicion in her eyes than he had seen from her before. She took a step back, as if to get away from Finn, and clutched the rest of the cards close to her.

"What is it?" Finn asked.

"I am not sure, Finn. Something is unusual. Perhaps it is the attack. Or the berahn. Either way, it has influenced how the card responds to you."

"Has that ever happened for you?"

Esmerelda shook her head. "Not that I have ever seen

before." She studied him for a moment before forcing a smile. "I'm sure there's nothing for you to be concerned about."

Finn looked down at the card. The ink still swirled across the surface, revealing no real image. It was unusual for him to see the ink moving like that; it had a strangely golden, glittery appearance and seemed to slide across the card's surface, the image shifting and gliding as he held on to it.

"I think it is time for you to return to Henry Meyer. I'm sure he would be most interested in learning what happened to you."

He wanted to argue, but she wasn't wrong: It was time for him to return to Master Meyer, to return to his work, and even to return the horse to the stable.

Finn pocketed the card and felt something else in there. It took a moment for him to realize that it was the coin he'd taken from Reginald's home. He'd forgotten about it. "I'll let you know if the image resolves into something useful."

Esmerelda nodded.

He waited for her to turn back to him, but she did not. Instead, she sorted through the powders resting on the table alongside her, as if she needed to move them more than she needed to visit with him.

He headed through her home, picking his way past the table, the faded wooden chairs, and along the brightly colored carpet covering the floor. Finn breathed in deeply, inhaling the aromas of her home. When he reached the door, he glanced back to Esmerelda, but found that she still hadn't turned back to him.

The card had her bothered, but why?

Unclean.

Maybe he *was* unclean.

He had thought Lyle Martin had been touched in the head, but maybe Finn had been wrong. Maybe he had gotten the execution wrong.

He'd allowed the villagers to guide how he had handled the execution—something he didn't always do, but Finn had thought it was appropriate this time. Perhaps it was not.

As he looked around again, he couldn't help but wonder what more he might need to know about what Esmerelda had in mind for him—and what she feared—but he had a feeling she wasn't going to tell him anything.

"If you come up with anything I need to know, please find me in the city," Finn said.

Esmerelda nodded.

As he stepped out of the home, he knew she would not.

All the time he had been working with Master Meyer, and all the time he had come to know the hegen, Finn had never seen Esmerelda in the city other than when she had come with him. She had never willingly gone into the city for any other reason.

Once outside, a northern breeze gusted, cold and biting, tearing through his jacket. He clutched his sword, and realized he didn't have his pack that he'd carried with him, but he didn't need to be concerned. The gray mare was tied to a post outside of Esmerelda's home, and his pack was strapped to her back. In any other part of the city, Finn would've been worried about somebody taking his belongings, but there was no reason for him to be afraid of that in the hegen section—especially outside of Esmerelda's home.

He looked at the bright red painted door leading to Esmerelda's home, and found himself reaching into his pocket, pulling the card out, and looking at its surface.

Unclean.

Somehow, that was tied to why the card wouldn't resolve an image for him.

Finn started through the street, then turned a corner and came face to face with a reddish-haired hegen he had come to know.

"Danior," Finn said.

Danior glanced past Finn, looking toward Esmerelda's home. "Finn Jagger," Danior said. "I didn't realize you were in our section."

"Esmerelda was…" Finn glanced at the card again for a moment before sticking it into his pocket, but not before Danior had a chance to realize he had done so. The other young man flashed a quick smile at Finn. "She helped me. I'd gotten injured on the road leading back to the city."

"It seems you get injured quite a bit for a man who serves the king."

"Apparently, my line of work is dangerous," Finn said.

"Apparently?" Danior asked, chuckling. "You're the one who does the questioning, are you not?"

Finn had always found it interesting that most of the hegen were not at all bothered by the nature of his work.

Far from it. "Most of the time," Finn said. "But there are times when I run into trouble."

"Since you serve the king, I imagine any trouble you get into is supported by him." He nodded toward the main part of the city.

"Usually," Finn said. Did Danior know the king had come to the city?

It had been Finn's experience that the hegen knew things they weren't always supposed to know.

"How's Kezia?"

His face darkened. "More trouble than usual lately. You have a sister too, don't you?"

"I do."

"And you are the older one?"

"Technically."

"What does that mean? What is this 'technically'?"

Finn chuckled, patting the horse on the side for a moment and glancing over her shoulder to Esmerelda's home. He could just see it in the distance, and for a moment, he thought the red door had pulled open and her face had appeared there, as if she was looking down the street toward him.

"It means I might be chronologically older than my sister, but there are times when it feels like she's the older sibling."

"Kezia often acts the same way. She tries to intervene, and has even come to my woodsmith shop, as if to get in the middle of my responsibilities." He smiled at Finn. "Perhaps the two of us can meet at the next festival, share a mug of tea, and dance while we commiserate about our difficulty with our sisters."

Finn nodded. "Perhaps." He patted the horse on the side again and looked over to Danior. "I need to return to the city."

"Of course," Danior said. "It's always my pleasure to see you, Finn Jagger."

"Say," Finn started, "since you're a carpenter, have you ever seen anything like this?" He pulled out the wooden marker he'd found in Reginald's home. It was time to focus on his investigation again. Esmerelda would deal with the Alainsith. He tried to tell himself that was for the best.

Danior looked at it but didn't touch it. "Skillful work," he said. "It looks like three different inlays, and they're placed artfully. It could almost be done by one of the people." He laughed softly. "But it's not. We don't use junith tree, which is what that is."

"Why not?"

"Ask Esmerelda." He grinned at Finn, then went skipping off along the road, dancing away from him.

Finn had found Danior and his sister to be pleasant, but then again, he found most of the hegen to be pleasant. For all that they had terrified him when he was growing up, for all of the ways he and others had use the hegen as a threat, they were nothing if not kind and welcoming, not the fearsome people others often made them out to be.

Junith tree.

One more thing to think about and look into.

He guided the horse along the twisting roads through the hegen section. When he reached its outskirts, he slowed, staring off toward the city. Typically, the Teller Gate was open, letting travelers in and out of the city—but for the first time in Finn's memory, the Teller Gate was closed.

Travelers who had come to Verendal were forced to stand outside the gate, waiting. The crowd was a little unruly, filled with anxious energy and agitation. He approached carefully.

Most of them were road-weary. He could see it in their faces and their posture, recognizing that he felt something similar. There were far more people outside of the city than he had ever seen before. It was as if the walls of Verendal—and Teller Gate—were there for no other reason than to push back those who wanted the protection of the city.

Finn guided his horse forward.

As he neared the Raven Stone, he slowed, looking up to see that a new rope was hanging from the gallows. It was a marker of a coming festival. He hadn't seen it while traveling with Esmerelda, though the Stone should have been visible.

He'd only been gone two days, hadn't he?

Two days out of the city, but that didn't include the time he had spent recovering—or now wandering in the forest with Esmerelda. There might be something taking place with old Alainsith buildings, but there definitely was something going on in the city.

He studied the gallows for another moment, then headed toward the city gate.

By the time he reached the King's Road, he had an increased trepidation about whether he would even be allowed in. It was strange seeing the gate closed this way, and stranger still that he didn't have any way of knowing how to get inside.

He moved through the crowd, ignoring the annoyed looks in his direction. Most of them were suppressed when they saw the sword strapped to his back, though some of the travelers outside of the city still cast suspicious looks in his direction. Maybe they thought him some mercenary, though the kingdom didn't have many of those.

As he approached the gate, he found a pair of Archers standing guard, with a dozen, maybe more, standing along the wall, looking down with crossbows pointed toward the collected people gathered outside.

Thankfully, Finn knew one of the Archers.

"What's going on here, Ned?"

"Hunter." The Archer glanced from Finn to the other Archer. He was a bit pudgy, and young enough that he barely had to shave. "What are you doing out of the city?"

"I had to travel for work on behalf of the king."

"Out of the city?"

Finn nodded. "My work takes me beyond Verendal from time to time."

"I didn't realize that other places need the service of the hangman."

"Other places have crime," Finn said.

Ned chuckled. "And the Hunter has to hunt."

The other Archer laughed, a bit of darkness in his tone.

Finn looked over to him, shooting him a hard-eyed gaze. He didn't know this man, though he was a little older than Finn. Brown hair poked out of his silver helm, and his slender jaw had the traces of a beard he'd shaved. Finn favored the look that the iron masters preferred, keeping a clean-shaven face, a way of setting themselves apart from the prisoners they confined.

"Why is the gate closed?"

"King's orders," Ned said.

Finn looked behind him. There had to be a hundred people, maybe more, and all of them were held back by these two Archers and the six along the wall?

Of course, it wasn't really the eight Archers who held them back. The Teller Gate was closed. The massive wooden doors blocked access to the city.

"I need to get inside."

"You have to wait, like everyone else," the other Archer said.

"This is the Hunter," Ned told him.

"Don't care who it is. We have our orders. You know what would happen if we let somebody in," the other Archer retorted.

"And this isn't just somebody." Ned glanced over to Finn. "Don't mind Willian. He's pretty new to the Archers."

He may have been new, but he looked older.

Finn immediately found himself suspicious of Willian, though maybe that was a mistake. The Archers had been more difficult to bribe lately, thanks to Finn. He had tried to ensure they weren't influenced by some of the local crews, adding that to his list of responsibilities. He had enough experience with crime lords buying their way to a measure of protection and had attempted to prevent others from gaining a foothold in the city by working with Meyer to have the Archers' pay increased, along with watching them more closely.

"I need to get into the city," he said to Ned. All thoughts of the Alainsith faded from his mind.

Ned shared a look with the other Archer. "This is the Hunter," Ned repeated softly.

The other Archer looked over to Finn. "And what do you hunt? You certainly smell like you've been out hunting."

"He hunts criminals," Ned said.

"Is he an Archer?"

"No, he's the hangman." Ned shrugged. "Well, he works with the hangman. I suppose that makes him a hangman too?" Ned's face wrinkled in a confused frown. "I don't really know how it works."

Finn wasn't in any mood to explain the relationship, and at this point, all he wanted was to get inside, leave the horse behind, and get to Master Meyer. Now he felt as if there was something more he needed to understand. If the gate had closed, then he wanted to know what had taken place to cause that. Something had changed while he was away.

He could ask Ned or Willian, but he suspected they wouldn't truly know.

Meyer would know.

The order would likely have been from the king himself—which meant Porman was still in the city.

"You just have to open it wide enough to let me slip in," Finn said.

"The gate opens at eight bells," Willian said.

Finn glanced at the sky. The sun was a little past midday, which meant he would have quite a few hours remaining before eight bells. He could return to the hegen section if they were really going to restrict his access to the city, or he could push the issue here.

How badly did he want to push the issue?

He wanted to figure out what was going on. Besides, there *was* a sentencing soon.

Finn nodded to the Raven Stone. "You need to let me in so I can prepare for the festival. Otherwise, you might end up at the end of the rope," Finn said, looking over to Willian.

Ned started to chuckle, but when Finn shot him a hard-eyed stare, he trailed off before nodding hurriedly. He looked to the Archers standing along the wall. "Open the gate. Need to let the hangman in." Somebody from the side shouted something, and Ned shook his head. "Just open the damn gate."

Willian glowered at Finn. "If you end up getting us charged for this, I'm coming for you myself."

"If you end up getting us charged for this, Willian's going to come for you," Ned said.

The gate started to open, stopping only a few feet wide.

Finn nodded to Ned, then to Willian, before leading

the horse inside. He'd just passed through the gate when the crowd behind him started to surge forward. Ned shouted, and the gate started to close far more slowly than it should have.

Ned cried out as several people converged upon him, and Finn tried to turn, but the gate was already closing. The Archers along the wall shouted, then he heard the sound of a crossbow firing, then another.

They came in rapid succession.

People shouted, then a pounding upon the gate thundered.

Finn stared at it.

That was my fault.

Had he only waited…

He had to stop thinking like that.

More than that, he had to get over to Master Meyer to understand what was going on, why the upheaval had persisted in the city, and how Meyer expected to carry out a sentencing in the current climate. If the people were so unsettled, how did they hope to carry out a sentencing without drawing another protest? If him just passing through the gate led to violence like that, how could they succeed in carrying out the king's justice?

Finn didn't have the answers as he continued weaving through the streets, making his way toward the stables. By the time he dropped off the horse, paid the fee, and started back toward Meyer's home, he found himself feeling the unease in the city, all too aware of just how unsettled everything was. It wasn't just the people at the gate.

The people in the city itself still had an edge to them.

232 | D.K. HOLMBERG

It was the Archers.

And now his coming back to the city had caused the Archers to take more action. There would be repercussions because of it. And Finn would have to be ready for it.

There were far more Archers patrolling the city than usual. Many of them weren't even from the city. Many of them were palace Archers. Not only that, but there were several who were Realmsguard, which meant the king was much more concerned about what was taking place than what Finn had believed.

As he headed to Master Meyer's home, he shifted the sword, reached into his pocket, and pulled out the hegen card. He stared at it for a moment, looking at the surface, and wished he understood what it intended for him.

But the card had not changed. The ink remained unreadable.

CHAPTER FIFTEEN

Finn's mind did not stop churning during his walk back to Master Meyer's home.

The city was quiet, which he thought was a positive sign, given the way he had left it, but he did worry about additional protests during the time he had been gone Not only that, but there was a part of him that wanted nothing more than to send Archers out of the city to investigate whether there were others involved in his attack. Finn doubted there would be much benefit to that, but someone attacking and trying to claim his sword suggested that the danger was far more real than he had known before.

Hopefully Meyer would understand.

Or maybe he wouldn't.

That was the other concern Finn had.

Meyer didn't always agree with Finn's investigations, and before Finn's departure, Meyer had made it quite clear that he felt Finn had been looking too deeply into details that were not necessarily crucial to their current investigation.

He limped forward, and by the time he reached Master Meyer's home, he was moving even more slowly. His body still ached, and he waited at the gate for a moment, looking at the home. It was early in the day. He had taken longer outside the city than he suspected Master Meyer would have preferred, which meant the master executioner would've been responsible for more tasks during Finn's absence. He doubted that Meyer would comment on that, though Finn felt the delay.

Even though he had taken more time, he still questioned if he had taken *enough* time. One thought stayed with him: He needed to question the prisoners.

He pushed into the gate, walking along the path, and stepped inside of the home. He put the sword back into the closet, reminding himself that he would need to clean and polish it later, before dropping his pack in his room. Everything was as he had left it.

There were times when he felt as if he were still the apprentice who Master Meyer had saved from execution. Often he was given freedom to operate as he felt necessary, but there were times when he was not. And there were times when the past seemed to come back and strike him, giving Finn a reminder of what he had done and been before.

He heard voices in the kitchen and Finn limped toward it.

Lena was there, but she wasn't alone. He had thought it

was Master Meyer with her, but it was somebody whom Finn had not seen in quite some time.

He bowed his head politely to his sister and Helda. She was a lovely woman, though had been less than sympathetic to the kind of work Finn had to do, resulting in the two of them never having the opportunity to progress to something more than friends. That seemed to be his ongoing challenge.

"Finn. Henry thought you would return soon, but he wasn't sure when," Lena said.

Finn nodded and limped forward before taking a seat.

"You were out of the city?" Helda asked.

"I was."

He never knew how much to reveal to anyone about what he was tasked with doing when he left the city. The investigation was easy enough to explain, but the rest of it was more difficult, and less pleasant, to describe. This last investigation even more so than others. There was something about what had happened in the village of Weverth that had bothered him.

"How has the city been?" Finn asked.

Lena glanced over to Helda for a moment before turning her attention back to Finn. "Relatively quiet. Henry has been looking into some of the protests while you were gone, and he said there was something about a man who died…"

Finn had almost forgotten about Reginald, but it was one more thing he needed to look into now that he was back. Reginald had killed himself, or seemingly so, though there was something about his death that troubled Finn.

He had Reginald's journal, which he would need to go through and look into more to try to find some answers.

"There was a man who died before I left," Finn said, "but I think the protests have taken priority. Or they had up until I left."

"I think the Archers have been too hard on the protesters," Helda said. When Lena looked over to her, Helda shrugged. "Well, I do. These are people who have nothing, Lena. I know it's hard for you to remember what it was like, but all they are looking for is a measure of respect from the king."

Lena frowned at her friend. "It's not hard for me to remember what it was like," she said. "In fact, it's easy. I know that if Meyer were to send me away, I wouldn't have anything. No way of taking care of myself, no way of providing for myself, and no way to find a place to stay safe."

"You don't have to worry about that though, do you?"

Lena looked over to Finn for a long moment, holding his gaze. "I hope not. Henry has been kind, and he has permitted me to remain. I hope he does not change his mind."

Finn thought Lena was well beyond worrying about that, though maybe she wasn't.

She did worry about whatever she might offer Henry. He wasn't looking for a relationship, Finn knew. The very few times Finn had ever spoken to Meyer about his lost family, the master executioner had made it quite clear that those wounds had not fully healed.

But Lena was something like a daughter to him.

Meyer would never banish her. In fact, he thought Lena had less of an issue concerning that than Finn did; he could disappoint Meyer far more easily than Lena could.

"You don't have to worry about that," Finn said. "He's not sending you anywhere. Besides, I think he likes having somebody who has a way with apothecary medicine like you do."

Lena blushed briefly and turned away from Helda's stare.

He needed to ask about the prisoners.

"Has your other project been successful?" Finn asked.

Lena frowned at him. "Not completely."

"You have another project?" Helda asked.

Lena glanced over to her. "Henry had me gather some items of importance and try to keep them coordinated."

Helda frowned.

Lena chuckled. "In his garden," she said quickly. Finn smiled at how quickly she found the lie. "He has some plants that are important to him that he has been trying to keep alive."

"And he asked you for that help?"

Finn leaned forward. "Master Meyer likes to think he has a green thumb, but he doesn't have the same skill as Lena. She's not just a healer." He winked at his sister and got to his feet. "I need to go looking for Meyer."

"I don't think he's gone terribly far. He made mention of visiting the site of the protest. He's been trying to piece things together. I think he does that because he believes it's what you would do."

"Say, would you look into something for me?" Finn asked. His sister would be able to go places he couldn't— and she'd probably draw very different attention than he would.

"What?"

He glanced to Helda. How much should he say in front of her? "I'm curious about the posters that have started appearing around the city."

"The Rose," Helda said. Finn turned to her and she shrugged. "I've seen them too."

"Do you know anything about them?" he asked.

"Nothing more than most. They want people from the outer sections treated better. They want the Archers to be…" Her eyes widened slightly as she looked at Finn. "Anyway, they want more."

Finn looked to Lena. "If you can find anything else?"

"I'll let you know," she said softly, seeming to avoid Helda's gaze.

Finn smiled. "Thanks. I can check on you later, Lena."

She nodded slowly.

He grabbed his cloak and limped out of the home.

His injury made everything a little uncoordinated. Though he ached, he still managed to move with a steady step, limping slightly as he weaved through the city. His side didn't hurt the way it should, but that had to be because of the hegen healing. He'd experienced it enough times now that it didn't impress him quite as much as it once had.

He reached the far side of the bridge when he saw Meyer.

"You're back," Meyer said.

Finn nodded and proceeded to tell Meyer everything that had happened to him while he was gone, including the attack and his concern about witchcraft. "I'd like to go back and bring men—"

"That's not what we need to be concerned with right now. We're still working through the situation with the protesters—something I believe you wanted to do."

Finn sighed. It *had* been his idea. "We need to know more though. If this Black Rose thinks to attack—"

"It's not only about you, Finn," Meyer chided. "Remember what you saw in the city."

Meyer was right. It *wasn't* just about him. "I remember."

"They gathered here," Meyer bent down next to the crooked iron gate of the wool warehouse. Finn had wanted to come back to see it since *he'd* been attacked. Meyer was staring at something, though Finn couldn't tell what it was. "But they didn't go any farther."

Finn squinted out over the shining water. "Because the Archers were on the far shoreline."

Meyer straightened, and Finn saw that he was carrying his walking stick. He didn't need it, but he had seen Meyer carrying it when he wanted a weapon.

All of this had Meyer feeling more unsettled than he was letting on.

"Too many were lost," Meyer said, shaking his head. "And all for what? Haven't found much about the Black Rose movement while you were gone. It's tied to the king."

"Not the Archers?"

"Not the movement. They care more about what the king has done, or so they say. But when the Archers cut down the protesters, it escalated. Next we'll see protesters executing Archers." He shook his head.

"They wouldn't."

"I'm not so sure about that. Men get angry enough and they'll do things they wouldn't tolerate otherwise."

"You still think this was just a spontaneous protest? Even with the posters and the coordinating whistles?"

Meyer shook his head, letting out a frustrated sigh. "Probably not, though it could be. When I was still in my training, living north of here, there was a protest. A man was cut down by the Archers." He shook his head again. "The Archers claimed he was guilty, though evidence later proved that he was not."

Finn watched Meyer. This was similar, though on a much greater scale. Maybe that was Meyer's point.

"It was difficult reporting to the magister and the jurors that the Archer was guilty," Meyer said.

"We've seen Archers bribed and worse."

"We have. It was that event that helped me see that any man can be tempted." Meyer headed deeper into the section, moving slowly. His gaze swept from one side of him to the other, looking at areas of the ground that Finn couldn't quite identify. It wasn't until Meyer stopped again that Finn realized what he was doing. He was looking at bloodstains. Some of the cobblestones appeared entirely maroon. "This occurrence has a different feel to it. The king was here." Meyer kept his voice soft, but there was still an edge within it. "They should not have known."

"How do you think they learned? From men like those who jumped me outside the city?"

"That is what we have to uncover."

"They have posters around the city. You've seen them, I'm sure." When Meyer frowned, Finn looked up. There would have to be one somewhere. He found one three buildings down, and motioned for Meyer to follow him until they reached it. The building had the smell of a butcher, though there wasn't a sign out front to tell him what it was. The poster was on the corner of the building. It looked no different from any of the others he had seen, featuring the shape of the black rose marked on the white background. "These posters," he said.

"I don't think there's anything to them," Meyer said. "We've been seeing these for months."

"We have, but now we've got someone with that same mark who tried to kill me." And take his sword. It occurred to Finn that though they had been seeing them for months, they had been increasing in frequency lately. More and more of these posters had started to appear. That couldn't be a coincidence. "It's all tied to the Black Rose."

Finn was convinced of it, but he didn't have the feeling that Meyer was.

They continued along the street, and Finn counted several more of the black rose posters. There didn't seem to be any pattern to them, nor was there any sort of organization to their distribution. Some were plastered to businesses, others to abandoned buildings, and one was on what looked to be a crumbling temple.

Finn heard a shout down the street and looked up. He tensed immediately, thinking back to the protest, but it was only a child running along the street, chased by two others. One of them laughed, then they disappeared around the corner.

"Is there a reason you're taking all of them?" Finn asked, looking over to Meyer.

"I want to study them later. I am curious if the design is the same for each of them. It is possible that some of these are copies of others."

"You're trying to see if you can figure out who printed them."

Meyer nodded. They had looped back around and stood along the river. "Why don't you finish whatever you have for the day and we can meet up later?"

Finn nodded and they parted ways. There were supplies to gather, and he had to stop at the prisons to see whether there were any new prisoners.

Return to normal.

It felt different though.

There was a strange energy in the air, and Finn didn't care for it. He passed one man who pulled a knife from his pocket. Most of the shops were closed. Most people he passed looked away, refusing to make eye contact. It was as if everybody in the city was on edge. He understood that, for he felt much the same way, feeling some of that tension, uncertain whether he could do anything about it.

As he made his way toward the prisons, he noticed a

black trail of smoke rising into the air. It wasn't in one of the outer sections.

Finn started off toward it.

He had seen too much fire in the city, and had seen how destructive it could be. He wasn't about to sit by and watch fire consume even more of the city. There had to be something he could do.

Finn wasn't entirely sure what that was though. He wasn't on the fire brigade, and he had no idea if there was anything nefarious about this fire. It might simply be accidental. But the timing of it, along with everything else that had been taking place in the city, made him question it.

He crossed the bridge, heading toward the center of the city, keeping the smoke in view. He followed the river, then veered inward.

Finn realized where he was going.

His heart started to beat faster.

He hadn't gone very far when he saw the fire licking at the sides of the stone building.

The Archers' barracks.

The fire brigade was already there, and they were pumping water to put the fire out. The stone had been blackened, and the windows on the front of the barracks had shattered or melted, leaving much of the building itself destroyed.

Finn strode forward, hurrying toward one of the head Archers. He recognized Tolsten.

"What happened?" Finn asked.

Tolsten turned. He was tall, though not quite as tall as Finn. His eyes glared until he realized it was Finn, then they softened slightly. "Hunter," he mumbled. "Didn't think to see you here so soon."

"I saw the smoke."

"Bastards didn't burn down the barracks. But they tried."

"What do you mean, 'they tried'?"

"They were throwing bottles of flaming oil. If they think they can intimidate us, they have another thing coming."

There was a dark glimmer in his eyes, and Finn resisted the urge to shiver.

How far would this go?

"Did you catch them?"

Tolsten glowered at him. "My men did. Nelshan. Yestel. Risah." He nodded, and Finn saw the three men standing on the far side of the street, five people lying in front of them.

"I need to ask your men questions," Finn said.

"Good luck," Tolsten said.

Finn frowned at him, but Tolsten strode away, heading over to talk to one of the members of the fire brigade.

Finn watched him for a moment.

He understood the frustration. Had the protesters targeted Meyer's house, he'd feel much the same way. In fact, if they targeted one of the prisons, he'd also feel possessive in a similar way. This was the Archers' base. This was their home, and Tolsten was their leader.

When he and Meyer had worked to try to expunge all within the ranks of the Archers who had been influenced by bribery, he didn't know if they had fully succeeded.

Tolsten had remained. Finn didn't know the man that well, though he and Meyer had quite a bit of experience together over the years, and Meyer had vouched for him. Finn figured that was more than enough reason to trust the man.

Others, though, were still being vetted.

Finn breathed out a sigh of frustration, making his way over to the three Archers who had captured the men responsible.

"You three are Nelshan, Yestal, and Risah?"

They all turned toward him.

"Who's this?" one of the shorter men asked. He had a broad face and a bald head.

"That's the Hunter," the taller man said. "You not met him yet, Risah?"

Risah grunted. He scrubbed a hand over his bald head, glancing down. "Nobody wants to meet an executioner."

"Don't mind him," the taller man said. "I'm Yestal. We were the ones to drag them down."

"I need to talk with them," Finn said.

"Good luck," he said.

Finn frowned. It was the same thing that Tolsten had said to him. "Why?" He started to wonder what had happened before looking past the three Archers, but didn't need to look long to understand.

Three of them had crossbow bolts sticking out of their chest. The other two were lying motionless.

"They're dead?"

"What can I say?" Yestal said, shrugging. "You bring it out here, you're going to face the consequences."

"Are you sure these five were involved?" Finn asked, sliding between Yestal and Risah. The third man still hadn't spoken yet. He crouched down next to the nearest of the bodies, checking for a pulse. There was none. He had no idea how long the man had been dead, though his body was still warm.

"We saw two of them with bottles in their hands," Nelshan said.

Finn looked up at him. He was the thinnest of the three, and the only one with the stripe on his shoulder. He had rank.

"What about the other three?"

"What about them? They were with the other two."

Finn moved past the first man. The next had a crossbow bolt in his belly. Finn checked him for a pulse.

There was a weak one, though it was still there. "I need you to gather a cot. We need to get this man to Declan."

"He already got his sentence," Risah said.

Finn stood. He had to handle this carefully, he knew, but he also needed them to realize they couldn't take action without the king's authority. Killing men in the street was not how the Archers were supposed to fulfill their obligations. "Gather a cot. Bring him to Declan. I will question him. If you challenge me, I'm going to have words with Tolsten, then you will find *yourself* in Declan."

Risah glared at him, but Yestal grabbed his arm and they headed off.

It left him with Nelshan.

He tested the next man. The crossbow had struck him

in the upper chest. There was too much blood. He knew he was down already.

"I see the crossbow bolts in these three," he said. He knew that three crossbow bolts were a result of the actions of the three Archers. "What happened to these two?"

"They ran," he said.

"And you chased them down?"

"Can't have them get away. One of the bastards did get free. We'll find him." He nodded to the others. "Besides, Hunter, you saw what happened earlier in the city. I heard you were there."

Finn checked on the first of the two without a crossbow bolt protruding from him. His neck was twisted strangely.

That wasn't the result of a fall.

He hurried around and checked on the next.

His head had been caved in.

Brutal attacks.

"What is this?" Finn said, standing.

"You see what it is," Nelshan said.

"I see what it is," Finn said, "but this tells me that you took these other two down with far more force than necessary."

"Who is to say what kind of force was necessary?"

Finn clenched his jaw. Was this retaliation for something?

"Did it not occur to you that we could question them?"

"Question them for what?"

"For what's going on in the city. The unrest. The protests. The attack."

"There's not a whole lot to question, is there?" He pulled himself up and held Finn's gaze. "We have five men who attacked the Archers' barracks. Seems to me it was pretty straightforward. Are you telling me that the jurors would see it differently?"

Did he really think to challenge Finn?

Finn glanced over to where Tolsten was talking to one of the fire brigade before turning his attention back to the Archer. "I'm saying that you had no reason to slaughter these two men. No reason, probably, to slaughter all *five* of these men. Not until the king has his justice."

"Slaughter?"

"That's right," Finn said, taking a step toward him.

The Archer reached for his sword.

Finn stared him down. "You do that and you're sealing your own fate." He said it quietly, but loudly enough for him to hear it. "I'm not going to drag you into Declan, but you and I are going to talk officially."

Nelshan remained tense.

"You need me to call out to Tolsten?" Finn asked.

He glowered at Finn. Finally, he relaxed, lowering his hand. "We didn't mean to kill them," he said.

"I'm sure you did not."

The other two Archers came out from somewhere carrying a cot. They looked over to Finn, who motioned to the still-living man and waved a hand. "I expect him to make it to Declan alive. If he doesn't, the two of you will end up staying there until I have answers."

Finn checked over the other bodies, knowing he wouldn't have the chance later. He found a tattoo of the Black Rose on one of the men's wrists, but only one of them. The others didn't have the mark. No other identification. No money. Nothing that would help him figure out who they were.

He would only be able to ascertain that from the man who'd lived.

If he could keep him that way.

After spending the better part of ten minutes doing his search, he made his way over to Tolsten. "I'm going to need to talk to you and your men."

Tolsten shot him a look. "Under whose authority?"

"The very same authority that I always operate under: that of King Porman."

"You're not talking to anybody unless the hangman is here."

Finn forced a smile. "I will make sure Master Meyer knows that is your preference." He nodded to the other three Archers, who were now hurrying away, carrying the fallen man toward Declan. Finn had more work to do. "Make sure none of them disappear."

Finn stormed away, making his way to Declan. He crossing the bridge toward the prison when he caught sight of his sister. He raised his hand, then lowered it.

Lena was walking with a tall, bookish-looking man.

He frowned. A priest.

She wasn't just visiting with him. She was walking with him. They headed across one of the neighboring bridges, making their way toward the center of the city.

She looked up at the priest, smiling, and at one point, he almost heard a laugh from her.

Lena never laughed.

Maybe he didn't have to worry about her. If she was finally putting herself out into the world, letting herself find someone, then there was no reason for him to worry about his sister. She deserved happiness. More than almost anyone else he knew.

As he continued onward toward Declan, he pulled Reginald's journal out of his pocket and thumbed through it. Finn remained convinced there was more to what was in the journal than what he'd seen so far, though he hadn't uncovered anything yet. His time out of the city hadn't given him any great insight, which he found disappointing. He stuffed it back into his pocket as he neared the prison, where he saw a dozen Archers had gathered.

Finn pushed through them.

"What happened?" he asked, looking over to the Archer with the stripe on his shirt. The man was short and stocky, and he knew him.

"We got three men down," Horace said. "Look, Hunter."

Finn looked at where he was pointing.

Three Archers. Each of them lay bound, heads tipped to the side, throats slit.

Nelshan, Yestal, and Risah.

Finn didn't need to examine them to know that all three were dead. There wasn't anything he could do for them.

The injured man was gone.

There would be no way to learn the names of the men involved in starting the fire.

"These two found them while on patrol," Horace said, pointing to two Archers. Both of them looked young, and one of them looked ashen, shaking slightly. "Just like this. Bodies still warm."

How did they act so quickly?

The Black Rose.

That was how.

Now they had Archers dead. Protesters dead.

And soon the city would explode.

Finn had to stop this. Somehow.

"Have your men move the bodies," Finn said.

"You aren't going to investigate?"

He debated what to say to them. These were their friends, he suspected.

"I don't need the bodies to investigate."

Horace held his gaze for a moment before nodding. He motioned to the others, and they quickly got to work carrying the bodies, two Archers to each.

When they were gone, Horace remained.

"They were good men," he said.

Finn knew the truth was more complicated than that. It always was. "I'm sure they were."

"They served the king."

Finn looked over to him, wondering where this was going. "We will find who did this."

"You damn well better," Horace said.

"I know my duty. And I expect you to do yours."

Horace glowered at him for a long moment, looking as

if he wanted to say something before thinking better of it and storming off after the other Archers.

Finn decided against going to Declan.

After visiting a general store, another apothecary, then the butcher, he was ready to return to meet Master Meyer. He found him in the kitchen. Meyer looked up at him, and Finn expected to have to tell him what was going on, but it was Meyer who looked more upset than Finn.

"What's wrong?" Finn asked.

"A summons." He held up a piece of paper, and Finn recognized the king's seal. "We've been called to the palace."

CHAPTER SIXTEEN

F inn and Meyer approached the palace slowly. The winding road leading up to it was meant to make it difficult for anybody to assault the king in the palace directly, but it did give flashes of the palace as they meandered along the street, putting it into view for brief moments before disappearing once again.

The sun had started to set, and the streaks of orange and pink on the horizon were beautiful in the autumn air. Fluffy white clouds swirled behind the palace, in front of the sun, but had the addition of the smoke from the city.

"I didn't realize when I came to work with you that I would visit the king as much as I have," Finn said.

Meyer nodded solemnly. "We serve his justice. Most who live in the city don't quite understand what that means, but the longer you serve, and serve within the executioner court, you'll come to see we have a pivotal role within the kingdom." He glanced over to Finn before turning and nodding to the palace that started to loom in front of them. Distantly, one of the church bells tolled—a deep, haunting sound. The Church of Fell. "We don't rule, and we don't offer any guidance to those who do, but we serve an important part of the kingdom. We serve to ensure justice is served."

"How often do you question what you're asked to do?" Finn asked quietly.

He had not struggled with that too much, but there were times when he did Some of his uncertainty stemmed from situations in which people were sentenced for crimes that Finn didn't necessarily view as severe as the king did. Having lived in the poorer sections of the city, and having struggled on the streets himself, he understood there were certain times and circumstances that drove a man to commit acts that he wouldn't otherwise. Those were the situations he grappled with the most.

Not so much when he dealt with arsonists, as he had several times, or murderers or rapists. Those were easy crimes to deal with.

"Every so often, you encounter a crisis of faith," Master Meyer said, not looking in his direction. Another church bell tolled, this one nearby. The Giver Bell. A reminder to offer a tithe to the church, though most of the churches had dedicated giving times that made a reminder unnecessary. "There are times when you have to find within yourself whether you're comfortable with what's asked of you."

"When was the last time you felt that way?"

"When I was to sentence you," Meyer said softly.

They reached the wall surrounding the palace and the two Archers standing guard at the gate. Finn doubted that was all who were there. Given the upheaval within the city, he suspected the king had far more men guarding the palace than usual. He had even caught sight of some of them coming into the city. Soldiers who were never stationed in Verendal now took up a place along the outer wall, and were occasionally stationed throughout the city along the streets.

"I didn't realize you considered that a crisis of faith."

"Did you think I wasn't aware of the reason behind what you did?"

"I told you why I did what I did," Finn said.

"You told me. And I corroborated it. I saw in you something I had gone through myself. A man who struggled with what happened with his family." Meyer looked to him briefly before turning his attention back to the palace. "And I have to say that I trusted myself, and my convictions. Had I not, think of what might have been lost."

"Lena would've been lost," Finn said, his voice dropping to a whisper.

"Your sister might be the most skilled healer the city has seen in over a century." Meyer shook his head, a hint of a smile twisting his face. "And had you told me that when I first met her, I would have thought it impossible, but she synthesizes information she reads in a way that no one I've ever met has been able to do."

"Even the hegen?"

"The hegen have their own ability, but it's one that

relies upon power. Your sister..." Meyer smiled slightly. "I suppose some would say that what she does is a form of magic. Some would claim that her ability to remember everything she reads, pulling it all together in a way that can build upon knowledge that was passed on before her, is a form of magic. And perhaps it is." Meyer shrugged. "All I can say is that because I trusted myself, trusted my convictions, and recognized something within you that could provide value to the king and the kingdom, there has been much more benefit than anyone ever would have anticipated."

Finn looked over to him. Meyer didn't often talk about that situation, and it seemed an unusual time for him to do so now, standing in front of the palace, but perhaps it wasn't. Meyer had needed to fight on behalf of Finn even then. Not only when he exerted his right, but then he had been forced to come before the king, to explain himself, and to justify claiming Finn—and not only had he claimed Finn, but he'd put his life on the line, risking himself in order to exert that right. Had Finn failed...

Not only would Finn have died, but Meyer would have as well. The kingdom would've lost two executioners. Bellut and the magister would have succeeded. The witch-craft attack on the city—and on the Alainsith—would have succeeded. And Lena would have never learned she could be the healer that she is.

Aside from all that, there was one part of him being claimed by Master Meyer that meant the most to him. Had Meyer not claimed him, Finn's mother would've suffered in her remaining days. Because of Master Meyer, she had an opportunity to live out the rest of her days in a better state than she had been before.

"I don't know if I've ever thanked you for what you did for my mother."

"You have," Meyer said.

"Have I? I don't feel like I've ever *properly* thanked you."

Meyer glanced over. "You do it every day in how you carry yourself." He took a deep breath and started forward. "Come along, Finn. It's time for us to meet with the king."

They reached the gate leading into the palace, and the two Archers regarded Meyer, then Finn, seeming to size them up. As they were both unarmed, other than the small belt knife Finn carried with him, they were not much of a threat.

Still, they didn't open the gate.

"What's going on?" Finn whispered.

"You will have an escort," the first Archer said.

He was heavily armored with his gleaming silver helm, his sword sheathed at his side, and the maroon and gold colors of the king striped along the armor plate on his chest. He was a powerful-looking man, and Finn had little doubt the man would have any trouble neutralizing Finn if he had posed a danger.

The other Archer was not nearly as large, but there was still a strange intensity to him. He stood casually, one hand near the hilt of his sword, and was dressed in leathers rather than full armor.

He might not be as well protected, but it would allow him more fluid movement. There was a twitchiness to him, and he shifted his feet slightly, sliding them from place to place, giving Finn the impression that he was ready to dart forward in an attack at any moment—which was likely exactly what he was prepared for.

Finally, a voice called from behind the gate. "You may open it."

The larger of the two Archers slid a bar across the gate leading through the palace walls, opening it. He stepped off to the side, though remained close, as Meyer, then Finn, passed through.

"I've never seen Archers like that before," Finn said softly.

"They have never been stationed here before," Meyer said. He glanced over his shoulder before turning his attention back to Finn. "Those are the Realmsguard."

Realmsguard. Even in his travels, Finn had never seen them.

The kingdom had regular soldiers. That was where the palace Archers were pulled from. The Realmsguard were different. More intense. They were soldiers without peer within the kingdom and beyond.

The gate swung closed, and Finn looked over to see three traditional-appearing Archers standing on the path. All had the stripes on their shoulders indicating they were palace Archers, and all carried both the crossbow and sword. Finn knew them to be deadly with both, and incredibly skilled, but it wasn't the Archers who drew his attention quite as much as it was the Realmsguard. Finn found something fascinating about them. Maybe it was a mistake for him to pay so much attention to them, especially as he and Meyer had come here to speak with the king; Finn didn't want to draw any additional attention and scrutiny, but he had a feeling from Master Meyer that even he was impressed.

The Archers took up positions on either side of Finn and Master Meyer, with one of the Archers—a gray-haired man with a grizzled appearance; heavily tanned skin; and deep wrinkles in the corners of his flat, gray eyes—leading them. They marched them forward. When they reached the entrance to the palace, a pair of massive doors with engravings of King Porman's wolf crest upon them, they paused while the lead Archer pounded briefly.

Another pair of Archers pulled open the doors, studying Finn and Master Meyer.

"This is the master executioner and his apprentice," a voice said from behind the Archers. The elderly man who had spoken shoved his way through the Archers and nodded to Master Meyer and Finn. "My apologies, master executioner. With the recent events, the Archers and the Realmsguard feel they must be as protective as possible in order to ensure the king's safety." He glanced over to the Archers, shaking his head as if to say just how he felt about that. "Of course, the king is perfectly safe within the palace, as are you. Would you come with me?"

The Archers stepped off to the side, allowing Finn and Meyer to pass through. Once inside, Finn glanced along the great entrance. Another six Archers were stationed inside, positioned along the wall.

The amount of preparation suggested to Finn a greater

concern for the king's safety than even the old servant had alluded to.

"Why has the king stayed here if he's concerned for his safety?" Finn asked, looking over to Master Meyer.

The servant glanced back at Finn. "He's here for a specific purpose," the servant said. "And while he must ensure he is safe while he's here, do not fear for the king. He has some of his most talented soldiers keeping watch."

He ushered them forward and left them in a large room. A navy carpet covered the marble tile, and flames crackled in the hearth at one end of the room. The curtains were open, letting sunlight in along with a bit of the afternoon breeze, circulating cooler air in with the warmth coming off the hearth. Flowers set into vases all around the room released a floral fragrance that filled everything.

Finn and Meyer stood in the center of the room, and Finn clasped his hands behind him as he surveyed his surroundings. The walls were all paneled wood, stained with a rich, dark brown. Sculptures were set on pedestals or situated around the floor, and one dark sculpture reminded him of a berahn, though it may have just been a wolf. He had a hard time thinking that the king would carry any decorations of Alainsith creatures, especially ones that were known as the silent killer.

As he turned in place, he noticed that the wall surrounding the door had swords crisscrossed along its surface.

"Some say those are the swords of the enemies who were vanquished by the kingdom," Meyer said softly.

"Alainsith?"

Meyer nodded. "Perhaps Alainsith, or perhaps one of the other countries we have warred with over the years. Yelind. Host. Nemenah."

Yelind had been the only one Finn had heard much about, while the other wars had been ancient, from a time long before Finn had been born, a time that might have even been before Verendal was a part of the kingdom.

He stepped out of the center of the room, making his way over to the wall so he could look up at the swords. "Which ones do you think are Alainsith?"

Meyer shook his head. "I'm not an expert in such things. I'm merely an executioner."

Finn chuckled. "You're not *merely* anything."

"The blades would be different," Meyer said. "And likely would be decorated with Alainsith symbols. Typically shaped like leaves or flowers. Something distinct."

He wandered along the wall, looking up at the blades. Many of them looked similar to the kinds of weapons he saw in Verendal: straight blades and simple steel, though some had more intricately carved hand guards and hilts. There was one with an enormous blue jewel at the end of the hilt, serving as the pommel. Nearest the corners of the room, the blades changed. They were more curved and made of a darker metal, one that almost seemed like it absorbed the light of the room. Finn leaned close, studying them and looking for any sign of Alainsith writing, when he heard laughter behind him.

He spun.

King Porman stood near the far wall. The king was not

a tall man, nor was he muscular, but there was a sense of intensity about him. Finn had noticed it during their first encounter. Perhaps it came from knowing that every command he issued would be followed. How could it not be? If Finn had that kind of power, he would certainly act similarly. The king was dressed in flowing blue robes that stretched down to his feet, though he also had a short sword sheathed at his side, which Finn questioned whether the king even knew how to use. Perhaps it was for appearances, or perhaps it was for protection against them. Though they were his trusted servants, the king might not trust them completely.

Finn wondered for a moment how the king managed to enter the room without him noticing. Then he realized a faint crack along the paneling. There was a hidden door. *That made sense.* There would be no reason for the king to head through the halls of the palace if he had some hidden corridors he could travel through. And it would be one more means of protecting him if he were under any sort of attack.

"I'm surprised you would be so intrigued by those blades when the one you wield is far superior."

Finn bowed, noting Meyer doing the same.

The king laughed again, and Finn flicked his gaze up.

"You don't need to be quite so formal. I did call you here to discuss the current circumstances, and I believe we will have an easier time talking if we aren't bowing and kneeling." The main door into the room opened, and a white-clad servant came in pushing a cart with a bottle of wine and three silver goblets. He bowed to the king before turning and leaving them. The king waved his hand toward the tray. "Please. I seem to remember the last time you were here, you enjoyed the wine."

Finn *had* enjoyed the wine, but he also recognized he should be careful around the king. He served at the king's behest, and all it would take would be for Porman to decide he didn't need Finn's service any longer and he would be banished from his responsibility.

Meyer took a glass of wine but made no attempt to drink it.

Finn followed his lead, though he sipped at the wine. There was no point in coming to the palace if he couldn't enjoy some of the benefits of it.

"I should start by thanking you for coming to visit," the king said.

"Of course, sire," Meyer said, bowing his head slightly.

The king headed over to the wall, looking up at the swords. "I find it intriguing you were interested in this," the king said, looking over to Finn. "Are you something of a connoisseur of weaponry?"

Finn resisted the urge to look over to Meyer.

"Not so much. I just appreciate how the blades all have different appearances."

"Ah. Of course." The king headed along the wall, keeping his gaze on the swords. "Many of these were claimed when my father ruled, and his father before him. It was a different time then, and we knew bloodshed in a way we don't know it now. Thankfully. Time has given us insight my forefathers did not have. They believed that testing one's mettle against even a foe as dangerous as the

Alainsith was necessary. Then again, had they not done so, the kingdom would not have advanced beyond its former borders, and we would not have begun to understand the dangers that exist..." He flashed a smile. "Perhaps I should not elaborate on such things. It is unsafe for me to share, especially for those who live out here on the border of the kingdom, in a place as dangerous as this one has become." He glanced over to Finn, taking a slow drink of his wine. "We have known peace for several decades."

Finn nodded. He didn't know where the king was going with this line of conversation.

"Verendal has known peace as well. We have such dedicated servants within the city that it's not surprising." He smiled and took a drink of the wine, looking over the top of the glass as he did. "Until now."

"We are looking into the protests," Meyer said. "There are rumors of a movement—"

"Not rumors," the king said, regarding Meyer for a moment. "I understand that you have a dozen or so men you've been questioning."

How would he have heard that? Finn thought Meyer kept the number a secret, as he had kept *where* they had been questioning them a secret. It was easier to prevent additional upheaval by keeping that hidden from others in the city.

This *was* the king though. If anyone would have access to resources throughout the city to find out what was taking place, it would be him.

"We have several of the instigators," Meyer said.

Instigators?

Finn looked over to Meyer, but he ignored Finn's glance.

Had Meyer learned something from them?

Not all of them could be instigators. Some of them might have been, like the older of the men, but Finn had a hard time thinking all of them were involved, especially the boy.

"Several." The king looked up at the swords. "There was a time when claiming the weapon of your defeated foe was considered a prize." He shook his head. "My father thought that way, though that was because he believed everyone was his foe."

"Even the Alainsith?" Finn asked.

When the king looked over to him, he realized he should be more careful.

"The Alainsith treaty has been tenuous. My father believed they were more of a threat than they presented, though not all of the men who served beneath him believed the same. Nor did I." He looked up and took a deep breath. "We have suffered over the years for our arrogance of believing we can understand them. They are different from us. Gods, they live lives three times as long as we do. How can we ever think we can understand what they are like?" The king turned to Finn. "One of the things I felt we needed to do when I began my reign was try to forge a peace—a real peace—with the Alainsith. We needed to be done with foolish fighting that would get us nowhere. We needed to ensure both of our peoples could thrive. Doing so has not been easy, and it has taken a considerable effort on my part, but I think it has been worth it."

The king turned away from the swords and sipped at his wine. "We must know who is responsible for these attacks," he said softly.

"We are doing all we can, sire," Meyer said.

"Then you must do more." His gaze lingered on Finn a moment. Then the king took a deep breath, looking at the swords again. "We don't need more blades of our vanquished foes hanging on my wall. What we have is enough." He turned and looked from Meyer to Finn. "We have seen Yelind attack. We have faced a magic that has tainted this great kingdom. And now this. I can't help but feel as if they are related."

The way the king looked at Finn and Meyer suggested they had no choice but to find those answers. That was their duty.

They were supposed to find the truth. They were the lead investigators for Verendal.

"I expect this resolved quickly. You know what must be done." The king looked at Meyer for a long moment.

Meyer gripped the wine glass, holding on to the stem tightly and twisting it in his hand.

The king turned away from them. "Enjoy the wine."

He headed to the door, pressing his hand up against the hidden section of wall. It slid open and he stepped through. The door closed, leaving Finn and Meyer standing in the room by themselves.

"What was that about?" Finn asked. "He called us here to tell us to do our job?"

"No," Meyer said softly. He stared up at the row of swords lining the wall, his gaze skimming along them before he turned to Finn. "He called us here as a reminder to me." Meyer stared at the doorway where the king had disappeared. "And perhaps to admonish me for sending you away during a time like this. Here I had thought it would keep you from interfering with the Archers during the protests." Meyer breathed in deeply.

That was why Meyer had sent him from the city?

Finn thought it was because he was the journeyman, but he also had proven himself to be too stubborn at times. Finn had a hard time letting some things go when he knew he should. "What do you mean?"

"The king," Meyer said. "The meeting was about you. He needs the Hunter." He looked up, holding Finn's gaze. "Find the Black Rose."

CHAPTER SEVENTEEN

Finn and Meyer parted ways outside of the palace, with Meyer heading off to run errands. It left Finn feeling strangely freed. He had become so accustomed to being the one to gather supplies and collect items from apothecaries, or visit general stores for different supplies, that he wasn't quite sure what to do now that Meyer had taken off to do it.

He needed to be the Hunter.

That was what the king wanted of him.

He'd gained the nickname through his dogged determination to find the truth, following instinct as much as the clues laid out before him, but that had been during a unique circumstance. Finn had done that when he had been after Bellut and the magister, looking for a bit of vengeance as much as anything else. It had been about revenge for him.

It couldn't be about that now.

Finn didn't even know if he *wanted* it to be about that now.

He had been the Hunter while looking into Holden and the danger of witchcraft. That had helped him understand a different threat to the kingdom, one that Finn still didn't fully understand now.

This time, he felt as if he were asked to serve in a specific way.

They wanted his stubbornness. In that regard, he was like his father, a man Oscar had nicknamed the Goat. He knew where he needed to go. While Meyer was off gathering supplies, it was time for Finn to start questioning the men they'd saved.

It was time to uncover the truth of the Black Rose.

He wondered how Lena would react. What would she think seeing how her brother had to question men and discovering how skilled he'd become at doing so? What would Lena think of him?

He was headed to the old prison when he glimpsed shadowy movement nearby. Finn ducked into a side alley.

"You're still soft," a voice growled from the other end.

Finn walked over. "And you're still too obvious," he said to Oscar.

Oscar remained in the shadows, though Finn didn't need to see him clearly to know it was him—the slight stoop to his back to conceal his height, the narrow frame, and the dark cloak that hung from his shoulders all revealed it was him, though the cloak cast him in even darker shadows.

"Obvious? I've been following you ever since you left the damn palace."

Finn had been caught up talking to Master Meyer.

He *had* gotten soft.

Then again, there had been no reason for him to keep up his skill. He didn't have to worry quite as often these days, and even if he did, he had others he could call upon for assistance if he was in trouble in the city.

"You told Annie you wanted to talk," Oscar said.

He had, and now he had even more reason to.

A thief like him would be connected to the Verendal underground in ways Finn was not—at least, not any longer. For Finn to understand the Black Rose and what they intended, he needed someone like Oscar.

And others like him, too.

That was something to think on later. Maybe he could start to come up with his own stable of informants. He knew Meyer had a few, though it was difficult to find anyone in the city who was eager to meet with the executioners.

"I figured you'd visit me at Meyer's home," Finn said.

"Where's the fun in that?"

"Why does there have to be fun in anything?" Finn asked.

"If you're not enjoying what you're doing, then why do it?" Oscar asked in return.

"Says the thief." Finn nodded to the street. "Would you mind joining me out of the alley?"

"I'll join you."

"Do you want to sit at the Wenderwolf?"

"No."

Finn started to smile. "Can we go someplace else to talk?"

Oscar took a step toward him and chuckled. "You don't like talking in alleys anymore?"

He looked around. The smell of smoke lingered in the air. He could almost imagine it infused with the blood of the men who'd died. "I would much rather us have a conversation somewhere else, if I'm being honest."

"Honesty from Finn Jagger. Will wonders never cease?"

"I've been honest with you," Finn said.

"Maybe you have," Oscar said, stepping into the faint gray daylight and flashing a smile that tugged on the long scar on his cheek. "But have you been honest with yourself?"

Finn chuckled. "Always the same Oscar."

"You'd be disappointed if I changed too much," Oscar said.

"Where would you have us go, if not to the Wenderwolf?"

"I might have a place," Oscar said.

Oscar turned away and headed down the alley, disappearing into the darkness before Finn had a chance to argue with him. Finn looked toward the street. This wasn't what he needed to be doing, but at this point, he wasn't entirely sure what he needed to be doing. Question the men involved in the attack, but then what?

The king wanted the Hunter. Which meant he had to

use all his contacts to help him be that person. Including Oscar.

Finn ran a hand through his hair, pushing it out of his face, and jogged after Oscar.

There was a time when he'd been comfortable navigating through the alleys. Probably more comfortable than Oscar was. When they'd worked together, Finn had grown not only comfortable, but competent at moving quickly and silently through them, having mapped most of them in his mind so he could get through the streets and avoid any Archers. That had always been the goal when he'd been working with the crews: avoid detection.

He caught up to Oscar at the end of the alley where it opened up on to Silven Street, a wide road that ran parallel to Porman's Path leading through the city. Unlike Porman's Path, Silven took more of a straight shot as it cut through the city.

"I wasn't sure if you were going to come," Oscar said.

"I was the one who suggested we talk. Remember?"

Oscar flashed a bit of a smile. In the overcast light, the scar gave him something of a grotesque grin. "Come along, Finn. Let's see if you can keep up."

Oscar started off, moving at a quick clip.

Finn didn't think he'd have any trouble keeping up with him, but the farther they went through the street, the more he realized that Oscar's movements had a different sort of purpose. He veered around a pair of Archers patrolling, twisting so they couldn't look at his face, then ducked down a narrow side street before returning to Silven. There weren't as many people out as there usually were. Those who ventured out seemed subdued, as if they didn't dare make too much of a commotion given the recent upheaval. Finn kept pace with Oscar, though the taller man's loping gait made it more difficult than he would have expected.

"Not going to be easy pulling jobs," Oscar muttered when they crossed another intersection and another pair of Archers who were out patrolling. One of them bore the stripes of rank on his shoulder, denoting him a palace Archer.

"I don't think you should be telling me about any jobs you're doing."

Oscar looked over to him. "Now I didn't say anything *about* the jobs. Just that it's going to be harder to pull them. You're the one who decided to make it into something it didn't need to be."

Finn just shook his head. The conversation with Annie came back to him. She didn't want Finn to get Oscar involved in what he'd be doing, but that was because she knew Oscar would probably want to help Finn. However, Finn wasn't sure if that was the case. Since he'd become an executioner, Oscar had come to Finn less and less often, though he'd still offered Finn help when it had been needed.

"I'm not trying to make it into anything," Finn said.

Oscar flashed a tight smile. There was a heat in it that made it look forced, but it could be hard to tell with Oscar. Since Oscar had taken on a more prominent role with his crew—becoming the crew leader, Finn suspected though had never proven—he had a hardness to him that he hadn't when he'd been running with other crews.

"It's always something, Finn."

They stopped at a narrow building with two unmarked shops on either side of it. The wooden storefront needed to be painted: where it wasn't peeling away altogether, the red color it once had been was now faded to pink. Iron bars crisscrossed over the windows, making it less likely they'd get broken in any sort of protest, though they were far enough away from any of the major streets that it shouldn't have been too much of a concern.

"What is this place?" Finn asked.

"You don't like it?"

Finn looked along the street. It curved in either direction, making it difficult to see much beyond the bend. Many of the buildings looked to be houses, most as narrow as the building they were in front of, though there were some with shops on the ground level. The wind gusted along the street, carrying the bite of the northern cold, but there was something else within the wind that Finn couldn't quite place. A strange odor. Maybe that came from this section, though they were in the Oldan section, which wasn't known to be one of the poorer parts of the city. There were middle-class merchants here, the kind of people he wouldn't expect Oscar to spend time around, mostly because they wouldn't want to encourage thievery. The people in this section would be hard workers, and many of them would believe they could make it into one of the nicer sections, if only they had the opportunity.

"It's nice enough."

"It's more than that," Oscar said.

He pulled a key out of his pocket, unlocked the door, and they stepped inside.

Finn had expected a tavern. When he'd met with Oscar in the past, they had *always* met at taverns. That was where the shady work of the crews took place. He hadn't expected Oscar to have a key, and certainly didn't expect him to have what amounted to some sort of private club.

The room was darkened, but it didn't take long for Finn's eyes to adjust.

Everything about the room spoke of comfort. A thick, plush green carpet covered the floor. Leather chairs were arranged throughout the interior, and a darkened hearth filled the space along the far wall. Tables were placed between the chairs, many of which were angled to form an arrangement so people could sit together, though some were situated apart to give somebody a chance to sit by themselves, in isolation, or perhaps just to relax. A stack of dice on a table in between three chairs caught Finn's attention, as did a pile of playing cards.

"This is a business venture I'm getting into."

"It looks like…" He had a hard time coming up with *what* it looked like. "Some sort of club?"

Oscar shrugged, motioning for Finn to sit with him in the center of the room. He grabbed a lantern off of one of the tables, quickly lighting it so it cast a warm glow over the entirety of the room.

"Are you trying to push Annie out of business?"

"Do you really think a place like this could compete with the Wenderwolf?"

Finn shrugged as he took a seat. The chair was comfortable, almost swallowing him. He settled back, crossing one leg, and looked over to Oscar. "Maybe not compete, but there's something about this place…"

Oscar grunted. "There's something about it, all right."

"What's that supposed to mean?"

"I wanted a place for men to gather."

"A men's club?"

"Something like that," Oscar said.

"You wanted a place for your crew to get together."

Oscar shook his head, glancing toward the door. "Not in this section of the city. They wouldn't tolerate those kinds of people here for very long."

"They would if they didn't know."

"That's not the kind of clientele I intend to attract here."

Finn leaned forward. The lantern light reflected off of Oscar's face, making the scar far more pronounced than it had been before. "You want to become an honest businessman."

"And if I do?"

Finn smiled, but a part of him hesitated. He'd come to Oscar looking for his connections to the underground. If he'd decided to go honest, should Finn pull him back?

"I never expected Oscar Richter, the Hand, would want to become honorable."

"We can't stay the way we have been," Oscar said softly, leaning back and closing his eyes for a moment. "After I was jumped, I decided maybe it was time for me to get out of that kind of work."

"That's why Annie didn't want me to pull you back in."

"Annie wants me to be safe. She figures she knows what I'd been up to before, and she doesn't want me to get involved in it again."

Finn knew the answer to his own question without even thinking. He couldn't demand anything of Oscar. "You *shouldn't* get involved in it again."

"Not you, too," Oscar said, winking at him. "Besides, this way, I can still use my connections, but I can look a little bit more honorable."

Finn frowned at him. "You aren't giving up your position on the crew?"

"Oh, I'm not going to be leading crews anymore, but once you have a foot in that world, you never really leave it, do you?"

Oscar watched him, a lingering question in his eyes that suggested something beyond what he had actually asked.

"So you're saying I never left my crew?"

"Only if you feel that way."

There was a time when such a comment would have bothered Finn, but not any longer. Now he had a different crew, though perhaps it was no less dishonorable.

"You want to tell me what you talked to the king about?" Oscar asked.

Finn looked around the inside of the room. He could imagine the place bustling with activity—people sitting around, gaming, drinking, even the din of conversation.

"It doesn't matter."

Oscar looked over to him. "You wanted to see me. I figure it has something to do with whatever the king wanted you for. Now, if you don't want to tell me, that's your prerogative, but I'm not going to be able to help you unless I know what sort of trouble you've gotten yourself into, Finn."

"What makes you think I've gotten myself into any sort of trouble?"

"I don't know. The fact that you came to me suggests there is *some* sort of trouble."

His friend was showing him that he wanted out. That was clear based on where Oscar had taken him to talk. And if that was what Oscar wanted, then who was Finn to force him to stay inside of the world he'd wanted to leave? All Finn had to do was ask and Oscar would help—but he didn't think he could ask.

There might be something Oscar could help with that wouldn't pull him in a way Finn didn't want to. Finn reached into his pocket and pulled out Reginald's journal, setting it on the table between him and Oscar. Oscar frowned at him.

"I'm not going to ask you to do anything dangerous here," Finn said with a smile. "I just want to know if you could make any sense of this."

Oscar pulled the journal over and flipped through it. "This? Why?"

"Just a feeling I have."

Oscar snorted. "A feeling? I didn't realize that executioners worked on hunches."

Finn suppressed the flush that came to him. "Meyer would prefer I didn't, but I can't help it. I feel like there is something to this that I haven't been able to uncover yet."

"Care to tell me what it is?"

"Probably nothing," Finn answered honestly. "I found it in the home of a man who had seemingly killed himself."

"Seemingly?"

Finn shrugged again. "That's just it. It doesn't really make sense that he would've killed himself. But I have seen stranger things, I suppose."

Oscar shrugged. "Can't say that I recognize anything. It looks like a financial ledger."

"That's what I figured, as well," Finn said, taking it back. "He owed money."

"There's your reason," Oscar said. When Finn looked over to him, Oscar shrugged. "The reason he killed himself."

"I don't know. It's probably nothing, but—"

"But it doesn't feel right to you," Oscar stated.

Finn shook his head.

"I can tell you what I would do."

Finn stuffed the journal back into his pocket. "What is that?"

"Nothing. Now ask me what I think you would do."

"What would I do?"

"Seems to me you have a problem letting things drop."

"From time to time," Finn said. It was fitting, given he'd just come from speaking with the king because of a similar issue. "But it's more of a bad habit than anything else. The kind of thing I've been cautioned to avoid."

Until now.

"Then look into it in your spare time. If it's bothering you, don't let it go. Trust yourself, Finn. It's gotten you this far."

Finn smiled. "Look at you, still trying to give me advice."

"Did you think I would ever stop?" Oscar grinned at him for a moment, then shook his head. "There was a time when I thought I had to be the one responsible for you. Can we really have gone so far that things have changed that much?" Oscar leaned forward. "You know I'm always willing to help you, Finn."

"I know," he said.

And he did. Which made it that much harder when Oscar obviously wanted something different for himself than the path he'd been on.

"You know, your father and I used to talk about having a place like this." He looked around, and his eyes took on a distant expression. "It was only in passing. Your father never thought we could actually make it happen." He smiled slightly. "There was a time when he and I would talk about what we might be able to do. Thought about what we might *be* if we were able to get some respectability."

"I didn't know you had conversations like that." Then again, it didn't surprise Finn that his father would have wanted to be something more than what he had been. Pretty much everybody living in the Brinder section wanted something more for themselves. It wasn't only

Finn and Oscar, but his sister. And Helda. So many others in that section.

"Not often," Oscar said, sweeping his gaze around the inside of the club. He started to smile, the first real emotion Finn had seen on his face. "But often enough that he and I thought we might be able to start a place like this. Maybe not quite like *this*," Oscar said, chuckling. "Your father liked a bit more of a traditional tavern. He would've loved the Wenderwolf."

"He would've loved Annie," Finn said.

"What are you getting at?" Oscar asked, though there was no real heat to his question.

"I guess I was just saying that he would've approved of you and her."

"Of that I have no doubt," Oscar said. He chuckled again, shaking his head. "I remember when he and your mother first met. We'd gone way back, you know."

Finn nodded. He had heard some of the stories about his father and Oscar before, but they always intrigued him. Partly because Oscar was so reserved, and partly because Finn had lost his father so long ago that he didn't have the opportunity to ask him.

"I remember. You were friends from childhood."

"Not always friends. He was bigger and stronger, though eventually, I got taller, faster, and sneakier."

"I didn't know he was bigger and stronger than you."

"Only when we were kids. That changes pretty quickly, and growing up where we did, we were forced to mature." Oscar glanced over to Finn. "Not that I need to tell you that. You went through it. Gods, had you grown up in this section, you would've had a different experience, wouldn't you have? Probably get an apprenticeship, something formal where you were given the opportunity to learn under some master instructor, and from there…" Oscar shook his head. "It's never easy in the kingdom."

"It never is," Finn agreed.

"He would have approved of you," Oscar said.

Finn nodded slowly. "You've said that before."

"It bears repeating. He would've approved of you. What you did for your mother. Your sister, especially. I worried about Lena, and thought the only way that you and I would be able to provide for her with him gone would be through running with crews. I never would've imagined she would have the abilities that she has."

"She doesn't quite know where she fits," Finn said.

It was more than her healing ability.

She had that, and because of it, she wouldn't need other work, but Lena wanted more. Family.

There were times when Finn felt like he'd helped his sister, and there were times when he worried that he'd held her back.

"I think the same could be said for you." Oscar regarded him, a bit of concern etched in his eyes. "At least, maybe it could have been said for you before. Lately, you look like you have grown more comfortable with your standing."

"What's that supposed to mean? Wait… how long have you been following me?"

"I told your father I'd keep tabs on you."

"I'm a grown man, Oscar."

"Just because you're grown doesn't mean I don't care."

With that comment, Finn realized he had not been as good of a friend as he needed to be to Oscar. This was somebody who had protected him and looked out for him in the way he knew how, first by offering him a place on the crew, then by trying to keep him from getting back into it. This was somebody who had come to see off Finn's mother when she died, had come into the Church of Heleth to mourn in a way that felt right in the way the Church of Fell felt wrong. Oscar had even admitted to sneaking into visit with her before she was gone. Oscar cared. He didn't have any family of his own, and though Finn had always viewed Oscar as family in some way, he had never made that clear to him.

That was a mistake he needed to rectify.

"Just because I'm a grown man doesn't mean I don't care, either," Finn said.

Oscar nodded slowly. "I know."

He looked around the inside of his lounge, the club taking on a different meaning for Finn. Oscar had done this for a reason. He wanted to leave the crew for a reason.

Was it more than just wanting to stop fearing that somebody might jump him again?

That had been an outlier. The attack had been unusual, even for Verendal. Something like that was not bound to happen again, so for Oscar to set up this sort of establishment, to present it in a way that would give him a chance to get out of his life of crime, meant that he was doing it for some other reason.

What if he was doing it for Finn?

"You don't have to do this for me," Finn said softly.

"Who ever said I was doing it for you?"

"I was just saying—"

"I know what you are saying. I'm not worried about making a mistake that's going to put me at the wrong end of your sword."

"You'd get the rope," Finn said.

Oscar glared at him.

"I don't say that to upset you, but you wouldn't get the sword. At least, not in Verendal. Maybe if I caught up to you outside of the city, I could offer you mercy."

"Am I supposed to be thankful for the offer?"

"You don't want to put me in a position where I have to choose whether to bring you in. I get that. And gods, Oscar, I appreciate it more than you can know."

"What makes you think that's why I'm doing any of this?"

Finn snorted. "I talk to men like you every day."

"There are no men like me," Oscar said softly.

Finn chuckled. "Maybe you're right. There are no men like you, but I still talk to men who intend to deceive me every day, and I recognize when someone is trying to get one past me."

"I see."

Finn looked around the inside of the tavern again, noting the paneled walls, the comfortable chairs, even the door leading to the back where he suspected there would be a kitchen, likely with ale-filled casks. Probably Annie's ale. "When do you intend to open?"

"Soon enough," Oscar said.

"Will you let me know?"

"I don't know if my establishment would do well with your kind coming to visit."

"Am I too honorable?"

Oscar shook his head slightly. "In the Wenderwolf, it's not quite as strange for an executioner to sit and have a mug of ale. There are plenty of other undesirables who come into the tavern, and visit Annie, that it doesn't draw any sort of extra attention. Out here…"

"You don't want me to defile your new business."

"It's nothing like that, Finn."

"I understand," Finn said, starting to get up.

"That's it?" Oscar asked.

"I do have my assignment from the king."

"Which you've never told me the details of."

He'd gone to Oscar and Oscar wanted to help. More than that, the king needed the Hunter. Finn had to use all his resources.

"The Black Rose," he said. When Oscar didn't say anything, Finn held his friend's gaze another moment. "I need to find whoever is responsible—and if it's one person or many."

"I'm sure the Hunter will find that out."

Finn just chuckled, though there was a flicker in Oscar's eyes that suggested he knew more. "You know, when I first heard that nickname, I didn't know how to feel about it."

"I thought you'd like it better than Shuffles."

"It's better than Shuffles, but I don't know if I even want a nickname."

"Your predecessor had one."

"And I don't know how he acquired his."

"I do," Oscar said and shook his head. "There were stories about him. They came with him when he first arrived in the city. You know he isn't from here, don't you?"

"I've heard." Meyer had told him a bit about his own past, and had given Finn some insight about the journeyman who'd worked with Meyer before Finn had come to serve as his apprentice. He'd been assigned by the executioner court, tasked with serving Meyer, assisting him in his responsibilities throughout the city, since Meyer had been unwilling to take an apprentice.

What would've happened had the Lion not been killed?

Finn hadn't asked Meyer that question, though he suspected Meyer wouldn't have been able to pull him in as his apprentice. It was only because the King and Wolf—as far as Finn had come to know—had killed the Lion that Finn had been given the opportunity that he had. Everything connected, lining up almost as if it had been ordained in some way. It was the reason Finn had suspected hegen involvement all along, even if he didn't think that anymore.

"Well, when he first came, word got out about those who were questioned by him."

"I was questioned by him," Finn said.

"I know," Oscar said. "He took joy in it. Almost as if he

liked to hurt others. He liked to torment. Can't say that I understand wanting to do something like that, and if he weren't in his position, he'd be picked up by the Archers and placed in the very same location he worked."

Finn grunted. He couldn't deny that.

One of the things Meyer had instructed Finn about was to not take any satisfaction in questioning. Of course, Finn hadn't needed to be instructed on that. Questioning was just a part of the job, and one of the worst parts. What made it easier was knowing he could find information to help others within the city. It was the same reason he valued the healing knowledge he'd gained. Having that knowledge, learning ways he could help others, made everything bearable.

"More than a few bastards were left barely able to make the walk to the gallows."

"I didn't know that," Finn said.

"There were also rumors your mentor didn't much care for the Lion."

Finn shrugged. He'd heard enough from Meyer early on to know how he felt, but those rumors didn't need to get out. "Even if he didn't, I doubt Meyer would say that."

"Probably not. If I've heard any story that I believe about the old executioner, it's that he is nothing if not dedicated to his job, but he's not dedicated to the act of killing."

"That's true," Finn said.

"I figured if it weren't, you wouldn't have stayed. Regardless of what you might think, Finn, you got a good heart. You always wanted to do the right thing. Not only when it came to taking care of your mother and your sister, but…" He shrugged. "You always wanted to take care of those around you. It made it easy for me to bring you along in the crew, but it also made it hard, if that makes sense."

"Not really."

"Because I knew what I was asking you to do was wrong. Even if it did put more coin in my pocket." Oscar grinned. "I justified it by thinking we were taking from those who had more than they needed, and we deserved more than the little we had."

"Meyer would say even those who have more than you can still suffer."

"I'm sure he would, but you got to justify what you do."

"He also said that stealing from somebody with less hurts them more than stealing from somebody with more."

"See? Maybe I can agree with the old executioner on a few things."

"I don't know how much the two of you would get along."

"We both want you to do well," Oscar said. "So in that, I suspect we would get along just fine."

Finn took a deep breath. It was time for him to get going. He really did have more he needed to do, and visiting with Oscar wasn't getting it done.

"Maybe I can stop by after hours sometime once you open. That way you don't have to worry about having an executioner here."

"Maybe," Oscar said.

Finn got up and headed to the door.

"Listen. If I do hear anything about the Black Rose, I'll send word. Can't guarantee anything."

Finn wasn't sure how he felt about that.

"You don't need to do anything, Oscar."

"Who said I was going to do anything? I just said that if I heard something, I'd send word, not that I was going to do anything about it." He looked down at his hands and leaned back in his chair, a tight expression on his face.

Finn pulled the door open, a gust of wind coming with it.

"I've been looking into your father," Oscar said.

Finn froze. "You've been doing what?"

Oscar nodded. "I don't know what happened, but after you told me that the only reason he'd be brought out of the city and imprisoned was treason, I thought I could check with some of my sources."

All that time, and Oscar hadn't even known?

Finn had wondered if Oscar had been a part of it.

"You don't need to do that," Finn said.

"I do," Oscar said, looking up. "Because that's not the man I knew."

"No?"

Oscar shook his head. "Your father never got involved in anything treasonous. All he wanted was to help your Ma. That was the only reason he wanted to take any jobs. He wanted to provide for her, and if that meant stealing a bit from those who had more than their share, then so be it. Besides, most of the time, he spent that coin and put it right back into their pocket."

"I know," Finn said softly.

It was even harder knowing his sister's healing skills would now be able to help their mother, if only they would've had the time.

"I haven't found anything though," Oscar said, looking back down at his hands. "I can let you know if I do."

There was a hint of an accusation in it, something that suggested Oscar was disappointed in Finn. Maybe it stemmed from the fact that Finn hadn't found anything out about his father. He hadn't looked, at least not recently. After learning his father had been brought out of the city, there hadn't been anything he could have done anyway. He didn't have connections in other cities or other prisons, and even Master Meyer hadn't known where Finn's father had ended up. There wasn't any way for him to figure that out short of the king telling him.

"Thanks," Finn said.

"And if *you* hear anything…"

Finn just nodded. "I'll let you know."

Oscar looked up at him, holding his gaze for a moment before looking down at his hands again.

Finn sighed, then stepped into the street, pulling his cloak tightly around him as the bitter wind threatened to blow him over.

CHAPTER EIGHTEEN

The inside of the old prison had a foul stench to it—a mixture of the wounds that had festered, despite Lena's and Wella's ministrations, and the medicine that had been used. Wella had taught Finn how to identify most medicines by scent, and even now, as he breathed in their aroma, he could pick up on so many of them without any difficulty. He could piece together the different oils, along with the dried leaves, and even a hint of flower, perhaps a rose.

Finn stood at the edge of the makeshift hospital, surveying the medicines arranged neatly on a table before looking at his sister in the distance. She was working her way from bed to bed, checking on each of her charges.

There was no sign of Wella, but as Finn turned his attention back to the table, he saw her jars of medicines, powders, and creams all lined up, most of them labeled so Lena wouldn't have any question as to what Wella had mixed. He noted that there were many antiseptics, designed to stave off infection, as well as a few pain relievers. Some were less obvious to him, and he held up one jar with dark powder in it, shaking it slightly.

"That is borgan leaf and vilth," Lena said, standing a few steps behind him.

Lena pulled out a small ledger, flipping through notes that she had made. Finn smiled to himself. She used the same organization as Master Meyer. She probably even had a series of notations on supplies that had been used so that they knew what needed to be restocked. He wouldn't be overly surprised to learn that she kept notes on how much everything cost, as well.

"We use it to get the men to come around if we've over-sedated them."

Finn snorted. "You've thought of everything."

"You wanted me to help."

Finn ushered her to the side of the room. "Which of the men has recovered the most?"

Lena's eyes narrowed for a moment. "Why?"

Finn looked at the row of beds. "Which one, Lena?"

"So you can hurt him again?"

He had dreaded this part of his profession. He knew how his sister felt, and it wasn't even misguided. She had done all she could to help these men recover, and now he was going to come in here, question one or more of them, and likely cause more injury.

It was a part of the job he'd preferred keeping from her.

She could come to the gallows festival, and there was

no way he could hide that aspect of his responsibility, but what he did there was quick—often brutal, but still quick. It didn't take long to hang a man, and even less time for him to use the sword.

"Whom can I question?" he asked Lena.

She flicked her gaze over to the table, sweeping it across the various medicines, before looking over to Finn. "You could—"

"Who is the least sedated?"

"Why?"

"If you don't want me to need to question them to the fullest extent, then I need to know who's been sedated the least. Anyone who has enough of that medicine in them is not going to tolerate my questioning as well as others."

He might as well be honest with his sister. At this point, he didn't want to have to acknowledge what he was doing, but he also figured she deserved the truth.

"Usually I can scare men into talking," he added, though he doubted he would convince her. Lena often saw through him.

"I see."

"I just need to get answers, Lena. The king asked that of Meyer and me."

She stiffened, looking at him with a new light in her eyes. "You spoke to the king?"

Finn nodded. "We went to the palace yesterday."

"I didn't know."

"Over one hundred people died during the last protest," he said. "We can't have the same thing happen again. We need to do everything in our power to *prevent* that from occurring. If that involves questioning one man, somebody who attempted to attack the Archers…"

Lena licked her lips, then swallowed.

He had to be careful here. He didn't want to bring her too deep into this aspect of his job.

"There's one man. He had a wound on his side. He's been recovering quite well," she offered.

"Have any of them said anything about their role in the attack?"

"None of them talked, Finn."

"None?"

"Well… some of them have muttered about what happened to them, and others have been in enough pain that they basically cry out until we sedate them, and still others just moan, whether sedated or not."

Finn frowned, looking over at the men gathered in the hospital beds. "What I need is somebody who might have had some influence on what happened." He wasn't sure how to find that person, but there would have to be something, wouldn't there?

"Like I was saying," Lena went on. "There's one man."

"You said he was the least injured."

"If you would have let me finish, I would've told you he's been trying to silence the others." Lena lowered her voice, stepping closer to Finn. "He scares me a little bit, Finn. I've had to keep him sedated just so I can make sure he doesn't do anything to me, but…"

Finn hadn't even considered that, but he should have. With as many men as there were here, and all of them recovering, attacking Lena might be the only way they could escape. They were chained to the bed, but desperation still made men dangerous.

"I think I'm going to have to talk with Master Meyer about having some Archers stand guard to keep an eye on things," Finn said.

"That's not going to be necessary," Lena said, waving her hand. "I told you I can sedate them, and it keeps them from trying anything. Between that and the chains he has on them..."

"But how long will that last?" Finn asked.

"Long enough."

"These men aren't all going to recover at the same time," Finn said. Besides, that wasn't even the point. The point of having them here was to get them to recover enough so Finn could ask the questions needed in order to learn who was responsible for the protests. "Maybe it's time we move them to a more traditional hospital."

"I thought they were here because they're a threat to a more traditional hospital?"

"They might be, but if we separated them, at least they wouldn't be all together and possibly putting you or Wella in danger."

"I'm fine, Finn. Really, I am."

Finn let out a long sigh and glanced back at the table. "Show me this man."

She brought him over to a cot near the corner of the room, farthest from the door. Was that intentional?

Now that he considered it, he realized that he and Master Meyer hadn't thought everything through here nearly as well as they probably should have. By having all of the men gathered here, they created an opportunity for them to recover and attack.

That was a mistake.

"I can see the look in your eye," Lena said.

"What look is that?"

"One that tells me your mind is working."

Finn chuckled. He stepped forward and found the man lying with a thin white sheet covering him, his hands clasped over his chest, his breathing slow, but not completely regular.

"You can open your eyes," Finn said.

The man didn't move.

"He's sleeping," Lena said.

"He only wants us to think he's sleeping."

Finn pulled back the sheet. The man had his cuffed hands over his chest, and his elbow was pressing up against the side that was bandaged. The dressings circled the entirety of his abdomen, though they were dry, not bloody like some of the wounds Finn had seen.

He was fairly muscular, with milky-white skin and a tattoo across his upper abdomen. The marking was unfamiliar to Finn, looking like a series of interconnected lines.

"My name is Finn Jagger. I am the executioner to King Porman. I'm here to question you."

The man twitched.

Finn didn't move.

"If you'd prefer, I could bring you someplace that would make it easier to question you."

"I'll answer your damn questions," the man said, his voice a low drawl. He didn't open his eyes as he answered.

"Good." Finn made his way around the bed, positioning himself closest to the man's injury. He glanced up at Lena for a moment, nodding to her. He didn't want her to linger here while he did this.

She watched him, shaking her head, but then Finn urged her forward, holding his gaze on her. Finally, Lena turned away. She headed to one of the nearby beds, not so far away that she couldn't overhear what Finn was asking.

"What's your name?"

"It don't matter. If you're here to take me for sentencing, then go ahead."

"I'm here to ask you questions, not to take you anywhere for sentencing."

The man cocked one eye open, looking up at him. He had a trace of red around his iris, and in the dim, white lantern light glowing throughout the room, his skin looked almost colorless. "You're the executioner, aren't you?"

"One of them."

Finn had put himself between him and the wall, which might've been a mistake, but keeping himself where he was gave him a different advantage.

"What's your name?" Finn asked again.

The man closed his eyes, looking away. "It don't matter."

"If you don't want to tell me your name, then I have to assume you were instrumental in the attack. You should know the king has instructed the master executioner and me to find all of those who coordinated the attack on the city and bring them to justice."

"Justice," the man snorted, shaking his head. "There ain't no justice going to be had here, and certainly not for my kind."

"And what kind is that?"

"Nothing but a poor bastard," he said.

The choice of words might be coincidence, but Finn didn't think so. "If you don't tell me what you know, then I can guarantee you *will* be a Poor Bastard," Finn said, lowering his voice so his sister couldn't hear. She moved on to a cot that was a bit farther away, but she still tilted her head off to the side.

"What do you want to know?" the man asked.

"I want to know what happened. I want to know who coordinated the protest."

"So you can silence us?"

"So others don't get hurt," Finn said.

"Others get hurt every day. What's it matter if a few more fall, as long as this injustice stops?"

"What injustice do you see?"

The man shook his head. He hadn't moved his hands from where he had them clasped over his chest. "You can't understand what it's like to live where we live. To see what we see. To be taken and taken and taken from, but never given anything. You could never understand."

"You'd be surprised," Finn said.

"Really?" The man opened both eyes finally. "Maybe we should see."

He lunged.

Finn hadn't expected him to move so quickly. With an injury like he'd sustained, he wouldn't have expected him to be able to move at all. He unclasped his hands, and Finn realized that he had a slender piece of metal in between them.

He darted at Finn, and Finn twisted, barely avoiding the slice. He chopped at the man's arm with his own, trying to keep him from stabbing him.

The chains on his wrists caught him, but Finn had gotten too close.

The man brought his knee around, connecting it with Finn's midsection.

Finn grunted, but managed to stay upright. He grabbed for the man's wrist and twisted as hard as he could.

The only advantage he had was the fact that this man had been injured.

Finn continued to twist, pushing the hand away.

"Finn!"

Finn ignored his sister's call, focusing only on the man, who was now leaning on the bed, using it to push off of Finn.

"Drop it," Finn said, "or this is going to go much worse for you than necessary."

"This has already gone much worse than I wanted it to go," the man said. "My whole life has gone much worse than I wanted it to go. That's why we protest. Your kind don't understand."

"My kind *is* your kind."

"My kind is nothing like your kind," the man said. "You

have money. You couldn't understand what it's like to…"

The man looked over his shoulder, sagging to his knees.

Lena stood behind him, a syringe in hand, pushing it down and injecting the man with some sort of sedative.

She took a deep breath, letting it out slowly as she stared at Finn. "I didn't know," she said. "I didn't expect him to attack."

"You couldn't have known," Finn said.

Lena looked down at him. The man had crumpled to the floor, and the slender piece of metal was still clutched in his hand.

Finn stepped on his hand, reaching down and prying the metal free. He held it up, staring at it for a moment. It was roughly cut, and looked like an incomplete knife. If he hadn't known better, he would've thought it was one of the witchcraft wands, but the shape of it wasn't quite right.

"What is that?" Lena asked.

"Something he must've carried with him," Finn said.

"Can I see it?"

Finn slipped it into his pocket. "It doesn't matter."

"It's my fault," she said. "I didn't know he had it, and if I had—"

"I know you would have taken it from him," Finn said. "I'm not blaming you."

He scooped the man off the ground. He was heavy, and Finn grunted as he dropped him back onto the cot before pulling back the bandages to check just how wounded he'd been. He saw a slight wound that had already been stitched up by Lena.

"I need to get him out of here," Finn said.

"Where are you going to take him?"

"This is a prison, isn't it?" Or, it had been. Even though it wasn't used as a prison anymore, that didn't mean it *couldn't* still be used that way. Finn wasn't going to be able to carry the man all the way to the prison cell, but he could make sure he wasn't going to attack his sister too.

Finn wrapped the chains around the cot so the man's wrists were held down. He could move his hands, but that was it.

"What are you doing?"

"I'm going to make sure he doesn't hurt you when he comes around."

"I can keep him sedated, Finn."

"I know you can. But I want to make sure he doesn't have any way of hurting you when he does come around. In the meantime, I'm going to make arrangements for him to go to Declan."

It would be better anyway. Lena didn't need to see how Finn questioned those under investigation.

If he could protect her from anything, it would be that.

But he had to be the Hunter.

This was a lead he would follow.

CHAPTER NINETEEN

As Finn made his way along the street, a sign caught his attention.

Erichan Luthier.

He had seen that shop owner's name somewhere before. It took a moment to realize where: Reginald's journal.

He needed to finish his tasks, but seeing as how he still didn't have any idea what had happened with Reginald, or why he had killed himself, curiosity got the best of him.

He headed inside the shop and paused.

It wasn't a very large shop—probably only a dozen paces wide by twice that deep. The ceiling was low and the light was dingy, with little more than a few lanterns inside in addition to the dirty streetlight coming in through the window. Lutes lined the wall along with packaged strings, feather quills, and stacks of paper, which Finn suspected was for music. A man sat at the back of the shop on a stool, strumming a lute.

"That sounds lovely," Finn said when the man had stopped playing. His fingers were nimble, his strumming quick, and he would've fit into any tavern Finn had ever been to.

"Do you play?" he asked Finn.

"I don't." He fished into his pocket and pulled out the carving he had found in Reginald's home. "My name is Finn Jagger. I'm investigating Reginald Smith. This shop was listed on one of his ledgers. Did he owe you money?"

The shop owner rested his lute against the wall and got to his feet. He frowned for a moment, sweeping his gaze around the inside of the shop before turning his attention back to Finn. "Repair work," he said. "I never got paid for it. That happens from time to time."

He seemed more dismissive than Finn would have expected. "How much did he owe you?"

"I'd have to look in my books. A few silver, most likely. It is expensive to do the work." He hesitated. "Not uncommon for a man like that. Is there anything else?"

Finn looked around the shop, appraising it with a renewed interest. Something suggested to him there was more here. The shop was nice enough from the outside, but inside there were signs of disrepair. Hooks that had fallen. Shelves that were bare. Dust that hung over everything. A luthier should keep a neater shop. Perhaps he wasn't doing as well as he made it sound like, but if so, why downplay the few silvers Reginald owed him?

There was more here. Finn was certain of it. The problem was that he didn't have the time to dig into it.

This was the kind of time-wasting that he had to stop doing. Lena needed his help, and he'd been intending to go straight to the hegen.

"Thank you for your time. I just saw your shop and wanted to see how much he owed you."

The luthier nodded, took a seat at the stool, picked up his lute, and resumed strumming.

Finn listened for a moment before tearing himself away and making his way toward the Teller Gate, glancing over to the stables. He had spent quite a bit of time in this part of the city lately, more than he would've expected, but mostly because he had been coming here to use the stables for his journeys around the city. Since the protests had begun, Finn had not had the same opportunity to explore outside of the city as he had before, something that disappointed him.

He still didn't know what was going on with the Alain-sith structure, nor did he know why Esmerelda was so bothered by it, but he recognized her concern. She didn't have to say what bothered her for him to know something did.

"Mr. Jagger?"

He turned carefully, though was pleasantly surprised by the person he saw. "Jamie."

"I saw you in the street, and I followed you…"

As soon as she said it, he suspected why she was there. "I'm sorry. I haven't found anything more for your father."

She shook her head. "My father doesn't expect much,"

she said. "He never anticipated that he'd get the money back." She stepped close to him. She smelled vaguely of lilac. "I understand that Reginald killed himself."

"How did you hear that?"

"People talk," she said. "And quite a few people knew that my father did work for Reginald."

Finn nodded. "I'm sorry. I'm working with the crown to ensure those owed money by Reginald will be paid, but I don't know the timing of it."

"I'm sure the crown has other things to be worried about," Jamie said. She flicked her gaze around her before turning her attention back to him. "Have you been involved in what's happening within the city?"

"It's part of the job, unfortunately. I serve as one of the king's inquisitors. That means I have to look into various crimes."

"I've heard stories." She shivered, wrapping her arms around herself. "So I can't imagine what that must be like for you."

"Most of what you've heard are probably *just* stories," he said.

He thought about the circumstances of their first meeting and found himself wishing he had met Jamie under different terms, not while serving in his formal capacity.

"Well, Mr. Jagger—"

"Finn is fine," he said.

She smiled at him, a lovely expression. "I really need to be going. I have an errand to run for my father."

"I understand. I should go as well."

"I would be interested in talking more later," she said.

He smiled. "I would like that. When works for you?"

"Most evenings," she said. "Why don't we meet at the Giver's bell? The night after tomorrow?"

Finn nodded. "I would like that."

She headed into the city, and Finn moved through the heavily armed gate.

There were more Archers here now than there were before.

But the gate was open.

What message did the king want to send?

Finn should've asked him when he had the chance. Instead, he was left with questions. He passed through, glancing at the Archers for recognition and finding none, before making his way toward the hegen.

The hegen section of the city had a comfortable quality to it that Finn had come to appreciate the longer he'd served as executioner in Verendal. There was something about it that left him feeling welcomed in a way he didn't always feel within the city itself, where he felt tolerated, but not always welcomed. Oscar's comment about him coming to his club was all the reminder Finn needed.

Finn headed through the narrow streets, much more comfortable here now than he had been when he'd first started coming to the hegen section. There weren't many who weren't hegen who traveled through here, though Finn would occasionally encounter people seeking the hegen for their magic. Most of the time when he did, they made a point of looking away from him, as if him catching them with the hegen would somehow implicate them in some greater crime.

A younger woman ahead of him didn't appear to belong here, but she seemed to be traveling in the same direction as Finn. Her long black hair hung past her shoulders, and her yellow dress looked as if it could be hegen made, but the way her head turned from side to side, and the way her gaze darted all around, told Finn she wasn't comfortable.

He turned another corner, figuring he'd lose her, when he saw her stop.

She turned, facing him. Deep brown eyes looked at him. "Are you following me?"

There was a measure of steel in the question, which brought a smile to Finn's face. "I wasn't following you. I think we're going the same direction."

"You're not hegen," she said, tilting her head and regarding him.

"I'm not."

For a moment, Finn had started to question if *she* was hegen, but the way she phrased the statement suggested otherwise. The hegen didn't refer to themselves in that way. They were always "the people."

"What are you doing here?" the woman asked.

"I suppose the same as you."

She frowned. "What do you know about it?"

Finn shrugged, looking past her. A familiar face poked out of a few of the hegen in the distance and grinned at him. He hadn't seen Kezia in a while, and suspected she'd be amused by this woman verbally attacking Finn for having come here.

"I've got some experience with the hegen."

Her eyes widened. "You do?" She turned, looking behind her, as if she was suddenly concerned by what she might find. "What have you asked from them?"

"Most recently?" Finn chuckled. "I've asked them for help finding someone."

"Do they do that?"

"If you ask the right way," Finn said.

He remembered what it was like to be someone like this woman, how he had felt when he had first come to the hegen for help. He'd been nervous, much like her.

And he could easily imagine his sister and how she had been when she had come to the hegen for help.

Finn didn't think Lena had gone to Esmerelda, but there were other hegen who had the ability to help. Others who were willing to trade cards for favors, magic for requests that would be honored later.

"I was hoping they could help me find something," she said softly.

"All you have to do is ask," Finn said.

The woman straightened, gripping the fabric of her dress, and looked along the street. "I never thought I would come out here to them," she whispered.

Finn frowned. He recognized the derision in her voice.

Would the hegen she went to recognize it as well? Even if they did, what would they do or say? It had been Finn's experience that the hegen wouldn't take offense, or if they did, they'd never let someone know about it.

Finn suspected this wouldn't be the first time some-body came to the hegen feeling as if they were somehow above doing so. But most people who came had felt a measure of desperation.

Finn had seen what desperation could do and under-stood how it motivated. In fact, it was a bit of desperation that brought him out here now.

"Sometimes they ask for more than you feel comfort-able providing in exchange for their assistance," Finn said, looking around. "But you don't have to accept unless you want to."

"I didn't think they told you what they wanted until after they provided the service."

"That's true enough," Finn said.

"Then how do you refuse?"

"You choose not to come to them for help," Finn said. He took a step toward the woman, and she stiffened slightly.

"I thought you said you weren't one of them?"

"I'm not."

"You sound like you know an awful lot about them. Nobody knows much about the hegen."

"It depends on your experience with them," Finn said. He looked along the street.

Kezia had stopped and watched him. Her lips quirked in a playful smile, and she ignored the boy she was talking to. She and her brother Danior had welcomed Finn when he had first met them, and he never felt as if they were bothered by the fact that he was an executioner. He felt much different with them than he had in so many other parts of the city.

"I wouldn't have come if I didn't have a need," she said.

"That's how I felt the first time I came to them," Finn said.

"How many times have you come here?"

"More than I can count," Finn said.

The woman's eyes widened. "So many times? How deeply are you indebted to them?"

"As deeply as I need to be," Finn said.

Her eyes widened again, and she looked past him, her gaze darting along the street in either direction. She began to fidget even more than she had been.

"You know you don't have to come here if you don't want to. You can turn back," Finn said.

"It's just… I just wish there was another way."

"Sometimes the only way is through the hegen magic," Finn said.

"You've seen it," the woman whispered.

"I wouldn't keep coming back if I hadn't," Finn said.

"Is it as terrifying as they say?"

"More," Finn said, smiling slightly.

The woman licked her lips, swallowed, then nodded to herself. She hurried off along the street, and Finn didn't follow. At this point, he figured he had scared her enough, and whatever she was after was her own personal issue, nothing that he needed to get involved in. She didn't need for him to chase her and make her feel as if she had to fear coming here.

"You might have cost us a bargain," a voice said from behind him.

Finn turned to see Esmerelda. She looked lovely in her bright red dress in the early morning sunlight, her raven-black hair pulled back, sweeping along one shoulder. She had a band of silver around her neck, a different trinket than he had seen before.

"I doubt it. She's continued onward. Whatever she's after is something she thinks only the hegen can provide."

"Yes, I see that. Someone like that has an agenda," Esmerelda said.

"Everybody who comes here has their own personal agenda," Finn said. "I had one too when I first came out here."

"You came on behalf of someone else."

"Does that matter?"

Esmerelda smiled, but ignored the question as she looked along the street. "Why did you come this time, Finn? Not the Alainsith structures."

"Have there been more?"

She frowned slightly. "I haven't uncovered anything. I wish I had a better explanation, but unfortunately there is nothing."

"I just want to know if they might be connected to the Black Rose movement," Finn said.

She frowned, pulling a card from her pocket and flipping it from one side to the next before shaking her head. "I cannot say. But you're not here for that. And you're not here because you're injured, so that is an improvement."

He had to smile, though his mind worked through what other Alainsith structures might have been attacked. "I'm trying to piece together what's taking place in the city." He glanced over toward the city itself. Only parts of Verendal could be seen from outside of the walls. The church spires rose over the massive walls, and in the distance, the palace could be seen, but little else. "The king asked us—or, I guess, me—to look into what happened."

"Would you have not done so otherwise?"

"I would have," Finn said.

"Of course you would have," Esmerelda said, smiling at him. "You've become a faithful servant."

"You say that as if it's something I should regret."

"On the contrary, I say it as if it's something you should be proud of. You have committed to something more than just yourself."

Finn shook his head. "I'm just trying to find answers. I need to find the Black Rose. We think that's who's organizing the attacks."

Esmerelda smiled. "So you come here and scare people away." She laughed softly. "That young lady had come because she wanted wealth."

"You already knew?"

"I don't need to talk with her to know certain things," Esmerelda said, pulling another card out of her pocket and flipping it briefly. A series of markers on the card started to shift and shimmer, the ink a deep gold, looking like a stack of coins. "But unfortunately, she is looking for something that cannot be found quite as easily as she would like."

"Do people really come to the hegen thinking they can bargain for wealth?"

"You'd be surprised what people bargain for,"

Esmerelda chuckled, a soft, warm sound, and motioned for Finn to follow her as they headed along the street. She turned away from her home, away from the direction Finn would have taken. "Though none want to learn *how*."

"I'm not sure anyone not hegen would be able to learn your magic."

She paused. "Do you think you couldn't learn it? All who want knowledge can learn to find it. It's not so different from the way you have pursued the knowledge of your current line of work."

"Are you really equating magic to hanging someone?"

"Are you really trying to tell me all you do is hang people?"

Finn held her gaze, then looked away. "The other parts aren't quite what I'm known for."

"And magic isn't quite the only skill our people have, as I have shown you." She stopped in front of a home. She had taken him down a side street he had rarely traveled along, and now that they stopped here, he looked at the building, realizing that he hadn't seen it before, but it was incredible. Its sides were painted vibrant colors, and there was a mural painted along the walls. It looked to be a depiction of the forest, almost captured perfectly on the sides of the home. He could practically feel himself standing beneath the trees, the earthy scent of the forest carried to him, the air cool…

He stepped forward, studying the mural. "All of these murals are amazing."

"Those who work at this study and train no differently from those who work at other things," she said. "The time

I took to study my art of what you call magic is no less than the time it took to study this art. We have artisans, Finn. We have craftsman. I'm sure you've seen some of the carvings they make, some of the ceramics and textiles, weavings of such skill that they take hundreds upon hundreds of hours to complete." She shrugged, turning to Finn. "But what we are known for is what you call magic."

"I think it's called that because people don't understand it, or know what to call it otherwise."

"They don't understand it because they don't take the *time* to understand it. Even you, someone who has seen it more than most, still view it in a way that creates a depiction of power that is not founded in reality."

"I've seen what I've seen," Finn said.

"You've seen the barest edge of what *could* be seen. If you were to look, if you were to keep your eyes open and try to understand the powers in the world, then perhaps you would see—perhaps you would understand."

He shook his head. "I didn't come here to debate the merits of your powers," he said.

"No." She looked past him, back toward the direction of the city. "You came to talk to me about the unrest in the city walls."

"Only indirectly."

"Indirectly?"

"I'm looking for answers, but there are people within the city who were injured during an attack. I suspect one of them knows who is coordinating, if not instigating, the attack. The person behind the Black Rose movement."

Esmerelda smiled at him. "Is it one person?"

"I don't know," he admitted. "It's just that someone is coordinating things. There has to be someone in charge. If we can find that person, I feel like we can put a stop to the unrest. Which is why we need to question them."

"I remember stories of an old facility in Verendal. It's been long since abandoned, but it was a structure that once had been quite powerful. Many within the city had once been powerful, but this one even more so than others."

Finn shook his head, laughing softly. "I don't know why I would ever think you wouldn't know."

Esmerelda pulled yet another card out of her pocket, flipping it from side to side, and each time she turned it, the image on the card shifted a bit. The card flickered and he saw a building. It was simple, all stone, with traces of markings along it—markings Finn knew to be Alainsith.

"I didn't realize that it was Alainsith," Finn said.

Had Meyer known?

"There is much within the city that shares that heritage." She quickly glanced toward the city. "Perhaps in this our objectives align. I had not thought they would, but time… and other things… has made it more likely that they do." She pulled a card out of her pocket, turning it briefly as if looking for answers in the movement of the ink. "You would like to understand who is responsible for upsetting the balance within the city, and I would like to understand who is responsible for upsetting the balance *outside* the city. I have started to think this is all connected."

She held out a card and Finn looked at it.

It had an image of a small marker with a symbol engraved on it.

It took Finn a moment to realize what it showed him.

Then he knew. He carried it with him, and had ever since investigating Reginald.

He pulled the marker he'd found in Reginald's home out of his pocket. "This?"

"I've pondered what you told me when you were here last." Esmerelda didn't take the marker when he offered it to her, shaking her head instead. "There is some witch-craft in that. It's subtle, but the effect is there."

"What does it do?"

"I cannot say."

"If it's tied to what's happened outside the city…"

"Again, I cannot say," she told him.

Finn hadn't spent enough time looking into Reginald and now he started to wonder if that was a mistake. Maybe he needed to investigate his death more.

His experience outside of the city came back to him.

Unclean.

"I *was* unclean," he said.

Esmerelda frowned. "If someone was sensitive to magic, they may have recognized it."

Finn squeezed his eyes closed. He hadn't understood at the time. He still didn't—not really—but Lyle Martin hadn't been babbling. He'd *known.*

Finn had been unclean.

"What else did he know?" Finn asked. He looked up at Esmerelda. "I sentenced him, but what if he knew some-thing? What if it was all some way of protecting the village from witchcraft?" The bodies had been used similarly to hegen magic.

"I am sorry," Esmerelda said, her voice soft.

Finn squeezed the marker.

Witchcraft. Reginald. The protests.

He couldn't shake that it *was* all tied together, but he had no idea *how*.

It was time that changed.

Be the Hunter.

That would be how he'd find the answers. That was what the king wanted from him. The question Esmerelda had asked him not long ago came back, though, sticking with him the way it had too often of late. What did *he* want? What would be his path?

"We may need hegen help to heal these men," he said. "I know you don't like going into the city itself, but could you do this?"

Esmerelda held his gaze. "If you ask, I will offer it."

There was a weigh to the words that Finn wasn't quite sure about, along with something in the way Esmerelda looked at him. "I would be in your debt," he said. "Even more than I am now."

She touched his arm. "Help will be freely given. All I ask is what Meyer promised my people when he came to his position."

Finn frowned. "Why would that change?"

"I hope it does not, but as you take on a greater responsibility in the city, there is the possibility that you would want to see changes."

Was that what she feared?

All of this talk about his path, and could she be more concerned about *her* path?

That didn't fit with what he knew of Esmerelda.

"I would like the hegen to thrive," he said. "You've lived too long on the fringes of Verendal."

"Do you think we resent our place?"

Finn knew they didn't, but he thought about what he'd seen from the woman coming to the hegen for help. "You don't, but I'd like it if the people in the city could see you the way I see you."

"Ah. Well, that change takes time and influence. Perhaps you'll be the one to make that change." She smiled. "First, I fear we must ensure the city's safety. Then we can think about its future."

He glanced behind him. "I know where to start, but I'm not sure how it fits."

"I trust you will find it. You must trust that, too. Don't let others convince you otherwise."

Maybe that was what he'd been doing.

Finn had been at his profession long enough now that he knew what needed doing. It was time he did it the way *he* believed he needed.

CHAPTER TWENTY

The inside of Declan prison was quiet. There were times when it was loud, times when men shouted, crying out against their fate, but now wasn't one of those times. Finn had entered quickly, hurrying along the hall toward the stairs where he would reach the cells beneath the main part of the prison. They were inaccessible by most, difficult to easily reach.

When he neared the lower portion, he nodded to the two iron masters standing guard. He recognized them both, and while he made no attempt to socialize with them these days, he made a point of getting to know all of the iron masters, questioning them in his own way to ensure they did not try to harm the kingdom.

"Hunter," Billy said. He was a wide-faced man, his eyes farther apart than they should have been, with a sloped brow and close-cropped hair. "We didn't expect to see you today."

"I came to see the prisoner."

"The bastard hasn't said anything," Billy said. "He just sits there, staring at us. We can tell he knows something."

"You're damn right he knows something," Mason said. "And if he's responsible for what happened to the others…"

"He'll talk," Finn said.

"Of course he will. If anyone's going to get him to talk, it's going to be you, Hunter."

That was his reputation. Finn had thought he was getting used to the name, but now old doubts started to resurface. Was that all he was going to be?

"Bring him up to the chapel," Finn said.

"It's about damn time," Mason said.

Finn frowned at him. "What was that?"

"I don't mean no disrespect by it, Hunter," he said. "We're just saying that it's about time he gets what's coming to him."

"What's coming to him is providing answers for the king."

"Right," Billy said, "but when you go and visit him, you nudge him a little bit. We know you're going to get some answers that he's going to try to hide from you."

"I'm going to find the truth," Finn said.

"The truth is that bastard wants to kill our people."

Finn glanced from one iron master to the next. "See him brought up to the chapel."

Finn left them, heading to the chapel by himself. There was a time when he would've assisted the iron masters in escorting the prisoner up to the chapel, but that had been when he thought he needed to take a greater role in his work. Finn no longer felt that way. His was more of a supervisory role, and he had a responsibility to get the answers he needed. He needed to trust the iron masters to do what was asked of them, and nothing more than that.

He reached the chapel, pausing inside, looking up at the stained glass windows as he often did. This had once been an actual chapel, a place where the gods were celebrated, primarily Heleth, but now it was a place that did nothing to honor the gods the way Finn thought they should be honored—at least, not if the gods truly cared. Perhaps this was what the gods wanted of them. Perhaps the gods enjoyed having Finn torment the accused so they could exact their vengeance for men who did not celebrate them nearly as much as the gods preferred.

Finn headed over to the cabinets and tested the tools there. He kept them clean and neatly organized, arranged in such a way that he could find any implement he wanted quickly.

For his questioning of this man, he would start slowly, but perhaps not as slowly as he would have if the circumstances were different. He needed to find the truth.

The king wanted the Hunter.

Esmerelda's voice drifted into his mind. What did he want for himself?

Mason and Billy dragged the man into the room. He was rigid but didn't fight.

How much of Lena's sedation remained in him?

Some of the sedatives used in healing would linger, but most wore off fairly quickly.

The two iron masters strapped the man into the chair. When they were done, they looked up to Finn.

"You can leave," he said.

Billy nodded, and Mason looked as if he was disappointed.

That was the reason Finn sent them away. He didn't need anyone looking at him with that excitement in their eyes, a look that seemed to scream that they enjoyed the torment.

Once the door closed, Finn pulled the small metal stool over and positioned himself in front of the man. His arms were strapped to the chair, which was bolted to the center of the floor, with leather bindings, and his legs were bound the same way. He wasn't going to be able to kick or hit; he wouldn't be able to do anything other than spit at Finn, and Finn had come to recognize when a man would try something like that.

"Now that we have you in a more controlled environment, perhaps you and I can have a different conversation."

The man glared at him and brought his head back slightly.

Finn reacted, striking him in the belly before he had a chance to spit. "Again. You and I are going to have a different conversation."

The man gasped, struggling to take a breath, and Finn sat with his hands folded in front of him.

"You're in Declan prison. If you're from Verendal"—and there was a part of Finn that questioned whether he was, especially as there had been other attacks on the city recently that left him wondering what sort of plot against the kingdom there might be—"then you would know Declan is a place that imprisons men who are condemned to die."

The man took a few short, shallow breaths and looked up at Finn. "So you sentenced me already?"

Finn shook his head. "I haven't sentenced you. And I won't—not until I have answers." Finn flashed a tight smile. "Unfortunately, we don't have time for you to waste by trying to hide what you've been doing. I think I'm going to have to be a bit more forceful with getting the answers I need."

"You haven't been forceful already?"

Finn grunted. "We've only just begun." He frowned at the man. "There are several ways this can happen. My preferred method is for you to answer questions without me needing to do much else. I will know if you're being deceitful, and if so, I can assure you that I will do everything in my ability to find the truth." Finn glanced behind him before turning his attention back to the man. "The other option is for you to refuse. Unfortunately, that is not acceptable to me or the king. So if you refuse, I will need to draw upon more resources so that I can ascertain the truth."

"Resources," the man spat.

"Resources," Finn repeated. "Now, you can decide how

much I need to involve myself with the other aspects of questioning. Perhaps you would like to get through this as painlessly as possible. I highly advise that, especially as I have firsthand experience with some of these techniques."

"Firsthand. By that, you mean you've gotten your rocks off by tormenting other people."

"No," Finn said. "I mean I have experienced the pain from some of these techniques. I assure you, as soon as I begin utilizing my training, you will find you'll want to answer anything I have to ask. Now. Let us begin again. Tell me your name."

"You aren't getting anything from me."

Finn shook his head. "I'm afraid that is simply not good enough." He got to his feet, pushing the metal stool back, and looked down at the man. "As soon as you're ready to share with me what I need to know, including everything you know about the Black Rose movement, this will be made much less unpleasant."

The man cried out, and Finn leaned back from him, watching his reaction. It was at this point in a questioning where Finn began to struggle to determine whether someone told him information because they wanted the pain to end or because it was the truth. That was a difficult balance to strike. Sometimes it was challenging to know which way somebody would go. With somebody who had refused to even share their name, he was much less concerned about forcing the issue.

"You would like me to believe your name is Jonrath Barlon?"

Jonrath nodded his head. His jaw was clenched, but he had somehow managed to keep from tearing up.

"I will verify that with others who know you."

"You can do what you want," he cried out.

Finn glanced down to the cuffs squeezing around the man's shins. Metal rods, each touched with a bit of fire ash, pressed through the skin of his legs. They would burn, and the pain would be incredible, but the rods would leave very little marking.

If Jonrath was responsible for the protests, or at least tied to them in some way, Finn needed to keep him as intact as possible to face sentencing. The jurors would require that.

"What were you doing near the bridge?"

"I wasn't doing shit," he said.

"You were there?"

"Of course I was there. Why else would I have been in that hospital ward?"

Finn smiled tightly. "Why else *would* you have been?"

Jonrath glowered at him. "You think I wanted to be there? You think I wanted you to hold me?"

"To be honest, I can't say what you wanted. All I know is that you were there near the bridge."

"I was there," Jonrath sneered again. "And I told you, I wasn't doing nothing."

"I find that difficult to believe." Finn glanced down to the metal rods. "The king believes the protests were coordinated. Tell me about the Black Rose."

"There wasn't no coordination," Jonrath said. "And there ain't no Black Rose."

There was more to the protests. Finn was certain of it. Which meant he had to be careful. He couldn't push too hard based on his belief alone.

That was what Meyer had cautioned him against.

Be the Hunter, but not the Hunter.

"I see," Finn said. "Well, unfortunately, we have a dozen or so others who've recovered. Each of them will be questioned as well. I have a feeling some of them are more important to this cause, though I don't have the proof that I need. Yet. Eventually, I'll find someone who can lead me to the Black Rose."

Jonrath glowered at Finn again.

"Perhaps I should bring them up here. Once they recover, I will of course need to do that. They must face the same questioning as you."

"Go ahead," he spat. "No one is going to tell you anything."

"I hope that's not true. I hope others will recognize that they would benefit by sharing anything they can with me."

"And I told you I'm not going to tell you shit."

Finn just nodded. "I think we're going to need to move on to another technique." He got up, glancing down to Jonrath's legs. He couldn't help but be a bit impressed that he had tolerated the rod, touched with fire ash, searing through his skin. "Most of the time, I take breaks in between my sessions, but seeing as how there is a measure of urgency, I do need to have answers. I hope you understand. I would much rather do this in a more cordial manner, but you have given me very little choice."

"I've told you everything," Jonrath said.

"If you've told me everything, then none of this would be a problem." Finn flashed another smile, making it look as if he were truly saddened by what needed to happen. "I hope you understand that all I'm doing is serving the king."

"Serving the bastard of a king."

A comment like that was almost enough to get a man into a very different kind of trouble. "Be careful. You never know who's listening," Finn said.

"I know who's listening. Bastards who think to step on us. All of us!"

Finn looked at him for a moment before turning his attention to the implements on the counter.

Which technique was he going to use now?

In his mind, there was a linear pathway through the questioning process. It began with the leg braces, which influenced Finn since his very first days here, when he dealt with the same torment he now dispensed. He progressed from there to using the metal rods that he pressed into the legs of the accused, using that method to try to encourage them to share more than they would otherwise. After that, it became more difficult for him to know just what he needed to do in order to get answers. He could try water, though he didn't have a feeling Jonrath would respond well to that.

Finn paused at the implements.

There was something else he could try.

He thought about the sliver of metal that Jonrath had and pulled it out of his own pocket, where he'd placed it earlier, and took a seat back on the stool in front of him.

"What are you doing?" Jonrath asked.

Finn tapped the piece of metal in his hand. "You remember this?" Jonrath's gaze drifted to the piece of metal and Finn smiled tightly. "It seems you do. Why am I not surprised that you remember what you were using to try to attack me with? Of course, I wonder if you intended it for me or if it was meant for my sister." His eyes narrowed slightly. "Or perhaps you didn't know she was my sister." Finn shrugged. "All she wants to do is help. She's a healer at heart, and she would prefer to help as many as possible. You were one of the many she wanted to offer assistance to, yet here you are, a man who decided to try to instigate something very different from what you really should."

Finn slid forward. "But you had something in mind." He looked down at the metal rod. An unformed knife. That was how he had come to see it. Not witchcraft, but it looked so similar to some of the pieces used in witchcraft. "What was your intention with this?" Finn twisted the metal piece in hand, twirling it in place as he studied it. "Do you even know what this is?"

Jonrath looked up at him, meeting his gaze. "Do you?"

Finn chuckled. "I've wondered whether you even *knew* what you were using. Perhaps you believed you understood it, or perhaps you believed this was something that you had a right to. But I don't think you fully understand it." He twisted it again and smiled tightly. "Or maybe you do. If you do, it raises the question of why you would bring an item of witchcraft into the hospital ward." He watched the man's face as he said it.

There was a flicker in his eyes; a fleeting moment when it seemed Jonrath knew just what he had done. *Could he have known?*

"Do you believe you're untouchable?" Finn asked.

Jonrath glowered at him. "You are making a mistake."

"The only mistake I made was not bringing you to Declan sooner." He looked around. "I was here when an attempt was made to use power that others didn't fully understand." Finn turned his attention back to the man. "But I begin to wonder if perhaps you knew that." He gave him no sign that he did. Finn leaned forward, tapping the metal wand on his hand before holding it outward. "I understand how these things work."

"You cannot," the man said softly.

"And I understand how this power is broken." Finn shot him a look. "And what about these?" Finn produced a poster from his pocket and waved it at Jonrath.

"You'll never find them."

"So it was planned by the Black Rose."

"You can't understand," Jonrath said.

"Do you think you're the only one who has attempted to take action upon the city?" Finn shook his head. "And such *weak* action. Unfortunately, it took little more than an executioner—and an apprentice, at that—to stop the previous attacks."

Jonrath watched Finn. "What makes you think you're merely an executioner?"

Finn smiled at him. "I know what I am. I know *who* I am."

"Do you?"

There was a hint of danger in the way he asked it, but not enough to cause Finn any fear.

"We are going to continue," Finn said. "And I think this time, I'm going to use the very weapon you intended to use upon me." Finn leaned forward, and Jonrath tried to jerk free of the bindings, but could not.

Finn grabbed Jonrath's hand, prying his fingers out and holding the man's gaze.

"We will start with the index finger."

Jonrath's eyes widened.

Finn held his hand down, flattening it, and forced his fingers out again, then he began to press the wand underneath the nail of his index finger. This time, Jonrath did nothing to try to fight the screams. He cried out, unable to withstand it.

Finn held his gaze. "It is quite painful. I agree. The more you hold out, the more I will need to use this technique on you. It would be so much easier if you answered me."

The man tried to spit, but Finn was prepared for that, and he kicked, catching him in the midsection.

"I take no pleasure in this."

"I see it in your eyes," the man said through gritted teeth. "I see that you do."

"The only thing you see is my determination," Finn said. It was the determination of the Hunter. That was what he had to be, even if he didn't want to.

He pulled the wand out and smiled sadly at Jonrath. He couldn't really use it—Finn understood that pain gave power to it, but the man might not—but it served as a threat.

"We will continue on to the next technique."

CHAPTER TWENTY-ONE

Finn sat at the worn wooden table inside the kitchen of Master Meyer's home and looked around him. A hot mug of steaming tea rested in front of him—that was all he'd managed to do so far this morning: make tea. He hadn't even bothered starting breakfast. The dishes stacked in the basin waited for either him or Lena to put them away—Meyer didn't have to put up with such drudgery anymore—and a loaf of day-old bread rested on the counter, almost enough for him to get up and toast a slice, but he didn't have the energy yet.

For a home the size of Master Meyer's, the kitchen was a large room. It was a place where they often congregated, where conversation would often lead to questions and assignments, and where Finn had studied in his years working with Meyer.

Finn needed answers, and he'd hoped that coming here would help him uncover what he needed, but no answers had been forthcoming yet. So he sat, hands cupped around the mug of tea, lost in thought.

The kitchen was quiet at this time of day, his sister not yet up—or if she was, she hadn't come down for the morning. She had been up late working with the injured, and when he'd last seen her, she was exhausted from the time spent with them, so it didn't surprise him that she'd still be sleeping.

Finn was tired from everything, especially after interrogating the prisoner far too late into the night. He was feeling wiped, but he didn't think he had the luxury of sleeping in any longer than he had. Already, he'd spent too much time sleeping and not enough time trying to figure out what the others had intended for Verendal.

Footsteps coming down the stairs caught Finn's attention, and he turned to see Meyer coming into the kitchen. His eyes were drawn, wrinkles forming in the corners of them, and dark lines worked beneath the hollows of his eyes.

"I didn't expect to see you up," Meyer said.

"I couldn't sleep well," Finn said, leaning back in the chair. "I had too much on my mind."

Meyer frowned, glancing to the mug of tea. "Want to talk about it?"

Finn sighed then shook his head. "I'm not so sure it'll help."

"You discovered something." Meyer took a seat at the faded wooden table, resting his elbows atop it and frowning again. The table was probably older than Meyer himself.

"It might not even be anything."

Finn pulled the wand from his pocket, resting it on the table.

"What is that?" Meyer asked.

Finn looked up from it. "Have you seen anything like this before?"

Meyer leaned forward, looking at the rod. "Not that I can identify."

"I have." Finn rolled it across the surface of the table. He'd cleaned it after using it on the man, though he didn't know if the way he'd used it would have added power to it. It was possible that by tormenting him, he had done exactly what Jonrath wanted. One of the few things he knew about witchcraft was that its power came from places that Finn didn't want to understand. Pain. Torment. "When you were injured. There were things like this used in the attack on the city."

Meyer clasped his hands together. "You fear it's witchcraft."

"I'd like to think there is some other explanation, but that's what Esmerelda said about this." He pulled the wooden coin from his pocket and set it on the table. "She believes it has some residual power."

Meyer nodded slowly. "If that's the case, what purpose would the protests serve?"

"I've been trying to figure that out. Witchcraft needs power, and from what I've learned, their power comes from pain and darkness." Maybe that was all it was. Use the protests to find a way to increase the pain in the city...

Even that seemed a stretch. How would they harness that kind of power?

"What have you considered?"

Finn looked across the table, smiling slightly. He couldn't tell if Meyer was asking him or testing him. At this point, it could be either. Given what Finn had gone through, he thought he'd earned a measure of respect as they'd worked together, but there was also the possibility that Meyer still thought Finn needed to be tested.

He *was* still a journeyman executioner. Finn didn't know what would come next, or even whether there would be anything coming, but it was Meyer's responsibility to ensure Finn was prepared. How else could he do it but through testing?

"Probably more than I should have considered," Finn said. "I'll focus on the protesters, though. That's what the king wants."

Meyer frowned a moment before nodding.

"There's something else. I know you want to keep the prison a secret, but I'd like you to station some Archers there to keep Lena and Wella safe." And Esmerelda, when she went to help, though Finn doubted she would need the same level of protection—if any.

"I suppose you're right. I've avoided it to keep from drawing any attention to the protestors, but I think we don't have much choice."

Finn had been somewhat concerned that Meyer would resist. He'd hoped he wouldn't, especially since Finn knew Meyer had a fondness for Lena.

"What else did you uncover?" Meyer asked.

"Other than when I questioned him in Declan, he barely even told me his name, and I'm not convinced the name he gave me is really his. He knows of the Black Rose though." He took a deep breath. "I'll get through to him as quickly as I can. The king gave us only a little time to finish this. We need to get it done before…"

The problem was that he didn't know *what* it would be before.

Another uprising? Another protest?

"Let me make breakfast," Finn said. Maybe the work would help clear his mind.

Finn grabbed the lard, sausage, and eggs and set them on the counter, working quickly to get breakfast sizzling on the stove. Meyer joined him. Neither of them said anything as they worked in a comfortable sort of silence.

Finn looked over when his sister came down, coming over to help them, but he shook his head. "We'll make breakfast. You can sit."

Lena brushed a strand of hair back from her face, looking over to Meyer. "You shouldn't have to do that. Let me help."

He guided her to the table, forcing her to sit. When he returned to the stovetop, Meyer had a plate already prepared, and Finn took it and set it in front of Lena. "Trust me. You are helping."

Lena glanced to Meyer again before looking up at Finn. "I could do more…"

Finn patted her on the shoulder. "Just eat."

He turned back to the stove, where Meyer had finished preparing the rest of the eggs and sausage. Finn hadn't done much of anything either. Meyer handed him a plate, which Finn took then sat down with.

In all his time working with Meyer, Finn didn't remember the last time Meyer had made him breakfast. Even though Finn had been the one to start the cooking, it had been Meyer who really did it all. As Finn took his first bite, he understood why Meyer hadn't usually cooked. The eggs were harder than Finn preferred, the sausage burned.

"Maybe I should have left it to you," Meyer muttered as he took a bite.

Lena smiled. "I think it tastes wonderful."

"I think it tastes like a brick," Meyer said.

Finn smiled slightly. "I think you're overselling it," Finn said, glancing over to Meyer. "I think it tastes worse than a brick."

Meyer glowered at him. "I should know better than to get in the way of your work."

"It's supposed to be my work," Lena said softly.

Meyer grunted. "For as much as I like your cooking, you're far more valuable doing other things." He nodded to Finn. "Him, on the other hand… He needs to perfect all aspects of his responsibilities."

Finn just smirked at him. He finished the eggs and the overly crisp sausage, then carried his plate over to the basin.

"I would love to spend time learning to cook from the master this morning, but there are other things I need to be doing."

Meyer looked up. "What else do you intend to do today?"

"I thought I might go back to visit Declan, see if I can't uncover anything with this man, and from there, maybe return to the hospital ward and figure out who the men were trying to protect. One of them has to know about the Black Rose and has to eventually talk."

Lena sat up. "What if none of them know anything? They've all been sedated enough that they would say something though. They certainly share a little too much with me."

That would work with some of them, but the man who'd attacked him hadn't been fully medicated. "Maybe most of them," he agreed, "but not all."

"Not all react to treatment the same way, Finn," Meyer said.

"Or they had built up an immunity to it," Finn replied.

"An immunity to sedatives? That seems to be a bit of a stretch," Lena said.

Finn shrugged, glancing over to Master Meyer, who sat with his hands resting on the table, looking over at Finn. He could see the look in Meyer's eyes, the question written there.

"If they know what sort of medications might be used, they could counter their effects." Finn glanced over to Lena. "What were you using on them?"

"A fairly standard regimen," Lena said. "We had a mixture of ostia and melander and clorath and—"

Finn started to laugh. "A fairly standard mixture? There's nothing standard about that."

"Well, perhaps not in acquiring the supplies, but it is certainly a fairly standard concoction. Wella had the supplies, and we used them to try to ensure the poor men wouldn't suffer too much."

"Maybe that's where I need to start," Finn said.

"With testing it?" Lena asked.

Finn shook his head. "With Wella."

"You can't think she has anything to do with it," Lena said.

Finn didn't. He'd known Wella too long, and she had assisted Meyer for such a long period of time that he couldn't imagine her getting involved in something that would cause harm to either Master Meyer or Finn. That wasn't to say that she didn't have knowledge of different techniques that might cause problems for them, but if not for her, he wouldn't have uncovered the strategy for stopping the fire ash.

"What she does have is the kind of knowledge we'll need in order to determine if they could have neutralized the effects of the sedative."

"Well, there are a few different compounds that might be effective," Lena said, resting her elbow on the table and leaning forward. She pinched her chin. "I suspect you could use a combination of thelen berry along with ghelum root, but both of those are somewhat difficult to acquire." Lena leaned back. "I can look into it as well."

"That would be great," Finn said. He didn't need to say anything about ensuring Lena made certain to keep working with the men. She would do it regardless. And having his sister's mind employed in other ways would only keep her engaged with what they were doing and what they needed to uncover.

She pushed the plate away. "I'm sorry, Henry. I know you mean well…"

"I meant well, but we can both agree that what I meant and what I managed to accomplish are vastly different things."

Lena smiled, reaching across the table and patting his hand. "You do many other things well. You don't have to be an expert in breakfast."

"I'm just glad I have him around to take care of things."

Lena frowned. "Just him?"

Meyer shook his head. "Glad I have you around, too," he said.

Finn groaned. "I'm leaving before the two of you decide to remind me of how much more I need to do."

He grabbed his cloak out of the closet, his gaze lingering on the two executioner blades in the back, both of them stuffed there unceremoniously, before closing the door. The only blade that had value was Justice. It was an ancient sword, one that had been in the kingdom for centuries—not at all like the sword Finn now used. His was a new creation, made for him, yet there were times when Finn preferred to use his sword rather than Justice. Not that he didn't appreciate the weight of Justice or value its history, but there was something refreshing about not having to consider the expectations associated with the old sword if he used it.

He closed the door behind him as he stepped outside.

The wind gusted along the street, carrying the cold in

the air that had been there for the last few weeks. The cold seemed to be coming with an increasing fervor, and Finn could imagine that within another few weeks they'd see the first snowfall. It was a time when things in the city tended to slow down, if only a little bit. Maybe that was all they needed. Let the seasons change, let the cold come on, and the people in the city who had begun their protests would find themselves distracted by the shift. It would be easier to stay indoors during those times.

Wella's apothecary shop wasn't terribly far from Meyer's home. It was close enough that Finn would know the path even if he were blindfolded. The streets were active, as they often were, but the people were more subdued than usual. Most of them walked in pairs, as if they needed the support of somebody with them, and even they hurried along the street, saying nothing, moving with a steady, determined pace. It seemed as if they wanted nothing more than to be out of the street and to be wherever their destination was. People looked askance at Finn as he passed them, and some even quickened their step as he approached.

The level of suspicion out in the city was elevated far more than it ever had been.

He found several other markings of the Black Rose etched onto buildings and a few posters. More than he had noticed before.

Finn slowed each time he saw one. Someone was putting these markers around the city, but for what reason?

As he reached Wella's shop, he heard a shout at the end of the street.

He hurried along the street, and when he reached an intersection, he found a small crowd gathering. One of the protesters whistled.

Soon more whistles rang out, a half-dozen, then a dozen.

The crowd began to build.

Finn shook his head.

How long would it be before the Archers arrived?

As soon as they appeared, the protests would be quashed, and unfortunately, he feared there would be lives lost, the same way there had been before. He wanted to wait, to see who was here, but as the crowd continued to swell, and people started to push and shove, Finn decided that this wasn't where he wanted to be.

Let the Archers deal with it.

He wouldn't be able to get near enough to the man who'd whistled to start the protest anyway—and getting near him would only matter if the man had anything to answer for.

Finn heard the protesters shouting—some decrying the king, while others dared the Archers to attack—and as he backed along the street he'd come down, he saw smoke beginning to rise.

More fires.

So much for the colder weather preventing the protests.

When he reached Wella's shop, he ducked inside.

It was gloomy, and the air smelled of all the various

medicines, herbs, leaves, roots, and oils that she gathered, all of them making her apothecary shop unique. He hurried toward the back of the shop, passing by a row of jars that contained human remains. There was one jar with only fingers, another only toes, and still another that held eyeballs. All of them had been harvested from men—and a few women—who had been sentenced.

Wella came tottering out from the back of the shop, running her hand through her hair as she looked over the counter and toward Finn.

"Finn." Relief swept through her voice.

"The protesters are gathering outside your shop," Finn said.

"I noticed," she said. "I heard the shouting and went to take a look…" She shook her head. "They don't know what they're doing, and if they did, perhaps they would act differently."

"Some of them do know what they're doing," Finn said.

Wella sighed. "What can I do for you? I thought, with everything taking place, Henry might decide to slow his purchases."

"I'm not here for supplies." She frowned and Finn shook his head. "That's not to say that I wouldn't purchase any." He needed to keep Wella happy, and happiness involved her staying in business. Finn knew that he and Master Meyer were some of Wella's best customers, and because of that, he felt an obligation to ensure she stayed open. Besides, there were too many apothecaries in the city that he didn't trust quite as much as he trusted Wella. She had far superior supplies. "I just came to ask about the sedative you've been using on the wounded men."

"What about it? It's a simple concoction."

"You sound like Lena," Finn said.

"Well, your sister was the one to suggest it. Not that I wouldn't have considered it," Wella added quickly, "but I must say, the idea behind it was a bit unusual." She shrugged. "I should have considered it myself, especially in light of the shortage of supplies."

"What supplies?"

"Well, we have dealt with a shortage in orphum, which, as you know, is the most often used sedative."

Finn nodded. He had been surprised that his sister hadn't used that on the prisoners, but if they had difficulty acquiring it, then it made more sense that she hadn't.

"I've never known there to be a shortage of it," Finn said.

Wella's face clouded. "No. There should not be. It's such a common root, and easy enough to acquire, but…" She shrugged. "We are at the whim of Heleth when we search for medicinals. We must make do with what she provides."

Finn smiled at Wella. He had never known her to be particularly faithful, though he had never really spoken to her about her faith. "What if Heleth wanted to challenge you?"

"My days have been nothing but challenging."

Finn cocked his head to the side, watching her. "Why do you say that?"

Wella waved her hand. "It's of no matter, Finn Jagger.

And it's not the reason you came here. I suspect you came to learn if there is any way to counter this sedative. Ostia and melander are typically rarer than orphum, but for whatever reason, your sister has come into a significant supply of them."

"She didn't tell me that," Finn said.

"Oh, don't be upset by Lena. I don't think she wanted to admit that she's been shopping at other apothecaries." Wella tapped the counter, and a bit of dust swirled. "Not that I could blame her. My suppliers have been a little less than satisfactory recently." Wella looked up. "Someone with her knowledge needs to make sure she has the right kind of supplies for all that she does."

"Is there anything I can help with?"

"Do you intend to go out into the forest and harvest for me, Finn Jagger?" When he shook his head, Wella cackled. "Then don't you worry your pretty little head. Supply constraints are something I deal with from time to time. I just need to shift my suppliers. Or perhaps I need to venture out beyond the walls myself." She frowned, her gaze drifting toward the door. "Given the current political climate in the city, that might not be all bad. I could go and gather my own supplies, and when I return, I wouldn't have to worry quite so much about these so-called protests."

"Why do you call them 'so-called protests'?" Finn asked.

"Because they are protesting out of spite, not out of any desire to garner favor or promote change. If that were the case, I might even get behind them."

"You would?"

Wella shrugged. "Should I not? I've lived in the city long enough to know that there are some who are treated well and others who are not. Even those who *should* be treated well are not." She offered Finn a pointed look. "And those who act in a vile manner often get away with their behavior." She drummed her fingers on the counter. "There was a time when I believed the gods would ensure only the faithful were given the upper hand, but over time, I've begun to realize that the gods don't care who is faithful and who is not. All the gods care about is men and women celebrating them."

"You just said that Heleth would—"

"I know what I just said," Wella said. "And I'm not foolish enough to risk angering the gods, but that's not to say that I think the gods are right in all things."

A shout drifted into the shop, and Finn shared a look with Wella before heading over to the door and pulling it open just a crack.

The crowd had moved along the street and one of the men carried a staff, tapping it on the ground from time to time, the sound of it ringing out loudly. He prodded everyone forward, and Finn pulled the door closed before anyone saw him looking.

Wella pushed up close to him.

Finn shook his head. "We should stay inside," he whispered.

"They wouldn't dare attack an old woman in this part of the city," she said.

"I don't have the sense that they care so much where they attack."

"The damn fools don't know that the Archers are going to sweep through here," Wella said, shaking her head. "So many people are going to be caught up in this."

"So many people have *already* been caught up in this," Finn said. "The last protest saw nearly one hundred people die."

"So many," Wella said. "Something like that requires organization."

"I'm looking into that."

"And it requires funding."

Finn frowned.

He should've thought about that. Men could organize freely, but to coordinate in such a way, and for people to be driven like that, it would take more.

"Finn?" Wella asked.

"I hadn't considered that before," he said.

"You hadn't considered what?"

"Where they were getting their funds."

"I don't know that you would be able to find anything. I was just saying…"

"I know what you were just saying," Finn said and smiled at Wella. "And I think you were right. They wouldn't be able to do this without funding. I think what I need to do is chase down the source of it. If I can uncover that, then I can get to who might be responsible."

"And if no one is responsible?" Wella asked.

"Why would you say that? You just said that this had to

be funded. And we know there's the Black Rose movement."

"Or perhaps there's another possibility. Perhaps the protests have happened naturally." She glanced to the door. "It didn't take long for word to get out about the iron masters, the wardens, and the prisons, and people have started to hear about graft within the Archers. Rumors have been spreading. As they spread, it doesn't take long for things to shift. The wind can change, and those who were content can find themselves unsettled and angry, and you know what happens when men become angry."

That may be all it was. If so, it was almost understandable, especially given what people had gone through lately, but he had a feeling it was something else. He had a feeling it was more than just that.

Finn pulled the door open again, glancing outside for a brief moment, and noticed that the crowd had moved past. "You never said if there was an antidote, or some way to avoid the effect of the sedative," Finn said.

"None that I know of," she said. "Like all things, a tolerance can be built, but it would be unusual unless you had plenty of access to it. There's only one place in the kingdom with that."

"Where?"

"The valley around Evertin in the north. That's why it's difficult to acquire in the first place."

Finn nodded. "Stay inside. Stay safe."

"I won't be able to do that, Finn." When he looked back

at her, she cackled softly. "Much like you, I need to help those men."

Finn nodded. "Just be safe."

He stepped out into the street, pulling the door closed behind him, and wrapped his cloak around his shoulders as he hurried along.

He wanted to avoid the protests, but more than anything, he wanted answers. If this was somehow instigated by people within the city, he needed to know. If it wasn't...

If it wasn't, then it was even harder for him. If this was just angry people, there might not be anything Finn could do about it. And that was the most difficult thing to comprehend.

CHAPTER TWENTY-TWO

M eyer approached Finn as he headed toward the old prison. Meyer's brow was furrowed, and he wiped his hands on a towel, leaving Finn to question what he'd been doing. Lena was there, as was Wella, so Finn didn't think Meyer would have been questioning the prisoners, but it was possible that he had dragged some of them away to ask them more about the Black Rose.

"Anything?" Finn asked.

He didn't need much of a preamble at this point. Not now. Not with what they were dealing with.

Meyer shook his head. "They don't want to speak. And I'm starting to question whether they know anything." He shook his head again. "None of them seem to believe there was anyone coordinating anything."

"Jonrath—"

"I'm well aware that his presence complicates things,"

Meyer said. He glanced along the street. Finn knew he was looking toward Declan.

"I'll get through to them," Finn said.

"I don't like this," Meyer said. "Citizens were killed during protests, protesters have attacked the Archers' barracks, and then there were Archers murdered in response. None of this is going well."

It was more than just that. Even walking through the city, Finn felt the undercurrent of anger that simmered everywhere. People, especially in the outer sections, had an energy to them that he couldn't quite place. Maybe it was the anger that he detected, but it might be something else—the rage that bubbled up, the fact that the protesters who killed the Archers would face one fate, while the Archers managed to escape any real consequences.

"I wish the movement wouldn't have killed those three Archers," Finn said.

Meyer held his gaze before turning his attention back to the prison. "Sentencing the Archers for killing the men might've gone a ways toward appeasing this," Meyer said.

"You would've agreed with that?" Finn wasn't sure. He had a hard time reading Meyer these days. Since the protests had begun, he had been reserved.

"All men need to face justice," Meyer said. "And they had taken justice into their own hands. Just because they were Archers didn't mean they had the right to do that. Even the king would see that."

Finn hoped that were true, but until they had a chance to prove it, he had no idea if there was going to be any way to convince the citizens of the city that even the Archers were not above reproach.

"I haven't found anything about the Black Rose," Finn said.

Meyer breathed out slowly. "I'm not sure we will find a singular person. There might be many people involved in this."

Finn had come to feel much the same way, but if there was more than one person involved, then they would have to bring down the entire movement.

But there was something that made him question whether more than one person was involved. A hunch suggested this more than just a faceless movement. Somebody guided it. One person had to be responsible.

"I've been looking through Reginald's books, as well. If I chase the money, I think the answer is there, but that hasn't been useful. Something Wella said to me suggested I needed to be more strategic, but with the protests and everything else, I guess I've been distracted."

Meyer chuckled. "It's more than just the protests distracting you, isn't it?"

"Why is that?"

"I saw you shining your shoes this morning."

Finn frowned. "I was going to meet with someone later."

"You don't have to conceal your romantic interests from me, Finn. If you want to go visit with the hegen woman—"

"It's not Esmerelda." Finn couldn't even imagine

pursuing her. "It's a woman I met while investigating Reginald."

"You should be careful," Meyer said.

"She's not guilty," Finn said.

"You want to make sure there are no perceptions of impropriety. That is always a challenge for us."

Meyer had cautioned him on that before. Usually it was about his connection to Oscar. It had never been about a woman.

"In this case, Reginald owed her father some money, but I doubt she's going to get it back from the crown."

"Can I offer a piece of advice?"

Finn cocked his head to the side.

"Don't talk about your day with her."

"What?" Finn was surprised that Meyer would offer any sort of romantic advice.

"Well, she will obviously know what you do, but she won't want to know anything *about* what you do. You will find that it will be easier to avoid talking about it altogether."

"Was that what it was like for you?"

"It was different then," he said, his voice going soft. "But I didn't tell her at first. I think I spoke of this with you once before, and how she was disappointed that I had hidden what I did from her."

"I won't be hiding anything from Jamie."

"And you should not," he said. "But steer the conversation toward something more pleasing. You are not merely an executioner."

"I know," Finn said.

Meyer clasped his hand on Finn's shoulder. "You are not merely an executioner." When he said it again, he looked into Finn's eyes. "It is *one* aspect of what you are, one aspect of what you do, but even in that, you serve in a greater way."

Finn could only nod. He had never had a conversation like this with his own father, and having Meyer now speak to him like this felt strange, but also strangely comforting.

"I just want to do what is asked of me," Finn said.

"Maybe it's time you stop worrying about what the king wants out of you, or what I want out of you."

"I'm your apprentice," Finn said to him.

Meyer chuckled. "You are a journeyman now, so you have a measure of independence. But you still serve. I'm not saying that you won't," Meyer added, smiling slightly. "What I'm suggesting is that perhaps it's time you do what you do best. Trust yourself. Trust your own instincts."

Finn had been trying to find answers the way he thought Meyer wanted him to. The way he thought the king wanted him to.

But that had never been how he had found answers, had it?

He had always relied upon a certain part of himself to find answers that others wanted to keep hidden. It was how he had thwarted multiple attacks on the city already.

Could he do so again?

"There's still quite a bit of the day left," Meyer said, releasing his shoulder. "And you aren't needed here. Your sister and Wella have things well in hand, and I can manage with questioning. If I uncover anything, I will let you know."

There was something in the way he said it that suggested Meyer didn't expect to uncover anything.

"I think I'm going to visit Oscar again," Finn stated.

"Will he know anything?"

Finn shrugged. "He doesn't want to get in the middle of everything, but I think he still wants to help. And with what we've been going through, I think we need as much help as we can get."

Meyer nodded and turned away.

Finn made his way through the streets. He passed patrolling Archers, many of them glancing in his direction, looking at him with suspicion until they either recognized him or questioned him, taking his word for his position. There were very few people out shopping. The protests had forced so many people inside.

The city felt wrong.

That was the only way Finn could describe it. Throughout his years in Verendal, he had never seen anything like this. Even when there had been a magical threat within the city, it hadn't felt quite so extreme.

Worse, it made it seem as if the king was crushing the people.

Which was the very thing the protesters were angry about.

He reached the Olin section and the Wenderwolf. There were no Archers here, thankfully. Finn was acutely aware of how he might bring attention to the Wenderwolf, especially considering how he had already brought it more than enough attention. He stepped inside and frowned.

Everything was quiet.

There was no music. No activity. No patrons, really.

The door to the kitchen opened, and Annie poked her head out.

As soon as she saw him, she frowned.

"I just have a question for him," he said.

"Like the last time?"

"Nothing like the last time," Finn said.

The door closed as she disappeared into the kitchen. Finn stood, not wanting to take a seat. It felt strange being in the Wenderwolf when it was empty—at least in the daytime. Finn had been here late at night when it had been empty, and there had been plenty of times when he had come in during the day when it had been quiet, but this was something else.

When Oscar appeared, he had one hand near his waist. A knife.

When he saw Finn, he relaxed, though not entirely.

"Damn, Finn. I didn't know it was you."

"I thought Annie would've told you."

"She only told me that we had a visitor."

Finn frowned. "I wasn't trying to scare you." He motioned to one of the tables. "Can we sit?"

Oscar nodded. They took a seat at the table, across from each other. It was a far cry from when Finn used to sit in the booth with him. Now it felt so much more formal. There was nothing relaxed about sitting with Oscar. And this was supposed to be his oldest friend.

"We're still looking into the Black Rose," Finn said.

"That's why you came here?"

"I just wanted to know if you had come across anything." He glanced behind him. "I don't know how much time you've spent out in the streets, but things are unsettled."

Oscar grunted. "I've spent enough time to know that much. Men can't move anywhere without having a pair of Archers trailing after them. I didn't know we had so many damn Mark Archers in the city in the first place."

"The king has brought palace Archers out to patrol." That wasn't all, though. There were the Realmsguard, though Finn hadn't seen many of them. "He wants to keep everything calm."

Oscar grunted again. "He's not going to calm things down that way. People are upset, Finn. You don't just wipe that away. It takes time. It takes change."

Finn nodded. "I know. And with the Archers dying, there won't be the justice there should have been."

Oscar leaned forward, resting his hand on the table. "You should know that quite a few men are claiming responsibility for that."

Finn shook his head. "I'm not surprised."

"Have you been chasing down leads?"

"I doubt there are going to be many useful leads with a crime like that."

"Maybe," Oscar said. He watched Finn, and there was a question glittering in his eyes, one that Finn wasn't quite sure how to read. "Would you—"

"They would need to face justice," Finn said.

Oscar nodded slowly. "Not that I know anything," he went on, leaning back. "Just rumors. You know how those can be. Especially in the outer sections of the city."

Finn regarded him, waiting for Oscar to say something more, but he didn't. "Have you found anything?"

"I thought you didn't want me to look."

Finn had told him that, but he had known Oscar would look. Even though Finn wanted his friend to find his way out of Olin, and for him to have the opportunity for respectability that he wanted, Finn also wanted answers.

There was too much at stake otherwise.

"I figured that you would dig regardless," Finn said.

"Might be that I would," he said.

"What did you find? Have you discovered anything about the Black Rose?"

Oscar watched him for a long moment. After a while, he slipped his hand into his pocket and pulled something out, setting it on the table.

It was a small pamphlet stamped with the symbol of the Black Rose.

"What is that?" Finn asked.

"That's what I found," Oscar said.

"And?"

"Look through it. Tell me that you disagree."

Finn frowned.

He pulled the pamphlet toward him and opened it.

Finn had learned to read at a young age, and he had been forced to read even more in the time he had been working with Master Meyer. Most of the time, he read about anatomy and healing—plenty of different ways to help people. He almost never read about torture, techniques for execution, or anything along those lines. It simply wasn't necessary.

This was simple. Not at all like some of the apothecary medicine texts he had read. Those could be complicated, and written in ways to make the author sound more intelligent than they might otherwise. This pamphlet seemed as if it was designed to be read by someone with almost no education.

It was designed for those in the outer sections.

"This describes the Black Rose movement," Finn said, flipping through the pages.

Oscar nodded. "That's exactly what it describes."

Finn looked up. "Where did you get this?"

"They are all over the city. Any place you see one of the posters on the wall has these," Oscar said. He shrugged and reached for it back, but Finn held on to the pamphlet. He had only skimmed it, but he immediately understood its purpose. It was the movement's way of getting others to side with them.

But there was very little convincing they had to do. It spoke of wrongs that men had suffered under the king. It spoke of abuses, the way that those with money took advantage of those without. It spoke of how difficult it was for someone to gain footing in the world, especially in Verendal.

All of it hit home for Finn.

"You understand what you're going against," Oscar said.

Finn sighed. "I understand."

"Still think you are in the right?"

"We can't have people killing themselves."

"Sometimes the only way to change things is through violence," Oscar said.

"Do you really believe that?"

"When it comes to pushing against those who have…"

Finn fingered the pamphlet. "When I was on the crew, we didn't have any problem taking from those who had more than us."

"I still don't," Oscar said.

"Meyer has trained me to try to find a balance."

"Not in your position," Oscar said. "There is no balance. You serve the king, or you don't. That's it. And if you don't, then you are against him." He nodded to the pamphlet. "Which means that you would be with them."

"I don't know," he said, shaking his head.

"You wanted me to see what I could find, so I'm telling you what I could find. And you can make up your own mind. You're a smart man, Finn. I'm sure you can look through there and come to terms with what you feel."

Finn wasn't entirely sure what he was supposed to feel.

The movement fit with his experience.

Had he seen this pamphlet even five years ago, it might've called to him even more.

But he had seen things.

He had done things.

There were ways the king protected the people that they didn't even know about.

Maybe they couldn't understand.

At least, that was what Finn had to tell himself.

"When you are running around and interrogating your prisoners, I want you to think about that," Oscar said.

"I will," Finn said.

He started to get up, and Oscar watched him.

"Tell Annie that I appreciate you providing this for me."

"That's it?"

"I plan on finding who printed it."

Oscar snorted. "Don't bother. I recognize the typeface. The printing house that used it burned down a year ago. And the owners died in the fire. More likely than not, someone scavenged the equipment and is printing it out of their home."

One more lead gone before he even had a chance to dig.

Finn stuffed the pamphlet into his pocket. He would look at it later. Meyer would need to see it.

How had they not come across it until now?

The answer came to him easily. It was the same reason that the men had accosted him, seeing him as rich.

It was in his clothing—the way he was dressed.

Meyer had ensured Finn was dressed appropriately to serve as an executioner, but it had separated him from his roots. Finn had been all too eager to embrace the style of dress when he had first taken up the job, but it had made him stand out, setting him apart.

Finn turned to the door. "Be careful when you're out in the streets," he said to Oscar.

"I always am."

He swung his gaze to the kitchen, but there was no sign of Annie.

He left. When the door closed, there was a feeling of separation once again. He stood in the small square outside of the Wenderwolf and noticed several buildings with the poster for the Black Rose on them.

It was a movement that had to be funded somehow. Somebody had paid for those posters. Somebody had paid for the pamphlets. Maybe that was where he should start.

He finished the rest of his errands with his mind churning. He didn't have the desire to go to Declan and interrogate anyone, so he avoided it. There were plenty of other things he could do anyway. He paused every so often, pulling out the pamphlet and flipping through the pages. He tried to make sense of what was there and whether it would provide any insight as to who had written it, but there was nothing. It was not even printed on high-quality paper.

He paused at the river, staring at it as the sunlight shone down. A couple of barges had made their way farther to the northwest, carrying goods to the city. They were always unloaded in the central part of the city. Never on the outside. Finn tried not to think about that.

He pulled the pamphlet out and flipped through its pages again.

Why would the protests have begun now?

Oscar wanted him to believe that the people were just angry. It was an anger he understood, but there was more to it.

Unless there wasn't.

They had known the king was in the city. That was when the protests had begun in full. They hadn't been instigated. Not with any real intent. It had just been an uprising.

That was the part of all of it that troubled Finn.

Men had been unhappy with their place in the world for years. It was something Finn understood. When he had worked with the crew, he had been unhappy with his place in the world, wanting to move beyond poverty, to find a way to not have to fight for scraps of food, for healing for his mother, or for a place to stay.

Something else had triggered people.

And maybe it was simply the movement coalescing.

When he heard the evening Giver's bell, Finn stuffed the pamphlet back into his pocket.

It was time to meet Jamie.

He had to push all of the thoughts of what he had been dealing with out of his mind. Now was not the time. Now was when he wanted to enjoy his evening.

He looked down at himself. He should have returned home, changed his cloak and shirt, but then he hadn't done anything that would have dirtied him too much. Besides, he wasn't going to be able to take Jamie too many places within the city—not with the city as it currently was.

He met her near the Giver's bell.

She had on a pale-blue dress and clutched a bag in her hands. A wide smile spread across her face.

"I wasn't sure if you were going to come," she said.

Finn grinned at her.

"Of course I was. You told me to meet you at the bell."

She looked up at the tower. It stretched high overhead, sending a shadow streaming across the ground. "I didn't want to show up late. What should we do?"

Finn had been preoccupied and hadn't come up with a plan.

"We could walk."

She arched a brow at him. "Is that safe?"

"There are quite a few Archers out," Finn said. "But I think we should be safe."

"You would probably know. I imagine you know the Archers, as well."

"I know some," he said. Meyer's words came back to them, a reminder not to talk about his work. "I can show you some of my favorite parts of the city."

"I might be afraid to ask what those are."

"I like walking along the river."

She regarded him. "I've never found walking along rivers to be all that peaceful, but partly that comes from having to traverse them while traveling with my father." She chuckled. "He doesn't really give much thought to how difficult a journey is going to be when we take it. Oftentimes, we end up searching for just the right species of wood, and all he wants is a branch." She shook her head, smiling to herself. "But with one branch, especially of the right species of wood, and with his skill, he can sell it for so much more—at least, most of the time."

Don't talk about your job.

That was Meyer's advice. He couldn't talk about what Reginald owed her father, or anything more about him.

That would only draw up more questions about what he had been up to.

"I find the river peaceful. At least as it flows through here. I've seen other rivers in my journeys that are wilder. I probably haven't traveled nearly as far as you and your father have though." She joined him, walking alongside him and looking up at him every so often. "When I was younger, I used to come to the river—never any farther. My father had warned me not to cross the river. He always told me that the Archers would shoo me away." Thinking of that made him smile.

"Tell me about your family," she pressed.

"My father is in prison somewhere," he said. "I don't know where. I don't know what he did. And I don't know if he's still alive." He probably shouldn't have led with that. "My mother passed away a few years ago. She was sick. We did everything we could for her, but I think she was ready to go at the end. And my sister lives with me."

"She lives with you?"

There was something in the way she said it that caught his attention, though Finn wasn't sure what. "We both live with Master Meyer."

"Doesn't he have a family?"

"He lost his family. I think he likes having us around, though he would never say it. He took us in when I started working for him, and he's training my sister in healing."

"She's lucky," Jamie said.

Finn nodded. "She really is."

"When I was younger, I remember my father toiling away in a small shop. It was barely larger than a closet.

Our room was above it. A single room. There were four of us."

Four. That meant she had a sibling.

And she'd said "*were.*"

"You can ask about them," she said softly.

"That's not my place," he said.

"My older sister had an accident when I was young. She fell." She shook her head and swallowed. She still struggled with it, regardless of what she claimed. "I didn't get to know her. My father tells me stories. My mother did, too, until she got sick. Like your mother. We couldn't afford the medicine she needed, and…" She looked up at him. "You were afraid to ask about her, too."

Finn swallowed. "I suppose I was."

"Are you always afraid to ask questions?"

"Not usually."

They reached one of the bridges leading across the water, and though Finn hadn't intended to, he had brought her toward one that had been blocked by protests at one point. He turned away, and Jamie watched him.

They passed several children huddled near an alley, and Jamie turned her attention to them for a moment before pulling Finn ahead to a fruit stand. She bought several apples, some pears, and a full bag of what looked to be overly ripe blueberries.

"Are you hungry?" he asked when she'd finished haggling with the man.

"They are." She brought the fruit over to the children, who took it but darted into the shadows of the alley immediately afterward.

They walked in silence for a few more moments. When a pair of patrolling Archers appeared in the distance, she shrank in closer to him.

Finn looked over, and she smiled sheepishly.

"I don't like the way things have gotten," she whispered.

"I can't say that I do either," Finn said, looking along the alley where the children disappeared. It was a direction he'd once taken many times. From here, he knew how to reach a section of the city that was several streets over, then he could take a different path that would even reach her father's shop. "All I can tell is that people are tired of what they perceive as injustices. I've been trying to look into the Black Rose movement—"

"You think it's tied to that?"

"I don't even know anymore," he said. He tried to keep his frustration out of his words. "But people are getting hurt. That's what matters to me."

"There have been rumors," she said. "They reach us even in my father's shop. I heard some Archers were caught in one attack."

She looked over to him, and Finn nodded before guiding her across the street, into another alley. He hadn't seen anything along the other street, but he wasn't going to take any chances of getting caught in a protest. He could protect her from that.

"Archers. Protesters. Too many." And there wasn't anything Finn could do about it. He'd been trying, and felt helpless at this point. Not that he could say that to Jamie. "Has your father been impacted?"

"In a city like this, I don't see how anyone *couldn't* be impacted," she said, her voice low. They reached another street, and Finn guided her to another alley farther down. "The hard part is that I understand."

Finn was quiet as they entered the turned the corner away from the Archers. "I understand what they want too. If I hadn't left my section, I think I might be a part of the protests."

"You wouldn't be now?" She looked up at him.

"There are other ways to accomplish change."

She looked as though she wanted to debate with him, but instead smiled widely at him. "I'm happy to walk wherever you want to go, Finn, but I'd be just as happy to sit, have a drink, and just talk." She looked around. "With the city the way it is, that might be better, anyway. I don't know if you have a place that might work, but…"

He held out his arm, and she looped hers through it. "I might have a place."

She smiled at him.

And he smiled back.

He could already imagine Oscar's teasing, but it was the first place he thought of, and the only place he'd want to sit and share a drink with her.

They passed by City Hall, and Jaime pulled on his arm, but not before he noticed the corner of the building had crumbled. Had it always been like that? He paused, looking down, when shouts in the distance caught his attention.

Finn straightened and stiffened. Another protest.

How had he thought he could have an evening to himself?

"I'm afraid I might have to cut our night short."

Jaime looked up at him. "I understand."

"I wish I didn't have to. Thankfully, I think I'm close to answers. Once I get the prisoner I have in Declan to…"

Another shout rang out, followed by a brief flash of light. Flames danced against the night. It silenced Finn, who realized that he'd been talking to her almost the same way he'd talk to Esmerelda. Jaime didn't want to hear about Jonrath.

Jaime squeezed his arm. "You should go. I can tell you need to. We can do this another time."

He took her hands, squeezing them briefly. "I *am* sorry."

"Another night, then."

He nodded, hating that it had to be over so soon. If he could get the answers he needed, then the protests wouldn't keep him from the next night he planned with Jaime.

Now Finn just had to get Jonrath to talk.

CHAPTER TWENTY-THREE

Finn sat in front of Jonrath once again.

After having met with Wella, Finn had shifted the direction of his questioning. No longer did he simply want to know who he was, but he wanted to know more about who funded the Black Rose. However, in order to learn that, he couldn't simply come out and ask him.

"When we talked last, you told me your name, but little else."

Jonrath jerked on the leather bindings around his wrists and ankles. "You aren't going to find out anything else about me."

"Not unless you share it with me. Remember, we will have a conversation, if you permit it, but otherwise…" Finn's gaze drifted intentionally to the cabinet behind him, lingering there for a long moment, and when he turned back to Jonrath, he shrugged. "It is your choice."

"Go ahead. Do what you need to do to get your rocks off."

"All I want is a conversation," Finn said.

"You don't give one shit about a conversation," he said.

"You're right. I give much more than that. I would much rather have a dialogue with you than go through all of this."

"Even if I told you something, you aren't going to believe me."

"I will believe you if you tell me the truth."

"Whose truth?"

"There is only one truth," Finn said.

Jonrath leaned his head back and laughed bitterly. "See? You tell me all you care about is the truth, but you don't care about the fact that the truth is different depending on which way you look at things. My truth is different from your truth, and I guarantee you that my truth is not the kind you care anything about."

"Why don't we stick with facts and worry less about the truth?"

"Facts," he said, shaking his head again. "You don't care much about that either."

"What makes you think that?"

"Because you're here."

"Just because I'm here doesn't mean I don't care about facts," Finn said. "You could argue that my presence here would indicate that I care very much about them. Now, why don't you tell me a little bit about yourself? Maybe you can tell me where you live."

"Why? So you can go and round up my friends and

family so you can torment them the same way?" He leaned his head back and Finn anticipated him spitting on him again, but instead, he just clenched his jaw, looking as if he intended to refuse any further answers.

"That's not how I do things," Finn said.

"I've heard about you," Jonrath said.

"Yeah? Rumors have a way of spreading in the city. Not all of them are true."

"Enough of them are true," he said.

Finn studied him, trying to decide how best to approach him. At this point, he no longer knew the proper technique.

In the back of his mind were the prompts from Master Meyer, from the king, even from Esmerelda. All of them were warnings, messages to him to find answers. The king wanted the Hunter. Meyer wanted Finn to be a skilled executioner. Esmerelda wanted him to find his own way, but what did that mean?

"I won't round up any of your family, but I will question them," he said.

Jonrath watched him. "What reason should I tell you how to find them, then?"

"Because you know I'm going to find them anyway."

Jonrath laughed darkly. "You aren't going to find shit."

"You said that you heard rumors about me."

"I did."

"And what did those rumors tell you?"

"They don't tell me shit."

Finn smiled tightly. "Perhaps not. But I can tell you what I know of those rumors." He leaned forward, holding his gaze on Jonrath, forcing him to meet Finn's eyes. "You would have heard rumors of my persistence. If there's anything that I'm known for, it's stubbornness. When I have a nugget of truth, I keep digging and digging until I dislodge it in its entirety. In your case, I know there's a nugget of truth in what I have already uncovered. And I will keep digging."

"So?"

Finn leaned back. "So you either give me the opportunity to approach those who know you and find the truth about the Black Rose, or you force me to find them on my own." He left the threat there and waited.

Jonrath didn't say anything, and he gave Finn no reaction, but Finn wasn't sure what he might do anyway.

"If you hurt any of them…"

"Yes?"

Jonrath regarded him for a long moment before shaking his head.

Finn just smiled again, making a tight expression as he watched him. "That is your choice. Not a choice I would make, but I respect that it is your choice." He got to his feet. "What I ask of you today is far simpler than what I asked of you before. I only want to know about the Black Rose." Finn looked over his shoulder at Jonrath as he moved past, heading toward the cabinets. "Anything you know."

He needed information. The attacks in the city would only escalate.

He *needed* to find the members of the Black Rose movement.

This was what the king had asked of him.

Something more *was* taking place. The slender rod might simply be a weapon—but it *might* be something more. He didn't know if this was connected to what he'd faced with Holden and Elizabeth Jarvis when they had attacked the city with magic, or something altogether different.

He returned to the stool. "I might have been a little too eager," Finn said.

The man glowered at him. "Now you're thinking you were too eager?"

"I thought I could get you to share a bit about yourself with me—so I could understand you." He reached into his pocket and pulled out the rod, tapping it on his hand. "That was a mistake. You see, I think I already understand all I need to about who you are. And I can see you're hesitant to speak about the Black Rose." Finn needed to find something to help with that, but he kept coming up with nothing. He held the rod up. "Why don't we get into where you acquired this?"

Jonrath's gaze lingered on the rod, though not for long. He turned his attention back to Finn, then looked down, as if to try to work free of the leathers holding him in the chair.

"Do you remember what I told you about what happened in this space?"

The man glowered at him again.

"That's right." He held out the rod. Wand? He couldn't tell. To get him to talk, Finn would have to reveal more. "We've had others who thought to use something similar to this. They were stopped." Finn rested the wand in front of him. "I don't suppose you know the name Holden?"

He watched for any sign of reaction, but either Jonrath didn't know the name or he was skilled enough to avoid reacting. It could be either.

Esmerelda's conversation after the sentencing came back to him. She had been concerned about something more—something worse than Holden. And he had been incredibly difficult for them to deal with. If there was something else coming, another attack that would be similar, Finn needed to do whatever he could to stop it. The problem was that he didn't know what it would take or whether he was even the right person to do so. He wasn't magically powered. The sword Justice might have enough power in its blade to do so, but him?

He didn't have answers. That left Finn irritated, which wasn't the right frame of mind to be in to do what he needed to do, but that didn't change the fact that it needed doing.

Finn thought about a different tactic.

"Have you heard of ostia and melander?"

He said it casually, but watched Jonrath nonetheless. Lena suddenly coming into a supply of ostia and melander —two rare medicines—might be connected to the movement, though he wondered if he were just grasping for answers now.

"Are they flowers?"

Jonrath seemed genuinely confused. Maybe there was nothing to that.

Finn sighed. If there wasn't anything to that, then he

had to get back to his original concern: money. "Someone is funding the Black Rose. That's what I need to know about," Finn went on. "Share what you can."

"I'm not telling you shit."

Finn held on to the wand, tapping it on his hand as he regarded him. Someone had to be financially supporting the movement. There were posters. Pamphlets. Organization. If he could find the money, he thought he could uncover the truth about the Black Rose—and bring the answers the king wanted.

When Jonrath stared at him defiantly, Finn finally let out a sigh. "I'm afraid that's not acceptable to me, so we will continue the questioning process."

The iron masters dragged Jonrath away, and Finn didn't have any clearer answers about what he might have been responsible for doing than he had before. He rarely encountered someone so determined to avoid answering questions. Any at all. His refusal was all the answer Finn needed about whether he was guilty. The problem was that Finn didn't know what he was guilty of.

He reached the main hall in Declan and came across one of the iron masters he had once been friendly with. There had been a time when Finn had tried to be friendly with all of them, but that had proven to be a mistake. There wasn't anyone in the city with whom he should connect. Not anymore.

"You come to see the bastard responsible for killing those Archers?" Norem asked.

He was a smallish man, though looked to have a strong frame. All iron masters had to have a certain physicality to them in order to do their job; otherwise, they'd be over-powered by their charges.

"What man is that?"

"Ah. Thought you heard already and that was why you were here. Just brought him in. Got caught after the last protest. Damn thing burned down two shops and trampled a few other bastards."

Finn just nodded. He'd been there for part of that protest—and had been more involved than he had wanted to be. He kept waiting for the Archers to react to the killings, but with the Palace Archers now a part of the patrols, there was a more militaristic approach.

Still, all of this felt like kindling getting ready to be set on fire. All it needed was a light.

"When did he come in?" Finn asked.

"Not long ago. He's down in his cell."

Finn nodded and veered off. He'd probably need to question him, but first he figured he would try to see if he could uncover anything from him by just seeing him in captivity. The lower level of Declan had a stench to it. Today it seemed worse. There was something almost rotten about the odor.

Finn wrinkled his nose, nodding to the pair of iron masters who had dragged Jonrath back to his cell and had taken guard near the stairs, before heading along the row of cells.

Declan was designed specifically to be a prison, not at all like what he'd seen from Hecindan prison, a place that had been converted from something else. Declan was stout, impenetrable, and the rows of cells were designed to be as unpleasant as possible while containing the prisoners.

He stopped in front of a cell that held a man he didn't recognize. The black metal bars of the cell were thick, nearly four fingers across. Men had scraped at the metal over the years, leaving some of it grooved, though because of the thickness of the bars, it made little difference.

He looked between the bars, peering at the man.

He was young, barely twenty years old. He had a bit of scruff to his cheeks, dirtiness to his arms and legs, and close-cropped hair. He was dressed in the prison gray, and cowered in the back of the cell.

"What's your name?" Finn called through the bars.

"He won't talk. That one is too precious to say much of anything."

Finn looked over his shoulder to see Olivan, his hands gripping the bars. The older man had been imprisoned in Declan for the last few years, held here as his sentence. It was a foul sentence, but one that was deserved given his crimes. Olivan was a repeat offender, having stolen from people all over the city. He had another year left of his sentence, then he would be released. At that point, Finn had no idea what would befall him. Somebody like Olivan, someone who had been imprisoned as long as he had, might not know what to do with himself other than live in the prison.

"Stay out of it," Finn said.

Olivan laughed and banged his hands on the bars. "Listen to the hangman. Gets all excited when he got a new charge to question."

"Not excited," Finn said, turning away from Olivan and looking into the cell.

"What's your name?" Finn asked again.

The boy looked up, a hint of uncertainty in his eyes. "Walter Briggs, sir."

Finn grunted. He recognized the name. Worse, he knew why.

He was from the Brinder section. Finn hadn't known him well, but he *had* known him. When Finn had last lived in the section, Walter had been a young man, barely into his early teens, running through the streets, and now…

He looked through the bars of the cell, regarding the boy with a renewed interest; he took in the sight of him, trying to measure something about him.

This was somebody who'd killed an Archer?

Finn had been around killers before and Walter didn't seem the type, though he knew accidents could happen.

"Come over here," Finn said.

The boy looked up, locking eyes with him. "Is it time?"

"Time for what?" Finn asked.

"Time for me. You're here to execute me, aren't you?"

Finn frowned and shook his head. "That's not how it works."

"But he called you the hangman."

"Because I am," Finn said.

"So you *are* here to take me."

"I'm not here to take you, but I can't deny that you might be sentenced. It remains to be seen what that sentencing will be."

"I deserve anything that happens to me," he said, his words soft, reserved.

"Why do you say that?" Finn asked.

"Because I..." He looked down at his pants and picked at the fabric. "I did it. That's what you want to hear? I did what they said I did."

"You killed the Archers?"

"I did."

There were times when Finn got confessions easily, though lately, most of the confessions he got were forced, requiring him to work at them. Getting one so simply, hearing it from Walter in this way, was almost anti-climactic.

It made up for how difficult it had been with Jonrath.

"You will come with me," Finn said. He nodded to the iron masters at the end of the cell. "Bring him up to the chapel. He doesn't need to be strapped."

At the mention of strapping, the boy's eyes widened, and he started backing away from the bars of the cell.

Finn just grunted.

He headed through the prison, making his way up the stairs, back to the chapel, and paused. The room stank from when Jonrath had been here, and it was more than just the stench of somebody who had been imprisoned for a while. It was the stink of rot.

He hadn't noticed it before, but maybe having come through the hallways made him much more acutely aware of it now, or maybe it was simply the fact that it didn't smell quite right.

He covered his nose.

Could he really be getting that sensitive to smells? Finn had to come to Declan regularly, so there was no getting away from the smells of this place. He didn't have to like them.

It didn't take long before the iron masters brought the boy in and tossed him into the chair. He looked up at them, his eyes wide, before jerking his head around and looking at Finn, taking in the sight of the metal implements resting on the counter. There was a purpose in having them there, and the boy started whimpering immediately.

Finn looked over to the iron masters. "You can go."

"Are you sure?"

"He's not going anywhere," Finn said.

They nodded and pulled the door closed, leaving Finn with the boy.

"Why don't we start with you telling me where you're from?"

It was the same conversation he'd been having with Jonrath, and while that had gone slowly, almost painfully, he at least felt he could get somewhere with this boy.

"I'm in the Brinder section."

Why did it have to be Brinder?

"What street do you live on?"

"Graned Street. It's a small house. My papa tried to keep it up as well as he could, but when he got sick, he wasn't able to do it."

Finn pulled the stool over and took a seat in front of the boy. "Tell me what happened."

"You already know what happened. I'm sure of it. That's the only reason they have me here, isn't it?"

"Tell me what happened," Finn said again.

The boy shook his head and craned his neck, looking behind him toward the counter. "You don't need to use any of that stuff. I'll tell you what you need to know. I'll tell you whatever you want to hear."

"What I want to hear is what happened," Finn said.

"I… I got caught up in the crowd. We all did. When the protests came through, we sort of slipped into it. They were heading out to the old temple in the Brinder section. It's a small building, a place where the ancients celebrated the old gods."

Finn stared at him.

This was a different killing. One he hadn't heard about before.

The protests had persisted, despite the king increasing the Archer presence in the city. There was a limit to how long everything would simmer before it fully exploded.

Another Archer dying…

Gods. What's going to happen now?

Finn knew the place. And it was more than just an old temple where the old gods were celebrated. It was a place of the Alainsith. There were many places like that throughout the city.

"And?"

"And everything sort of got chaotic. A building nearby was burning. We were shouting. And then the Archers came. I threw something. Didn't see where I threw it, or what I threw it at, but they tell me that it hit one of the Archers on the head, and it... it killed him." His voice trailed off at the end, though he had been speaking quickly, almost as if to get out everything as fast as he could. "I didn't mean to kill one of the Archers," Walter said. "I was just caught up."

"How many were with you?"

"How many what?"

"Protesters?" Finn asked.

"There were a bunch of them. The streets were filled. Never seen anything like it. Not too many people want to come into the Brinder section. Those who do usually want to get out, you know?"

"Yes," Finn said.

"Anyway," Walter said, looking up at him and holding his gaze. "I just went along. I mean, who wouldn't want to go along when they are demanding more? I want the same thing as everybody wants. I want to make it out of my section. I never wanted to hurt anyone, though," he said, his voice dropping to a whisper.

Finn sighed. He pushed the stool back, placing it along the wall, and glanced over to the tools. None of them would be needed.

Worse, nothing this boy knew would help Finn understand what had been taking place in the city. He was just one more person who'd gotten caught up in the current, a pebble washed along in the stream of people.

"You will be brought before the jurors. They will decide your fate," Finn said.

"What's going to happen to me?"

Finn wished he could tell the boy anything but the truth. "If you didn't hit the Archer, you'll be fine, but if you killed him, then you'll likely be sentenced to hang."

Walter started whimpering.

"I'm sorry."

He stared at the boy for a moment and realized just how similar his experience was to Finn's. Had Finn been in the Brinder section under similar circumstances, wouldn't he have done something like that?

Finn couldn't deny that he would. He knew the kinds of things he would've done, knew how he had felt—and he knew he would have been just as likely to have thrown a rock, trying to rage at his place in the world.

And he also knew it wouldn't have made a damn bit of difference. As he pulled the door open, glancing out to the iron masters, he wondered if perhaps that was the point.

Regardless of who was a part of the Black Rose movement, or why they organized the protests, they fed on emotions that existed within the city. They were emotions that a part of Finn still held, even though he had escaped from that fate—at least, mostly—but just because he had didn't mean that others could.

And how was he supposed to carry out the king's justice when he wasn't completely convinced that it *was* justice?

CHAPTER TWENTY-FOUR

Finn hadn't been back to the Brinder section in a while. There wasn't much reason to, most of the time. He didn't have anything in the section anymore. His sister was with him at Master Meyer's home, and he didn't have any friends in the section. He did have a few friends there when he'd been growing up, but by the time he had started working with the crew, Finn didn't interact with anybody in his old section.

It was strange coming back here. Stranger still was knowing he didn't fit there the way he once did. Even his clothing didn't fit, which made Finn question whether he should change into clothes that were more suited for the Brinder section. He had on flowing pants, a custom-stitched shirt, and a black-dyed leather belt. All of that would've been far too expensive for him to have afforded when he was younger.

Not that Finn hadn't been able to afford anything.

Stealing had afforded him a lifestyle and a measure of comfort that he wouldn't have been able to have otherwise, though Finn wasn't necessarily proud of the fact that he had been a thief. He had learned much, though—how to survive, how to fend for himself, and he had learned that he was the only one who would care for him. The world didn't care for him, and the gods certainly didn't care for him.

Only, Finn had been wrong. Others did care for him.

Oscar had always cared about him, though Finn had taken that for granted. He had ignored his oldest friend's intention, mistreating it and abusing it, much like he had mistreated and abused so many other things when he was young. Time had given him insight and wisdom, but not all would get that time. Finn almost hadn't. The boy certainly wouldn't.

There was no reason for him to come to the Brinder section. Nothing that would provide him with any greater insight as to what Walter had been doing. Still, Finn couldn't help it. He felt compelled to come out here to see what had taken place—and perhaps also to be reminded of who he had been.

He'd finished his errands at Tahn's general store before coming here, which was probably a mistake. His satchel nearly burst with items that he and Meyer needed, along with a few extras he'd purchased.

The streets were narrower here than in many of the other sections, and the houses more rundown. They were almost to the outer wall surrounding the city, and the slaughterhouse in the section that gave it much of its stench. Even now, Finn could smell the odor from the slaughterhouse, a mixture of the coppery scent of blood and the overwhelming stink of meat and death. Several butchers and smokehouses surrounded the slaughter-house, as if to try to smoke out its smell, but they didn't manage to succeed.

Thankfully, there weren't many people out in the streets. Considering recent events, especially the protest and how the Archers had suppressed it, Finn wasn't surprised. But he was surprised by the heaviness of the patrols in this area. Most of the time, the Archers left the poorer sections of the city alone. Partly that was out of graft. Many of the Archers in these outer sections were paid—well, bribed—to shift their patrols, to avoid crews that might be operating, but now he wondered if the Archers would finally stop that behavior.

It was difficult for them to avoid it, though. Archers were not paid well, and while Finn didn't know exactly how much they made, he understood the need to supple-ment income. How could a man provide for his family when he could barely afford food?

Finn headed toward the old temple.

That was where the protests had congregated. That was where the Archer had died.

That was where he needed to go.

Mostly, he felt he needed to go so that he could see where the Archer had died and he could feel as if he had done his due diligence to ensure he had looked into all aspects of what Walter had told him.

Finn should have known better than that, though. He

should know that heading here now, allowing himself to be drawn out here, had little bearing on anything else.

It *wasn't* what he needed to be doing. It wasn't the way the Hunter needed to be searching. The Hunter needed to be looking for answers. He needed to be investigating Jonrath—what he told him and his influence on coordinating these attacks.

Finn slowed and frowned to himself. In the distance, a lamplighter lit one of the rare streetlights in the Brinder section, holding the flame high overhead, his hands trembling and his gaze drifting in either direction, as if he was afraid he might get jumped.

Even such simple work was dangerous in these times.

What if he brought Walter and Jonrath together to see what they might say to each other? It might lead him nowhere, but there was the possibility that idle conversation would give him answers he hadn't uncovered anywhere else.

He could certainly arrange for them to have cells close together, and perhaps he might find some answers by doing so. He could pitch the iron masters nearby and see if they might overhear anything.

He didn't know how much time he would have though. Once the jurors met to discuss Walter, he suspected the sentence would be swift. They would have two days, three at the most, to prepare the gallows for the festival, and then what?

Given the current climate, Finn was uncomfortable with what might happen. A festival would draw attention, and it would bring out the kind of people who would

THE EXECUTIONER'S REBELLION | 389

likely still resent the injustices in the kingdom. The festival would certainly further the belief that the king doesn't care about those in the outer sections.

Most of the time, the gallows festivals were meant to be a way of encouraging people to reflect upon their own behavior and deter crime, but if they were to hang Walter publicly…

Finn didn't know if it would still have the desired effect. Given everything that had been going on in the city, it might actually work against them. He would have to talk to Master Meyer about it.

Finn headed onward. When he reached the streetlight, he looked up. Night had not yet started to fall, but the lamplighter was already out?

It suggested that not only was the lamplighter concerned, but the section chiefs were concerned enough to permit the lamplighters to come out this early. It meant using more oil, but if it prevented further attacks…

Several of the buildings along the street had their windows caved in. The people here didn't have the same wealth as others had in different sections, and many of the damaged windows had been left open, not boarded up in the same way the others had been.

Finn passed a row of houses that reminded him of where he'd grown up—they were damaged in some places and looked as if the people who lived there wouldn't be safe, not with their windows cracked open like that.

None of this would be safe.

None of this would be fixable, either. The people in the Brinder section didn't have the money to do so. The poor became poorer. And that alone was depressing to Finn. So far, all of the attacks had been in the poorer sections of the city—none had occurred in any of the wealthier sections.

Maybe that was only because of the Archers who guarded those sections, and the fact that many of those central sections of the city had hired their own security, but what if there was something else to it?

Finn had to stop seeing shadows that weren't there; he had to stop seeing connections that didn't exist. It was a crime of convenience, little more than that. They committed the crime because this was where they could do it. This was where the people had gathered. This was where the people were angriest.

He found himself heading toward the old temple and stared when he finally stopped at it. It was growing dark, the day starting to fade, and he hadn't given much thought to this place in many years. He remembered when he was a child climbing over the stone and the mossy surface, jumping down the street. This was one of the few places where children's laughter could be heard. Few people grumbled when kids ran around the old temple. The old gods weren't celebrated here anymore, and even if they were, the temple itself had faded into disrepair. Still, the stone was mostly intact, though much of the stonework of the old Alainsith buildings remained intact.

He didn't see any sign of violence here.

Whatever had happened was gone. The evidence faded. There was nothing other than the emptiness of the streets. Finn clasped his hands together, staring.

As he wandered through the temple, he couldn't shake the feeling of something bothering him. This was the kind of thing that Meyer would never have done, but it was the kind of irritant that Finn simply couldn't ignore.

He didn't understand *what* bothered him, exactly, and he didn't know why, but something prompted him to look.

As he studied the broken remains of the ancient temple, he saw that it was starting to crumble—not quite like what he saw in the village outside of the city, nor like the Alainsith building he'd seen when he'd been with Esmerelda. There was something about this that left him feeling a bit unsettled.

"Even now, you keep coming out here."

Finn spun, turning toward the voice that came out of the darkness, and shook his head. "Dammit, Oscar. What are you doing?"

"The same as you, I suppose. A friend of mine asked me to see what I could uncover."

"This friend of yours doesn't want you to put yourself in any danger," Finn finally said.

"There's no danger, Finn." Oscar looked toward the distant streetlight. "I know you think there's some mysterious connection taking place, but that's not what I'm finding. People are angry." Oscar shrugged. "People are always angry, but for whatever reason, they decided to do something about it this time."

"It's one thing to be angry," Finn said, "but now people are dying."

"People are always dying too."

Finn just shook his head. He wasn't nearly as prag-
matic as Oscar. Maybe that was part of the problem.

"You know that's all they want," Oscar said. "That's the
entire purpose behind the movement. I know you want to
think there's some grand conspiracy behind everything,
the same way I've heard the Hunter believes there's a
grand conspiracy behind everything, but I've started to
think this is nothing more than what it appears. Oh, the
Black Rose might be real enough, but this is about men
and women fed up with their station." Oscar watched him
for a moment. "Time was that you felt the same way."

Finn regarded him, unsure what he could say in
response. Maybe there really wasn't anything to say in
response. Oscar was right. There had been a time when
Finn had felt much the same way. To be honest, he still
understood those sentiments even now. The people in the
outer sections, the poorer parts of the city, had very little,
and they rarely had an opportunity to rise beyond their
station. Those who did…

They ended up abused. They struggled. Or they
remained shunned, much like Finn was typically shunned.

None of that made it any better, though. None of that
solved problems. All it did was cause more problems.

He looked over to Oscar, and all he saw was his friend
and the disappointment in his eyes, along with a reflection
of the anger that Finn had once felt. It was an anger he
had seen in the protesters.

Oscar was like all of those protesters.

He was a thief trying to rise above his station in life.
That was the reason behind his club. If not for his thieving

crew, and the days spent in the underbelly of the city, Oscar wouldn't have even had that opportunity.

"It has to stop, Oscar."

"I'm not sure it can be stopped," he said. "Short of the king taking more decisive action, I doubt anything can be stopped."

Finn couldn't shake the feeling that there was more to the situation than what there appeared to be on the surface—not only because of the wand he had recovered from Jonrath, but also because of the men who had circulated through the crowd, directing the protestors.

"Were you here before?" Finn asked.

"No. I was at the Wenderwolf. Heard there was a gathering though. I think most in the sections heard."

"An Archer was killed."

"You mean another."

Finn nodded. "We don't know who killed the last ones, but we know those were revenge killings. The Archers kept a handle on that." *For now*, Finn thought, though he wondered how long that could be the case. "This one is different. The boy responsible is probably going to hang."

Oscar took a step toward him, the wind catching his gray cloak hanging around his shoulders. "Why does it look like that bothers you?"

"I'm not sure why. He was from this section. He got caught up in the crowd. He threw a rock. And—"

"And you can't do anything to help him."

Finn looked over, nodding. "There's nothing that *can* help him. He committed the crime."

"He reminds me of someone else I know."

"I committed the crime, as well," Finn said.

"Not one that deserved hanging."

Finn turned toward the temple, shaking his head. "I know." That was what bothered him the most. "If the boy was caught up in the crowd, I'm not sure he deserves hanging, either."

"Even though he killed a man?"

"Even though," Finn said softly.

"I doubt the king is going to be too pleased with that assessment."

"I don't make the decision," Finn said. "I present him to the jurors, recommend sentencing, but…" Finn shook his head again. He had little doubt how the jurors were going to react in this case.

The jurors were comprised of men and women from the wealthier sections. There were no representatives from the poorer sections, and though the magister was there to ensure the king's rule of law was applied equally, that didn't always happen.

"I remember coming out here with your father."

"My father again?"

"I haven't given up on him," Oscar said.

"I haven't either," Finn said softly.

"Haven't you?"

Finn shot him a hard glare. "There's only so much that I can do in my position. You're better equipped to help him than I am."

"I know," Oscar said.

"Why did you and my father come out here?"

"It was an easy place to meet. And before we'd established ourselves, it was an easy place to hide." He nodded to the stone. "These old buildings are stronger than you would think."

"They're Alainsith," Finn said.

"Is that right?"

"There are Alainsith buildings all throughout the city," Finn said.

"Not too many like this," Oscar said. "Most of those are near the palace."

Finn nodded. Most of them were. City Hall was one of the largest of the Alainsith structures, and the king had turned it into something of prominence within the city.

"You only came out here to figure out whether this boy did it?" Oscar asked him.

"No. He admitted to what he did."

"Then why did you come here?"

"I don't know," Finn said. "Maybe because I want to know that there's a reason behind things, or maybe because he reminded me of myself, or maybe because all of this has me questioning my purpose." He said the last part of his statement softly, and he looked over to Oscar, shaking his head. Or maybe because he wasn't the kind of Hunter who the king—or Meyer—believed him to be. He had his own way of searching and following up on what bothered him. "It probably shouldn't, but I can't help it. With everything that's been going on, I start to wonder if I'm really serving justice or not."

"You have to decide what you want to follow."

"I thought I knew," Finn said.

"And now?"

"Some think the king's authority is absolute," Finn said. "Others believe the king serves on behalf of the gods."

"I think the king follows his own guidance," Oscar said.

"He does, and I guess the question is whether we serve him, or whether we serve the people he's supposed to rule."

What was more, Finn wondered if he could do both.

He felt as if he needed to somehow find a way to do both, though he didn't know what that would take or how he could even do it.

"You don't have to follow me," Finn said to Oscar.

"I wasn't following you," Oscar replied.

Finn arched a brow at him. "You wouldn't have found me so easily otherwise."

Oscar grunted softly and stepped toward Finn. "You really aren't all that difficult to find, Finn. You head through the streets, dressed the way you are, and don't even pay any attention to the Archers." Oscar turned from side to side, glancing in either direction along the street, and hunched slightly, as if to conceal his height. "Not too many people in this section don't even give the Archers a second look. You look like you're royalty yourself."

"You know that's not true."

"I know you have protection that others don't."

"If I committed a crime, I would face the same sentencing as anyone else."

"Are you sure?"

"You know I would."

"Let's see. Here's a man who has broken into the

viscount's manor and sentenced to hang. He was rescued, then given the opportunity to serve the king directly." Oscar looked over to him. "He is given access and resources that others would kill for, and with those access and resources, he's uncovered… what, do you think?"

"A plot against the kingdom," Finn said. "An attempt to destroy much of the city."

"What you call 'a plot against the kingdom' some would call a chance for a revolution."

"That's not the kind of revolution they should be having," Finn said.

"Maybe not," Oscar turned away. He stepped back in the shadows, moving away from the temple—away from Finn. "You need to stop thinking there is more to this than there is. You have an angry populace. That's all this is." Oscar tipped his head slightly, then he backed even farther away, disappearing into the shadows.

Standing here in this section, looking all around, Finn still felt as if there was more going on than he knew. He didn't see any sign of blood on the cobblestones, nothing to indicate the fallen Archer. There was nothing notable here. No sign of the commotion that would've come through. No sign of the protests, other than the broken windows along the street.

No sign of anything.

He made a small circuit around the temple, then stopped again.

It was time for him to head back.

The streets were dark. Quiet. Finn moved quickly along them, glancing every so often down side streets before hurrying forward to get back to Master Meyer's home. He'd been away for too long.

He hadn't gone very far when he thought he saw someone behind him. At first, Finn thought maybe it was Oscar trailing him, but Oscar wouldn't be quite so obvious.

Finn knew the streets of the Brinder section; even though he hadn't lived here in years, he still knew his way around them. He knew the alleys too. There had been a time when he'd run through these alleys, picking his way around them to sneak as quickly as he could. When he was younger, his father had practically encouraged it, and as he had gotten older, it was part of the game Finn had played with himself so he could know the city better. In his mind, he needed to know the alleys and streets better than any of the Archers in case he was pinched.

When he turned a corner, he caught sight of shadows moving.

Three figures headed along the street—Archers.

They had a much different appearance than usual, and rarely patrolled in threes, though given the current climate, maybe it would be safer for them to have more patrols. Considering the potential for attack, he could understand why they would have wanted to do so, but that didn't seem to be the case.

Finn ducked into a nearby alley. He backed along it, wrinkling his nose at the foul odor—stale water mixed with mold, and trash piled up into the alley.

He waited.

He didn't see anyone. Maybe they hadn't been Archers.

Archers would've made a steady circuit, and they wouldn't have moved under the cover of darkness like those men had. Or women.

Finn considered going farther down the alley, but it smelled terrible, and he had no interest in trudging along it. He waited until he was convinced there was no other movement, then he hurried forward, out into the street, and nearly collided with one of the figures he'd seen.

It *was* three men.

One of them had a small insignia on his cloak, and Finn stared for a moment, realizing almost too late what it was.

The Black Rose.

They have to be with the Black Rose.

The man had his cloak's hood up to cover his face and held a long wooden staff. The other two men were older and burly, with dark hair, dark eyes, and tattered, worn clothing that had no insignia.

They could be from Brinder.

"Lookee here. What do we have?" The man took a step toward Finn, leaning in, and Finn caught a wafting stench coming off of him.

He backed toward the alley.

"My name is—"

The man didn't give him a chance to answer.

He lunged at Finn.

He was quick—quicker than Finn would've expected given his size and the way he was dressed.

Finn spun, turning to the alley.

The other tried to block him off, not giving him any place to go.

"You don't look like any Archer," the other said, his voice a low drawl. "But he's got the smell of money."

"Probably an Archer."

They couldn't really think he was an Archer, but knowing what had taken place earlier in the day, Finn wasn't about to linger. He had the alley to his back and the two men blocking his way, but neither of them really drew his attention—not like the man holding the wooden staff with his hood covering his face.

Someone with that insignia on his cloak would have to know something. If only Finn could capture him to learn what.

"You shouldn't be out," Finn said.

The man who had first spoken to him laughed. "See? Even speaks like he's trying to be an Archer."

Finn looked along the street. There was no sign of any actual Archers, though given the time of day, and the protests that occurred earlier, there should have been some here. There should be some way for him to have safety, but…

He was going to have to run.

The other two men converged upon him, lunging toward him. Finn darted back.

Doors opened along the street. Finn caught sight of them for only a moment before he turned and started down the alley. He raced along, reaching a side street, but the men were behind him, coming quickly.

He wouldn't have much time.

Finn looked over his shoulder.

From here, he wasn't going to be able to reach Meyer's home. He was going to need to take a different route back.

Shouts rang out behind him.

As he hurried along the alley, more doors along the street opened. A crowd was forming.

Finn raced as quickly as he could, trying to stay ahead of the crowd, before veering in a different direction. Somebody threw something at him, striking him in the back.

He stumbled, catching himself, then lumbered forward.

He looked around. Panic started to set in.

It was strange that he would feel so panicked in the Brinder section. He could take a right, and it would lead him toward the Olin section, and the Wenderwolf tavern.

He would draw attention to the tavern if he didn't get away from here.

Finn had to get even farther ahead of the crowd.

A wave of people began to follow him, and as he ran, he looked for signs of Archers, but there were none. Finn started taking side streets, heading toward the central section of the city. If he could reach that part of the city, he could find Archers.

This is ridiculous. The idea that he would be running through the city, away from protesters, left him feeling as if he were a criminal himself.

He whistled, trying to draw attention from some of the Archers.

He caught sight of a bridge leading over the river and knew he could find Archers from there.

Another group of protesters appeared in front of him, and Finn veered away, darting toward another side street. As he popped over the street, he looked toward the bridge in the distance, but a crowd had formed that prevented him from heading through.

He reached another section where the crowd grew thicker and was forced back.

He wasn't going to be able to reach Meyer's home until the crowd settled down. All around him were the sound of shouts and occasional screams, as well as flames that lit up the night sky.

He couldn't stay here.

Maybe there was someplace else he could go.

Finn hoped the hegen would welcome him while he waited out the protests. When it calmed down, he would have to get back to work.

CHAPTER TWENTY-FIVE

Finn reached the Teller Gate and found it guarded by only a small number of Archers. He hurried through, pausing for just a moment to make sure nobody was following him before jogging into the distance. The hegen section glowed with pale light, and as he rushed over to it, he paused at the Raven Stone long enough to look at it for a moment, then tore his gaze away.

He watched behind him, but saw no sign of anybody coming out of the Teller Gate.

There was no reason for it.

Finn reached the outskirts of the hegen section.

Music filled the air, a stark contrast to what he had experienced in the city. There was a joyousness here, a festivity, a happiness, and as he headed in, Finn couldn't help but feel as if a wave of relaxation struck him—as if the hegen section itself had some sort of magic that sent him into that state.

He breathed out as he jogged along the street, hurrying toward Esmerelda's home, and when he reached it, he knocked. It was late enough that he worried how she would react to his presence.

The door opened and Esmerelda greeted him with a wide smile. She had on a white gown, cinched at the waist with a maroon sash, and her black hair hung loose around her shoulders.

"Finn. I was not expecting to see you this evening."

"May I come in?"

"Do you need something?"

Finn looked over her shoulder. In the distance, he could see a hint of orange on the horizon, evidence of the flames in the city.

"Safety. And I brought you something."

Esmerelda frowned.

"I was bringing this for your school," he started, pulling out the colored chalk he'd found in Tahn's. "Then I got caught up in a protest in the city."

"I see," she said, taking the chalk. "Thank you. The children will appreciate your gift." She smiled and some of the pale moonlight reflected off her cheeks. "You may come in, but I'm afraid that I have been working with someone, so you may have to wait until we are completed."

She escorted him inside, where he found a man about his age, with pale skin and neatly combed black hair that matched Esmerelda's. He wore a deep-blue jacket with yellow pants and sat in a chair in her kitchen, lounging back with a mug of tea.

He glanced over to Finn. "Who might this be?" the man asked.

Esmerelda nodded to Finn. "Themen, this is Finn Jagger. Finn Jagger, this is Themen Mavoy." She headed into the kitchen, lifted a pitcher, and poured a mug of tea for Finn, which she then handed to him. "You may sit in the other room until we are finished," Esmerelda said.

Finn took the mug and carried it to a chair in the other room. Her home was always tidy, and this time was no different. She had the comfortable, brightly colored carpet, and the table ringed with chairs. A shelf beside it displayed strange carvings.

Finn took the chair and sipped at the tea.

There was a time when he would've hesitated to take tea from the hegen, especially from Esmerelda, but he trusted her.

Obviously. He had found himself coming here, of all places.

What did that say about him?

It said that he felt safest with Esmerelda.

At least, relatively safe.

Finn glanced toward the window that looked over the street. A curtain was drawn, and he couldn't see much, though the sound of music drifted along and came through the door. The hegen music was always buoyant and festive, filled with the sounds of horns and strings, along with the distinct, staccato sounds of the voices that sang with it. Finn tapped his foot as he listened.

He tried not to listen to Esmerelda and Themen, but curiosity overwhelmed him.

"You must focus," Esmerelda said.

"You don't want me to focus," Themen said. "In fact, I think you called me here for something else."

Finn glanced back before shaking his head and turning his attention back to the window. Esmerelda wanted a measure of privacy, he was sure, even if she would never demand that. She wouldn't have allowed Finn inside if she was concerned about him overhearing anything.

"I called you here because you are reported to have some talent," Esmerelda said.

"Is that what you call it?"

Esmerelda fell silent.

Finn suspected she said something more, though he couldn't hear what it was.

Themen laughed. "There it is. There's the fire I expected out of you."

Finn couldn't help himself; he looked over his shoulder.

Themen seemed to sense him looking and he turned in Finn's direction, grinning widely. He winked, then turned back to Esmerelda, leaning toward her, touching her knee.

There was something far too familiar about the gesture for Finn. Not that he felt as if he had any ownership of Esmerelda, but he wouldn't have expected her to welcome that kind of touch.

Esmerelda got to her feet. "Seeing as how Finn has come and does need some assistance, perhaps the two of us can continue this conversation later."

Themen chuckled. "I'd like that. Would you like me to come back in an hour?"

"I was thinking you would give it a few days," Esmerelda said.

"I don't know if you really want me to wait a few days," Themen said.

Esmerelda tipped her head to the door. "I believe you can show yourself out."

He chuckled and sauntered toward the door, glancing over to Finn one more time before winking and stepping out into the night. He whistled as he did, his voice joining the hegen song.

Finn got to his feet, holding on to the mug of tea. He turned to Esmerelda. "I'm sorry if I interrupted."

"I had the understanding that he had an interest in learning about the art, but..."

"I think he's interested in you," Finn said.

She sighed. "It might not be entirely his fault. There are some who believe it's time for me to choose. You aren't of the people," Esmerelda said. "And I suppose you can't and don't understand."

"I understand feeling like you need to find someone."

Esmerelda watched him for a moment, then she turned away, heading back to the kitchen. "Would you like to take a seat?"

"I shouldn't have interrupted," Finn said.

"You should have done whatever you needed to do, Finn," she said.

"I wasn't sure what to do," he admitted. He joined her in the kitchen. He deeply inhaled the steam and scent of the tea, then breathed out in a sigh. "I was looking into a man who had died in the Brinder section, then I was nearly attacked."

"I believe that section is familiar to you."

"That's where I was raised," he said.

"That is what I thought," Esmerelda said. She poured another mug of tea and turned toward Finn, smiling tightly. "You look as if it troubles you."

"It troubles me that I didn't feel safe there."

"Was it a safe section of the city?"

Finn took a seat, and Esmerelda joined him, setting her mug of tea on the table. She looked at him, a brightness in her eyes.

"No," Finn said. "It wasn't. At the time, I didn't know any better, and it was only after I left that I really began to know anything about safety."

"A child should feel safe," Esmerelda said.

"Are the children of the hegen section safe?"

"The hegen children are prized," she said. She took a sip of her tea, setting it down again. "You saw the school."

"Is that where you learned?"

Her eyes narrowed slightly before relaxing again. "My experience was different."

"You called it the art," Finn said.

"Yes."

"Not magic."

"You may call it magic, if that is more comfortable for you."

"I want to refer to it by its proper terminology."

Esmerelda smiled. "Very few people find that matters."

"Considering how much you have helped me, and how

much of an interaction there is between my line of work and yours, I prefer to respect what you call it."

"You may call it magic, Finn. What is magic but the unexplained?"

"But you called it art."

"I called it *the* art. There are many forms of art, as you have seen from the displays my people have created."

"The murals?"

"Those are an example of one of the forms," she said.

"The music?"

She smiled, tipping her head to the side, and drummed her fingers on the table for a moment, working them in time to the sounds that Finn could hear just beyond the walls of the home. "That is another form. My people find that there are many reasons to celebrate, and not all are tied to the gallows."

"I wouldn't have accused them of that," Finn said.

"Perhaps not you, but others would have."

Finn chuckled. "You have craftspeople who have their own sort of work. You mentioned the weavers. All of the hegen's work is art."

Esmerelda smiled. "Very good, Finn," she said, lifting the mug to her lips and slowly taking a sip. "What is art but a celebration of life?"

"Even though the kind of work you do deals with death?"

"Death is one source of power. Death is a part of life, the endpoint, and it is through death that we can fully appreciate the power of life."

Finn smiled. "I wish I believed that. I deal in death.

Unfortunately, I have a hard time thinking it connects me to life in any way."

"More than you realize," she said.

"What was it like when you learned it? The art, that is."

"Would you be interested in learning of the art?" There was a weight to the question as she watched him, an intensity he could feel, as if his answer mattered more than anything else.

Finn chuckled. "I don't think I have the same talent as you. I have my own set of skills, but I doubt I can do anything quite like you."

She regarded Finn before taking another sip of her tea. "It was isolating. When I learned the art, it was a different time. I lived in a different place."

"I thought you were always in Verendal."

"As you have observed, the people move. Some are born here and stay, and some migrate, looking for an opportunity to learn about and find their calling."

He'd learned that when he'd met Jasmine. Her parents had moved around, which was how she had ended up with her grandfather, then moved on here. "How long have you been in Verendal?"

Finn hadn't even considered that question before. He assumed she had been here her whole life, especially given her level of responsibility to the people.

"Long enough," she said.

Finn waited for her to explain more, to share something else, but that was all he got.

He chuckled. "Long enough? That's the kind of answer

Meyer would give me, not the kind of answer somebody whom I have..."

Esmerelda looked at him, waiting. "Yes?"

". . . Not the kind of answer somebody whom I have come to be friends with," Finn said, picking his words carefully, "would give."

"There are some things even friends don't care to talk about," Esmerelda said. "Some memories friends would like to forget."

"What happened to you?"

She shook her head. "As I said, it was a lonely time for me." She leaned down, looking at the mug before taking a sip. When she set it on the table again, she rested her hands on either side of it. "Those of the people who have potential to learn the art are often separated from others. Not because we're feared, but because there is something in the learning that requires isolation. Unfortunately, my isolation was almost more than I could tolerate."

"I'm sorry," Finn said.

Esmerelda smiled at him. "I don't need your pity, Finn." She laughed. "Besides, ever since I have come to Verendal, I have experienced a stronger feeling of welcome than I ever have before. Henry Meyer has ensured that. He has worked with the people in a way that very few others have."

"Are you afraid of what will happen when he's gone?"

"Are you?"

Finn shrugged. "I don't think Henry is going anywhere anytime soon. He's still the master executioner in Verendal."

"All men must find a new calling," she said.

"All?"

"Even if that calling is to pass on from this world," she said.

"So you're saying that Meyer has to serve until he dies."

"Am I saying that?"

"I don't even know what you're saying," Finn said, laughing to himself.

Esmerelda pulled out a card from her pocket and set it on the table. "I found this today. I do not know how to read it." She showed Finn, and he saw the golden ink start to swirl before taking on the shape of a noose. "All I know is that it leads to you."

Finn stared at the card. "What should I do?"

"Do what you always do, Finn. Do what is right." She stared at the card, leaving it in the center of the table. "How long will you be staying?"

"I had hoped to stay long enough to ensure my safety."

"I think the city has quieted down," she said.

"How do you know?"

She pulled another card out and slid it across the table.

It looked like Verendal. The detail was strange, but it looked as if the city itself was normal. He could see the spires of the church of Heleth rising up over it, the palace, and even the newer church of Fell.

"Then I should be getting back," he said.

"If you must. Be careful, Finn."

Morning came quickly, and when he woke up, he found Meyer in the kitchen. He was dressed for the day in a deep-brown jacket and matching pants, a pack resting on the table.

"You came back late," Meyer said.

"I got caught up in one of the protests," Finn said. He told him about visiting with Walter, heading out to the Brinder section, and encountering the three men, including the agitator. He skipped his visit with Jamie, however. Finn didn't want Master Meyer knowing everything going on in his life. The more Finn shared, the more Meyer's eyes narrowed.

"Another dozen died last night," Meyer said. "Most of them protesters. Another pair of Archers." He slid a folded piece of parchment toward Finn. "I've been questioning the men we healed, but none of them know anything."

"Not even about the person behind it? The Black Rose themself?"

"I suspect there is no one person who is the Black Rose. This is a movement, Finn. Not a person. As you've seen." He flicked his gaze to the pamphlet that Oscar had given him.

Finn picked up the parchment Meyer had offered, skimming through. It was a missive from Tolsten.

"The magister wants to make a demonstration," Meyer said.

"Tolsten is going to use Walter," Finn said.

Meyer nodded. "Unfortunately."

"He admitted to the crime," Finn said.

"I got word from the warden that he acknowledged

what he did. With an admission of guilt, there is no reason to delay his sentencing."

"Even if he was drawn into something that he didn't really understand?"

"Killing someone accidentally is still killing them, Finn. The king still demands justice. In this case, the justice has a different meaning. It has a different need."

Finn glanced back toward the door, looking for his sister, but she was not yet up.

"Lena got back late, as well," Meyer said. "Let her sleep."

"Maybe I'll make breakfast today," Finn said.

Meyer chuckled. "Maybe that would be for the best."

Finn prepared their breakfast and they ate in silence. Only when they were done did they get to their feet. They headed out of the house, pausing at Declan for Meyer to head inside, with Finn accompanying him, to gather Walter Briggs. He glanced from Finn to Meyer, his eyes growing wider with each passing moment. They led him through the streets, which were strangely quiet this morning. There *had* been fires during the night—he had seen the flames when he'd left the city—but there was no sign of those either. No windows were broken like he'd seen in other parts of the city, and there was no debris to indicate any damage.

By the time they reached City Hall, Walter had already started to babble.

It started slowly, but the farther they went, the more he started to tear up, to the point that he was shaking his head, his eyes wide, his mouth working as if to say something he'd never said.

"You're going to want to speak on your behalf," Finn said.

"I've already told you that it was an accident." He looked over to Finn, his wide-eyed expression begging him to help. "I told you that I didn't mean to do it. I told you that—"

"You are going to want to speak on your behalf," Finn said again.

Walter bobbed his head, nodding at him. "I... I didn't mean to."

"Whether or not you meant to is immaterial now."

They climbed the steps to City Hall, the old stone of the Alainsith building giving a sense of weight to the proceedings. He looked to Walter, and his shoulders were slumped, his head bowed, and his hands clenched in front of him.

Finn took a deep breath and pushed open the doors, guiding Walter inside. City Hall often caught Finn's attention, much like it did today. There was something impressive about it, which was the intent of its design. It drew the eye, from the gleaming white floor, to the smooth walls, to the enormous wolf head emblem etched into the stone—a reminder of the king and his authority over all of this, despite how City Hall had once been an Alainsith structure. Pale light poured in through the windows and wall-mounted lanterns glowed, as if guiding the condemned toward their fate.

Once inside City Hall, they headed toward the juror

chamber, and to Walter's sentencing. Finn knew what his sentence would be.

The jurors were all present. As was the magister.

They waited as he and Meyer guided Walter in.

Throughout the time Finn had served as executioner, the jurors had changed. They all still came from wealthier sections of the city. Finn still found it troubling that the jurors were always wealthy, perhaps more so now that they would be deciding the fate of people with so little. It was the exact thing that the Black Rose railed against.

Finn tried not to think about that, and tried not to think about the fact that all of the jurors were selected from the innermost parts of the city, the wealthier parts. Those from the outer sections, the poorer places, did not have any real representation. They relied upon the kindness of the others.

Meyer nodded to Finn, who guided Walter forward.

"Jurors. I present to you Walter Briggs, accused of killing an Archer"—it occurred to Finn that he still didn't even know the name of the Archer, or whether the Archer had actually died—"during the protest in the Brinder section. The accused has admitted to his crime, though he states he didn't intend to harm anyone."

Finn looked up at the jury, taking them in. They sat behind a long table on a raised platform, giving them the appearance of looking down on others in the juror chamber. A lantern hung on the wall at either end of the room, spilling light inside—the flame of justice, as the magister had once called it. That light wasn't fully necessary, as there was plenty of natural light coming in through a row of windows seated high in the wall, though the lanterns cast a warmer glow.

The current jury was comprised of four men and three women. All looked as if they were displeased they had been asked to come to the City Hall for this, though Finn suspected it was more of a displeasure in what Walter would force them to decide. None of the current jurors seemed to take any satisfaction in the convicting and sentencing of criminals. That was better than enjoying the process, he supposed, especially as they were often the ones to decide who lived and who died.

The magister leaned forward. Dressed in the black robes of his office, his flat, gray eyes looked out at Finn, then he turned to Walter Briggs with an expression of disdain before turning to the jurors.

Finn didn't know Magister Yolath well. Like all magisters, he had trained at the university in the king's law and served as guidance with respect to sentencing. There were times when he inserted himself into the sentencing more than others, though this magister did so less often than his predecessor. From what Finn knew, the role of magister was supposed to be merely advisory, but seeing as the magister was the one position that rarely changed, that often didn't happen. Too often, the magister defaulted to making the sentence and the rest of the jurors had to decide whether to go along with the decision.

"As he has been accused and admits to his guilt, the decision is clear," the magister said. "He would serve as an example to the others and—"

"I have not had the opportunity to speak to the captain

of the Archers," Finn spoke up, ignoring the quick look from Meyer. He knew where it came from, and he knew it didn't matter. If he didn't speak on behalf of Walter now, there wouldn't be another chance. "I have not confirmed that an Archer was killed during those protests."

The magister leaned back, resting his hands on the table in front of him. "That was not the report."

"I understand the report is that Mr. Walter Briggs killed an Archer, but I didn't have an opportunity to confirm that before we were summoned here." Finn preferred to be thorough, and not having that opportunity made it harder for him to feel as if he'd done everything he needed, especially when he didn't know if there was something more he could do to help Walter.

He didn't even know if he should help, but there had been so few times when he had come across someone for whom he had a desire to intervene.

That wasn't what fully motivated him though.

It was twofold.

Walter could have been him. Gods, Finn practically *had* been him. If he had still been running the streets during the protests, Finn suspected he would have been caught up in them and pulled into many of the same actions as Walter. How could he blame the man—rather, boy—for actions like that?

The other reason was harder.

Finn knew him—not well, but he *had* known Walter's name. And the boy was from Brinder. Like Finn.

But it was about more than simply recognizing his name.

It was about the fact that this was someone he knew—and someone he could offer a measure of help to. If he was honest with himself, he couldn't help but wonder if he would do the same thing for Oscar if he were in this situation.

That question had stuck with Finn ever since he'd come to his position. If his oldest friend in the city—and his father's closest friend—had needed him because of a crime he'd committed, what would Finn do?

There wasn't a good answer.

Finn thought he would serve the way he'd been instructed to serve—he thought he would want to fulfill the king's justice—but there was a part of him that wondered if he would really do that. It had never been tested, and Finn didn't *want* for it to be tested, but if he were to be challenged, he knew he would find it difficult to turn away from helping Oscar.

"What is this about, Mr. Jagger?" the magister asked.

"Nothing more than what I've told you." Finn could feel Meyer's gaze on him, but he continued to ignore it. "In most cases, I would have taken the opportunity to confirm all aspects of the accusation, but I didn't have the time to do so with Mr. Briggs."

"Would you care to tell us why you did not and what you *have* been doing?"

Finn finally did look over to Meyer at this point.

Meyer didn't have anger in his expression, as Finn feared he would, but there was worry, maybe a hint of sadness, and perhaps even disappointment.

It was that last feeling that troubled Finn the most. He didn't want to disappoint Meyer.

That, more than anything else, was the thought that stuck with him.

He couldn't disappoint him.

He turned back to the magister and glanced to the jurors, his gaze sweeping over them. "We have been investigating the Black Rose movement. That's what is responsible for the protests." He took a deep breath. "I'm not saying he didn't commit the crime, only that I have not had the opportunity to fully determine the details of what occurred. He stands accused of killing one of the Archers, and given the current situation in the city, I think it prudent to ensure he actually *did* kill one of the Archers."

"The accusation is sound," the magister said. "We have corroborating stories."

"From other Archers? Or from others within the crowd?"

Finn had to be careful here, and even if he managed to get a stay of execution, a little more time, would it matter?

Given what Finn had seen with the crowd in the street, how the protesters had converged as quickly as they did, he didn't think he would even have an opportunity to uncover anything more than what he already had. It was unlikely to make any difference for him, and certainly not for Walter Briggs.

"The other Archers who were on duty at that time," the magister said. "They observed the violence, they grabbed the one responsible, and they placed him in prison. Surely you have pieced that much together, Mr. Jagger."

Finn looked over to Master Meyer, and knew he still needed to be careful, knew he shouldn't be pushing so hard, but he felt as if he wanted to question more than he had.

"I understand," Finn said.

"Good. Then it is decided." The magister turned to the jurors. "In the matter of Walter Briggs, I recommend, on behalf of the king, that he be sentenced to hang. He can serve as an example to the entire blighted movement that they cannot oppose the king and his justice."

Finn closed his eyes and breathed out slowly. He knew this was the inevitable outcome, but he didn't like it any better than he had before. Worse, he didn't think the magister was right. Walter's sentence wouldn't deter the movement. It would only fuel it more.

The jurors leaned back, speaking softly to themselves, but Finn knew it would only be a matter of time before they came back with the conviction, and when they did, there wasn't anything he would be able to do on Walter's behalf. He didn't even know if there was anything he *should* do on his behalf.

They finished their discussion and leaned forward, the magister leveling his gaze on Walter Briggs.

"The jurors, serving on behalf of King Porman, have agreed that Walter Briggs will be sentenced to hang in two days' time. May the gods welcome you back."

CHAPTER TWENTY-SIX

The days leading up to the execution had been fruitless.

Finn had learned nothing more about the Black Rose, though he kept searching, questioning the men who had recovered enough to answer—but they knew nothing. All were at the protests out of anger with the king.

Finn hated his failure. The king had asked for the Hunter, but he had found nothing.

Now he sat at the table, resting his hands in front of him and looking at his mug of tea. He couldn't help but feel as if something was wrong, as if all of this was heading in the wrong direction, cascading uncontrollably.

The mug of tea steamed in front of him, but Finn hadn't touched it, his stomach roiling, leaving him with a hint of nausea that was unusual for him on a morning like this. He had a piece of toasted bread and a few bites of sausage, but nothing more than that. Normally, on the morning of an execution, Finn would eat more than this, but for whatever reason, he simply didn't have the stomach for it today.

Lena stood near the stove, her back toward him as she worked on breakfast for Master Meyer and herself, humming softly.

"What's that?"

Finn looked up from staring at Reginald's journal as Lena leaned over him, frowning. "It's nothing—at least, it's probably nothing," he said.

"It looks like it's something." She took a seat across from him and grabbed it, flipping through. Her brow furrowed. "Payments."

"No," he said, reaching for it. "Debt owed."

Lena shook her head, tapping on it. "No. These are payments. Meyer uses something similar, but not quite the same. There is a different organization to this one. I'm not a bookkeeper, but if you follow it, these are payments received."

Finn frowned, pulling it back to him. Why would Reginald have killed himself if people were paying him?

"I could be wrong," she said, but from her tone, Finn could tell she didn't think that was likely.

"Thank you," he said. "You've given me something to look into."

"Does this have anything to do with the protests?"

"Probably not," he said.

Payments might mean funding. What if it *was* tied to the protests? Then Reginald had been more tightly involved than he'd known. If that were the case, then Finn had overlooked something with Reginald. Perhaps much about Reginald. He needed to revisit the ledger, along with all of the shops listed within it, and go back and question all of them. It would take an incredible amount of work, but it felt like the right thing for him to do. It was the kind of thing that the Hunter would do.

"It's about something I thought had been resolved."

And it still probably was. Finn knew it didn't matter at this point. At least, it shouldn't matter. It bothered him though.

She pointed to his plate. "You need to eat more than that, Finn."

"I know," he said softly.

"I know you know; it's just that…" She trailed off as Master Meyer came in, dressed in his executioner leathers, and took a seat at the table. He nodded to Lena as she placed a plate in front of him, then he turned his attention to Finn.

"Are you still displeased?" Master Meyer asked.

"How am I supposed to be pleased with this outcome?" Finn asked.

"I understand it's difficult for you since this is some-body who came from your section, but there was bound to be a time that would happen."

Finn sighed. If only that were it.

"We've had other people from the Brinder section."

"Not anyone you knew," Master Meyer said.

"We've had other people I've known," Finn said.

"The circumstances were quite a bit different," Meyer replied.

Finn breathed out and nodded. The circumstances *had* been different. When he had been tasked with executing his crew boss, a man known as the King, it had been easier, mostly because Finn had known he was guilty, but also because the King had truly been responsible for what had taken place.

More than that, though, the King had wronged Finn.

"I could perform the execution," Meyer said, lowering his voice and not looking over to Lena.

Finn just shook his head. "That is not necessary."

Meyer grunted. "You realize I'm still capable of it."

Finn nodded and pulled the tea toward him, bringing it up to his nose and deeply inhaling its scent—mint, which reminded him a bit of the hegen tea that Esmerelda always served him, though this was not nearly as refreshing. When she gave him mugs of tea, it usually helped clear his head, something that might be beneficial now.

He had to stop thinking about Esmerelda. He had to stop thinking about the hegen. He had to start focusing on what was to come.

"I realize you're capable of it," Finn said. "This is my responsibility though."

He had a feeling that this was another sort of test that Meyer had placed upon him—whether Finn could carry out an execution when he felt conflicted.

He had certainly been in enough situations where he knew he would have to carry out an execution even when he wasn't completely in agreement with it. For that matter, Finn had even carried out executions when he had not been fully convinced of the evidence, though he had always found a way to get himself comfortable with it. In this case, however, Finn wasn't sure he *could* get himself comfortable with it.

"Could you give us a moment, Lena?" Meyer asked.

Lena had a plate in hand for herself and looked over to Finn, then Meyer, then nodded. "I will take my breakfast in the office, if that is acceptable?"

"You know it is," Master Meyer said.

She left them, and Meyer sat quietly, chewing on his food. He didn't say anything until the door to the office closed with a soft click.

When it did, he rested his hands on the table and looked at Finn. "What is this about?" Meyer asked.

"It's nothing," Finn said.

"We know that's not the case. If it were nothing, then you would have eaten by now. You have been through many sentences at this point in your career, Finn. I recognize that there is something to this one, even if you don't want to acknowledge it."

Finn looked over to Meyer. "I thought maybe it had something to do with the fact that he's from the Brinder section, but I don't think that's what's troubling me."

"Then what *is* troubling you?"

"It's the details of this. All of this. It feels—"

"Wrong?"

Finn frowned, eyeing Master Meyer and nodding. "You feel it as well?"

"I can't say I feel good about what must be done," Master Meyer said, taking another bite of sausage and chewing slowly. "Unfortunately, there are times when we must take action that we don't always fully agree with when it serves a greater good."

"What if I'm not convinced this serves a greater good?"

"Why would you say that?"

Finn couldn't tell if Meyer was asking or testing.

"I'm just not convinced he's responsible for what he's been accused of doing."

"And I would argue that his death will possibly serve an even greater good than his life ever could."

There weren't many times when Finn had felt Meyer was heartless, which was strange, considering his occupation of an executioner; in fact, throughout the time he had worked with Master Meyer, Finn had found him almost compassionate. He had a unique combination of qualities for an executioner, but it suited him, and it suited the nature of the job. Finn feared what would happen if Meyer were to lose his compassion—and if he did, he worried he wouldn't ever be able to regain it.

"Why would his death serve the greater good?" Finn asked.

Finn sipped at his tea, staring at it for a moment before setting it back down.

"If the jurors and the magister are correct, his death will hopefully limit additional protests." Meyer smiled sadly. "It is a sad state of affairs to say that, but I can't help but think that if he were to serve any purpose, then it could be that. We could hope his death will prevent the protesters from continuing to riot and fill the streets with violence."

"What if it only prompts more protests?" Finn asked.

Meyer sighed. "That is always a possibility."

"So, you're acknowledging that it may not change a thing. You're acknowledging that it might make everything worse. And you're acknowledging that we—"

Finn cut himself off. He wasn't angry at Master Meyer. He was angry at the situation, but to be honest, it wasn't even that. If Walter was guilty, then he should face the punishment for the crime.

Finn didn't know, though.

He had spent time searching in the days since the sentencing, but all he'd found was that there had been an Archer who had died, and every other Archer whom Finn spoke to suggested it had been Walter who'd struck him.

Which was reason enough for Finn to believe that Walter was responsible and that they needed to carry out the sentence.

"You don't have to do this, then," Master Meyer said.

Finn shook his head slowly. "No. I think it should be me."

Meyer took a deep breath, nodding as he let it out. "Very well. If you are finished with your breakfast, then it's time for us to make our preparations."

Finn could only nod. The preparations were the easy part—if anything they did could be considered easy. They had to ensure the knot on the rope was tied tightly, and they had to head to the prison to question Walter Briggs one last time, giving him an opportunity to confess—though given that he had already confessed, there wasn't much else that could be done. He would need to make sure the priest of Heleth was ready for the procession, but that was about it.

Finn gathered himself, got dressed in his executioner leathers, and pulled the sword Justice out of the closet, holding on to it carefully—not that he had expected to use the blade during execution, as the jurors had convicted Walter Briggs to hang. It was a part of the attire expected of the executioner.

Meyer joined him and they headed out.

As Finn stepped out of the home, he glanced behind and saw Lena looking out the door, a hint of worry etched in her eyes.

"I didn't even ask her about the others," Finn said softly.

"There is not much to have asked about," Meyer said. "She has several of them coming around, and I think we are going to need to move them out of the old prison, but I didn't want to do that until I could ensure the riots wouldn't preclude us from doing so safely."

"I understand," Finn said.

"We might need to move them at night," Meyer said.

Finn looked over. That was unusual.

"I will do whatever you think is appropriate."

Meyer slowed, looking over at Finn. "And what about you? What do you think is appropriate?"

Finn kept his gaze locked straight ahead of him. "Not this."

They made their way through the streets, and the closer they got to Declan prison, the more Finn began to feel that something was not quite right.

At first, it was just an underlying sense of the city that bothered him, something that triggered a feeling deep within him, but it was a feeling that Finn didn't really understand. Maybe it was nerves. That would be unusual, as Finn no longer had nerves about going to an execution, though having a bit of nausea, the way he did this morning, wasn't altogether surprising.

It was possible it was something else though. The streets were emptier than he would've expected.

"There's no festival?"

"The Archers have a heavier presence today," Master Meyer said.

"I suppose that makes sense," Finn said. "A festival might cause more danger."

"That is what the Archers felt."

Finn looked over to Master Meyer, frowning. "The Archers, or you?"

"Both," Meyer said.

They made their way farther along the road, closer to Declan prison, and Finn looked over. "Are you concerned about what might happen?"

"I'm always concerned about what might happen," Master Meyer said. "In this case, it might be nothing, but I worry there will be an explosion of activity. Violence. All of it tied to what is to come."

Worse, even if they wanted to make it less of a public display, Finn didn't think that would accomplish what the magister and the jurors really wanted to. They *wanted* the public display, and they wanted to carry it out in a way that would deter others from protesting, from rioting, and from doing anything similar to the violent acts that had been taking place in the city.

By the time they reached Declan prison, Finn felt his unease growing.

He had been a part of so many executions in the time he'd served Master Meyer that he knew how each one should go. He knew how it should feel. What was happening now, the way the city felt now, was not the way an execution should feel. There was something off here, a distinct feel to the city that was wrong.

At the same time, the streets were empty and it was less of a spectacle than it normally was, which left Finn thinking that perhaps it was right.

"Have you ever given much thought to the gallows festival before?" Finn asked as they neared the prison. The dark outline of the building towered over them, casting a shadow over the street.

"I've often wondered whether there should be a festival celebrating the death of the men and women whom we bring to their sentencing," Master Meyer said, nodding slowly. "Though I think it gives the people in the city a chance to grieve, in their own way. If you've noticed, there are plenty of people in the city who mourn the dead. Some use it as an excuse to gather and congregate, and some use it as a chance to get vengeance."

"Our job isn't about vengeance," Finn said.

"Our job is not about vengeance for us," Master Meyer said. They reached the door leading into the prison. "For others, there is a measure of relief brought when they feel vengeance has been served. Even if they don't necessarily agree with the way that vengeance is carried out, there is something to be said about how people feel."

"They are going to feel that this is justice. Or vengeance."

"Not all of them," Master Meyer said.

"Not the people who come to the gallows festival," Finn said.

"Which is why we tried to limit the number of people who would come."

Finn wondered if such a thing would even be possible, if people decided to come out. There was no way to force people into their houses, to prevent them from coming out and watching, and no way for them to ensure the streets would be kept safe if they did come out.

That was what he had to keep in mind.

Finn pulled the keys from his pocket. He unlocked the door leading into the prison and nodded to Master Meyer.

"You can still step aside and let me carry this out," Master Meyer said.

"I don't need to," Finn said.

He made his way to the cell where Walter Briggs would be held. It was a different cell from the one he had been imprisoned in before—a place where he would've been given a chance to look out into the daylight, the sky, and have the opportunity to commune with the gods and decide if there was anything he could do or say that would sway them in his favor.

Finn remembered his own night sitting there, how he had lost hope, how despair had filled him as he realized his final days were gone—and that within hours, then minutes, he would die.

It was an empty, hollow feeling, and it didn't make Finn feel any closer to the gods. How could he, when he had to question why the gods would permit him to be brought into such a situation?

Would Walter feel the same way?

By the time they reached the room, Finn paused at the door. It was a stout oak door, with heavy bars criss-crossing it and a small open window that allowed him to peer inside. He looked through the window and saw a priest of Heleth bowing in front of Walter, his head bent forward as they spoke softly, whispering their voices in prayer.

Finn turned to Master Meyer. "This is the only time when I still think about my night. It influences so much of what I do, but I don't really consider it too much anymore. Maybe I should."

"The fact that you don't suggests you have moved on," Master Meyer said.

He tapped on the door, and the priest looked over to them. Finn recognized him. Garrett was a priest of Heleth, one who had a warm demeanor and who had served for many of the past executions. He was so different from the priest who had served during Finn's sentencing, though that priest had also spoken the words of Heleth in a way that had convinced Finn to say them alongside him. Maybe he wasn't so different after all.

He stepped over to the door as Finn unlocked it, pushing it open.

"He is ready to meet the Blessed Mother," Garrett said.

Finn stepped in. Walter sat on a ledge looking out a window, resting his chin on its sill, his back turned to Finn.

"Walter Briggs. I, Finn Jagger, am present to escort you to your sentence."

Walter looked over. "I don't want to go. I don't want to die. I don't deserve this. I—"

"I know," Finn said.

He and Master Meyer joined Walter, both of them standing on either side of him, guiding him to his feet.

Finn wasn't sure what kind of prisoner Walter was going to be. There were some who resisted. Some who tried to force him and Master Meyer to drag them through the street, whereas others simply came along with a determined stride, as if facing their death was some measure of manhood. Finn had gone with an emptiness within him, facing his fate, though he didn't feel as if he had done it to prove himself, but rather that he knew it didn't matter anymore.

Walter came willingly, though he looked up at Finn, his wide brown eyes beseeching him. "You have to do something. I know you can. You were saved. You could do the same for me. I could be an apprentice. All you have to do is say those words."

Finn licked his lips, then swallowed.

He couldn't deny the thought had come to him, but he was only a journeyman. Only master executioners took on apprentices, and he doubted that Master Meyer was going to do anything to delay this execution—not when so much he believed was at stake.

"Come with us," Finn said.

"What if I refuse?" Walter asked.

"We will drag you," Finn said.

"The gods don't want me dragged to my death," Walter said. He looked over at Garrett, as if looking for reassurance, but Garrett didn't say anything.

Garrett had risen among the priests of Heleth, but still chose to serve during executions. Typically, that was the responsibility of newer priests, though occasionally more seasoned priests would accompany higher-ranking criminals. Then there were times when the priests felt a calling. He wondered whether Garrett had felt called to serve Walter.

"The gods won't refuse us dragging you to your sentence," Finn said. "Don't make it be like that. Make the march with dignity."

Walter swallowed, then got to his feet.

Finn motioned for him to keep ahead of them, and Walter started forward, through the cell door. Once in the hallway, Garrett began speaking the words of Heleth.

They reached the entrance to Declan, and once they stepped outside, a pair of Archers joined them, taking a position on either side of Walter.

"Are you sure that's a good idea?" Finn asked, looking over to Master Meyer.

"It is tradition," Master Meyer said.

"Tradition or not, I wonder if perhaps in this circumstance it is not the wisest of decisions."

Meyer said nothing.

Archers were stationed throughout the city, far more than usual.

The two with Walter guided them along the street, heading toward Porman's Path, and once they reached it, they began the winding road toward the Teller Gate. The city had an eerie emptiness to it, as there were only a few people out.

There were no street vendors today and the crowd didn't line the streets, but that didn't mean there weren't people watching. Finn could see them on rooftops and packing side streets. He could see them in alleys, some poking their heads out to watch.

He swept his gaze around, looking for signs of agitators, but didn't see anyone.

Everything was quiet.

But there was the sound of Garrett murmuring the words of Heleth, and Walter speaking those words along with him, his voice filling the street. There was the sound of Finn's own boots thudding along the cobblestones, even the soft sound of Walter's slippers on the stones. Finn knew just how much he would feel through those slippers, each contour of the cobblestones, as if the walk to the gallows was one more torture before his hanging.

By the time they reached the Teller Gate, Finn couldn't help but feel as if the presence of the Archers in the city had truly pushed back the typical crowd.

Then they stepped through.

They were hundreds upon hundreds of people outside the Teller Gate. Thousands. It was as if the entirety of the city had emptied beyond the wall, filling the space. There was no festival feel here though—only an undercurrent of anger.

The Archers slowed, but Meyer pushed them forward.

"How are we supposed to get through the crowd?" Finn asked.

"By walking," Meyer said.

"I understand that. I'm just saying—"

"I know what you are saying," Meyer said. "But keep moving."

They headed forward. Other Archers streamed out of the city, joining them and creating a path. Shouts started to ring out around them, loud and angry. People threw objects, though for the first time in Finn's time serving as an executioner, no one threw anything at the one sentenced.

Instead, Finn and Meyer were the targets along with the Archers, and even Garrett.

An apple struck Finn, and it stung, but he ignored it, the way he had learned to ignore everything like this. He trudged forward, and with each step, he could feel the tension within the crowd beginning to rise, building around him.

It was going to explode.

"This is a bad idea," Finn muttered.

"We must carry out the sentence," Meyer said.

Typically, most of the jurors, along with the magister, came out for the sentencing, but Finn didn't see them in the distance near the Raven Stone. Occasionally, the viscount would come out too, though maybe he wouldn't for somebody like this.

Finn didn't know whether the king was still in the city, but he suspected he was, especially given the strong presence of the Archers, many of them palace Archers, along with some who had to be members of the Realmsguard.

Finn heard a grunt and looked over to Meyer. He'd been struck in the head, and he held it, a bit of blood streaming down from his temple.

"Meyer?"

"Keep moving," Meyer muttered.

The Archers flanked them, creating a path they could walk through, though it wasn't wide enough for them to make that much headway. Finn tried to keep his focus straight ahead of him, but he found it increasingly difficult with the crowd yelling and the agitation around him. He knew that if he was hit like Master Meyer, it would be difficult for him to carry out his responsibility.

Another apple struck him, catching his shoulder, and though it stung, it wasn't quite as bad as what he suspected Meyer had experienced.

Once they had reached the Raven Stone, they forced Walter up the steps.

There were still no jurors or magister.

This was going to be done out here like this?

"Where are they?" he whispered to Meyer.

"I don't know."

He stumbled, and Finn looked over.

"Stay down there. I will do this," Finn said.

Meyer looked as if he wanted to argue, but instead just clutched his hand up against his head.

Finn reached the top of the Raven Stone and guided Walter to the middle of it, holding on to the coiled rope in one hand, before looking out over the crowd.

"Walter Briggs, I, Finn Jagger, present you for execution before the people of Verendal. You have been accused and sentenced for the crime of killing a city Archer."

Walter looked over, his eyes still searching, hoping Finn might change his mind, but Finn knew he couldn't. It felt as if he had been forced in this direction, forced to do this, and yet...

He didn't like it.

Finn looked down to Master Meyer. He still had one bloody hand on his temple, holding it. He needed healing, but there wasn't going to be any—not until this was over.

Finn affixed the rope to the gallows, placed the stairs into position, then motioned for Walter to climb up.

"Don't make me do this," Walter said.

"Neither of us have a choice," Finn said.

Walter swallowed, then climbed the stairs.

Finn fitted the noose around his neck and looked over to him.

"Do you have anything to say before you go to meet the gods?"

Walter looked out over the crowd, then to Finn, terror filling his wide eyes.

All Finn could see was a reflection of who he would've been, the way he would have felt, and he hated that he had to do this.

He took a deep breath, then kicked the stairs out of the way.

Walter dropped. His neck snapped.

The crowd surged.

The Archers cried out, turning to face the crowd, swords and shields trying to push them back, while the Archers along the wall surrounding Verendal began to fire into the crowd.

Finn ducked down, hurrying to join Master Meyer.

"Did you know they had Archers on the wall?"

"No."

Other Archers surrounded them, guiding them toward the city.

Finn looked back toward Walter, seeing him swinging with the cool northern breeze, and noticed movement out of the hegen section, though he hoped that Esmerelda and the others would wait until the crowd departed to claim their prize.

In this case, maybe it would make more sense if they didn't claim their prize.

By the time they had reached the Teller Gate, the crowd had pushed toward the Archers, but thankfully, Finn and Meyer got into the city peacefully enough, and without any further injury.

Finn looked over to Master Meyer. "We need to get you stitched up."

Meyer just nodded.

CHAPTER TWENTY-SEVEN

The riot following the execution stayed mostly out of the city, but the Archers had squashed it as quickly as they could—using a level of violence that Finn wasn't entirely comfortable with. Meyer's injury had required Lena's deft hand to suture, but now he was well enough, which was good since he and Finn had to question some men about the protests.

Now Finn had something more to deal with.

Finn held the piece of paper in hand, the hastily written message all he needed, though it left him feeling cold. There was more going on here, though he didn't know what it was.

Jonrath was dead.

Another death in custody. First Reginald, now him.

Finn didn't *think* it a suicide but didn't know. The possibility that someone would be able to sneak into

Declan to get to a prisoner there bothered him. It should be secure. He had made a point of ensuring that.

Or thought he had.

Both dead men had ties to the Black Rose, and Finn felt even more uncomfortable with that connection. He wished he could understand it.

Everything continued to build, but Finn felt as if he was even further from answers than he had been before. He hadn't been able to find out anything, even though he and Meyer had chased leads and questioned the men who had survived. The only thing he had managed to come up with was that the Black Rose was a movement. Nothing more.

He should've trusted himself. He should've gone with his instincts to solve the mystery sooner. Maybe he would've even saved Walter Briggs.

If only he had.

Someone had suffered and died because he had not trusted himself.

Finn would not let that happen again.

He turned a corner on his way to Declan, and a flash of a black cloak caught his attention.

He had seen something like that before; it was similar to the insignia worked into the man's cloak.

The Black Rose.

He'd last seen it when he'd been chased out of the Brinder section.

It might be coincidence. They might've only worn it as a way to show solidarity with others, but Finn wasn't completely convinced that was the case.

He needed to follow this man.

Finn kept his distance, not wanting to make it too obvious that he was chasing him, but the streets were relatively empty these days.

There had been no further protests since the execution, but that didn't mean the movement had ceased; it had only gone quiet—for now.

He still hadn't managed to shake what Wella had suggested to him.

A movement like this would require funding. Reginald might have been a part of it, but he couldn't have been *all* of it. The protests had persisted after his death.

Which meant he was only one part.

Who would finance something like this? Better yet, *why* finance something like this?

Most in the city with wealth wanted to do whatever they could to *keep* their wealth. They wouldn't side with the poor whom they took advantage of.

None of this made sense to him.

The man ducked down a side street.

Finn noted the heavy presence of Archers. There were probably five in the street, all of them armed with swords and crossbows, and all of them staring at each person they passed with a dark gleam in their eyes. Most of them were city Archers, though there were quite a few more palace Archers than Finn was accustomed to seeing out in the city.

He turned the corner and lost sight of the man, but he couldn't have gone far.

Finn slowed and headed toward one of the bridges,

pausing in the middle and looking out over the river. The river itself seemed to serve as a boundary within the city. On one side was the poorer outer sections, its inhabitants often treated unjustly. The wealthy inner sections were on the other side, and the people there tended to *stay* there, closer to the palace and the viscount's manor.

From here, Finn could make out trails of smoke that drifted up from hundreds of chimneys within the city. He felt a strange energy in the crisp northern breeze, charged with the fear of the people who lived there, charged with the fear of those who had experienced the dangers that had occurred, and charged with the death of Walter Briggs.

Finn crossed the bridge, heading into the more central sections, wandering along the street that ran along the river. The River Walk was one of the nicer streets in the city, and though the nearby houses weren't the wealthiest, there was still something quite regal about them. Many of them were dated, and some were made of a dark stone that reminded him of the stone used in City Hall—and the stone used in the ancient temples.

There was still much he needed to do. He continued his walk until he reached a side street leading back over the river. He needed to go back to Declan, though something had prevented him from doing so ever since he'd hanged Walter Briggs. He and Meyer had been in hiding, for the most part, trying to keep themselves safe from the potential of danger during the unrest in the city, but Finn had to stop abandoning his responsibilities. It was time for him to focus.

If only Jonrath had lived. It made him think the Black Rose was more than just a movement, though Finn couldn't prove that. It irritated him—their way of showing they could get anyone, regardless of where they were.

Finn had already dealt with the iron masters showing loyalty where they should not, and he hadn't expected to struggle with that any longer. Perhaps continuing to struggle was to be his fate.

Instead of going to the prison, he turned and headed toward the Church of Heleth.

It wasn't all that far from Declan, and as he approached it, Finn shook his head, wondering why he was coming here. Maybe it was in search of answers, or reassurance, or maybe it was just that he didn't know where else to go.

He entered through the small door on the periphery of the church, and stepped into a narrow antechamber that led into the worship hall. He didn't expect there would be many priests available, and was surprised to see a younger priest of Heleth sitting in a booth.

As soon as Finn entered, the priest got to his feet, heading toward him. He had thick glasses, short black hair, and a beard. "May I help you?"

"Is Priest Garrett available?"

"Any of the priests can help you with your needs."

"Garrett is really the only one who can address these particular needs," Finn said.

"I'm sure all of us can answer to your needs and help you find the wisdom of the Mother."

Finn looked over to him. He didn't know this priest,

but there was something about him that reminded Finn of the young priest he'd seen Lena walking through the city with. "I just need to see Garrett."

"Has Garrett helped you on your path to understanding the Mother?"

Finn grunted, looking around the antechamber. There were markers of Heleth all over. She was the Blessed Mother, and she sat above the rest of the gods, which meant that everything here gave off a feeling of warmth. A portrait of Heleth hung on one of the walls, depicting her as a matronly-looking woman with a glow around her, her hands spread off to either side, as if looking down at the earth.

Several wall hangings were in the shape of the earth and moon, the sun shining over them and looking as if it were Heleth herself, the Blessed Mother, shining down upon everyone.

"You could say that," Finn said.

"Then you have already begun to understand your place with the gods."

"I have no place with the gods," Finn said, and immediately regretted it.

The priest frowned at him. "You said that Garrett has helped you."

"I am Finn Jagger, executioner for the king. Garrett has helped me as we've carried out sentences. I'd like to speak with him about the last sentence."

The priest stiffened, then nodded slowly, backing away and disappearing into the main part of the church. Finn should know better than to intimidate a priest, but he didn't want to sit and have a conversation about Heleth with somebody who didn't understand him.

He stopped in front of another painting. All of the paintings hanging on the walls were intricately done, and he thought of Esmerelda and the artisans within the hegen section—the way they depicted scenes of nature and the world. Perhaps they would be able to paint something as exquisite as what he saw in front of him now. Heleth sat among the other gods, though all of them were blurry, making their features difficult to discern. She sat at the head of the table in this portrait, the only one clearly rendered, while the other gods all sat farther away. There was Fell, Volan, Cranar, and even Jor.

"Are you trying to find the wisdom of the Blessed Mother?"

Finn turned to see Garrett approaching. His hands were clasped in front of him, and he looked over at the same portrait Finn studied, his mouth pressed together in a tight frown.

"I often come out here, like many of our parishioners, to see if I might be able to find the wisdom of the Blessed Mother myself. I find that these paintings inspire me." He turned, looking at Finn. "Do they inspire you, Mr. Jagger?"

"I don't know if I *can* be inspired," Finn said.

"But you have come to visit with the Blessed Mother," he said.

Finn took a deep breath, looking around him. The air was damp, still, and carried with it a bit of warmth. Heat seemed to radiate off of the stone of the church itself. It was almost as if somebody *could* feel Heleth here. "I don't even know why I came," Finn said.

"You came because you're troubled."

"Yes, I'm troubled," Finn agreed.

"What is it that troubles you?"

"What if I say everything?"

"Then I would say we have a long conversation ahead of us." Garrett motioned for Finn to join him at a booth, then he slipped into it, waiting for Finn to take a seat.

Finn wrapped his cloak around him, taking a seat on the booth next to Garrett, who was dressed in the brown robes of his office. Garrett turned so he could look at Finn, yet Finn stared straight ahead, not knowing whether there was anything he could say beyond what he already had. He wanted to be here for some reason, but why? Finn wasn't devout, so it wasn't a matter of devotion that had driven him here. It was fear. Worry. Uncertainty.

"Your last assignment troubles you."

"Was it obvious?"

"From the moment you came to the confession hall," he said.

Finn smiled. The priests referred to the final holding cell as the confession hall, though there was no confession happening at that point. By the time the prisoners were brought to that room, they had already confessed, or they had already been convicted. He supposed it didn't matter though. They called it that because it was meant to be the final place that prisoners could offer their confession to the gods, some sacred room that would give them an opportunity to reach for the gods' forgiveness. Finn wondered if the gods even cared.

Maybe that was why he came.

"He was used as an example," Finn said.

"Does that bother you?"

"I don't know," Finn said. "I don't know if it bothers me that he was used as an example, or that he's from the section I grew up in, or if it's something else entirely," he said and shook his head. "Maybe it's all of that."

"Was he guilty?"

"He said he was."

"Then he was guilty," Garrett said.

Finn looked over. "Normally, I confirm confessions so I can ensure those who have confessed to their crimes are actually guilty of those crimes."

"That's what makes you effective, Mr. Jagger."

"I don't always feel that way."

Garrett smiled sadly. "I have traveled much throughout the kingdom. I wasn't always stationed in Verendal, though I did ask to come."

"I didn't realize priests traveled."

"I didn't realize executioners traveled."

"I don't travel much."

"Yet you have been seen in the countryside, making journeys to different villages, offering the king's justice."

"The king's justice."

"The king serves the gods, Finn Jagger."

Finn wasn't sure if that was what troubled him, or whether it was merely a matter of not knowing what he needed to do—how he needed to serve.

"What if justice is a mirage?"

"An executioner who has begun to question his calling." Garrett smiled slightly. "I must say, I did not expect my day to go this way."

"I don't know if I'm questioning my calling so much as I'm questioning my role in it."

"If it's not you, then it would be another. As I was saying, I have visited other cities within the kingdom. I have served as well as I can, and have even traveled outside of the kingdom. Do you know what I have seen?"

Finn shook his head. "What have you seen, Garrett?"

"You aren't the only one who has this role."

"I know there are other executioners in the kingdom," Finn said.

"There are others, and not all are like you—or like Master Meyer. Far too many are like your predecessor."

Finn snorted. "From what I know, he was a bastard." He stiffened, shaking his head sheepishly as he looked around him. "Sorry."

Garrett smiled. "Do you think the Blessed Mother cares about the words you use?"

"There are some who would say she does."

"Those are people who don't know the Blessed Mother. Once you feel the warmth of her embrace, her touch upon you, you realize that she forgives all."

"If you accept that forgiveness," Finn said.

"And do you?"

He could feel the question, and he knew exactly what Garrett was trying to get at, but Finn didn't know how to answer.

Was *that* why he was here?

Did he want forgiveness for what he had done, or did he just want to talk to somebody who knew?

He didn't have anybody else he could go to. Master Meyer certainly wouldn't talk about it. When Finn had tried bringing up past executions with him, Meyer had simply told him that it was time to move on, to carry out their duty, then to plan for the next thing asked of them. He didn't want to talk about it with Lena, though he suspected his sister would understand. She had shown a willingness to at least listen to him, but it was something Finn wanted to protect her from. She shouldn't have to hear the details of his executions, and she didn't need to worry about his internal struggle. He had tried going to Oscar before, but Oscar had challenges of his own.

Who else *was* there?

Garrett wasn't a friend. Maybe that was what made it easier. He was someone who served the gods, and theoretically, that meant he served without question or judgment.

"I don't know," Finn said.

"The fact that you have come asking the question is enough, Mr. Jagger."

"It doesn't always feel like enough."

Garrett looked over, shaking his head. "Eventually, you will find that the gods, and especially the Blessed Mother, will make a choice on your behalf. When they do, I hope they choose the path of the righteous."

Finn sniffed. "I feel like someone has chosen on my behalf already."

"Ah. That's right. You were chosen for salvation. Do

you think that is the responsibility of the Blessed Mother, or perhaps you follow Fell? Many young men have been swayed by the promise Fell offers, that of wealth and power."

Finn looked up at the portrait depicting the Blessed Mother. "There was a time when I thought maybe it was the hegen."

"The hegen don't choose who lives or dies," Garrett said.

"They do, more than you realize," Finn whispered.

Garrett frowned as he looked at him, and Finn just shook his head. He needed to be careful here; he didn't want to get the hegen into trouble for his own crisis.

"I think I just needed to talk to somebody who was there," Finn said.

"It was an unsettling experience," Garrett said. "With the uprising, and the violence that followed, I can understand your difficulty processing it."

"It's not that," Finn said. And it wasn't. Even though there had been violence and bloodshed, and probably more deaths than he wanted to know about, none of that was what had really bothered him.

Sitting here, talking to Garrett, Finn began to realize what it was that truly troubled him the most: The jurors had decided Walter Briggs' fate, but then they hadn't been there to see it carried out. They had remained inside the walls. They had used Finn and Meyer as tools, nothing more. That was what they had been to them.

Was that what he was to the king?

The Black Rose movement pulled on a part of him that

he'd thought he'd moved past, but something else about it bothered him, and he continued to think it was more than just a movement.

Jonrath. Reginald. The mysterious Black Rose members themselves.

All of it smacked of a greater conspiracy... but was it really?

What if it was nothing more than his imagination? Finn *wanted* there to be something more so the movement wouldn't pull on him the way it did.

Perhaps that was all this was.

He stirred, getting ready to stand. "I think it's time for me to go."

"Did you find the wisdom you were seeking?"

"I think I found something."

Garrett looked up at him. "The Blessed Mother is always here for you, Mr. Jagger. When you're ready to follow her path, I may offer you guidance."

Finn didn't know what to say. Despite all of his protestations that he didn't believe in the gods, that he didn't follow their teachings, when it came down to it, when it had been *him* heading to the gallows, he had spoken the words of Heleth. When his mother had died, Finn had been there, in the church, celebrating with Heleth and praying for his mother to go to the Blessed Mother. And when he had this crisis, where had he gone?

Maybe he had more faith than he realized.

Would the Blessed Mother understand his faith was not absolute?

He looked over to Garrett. "Thank you."

Garrett nodded.

Finn headed back out and looked into the distance, along the street, and found himself drawn toward the palace. A dozen palace Archers stood outside, standing watch, but Finn didn't push forward, having no need to do so. That wasn't the reason he had come. He wasn't here to try to press for access to the king, though given the number of Archers here, he suspected the king was still in residence.

What he wanted, though, was to think.

He stared up at the palace, again wondering if he had only been a tool for the king.

Finn had thought he was providing a service, serving the king and serving justice, but maybe he and Meyer were nothing more than tools to be deployed.

If so, was that what he wanted for himself?

It was strange for him to question this so far into his apprenticeship, now that he was an established journeyman, and now that he had done what he had in service of the throne.

But at the same time, eventually, Finn would have to find his own path.

That was what Esmerelda had suggested to him, and he thought he understood the reason she had done so. Knowing her, she probably would have already anticipated his crisis of faith.

Her cards had certainly predicted other uncertainty. Maybe the cards had known he would feel conflicted like this—that the Black Rose movement would pull on him and make him question what he was truly meant to do.

Finn turned away from the palace.

If he thought too much about this, he wasn't sure he'd be able to do what he needed to. Maybe it would be best for him to find Meyer and his sister, then process his remaining tasks. Only then could he begin to work through his concerns.

He weaved through the streets until he reached the old prison. Finn and Meyer both had ways of sneaking in unseen. The old prison was a nondescript-looking building, a single story of stone, and it stretched far deeper belowground than he would've expected, though it didn't tower very high aboveground. Moss grew along the surface of the stone, crawling into the remnants of the windows, leaving it looking as if nature attempted to reclaim the old prison even though it was still inside the city. It was surprising to Finn that it hadn't been demolished, but old buildings like this were difficult to destroy, and they held an almost sacred quality for those who lived within the city.

He found the back entrance and snuck inside.

Finn made his way through the hospital ward, looking at the people gathered there. Most of them were still sleeping, or seemingly so, though he couldn't tell how much of it was from sedation, how much of it was due to their injuries, or how much of it was an act.

Meyer sat in front of a table, flipping through the pages of a book and marking them. Every so often, he would look up, seeming to see Finn watching him, before turning his attention back to what he was doing.

The scalp wound had been stitched and it was healing,

but slowly.

In the time since the hanging, there hadn't been any further protests. The streets still had an eerie, empty quality to them, partly because of the continued—and heavy—Archer presence. It made navigating the streets easier in a way, since there weren't nearly as many people out as there usually were, but it also made it harder in that anyone traveling through the streets had increased attention drawn to them. Finn didn't necessarily want that attention, but he understood the need for it.

He approached Master Meyer.

"This came," he said, sliding the parchment onto the table.

Meyer looked over. They had been staying in the old prison for the most part, avoiding Meyer's home for fear of reprisal. The Archers had kept the home from getting targeted, though Finn believed it a fragile peace.

"What is it?" Meyer asked.

"I don't know. It came while we were here. I snuck into the house to gather some supplies."

Meyer's face wrinkled. The idea that they would need to sneak into their home was bad enough, but Finn didn't know if they had much choice.

Meyer unfolded the paper, his gaze skimming across it while his jaw worked. "Maybe this is for the best."

"What is?"

He handed the paper to Finn.

It didn't take long for Finn to see what it was. Another request for an executioner.

"We can refuse. We have enough going on in the city.

We're close to finding the Black Rose—" Finn said before Meyer cut him off.

"We don't have so much work that we can abandon our other responsibilities," Master Meyer said. "And we haven't proven that there *is* a Black Rose, just that there are people who follow a movement." He sighed. "I know the king thinks there's something more, but we have to come to terms with the fact that there's not."

"I don't want anything to happen to you or Lena," Finn said.

Meyer grunted. "It won't. Can you do it?"

Finn looked over. It was from the village of Serat, which was only a half a day away. Finn had ridden through it before. "Are you sure we should do this now?"

"Not we. *You.* You need to get over your fear. That means going back out."

He swallowed. Meyer wasn't wrong. He knew that. "What about the protests?"

"There have been no protests," Meyer said. He turned his attention back to the book in front of him. "Hopefully, over time, all of that will begin to die down."

"Hopefully?"

"I can't say whether it will or not," Meyer said. "And I can't say how long it will take."

Finn wanted to argue, but he was still just a journeyman.

"I will gather my supplies, make arrangements, and leave in the morning."

Finn approached the small carpenter shop. Maybe he was getting ahead of himself, but since he would be leaving the city, he didn't want to leave Jamie thinking that he had abandoned her, nor that he would have ignored her. She probably wouldn't think that, but he also wanted to see her before he left. It was selfish of him, he knew, much like his desire to pursue the relationship was selfish of him. How could he have a relationship when he was expected to carry out sentences and be such a visible presence in the city?

He raised his hand to knock, when a slip of paper on a neighboring door caught his attention. The mark of the Black Rose.

It was here too.

Finn knocked, and when the door opened, Jamie looked out at him, smiling broadly.

"Finn. I was expecting you today." She glanced behind her before turning back to him. "I hope this isn't official business."

He started to flush before he tamped that feeling down. "I came to see you."

She stepped toward him, smelling of lilacs mixed with a little bit of the sawdust that he suspected was prevalent in the carpenter shop. "You did?"

"I had a nice time with you the other night, and…"

She smiled at him. "I had a nice time with you as well."

"I don't have too many evenings like that."

"Really? You seemed comfortable enough with me."

"Well, not so much these days," Finn said. "It's difficult with my position."

"It's a job."

"It's a job," he said. "And that's why I'm stopping by. I have to leave the city for a while. Hopefully not for long, but I have stopped trying to anticipate how long these assignments will take." Most of the time, they only took a few days to a week at most, but Finn was determined to make this trip out of the city as short as possible. He didn't want to be gone long. He had no idea what might happen in his absence—probably nothing, but there remained the possibility of something else happening. If so, Finn didn't want Jamie to think he had left her. "I didn't want to leave without telling you."

She smiled at him. "You were worried I'd be upset?"

"I wanted to give you the courtesy of knowing that I had a nice time," he said. "And I wanted you to know that I was hoping to see you again when I return."

She laughed softly and touched him on the arm. "I'd like that." She looked along the street before turning her gaze back to him. "I can't imagine the kind of supplies your job requires you to take out of the city."

He smiled to himself. She was trying to show interest in his job, though he didn't know how he felt about that. He didn't really want to tell her what he did. He worried that doing so would only push her away. Still, she knew what he was.

He had to trust that if she were interested in him, what his profession was didn't matter.

Besides, she might understand him in a way that others wouldn't.

Her family had come from nothing and had moved upward, much like he had.

And, much like him, her family still didn't feel as if they fit in.

"I don't have to take much. Food for the journey. Clothes. And, of course, my sword." He regretted saying that last part immediately, but Jamie didn't seem to mind.

"You have to bring the sword with you?"

"I shouldn't talk about that," he said.

"No. It's fine." She looked up at him, holding his gaze. "I know what you do, Finn."

His heart fluttered. He shouldn't feel like this. He was a grown adult. A man. She had him feeling like a boy.

But he had gone so long thinking that he wouldn't find somebody who could come to terms with what he was. Finn had tried to have relationships before. First with Jasmine, though that had never really flowered. Then there had been the start of something with Helda, but she had never been able to move past his occupation.

"I always take a sword when I leave," he said. "I never know what sentencing will be required. But you don't want to know about that." He forced a smile. "I can tell you all about the trees leading up to some of the neighboring communities."

"I have left the city and traveled before, Finn."

He flushed. "That's right."

"But I'm sure your experience in some of these villages is different from the experience I might have. I would be very interested to hear what you have seen in your journeys."

"We can talk about it when I get back."

"Where are you going this time?"

"A village not far from here. It's called Serat."

"I've not heard of it."

"It's along the border of the forest, near the edge of the kingdom, along the Alainsith lands." Hopefully he wouldn't see more Alainsith destruction when he left.

At the mention of the Alainsith, she frowned.

There were many within the city who felt a particular way about the Alainsith, so he wasn't surprised.

"We've never seen any Alainsith during our travels. I've always been curious about them."

"You have?"

"Only because they are rumored to be powerful. And the king fears them," she said.

That wasn't entirely true, but it was close enough. "I can tell you if I see anything of the Alainsith when I'm gone, as well."

She smiled and turned her head briefly, looking back toward the shop for a moment. "My father needs me. I'm sorry, Finn."

"No. I didn't intend to take you from your responsibilities with your father. I just wanted you to know that I'm leaving."

"I will look forward to your return, then."

She squeezed his arm, then headed into the shop.

Finn smiled.

Seeing Jamie again was another reason for him to hurry back.

CHAPTER TWENTY-EIGHT

Finn hadn't been gone from the city for very long. Only a day. Not so long that he would've missed much in Verendal. That was Meyer's point. Besides, Meyer was there. He could handle anything that came up, the same way he had until Finn had started working with him.

He had traveled to Serat, the ride uneventful, though Finn had been jumpy the entire time, something his horse had seemed to recognize. It hadn't made his ride any better or smoother. Confidence seemed to matter to horses, at least the ones he rented. He'd found the village quiet, which was a relief. There was no sign of the Black Rose, and no one in the village had heard of the protests in Verendal. It was almost peaceful.

The man he'd come to meet with had killed a neighbor over a stupid dispute: leaves had fallen on one man's roof and were tossed onto the other's. They had some history, so one had killed the other. There was no remorse.

A simple sentence and the king's justice was carried out easily.

It was almost as if it had been planned by Master Meyer to help him move past what had happened during his last journey out of the city. Still, while he was gone, his thoughts lingered on the city, on what he was missing, and on whether the protests would pick back up. Finn still wasn't convinced that Walter Briggs' sentence would take care of the unrest in the city—not based on what he had seen, and not if everything was coordinated the way he believed.

But the Teller Gate was open as he returned that evening.

He returned the horse to the stable, still feeling an unease within the city, but he wasn't stopped. He saw no one in the streets, which was typical these days, but the stable was empty as well. Finn returned the horse and paused in the street. He saw a trail of smoke in the distance, but it might have been there when he'd left, the remains of one of the fires in an outer section. There had been so many set during the protests that it felt as if the city had continually burned.

As he made his way to Meyer's home, he realized the smoke drifting around the city was more substantial than he remembered. Much more. And only in the outer sections. It was a wonder he'd made it into the city without seeing it better.

Shouts caught his attention, and he slowed long

enough to realize it was another protest. Finn knew better than to get caught up in that, so he hurried to Meyer's home.

The inside was quiet. He lingered for a moment in the entrance to the home, sweeping his gaze around it. Not nearly as much had changed for him this time, compared to the last time he'd left the city. He hadn't nearly died, for one.

He set the sword inside the closet, closing it, then paused in his room. The curtains were drawn, the bed was made, and the books he had stacked on his desk were untouched. The lantern looked as if it hadn't been lit in weeks, which was probably true. Ever since the protests had started, Finn had not paid much attention to his space, nor to his studies, though perhaps that was a mistake. He might have benefited from continuing to work on his training, learning more about medicine and healing, and trying to keep up with his sister. He didn't need to continue studying techniques of torment, as he felt he had mastered those. It was the other aspects of his job he needed to hone.

Finn set his pack down and headed through the home to see where Meyer and his sister were, but there was no sign of them. The kitchen was empty. The air had no smell of bread, meat, eggs, or any of the sweet treats his sister liked to bake.

There was no one here.

He thought they would have returned from the hospital ward by now.

Meyer might still be there, especially if it meant he'd

find more answers about the Black Rose—and if the protests had returned. Finn was tired, and he wanted to rest, but after having been gone for a little over a day, he didn't know if he would have missed anything. He grabbed his cloak, threw it over his shoulders, and headed back outside.

It was eerily quiet in the streets.

The air smelled of the smoke and something he couldn't quite place.

Finn hurried to the old prison. The only people he saw were Archers in the distance.

Something was wrong.

The old prison had a faint odor to it. Its usual mossy appearance suggested that nature still threatened to overwhelm it despite the city landscape, but for whatever reason, it now felt as if the city were pressing upon it, causing the stone to change.

To decay.

Finn frowned.

He approached it slowly.

The old prison was an Alainsith building. There were dozens upon dozens of those within the city. The only thing Finn could think of was what he'd experienced outside of the city, the way that the other Alainsith structures had collapsed. Esmerelda had warned him about others, though he'd been so focused on the protests, he hadn't had the chance to look into it. There had been the one he had seen with Esmerelda, then the one he had seen outside of Weverth. It was all somehow connected.

He swept his gaze over the stone, looking at the moss, then pressed his hand up against it.

It was cool to the touch.

Had it always been that way?

He hadn't taken any time to test the temperature of the stone, though he seemed to remember that Alainsith structures were always warm, certainly warmer than this.

Finn stepped back and looked along the street.

The fact that there was still no movement should reassure him, but there was a strange emptiness here, which was more than a little unsettling. Finn made his way around the back entrance to the prison and opened the door.

A stench struck him—foul and unpleasant, and different from what he remembered before.

Finn held the door open and looked around him. There was nothing here. It was empty. He hurried inside.

When his boots stepped on the stone, he felt a crunching.

He stopped.

Finn looked down. He crouched in front of the stone, running his hand along its surface. The stone had crumbled.

He shifted forward, and when he did, the stone crumbled again.

Finn got to his feet and hurriedly looked around the inside of the prison. If his sister and Meyer were still here, then they were in danger.

He rushed forward, stepping carefully as he went, but he needed to get down into the hospital unit.

He took the steps in long strides, careful not to put any more pressure on the stone than necessary. Each time he touched a step, the stone began to crumble around him.

What's going on here?

Finn reached the bottom of the stairs and hurried along the hallway, the crackling of the stone loud in his ears. He didn't see any other damaged stone around him, which left him worried that something had happened to his sister and Meyer. If they were still inside the hospital ward...

He reached the doors and pulled them open.

It was empty. And it stank. The air was foul, filled with a strange odor of decay.

Finn swept his gaze along the empty beds, pausing in front of the table at the back of the room where Wella had left all of the supplies. It was empty now. In fact, the entire room was empty, the supplies gone.

With every step he took, the ground crumbled.

He needed to get out of here.

Where was his sister? Where was Meyer?

Most of the prisoners had been questioned and moved, but there were still a few here when he'd been here last. Where were they now?

Finn hurried back out, down the hall, all too aware of the trembling beneath him.

He quickly climbed the stairs as they collapsed with each step.

The ground rumbled. Finn fell, slipping down the stairs.

He scrambled for a handhold, but couldn't get one.

Finn tried pulling at the stone, tried to get his hands farther along, but each time he clawed at it, the stone collapsed under his hand, almost as if it were unwilling to let him touch it.

He cried out.

The walls were starting to crumble around him.

He had seen something like this happen before, had even experienced it firsthand, but had never expected that it would happen inside this old building. There had been nothing like this anywhere in the city.

Just outside it.

Unclean.

That word came back to him, as if it were a message.

He dug his toes in. Finn tried not to think about what would happen if the stone collapsed around him entirely, what it would feel like to be buried underneath it.

Finn slammed his hand into the crumbling stone, pulling himself forward. Each time he did, something shifted beneath the surface of his palm, but he still climbed, pulling himself up.

He was close.

Not much farther, and he would be able to get to the ground floor hallway, and from there he could get outside.

He slipped again, sliding down along the surface as the stone continued to crumble beneath him.

Finn tried to anchor himself, hold himself in place, but he could not.

Now the walls began to tremble.

He covered his head as the stone started to shower down around him. He wasn't going to be able to get out the same way he'd come in. Was there another way he might be able to escape?

The hospital section had a much higher ceiling, and there were tables. Beds. He could use something there.

He raced backward, ignoring how the stone cracked and broke with each step. When he reached the hospital unit, he dove toward the table that had once had Wella's medicines on it and crawled underneath—and not a moment too soon.

The walls trembled. The ceiling collapsed. Stone rained down.

Finn could do nothing more than just lie there.

When everything settled, daylight shone down. The walls still crumbled, but with less intensity. He would live.

Weverth. The Alainsith building. The attack—and attempt to take his sword.

He'd been so focused on the protests, but what if there was something more to everything that had happened?

Perhaps the Black Rose movement was involved in some way, but Finn didn't know how it could all be connected, or why.

Finn moved mattresses together, stacking them. He could use them to climb out. As he pulled one off of one of the beds, he heard a strange clattering.

He looked down. There was a small, wooden object resting on the ground. It was broken, little more than a chunk of wood, but he could imagine what it was supposed to look like: a black rose—and it had an engraving on the other side.

It was the same kind of engraving he'd seen on Reginald's coin.

Witchcraft. He didn't understand what the engraving was, or how it worked, but it had to be why the prison collapsed around him.

Finn started to climb up the stone. At first, it crumbled more, but the more he climbed, the more it held. It seemed as if the lower level of the prison had crumbled more than the upper level, and that was what had caused the collapse.

Once he got free, he stood on the street, backing into the shadows so he could look around. Someone had done this. Again, the only thing he could think of was witchcraft, but what kind of witchcraft was this?

He needed to find Meyer. His sister. The rest of the prisoners.

He needed to find answers about the connection between the Black Rose movement and the use of witchcraft, but Finn didn't know what that would involve.

He looked along the street, uncertain where to go. He reached an intersection, then soon realized something. Debris filled the air in another place. Finn had thought it was smoke, but that wasn't it at all.

He went toward it and found it brought him to a part of the city that Finn was all too familiar with.

The Brinder section. The temple had collapsed.

Finn reached it, then stopped.

There was a figure standing near the temple dressed in a long, gray cloak, and beneath the cloak were dark—the clothing of thieves.

Finn knew who it was. How could he not when he had seen those darks so many times over the years and pulled jobs alongside them?

"Oscar? What are you doing?"

"I suppose the same thing as you," Oscar said.

"This isn't the only one that collapsed." Finn took a moment, looking around before sharing with Oscar what he'd seen.

Oscar turned his attention back to the temple. "This always felt so impressive before," he said. "It always felt like something that couldn't fall. I can't believe it has."

"Somebody is doing this. It's tied to the protests."

He frowned. "Why would somebody care enough to destroy these buildings? That's not what the movement was about. You read the pamphlet I gave you. I know you saw what they wanted."

Finn shook his head. Oscar was right. The protests made a certain sort of sense, but this... "I don't have any idea. I need to find my sister and Meyer." Finn looked along the street. It was strangely empty, and even out here, there were no Archers. Why had they all disappeared? "The two of them are missing. I was outside of the city on an assignment, and when I returned, they were gone."

"I can look for them."

Finn smiled tightly. "Thank you."

Oscar just shook his head. "You know I would do anything for your sister."

Finn breathed out. He wished there were an answer here, or something he could say or do to get one, but there was nothing. He needed to know what had happened here, and he wasn't going to be able to do that until he had help.

This was magic. Which meant he needed to get Esmerelda.

Oscar started toward him, but then froze. He flicked his gaze past Finn.

Finn looked behind him. A pair of Archers were heading along the street, sweeping quickly toward them.

"It's fine," Finn said. "The Archers aren't going to do anything to you."

"They aren't going to do anything to *you*," Oscar said. "But they very much will do something to me." Oscar started to move away. "Let's get away from here. Find me at my club. Do you remember how to find it?"

Finn nodded as Oscar slipped away.

Out of the three in the patrol, one of the Archers peeled off, though Finn didn't see where he'd gone. One of them approached Finn, already drawing his sword.

Finn placed his hands in the air. "I'm Finn Jagger, executioner for the king."

The Archer watched him, hand on his sword, making Finn even more uneasy. He didn't recognize the man, but these days, Finn wasn't even sure if he would recognize the Archers.

"What are you doing out?" the man asked. "There's a curfew in the city."

"I've been away from the city for a bit," Finn said. "What do you mean, 'there's a curfew'?"

The Archer took another step toward him. "You are not to be out."

Finn frowned. Now he understood Oscar's concern.

"I'm in service of King Porman. If you question that, then we can go to Tolsten."

One of the other men motioned to the Archer, and they looked along the street.

More Archers.

The patrols were heavier than Finn had ever seen. The city had erupted in violence in the day he'd been gone. Would it have been different if he had stayed?

"Leave him," one man said.

The first Archer slammed his sword into his sheath and they marched away.

Shouts rang out behind Finn.

More and more people gathered in the street as a crowd started making its way toward Finn.

He ran, hurrying across the road after making sure no one was there. When he got to the opposite side, he slipped along in the shadows, reaching the next alley. He moved carefully and quickly, trying to ignore the stench of the alley and pausing when he reached its end. There was someone moving along the street. He didn't dare head out until he could tell for sure who was there.

A man called out to others. Finn recognized the black crest on his lapel—the mark of the Black Rose. The man led the crowd past, and thankfully, no one looked toward Finn. He stayed in the darkness, hiding in the shadows.

Now wasn't the time to go to Esmerelda.

Get to Oscar.

He didn't know if he was going to be able to take the alleys all the way to Oscar's lounge. Finn pressed his back up against the wall nearest him and closed his eyes. He had to think through his path.

He could get through Brinder. That was easy enough. Once he got outside of the Brinder section, though, passing from here to another section would be more complicated.

Finn darted forward. As soon as he crossed the street, there was a shout behind him.

The protesters moved toward him.

He was no longer accustomed to this.

He wasn't a thief anymore. He was an executioner. There was no reason he should have to sneak through the streets like this. No reason for him to have to hide who he was and where he was going. No reason for him to have to conceal himself.

Finn raced along the alley until he got to the next street.

Every time he thought there was a clear section of street, he heard chaos—fighting, violence, occasionally shouts. Every so often, an explosion echoed, thundering through the streets and carrying to Finn's ears.

He navigated slowly, carefully, pausing at each alley, looking along the street, and searching for any sign of the protest making its way toward him. At one point, Finn had to duck around the corner and hurry toward an alley, barely managing to stay ahead of them. He didn't know if they would recognize him, or if they would come for him, but he didn't want to take his chances.

He came across several other throngs of people, all led by someone with the mark of the Black Rose.

The city was in chaos.

Fires glowed everywhere. Smoke filled the sky.

And there was dust. Alainsith structures destroyed.

All he wanted was to find his sister and Meyer and get them to safety.

The only way he could do that would be by getting to Oscar. It was strange for him to feel that way. He had been the one to promise safety to Oscar, but he wasn't able to offer him that.

Not anymore.

But Oscar was there for him.

Oscar had always been there.

By the time Finn made it to Oscar's club, he was tired. Nothing he'd found helped him understand what was going on in the city around him. There had been no additional movement from the protesters or those with the marking of the Black Rose since he arrived, though every so often, Finn caught sight of shadows in the distance, and the sound of screams or shouts echoing. It wouldn't be long before everything exploded in violence.

But the king wasn't about to let the violence in the city build. Finn was certain of that.

He tested the lock on the door to Oscar's club. It was closed.

He tried to look inside, but the windows were all blocked, barricaded to keep him from seeing anything.

He knocked softly.

Finn stayed pressed up against the door, cautious here,

and worried that he might get caught by one of the members of the Black Rose.

He knocked again. Once again, there was no answer.

"Dammit, Oscar," Finn muttered.

He needed his old friend. Needed him for several reasons, not the least of which was to let Finn into the club.

He knocked again, this time more forcefully than the last.

Finally, the door opened, and Oscar poked his scarred face out toward Finn.

"You don't have to knock so hard," Oscar said. He glanced in either direction along the street before opening the door widely enough for Finn to come inside.

"I've been trying not to, but first you tell me to come here, then you have it locked, and—"

"Just get in here," Oscar said.

Finn stepped inside.

The chairs had all been pushed off to the side of the room. Annie sat in one of them, leaning forward, a frown creasing her brow. There were two others whom Finn didn't recognize, younger men he suspected were a part of Oscar's crew. One of them was tall and muscular, with a brooding expression that gave him the look of a bruiser. The other was short, and he pressed his mouth together in a disapproving frown as Finn came into the club.

There was one other person inside the room: a man with his wrists bound behind him and his legs bound in front of him, wearing the clothing of an Archer.

CHAPTER TWENTY-NINE

"What did you do?" Finn asked. He looked around the club for a moment, noting the dim lights, shaded windows, and stale air. Even though Oscar had claimed he would be opening his club soon, he still had not done so. Had the attacks of the Black Rose changed Oscar as well?

"Just get in here," Oscar repeated.

Finn stood for a moment, looking over to the Archer, then back to Oscar and the others. This was his fear. Now he would have to decide how to deal with Oscar, after everything he'd gone through with him.

But Finn didn't know if he could even do anything when it came to Oscar. He certainly couldn't take him to the prison, and he couldn't do that to Annie either, given what she had gone through, but the other two...

The other two would know if Finn didn't take Oscar in.

He turned to Oscar. "You can't do this to me," he said softly. "I know you side with them, but not this way."

Oscar took his arm and forced him forward. "You're damn right, not this way. I think the movement is right. They want people like you used to be to have a chance to live. Those fighting for it might not be doing it how you agree, but you need to take a look, Finn. Be the man you claim you are."

Finn looked down at the Archer, crouching on the ground in front of him. There was something wrong. The marking on his jacket was wrong.

Archers all had a single stripe, unless they were serving as palace Archers. This one had a stripe on his left shoulder, but the angle was all wrong. It looked to be made by somebody who had only seen Archers from a distance.

"He's not a real Archer," Finn said, looking the man over. He had dark brown hair, a lean face, and deep-brown eyes that glowered at Finn.

"That's right," Oscar said. "I was followed on my way back here. Bastard was a little cleverer than I would've expected for one of the Archers. Most of them don't care to take the side streets."

Finn looked over to Oscar and chuckled softly. Side streets to Oscar meant alleys.

And he wasn't wrong. The Archers generally avoided alleys. It was one way the criminals managed to stay ahead of them. They mostly avoided them because they didn't care for the smell, but it was more than that: it was the dirtiness of most of the alleys, and the darkness, along with the fact that they had to go down them single file, which meant any criminal hiding there had an advantage.

"How did you know?"

"He doesn't look quite right, does he?" Oscar said, looking over to Finn.

Finn regarded Oscar for a moment.

He didn't know quite what to say. He had a sneaking suspicion Oscar would have jumped him regardless. And if that was the case, then Finn was lucky this was a false Archer and not a real one. If it were a real Archer, what choice would Finn have had but to do the one thing he feared doing in Verendal and bring him in?

"Damn you, Oscar," Finn whispered.

"You're going to go on about that?" Oscar said.

"You're going to force me to make a decision one of these days."

"I'm not going to force you to do anything," Oscar said. "You do what you need to do. And I'm going to do what *I* need to do. You wanted to know who's organizing all of this. I told you I'd try to help you out. Why don't you start with him?"

Finn looked at the man. He still hadn't said anything.

"Who are you?" Finn asked.

"You're going to face the king," the false Archer said.

"I have. That's why I'm here." He leaned toward the man. "My name is Finn Jagger. Executioner to King Porman. And I'm here to question you."

The two men sitting off to the side groaned softly.

"If you serve the king, then you need to take him in,"

the false Archer said, nodding to Oscar. "He attacked a servant of the crown."

Finn shook his head. "I don't think so. In fact, I am quite certain you aren't what you claim yourself to be. I will give you only a few moments to tell me who you are and why you're dressed like that."

"Or what?" the man asked.

"Or you're going to see how I question prisoners." For him to get the information he needed, he was going to have to be forceful—and quick. If he couldn't find it from this man, he would have to ask others. The longer this took, the more likely the city would be under attack.

Unfortunately, he would need to question him around Oscar, unless he asked Oscar to leave.

"I've told you that you made a mistake. I serve the king."

Finn found a stout wooden chair pushed up against the wall and grabbed it, carrying it over to the center of the room. There, he hoisted the false Archer into the chair, his arms behind the backrest. He looked over to Oscar. "I need everyone out."

Oscar regarded him for a long moment. "This is my establishment."

Finn strode over to Oscar, lowering his voice as he flicked his gaze over to Annie, then the other two men. "Don't make me push the issue, Oscar. I just need a few moments to question him. We need to know what's going on. Something strange is happening in the city with the Black Rose and his men, along with the riots."

Oscar held his gaze before glancing over to Annie and nodding. He turned to the other two men. "Out."

The larger of the two frowned. "Are you sure you're safe with this one?"

"I'm safer with him than I am with anyone else," Oscar said.

The other man studied Finn, then the two of them headed out the back door, with Annie behind them.

Oscar looked over to Finn. "I'm not going anywhere," he said.

"Oscar—"

"Dammit, Finn. You asked for my help. I gave it to you. Now would you just do what you have to do?"

"You aren't going to like it."

"You asking a few questions?"

"*How* I ask the questions." Finn grabbed another chair, dragging it over and taking a seat in front of the false Archer. "I need to know about the Black Rose."

The man leaned his head back. It was slight, but enough that Finn knew what was coming. He tipped off to the side, grabbing for his belt knife, and waited until the man spit at him before sitting upright again.

"This isn't going to go the way you think it is," Finn said. "You're going to tell me what I need to know about the Black Rose."

"Fuck you," the man said again.

"I don't think so," Finn said. He scooted forward and jabbed the knife into the man's thigh.

Behind him, Oscar grunted.

Finn ignored it.

The false Archer glowered at Finn.

"Tell me what you know about the Black Rose," Finn said.

Finn had been less aggressive than he should have been when he had Jonrath captured in Declan. He wasn't going to take that approach now. He had an obligation to find answers, but he also had an obligation to understand what was going on and ensure it stopped.

This was what he had to do.

He served the king, but he also would do this for himself.

"Finn?" Oscar said.

"Don't interfere," Finn said. He glared at the man. "Tell me about the Black Rose."

Again, the man leaned his head back slightly.

Finn twisted the knife. The man cried out.

He tried to keep emotion out of this, but his irritation with himself made it difficult. Had he only followed his instinct, he might have found these answers sooner. Instead, he'd pushed himself to be what he thought others wanted of him.

"You will tell me what you know about them."

"I don't know anything. I was hired. That's it. They got money. Lots of it. We do what they want, and they pay."

"Hired." Finn shook his head. "I'm sorry, but I don't believe that anymore." He slid the chair forward, pulling the knife out of the man's thigh and jamming it into his other one. These wounds would take time to heal. He was being more aggressive than he would typically be when questioning. Most of the time, Finn went the route of trying to be friendly, trying to gain an alliance first, but he'd seen how unsuccessful that would be in this case.

"What do you want to know? They promised me ten gold coins. All I have to do is give them what's in my pocket after the job is done, and I get paid."

Finn pulled the knife out, twisting as he did, then he held it up to the man's neck while reaching into the man's pocket.

There, he found a circular wooden object.

It reminded him of what he had found in Reginald's home, but it was different. It was the same as what he'd found in the old prison, but this one was intact. If he could find who made these, maybe he could figure out the rest.

There couldn't be that many capable of carving a Black Rose medallion. The one he'd found in the following prison had been incomplete, but seeing this one now gave him all of the answers he needed—but he hated those answers.

He started to stuff it into his own pocket, when he felt something else.

Esmerelda's card.

He pulled it out and the ink swirled, golden shapes taking hold.

He recognized the storefront symbolized on it. A hammer and chisel.

It was Jaime's father's store.

Everything went cold for Finn.

"Where did you get this marker?" he asked, holding out the medallion.

"I told you. They gave it to me. It's a marker for the Black Rose. I get paid when the job is done. That's it."

"What is it, Finn?" Oscar asked, pressing up behind him and looking over Finn's shoulder. He tried to reach for it, but Finn closed his hand around it and stuffed the wooden medallion into his pocket.

Payments.

That was what this was about. The Black Rose medallions were tied to payments.

Reginald's journal was tied to payments.

He leaned down, looking at the man. "I need to know everything."

Finn had been right. All along, he had been right about this. Had he only continued digging into Reginald when he first ended up dead in the prison...

"I don't know what to say. I was supposed to get close to the old buildings. You know the ones—dark stone, impossibly old."

"Alainsith," Finn said.

"I was supposed to get close, wait until the crowd gathers, and..."

Finn clenched his jaw.

He wasn't entirely sure what to make of all of this, but it all fit together: Alainsith, the crumbled buildings, the crowds, and his belief that witchcraft was involved. And now he understood how Reginald fit in.

"Get rid of him," Finn said.

"*What?*" Oscar said.

Finn glowered at the false Archer. "When all of this

calms down, bring him to Declan prison. Tell the iron master there that I sent him."

"You can do that," Oscar said.

Finn looked up at him, and Oscar took a step back. He had worried what would happen if it came down to trying to capture and imprison somebody he cared about. All along, he'd feared it would be Oscar, or perhaps Annie, or any of the others within the Wenderwolf whom he had come to know.

Not Master James, the father of someone he thought he might be able to connect to.

Sadly, it fit. Uprisings spread in other places within the kingdom. Places where Master James could have visited. Places where the Black Rose could have been.

And now Finn would have to be responsible for stopping him.

Jamie would never forgive him.

Finn could choose. He could do nothing—let the fighting persist, and eventually, he had little doubt that the king would end it. And Finn didn't have answers yet either.

He still didn't know why witchcraft was involved, or why the Alainsith sites had been targeted and whether they were tied to the Black Rose, though he was increasingly certain they were, though he didn't know how.

"Finn? What is it?"

It was the one thing Finn had feared. Could he do his job, carry out his responsibility, even if it meant harming someone he cared about?

Esmerelda had talked to him about finding his path.

Finn had gone along with what was asked of him from the very beginning. When it had involved the King, then Bellut and the magister, it had been easy. When it had involved people getting hurt within the city, that had been easy, even if the task assigned to him was not. Now…

Now it was difficult.

All he had wanted was a chance at some normalcy.

All he had wanted was to have somebody he could spend some time with, somebody who could know him—somebody not afraid of his job and what it meant for him. For only a moment, he had thought that might be Jamie.

Now he would be taking her father into custody. He would be responsible for carrying out her father's execution.

Finn pushed down all of the emotion he felt, forcing it deep inside. "This has to end." He looked up. "I'm going to go stop the Black Rose."

"It's a movement, Finn. You can't stop a movement."

"It's more than a movement," he said sadly.

"You know who did it?"

"I do now." He looked over to the man. "I hope it was worth it for what you were paid," Finn said.

"They were going to pay. Everyone said so. Nobody in the city has got anything. Not unless you're on the right side of the river. Everybody else…"

"How many died because of what you did? How many more are you willing to sacrifice?"

"For change?"

Finn snorted. "You don't even know what you're trying to change."

Finn headed toward the door. He was going to have to sneak through the streets, but at least he knew where he was going. It would be a difficult trip, but at this point...

Oscar caught him as he reached the door. "Is that the kind of thing you're doing now?" Oscar asked, glancing over to where the false Archer sat in the chair.

"Don't start on me," Finn said.

"Not starting on you at all. Just trying to understand who you are and what you've become."

"I'm trying to find my place," Finn said. His gaze swept around the inside of the club. "Sort of like you're trying to find yours."

Oscar blinked. "I don't like this side of you, Finn."

"Which side?"

"The side willing to do that. That's not you."

"That is me," Finn said. "At least, it is now."

He pulled open the door, stepping outside. The wind had picked up and thunder rumbled as gray clouds thickened, becoming darker before rain began sheeting down.

It was fitting; given everything he had gone through, Finn thought the downpour suited his mood. He darted along the street, slipping through the alleys and avoiding the Archers. He found several pockets of them, though many were likely fake.

Finn reached the river, and he had to wait for one patrol to clear before he darted across. Once he did, he encountered a group of five Realmsguard dressed in heavy armor, rain dripping down the surface of it. One of the men had a long scar along his cheek and part of his nose had scarred in, making it look as if he'd lost it in some battle. There was no way these were false Archers. They certainly didn't serve the Black Rose.

They stopped him, swords pointing at him.

Finn frowned. "I'm the king's executioner."

One of the Realmsguard stepped forward. "The king's executioner is in the palace. You aren't him."

At least that explained what happened to Meyer. "His apprentice," Finn said. "And if you want to stop the Black Rose, you need to come with me."

The others looked around before turning to the lead Realmsguard.

"If you're misleading us…" he started.

"If I'm misleading you, then you take me to the palace and put me before the king."

Finn pushed past him, ignoring the soldier, and marched to the Yanish section.

A pair of the Realmsguard followed Finn, including the one who had stepped forward.

"What happened today?" Finn asked.

"People revolted. We tried closing the gates, but they pushed past them. The damn Black Rose got the people to uprise. Killed a couple dozen Archers."

"Is the king still here?"

The soldier frowned at Finn. "How did you know?"

"I told you," Finn said.

"You told me you were the executioner."

"I met with him not long ago."

It felt like ages ago, though it couldn't have been.

"Well, the king don't have much tolerance for that kind of uprising. We plan on squashing it."

Finn flicked his gaze to the palace. In the rain and the darkness, he couldn't make much out. If the king decided to squash a rebellion, he knew what would happen. People would be killed. The rebellion would be crushed. And all of the poorer sections in the city would be destroyed.

That wasn't what Finn wanted. That couldn't be what the king wanted either.

"We might be able to stop this before it gets to that point," Finn said.

"Why do you care?"

"Because those people don't deserve to be slaughtered," Finn said.

"Them people are nothing."

Finn turned and faced the Realmsguard. "Those people are citizens like anyone else in the city. And they deserve the same protections."

He hurried forward. He didn't want to argue about whether the people in the poorer sections deserve the same protections, and given what they had done, and how it had led to the uprising, Finn understood it was going to be difficult to convince anybody that they needed to do anything more than what they already had, but he wasn't going to stand aside and wait.

By the time he reached the carpenter shop, Finn was drenched. The two Realmsguard stayed with him, but they'd fallen silent.

Finn pounded on the door and ushered the soldiers back.

Master James pulled the door open, peering into the rain before beaming as he spotted Finn. "Mr. Jagger! Are you here to visit with Jamie? She's just popped out to get an elixir I need, but I'm sure she won't want to miss you."

Finn shook his head. He held out the coin. "Is this your work?"

Master James stared at it, looking up at him. Something in his expression changed. "You know it is, Mr. Jagger."

Finn nodded to the Realmsguard and they grabbed Master James. "What is this about?"

"Under the orders of King Porman, we're taking you into custody," Finn said.

"For what charge?" He looked at the coin. "It is not a crime to create carvings, even this one."

"It's not a crime, but you told me how much it costs you to make each one of these. And I can only imagine why you would have done something like this." Finn leaned forward, shaking his head. "Jamie will be so disappointed to learn that you're leading the Black Rose movement." Finn nodded to the Realmsguard. "Take him to Declan."

The Realmsguard dragged Master James along the street as he continued to try to protest, arguing for his innocence. Finn stood in the pouring rain for a long moment, debating what he would do.

They needed to end the violence.

Capturing the Black Rose would hopefully prevent the king from taking drastic action, but only if Finn could get to him and tell him that he had been captured.

"Finn?"

Finn turned to see Jamie coming down the street. Her

dark brown dress was drenched, and her leather satchel was completely saturated.

He swallowed.

Finn was going to be responsible for what happened to Jamie. He was going to be responsible for what took place with her father. And now he was going to have to be responsible for telling her.

"What are you doing here? After what you went through the last time you left the city, I figured you'd be gone longer." She glanced behind her. "The city is not well."

Finn nodded. "I know."

"Then you shouldn't be out. Gods, Finn. With the rain, you should just head back to your home and wait it out." Her gaze darted to the bundle he carried, then up at his face. "You aren't here to see me though. You aren't here to visit."

Finn shook his head. "I'm sorry," he said softly.

Her eyes widened. "What happened?"

"It's your father." He had to get the words out quickly, tell her then move on. She deserved that much from him. He glanced to the shop. "We can get out of the rain, if you would like."

She nodded, heading past him and into the shop, and looked at him in a way he had never seen from her before. Throughout the time he had spent with Jamie—especially when they had wandered the city, talking and connecting in a relaxed and peaceful manner—Finn had never felt that tension from her. There had always been comfort between them.

And now that was gone.

It would never return, especially after Finn told her what he needed to.

He stepped inside the shop and closed the door. Jamie had gone to one of the tables, grabbing a lantern and lighting it. She stood and waited, water dripping off her.

"I told you I had been on an errand for the king," Finn said slowly. He tried to ignore the water pouring off him too, as well as the puddle beneath his feet, the hammering of his heart, and the nausea within his belly that came from what he had to say. "He tasked us with finding the Black Rose."

"I figured as much," Jamie said. "With everything that has been going on in the city, it isn't surprising that the king would want to find this person."

"Well, I found him."

Jamie had turned away to grab something out of one of the cabinets, then paused. "What do you mean, 'you found him'?"

"I'm terribly sorry, Jamie. Your father is…"

She shook her head. "No. He couldn't be."

Finn sighed. "It fits." He wasn't about to tell her that she was responsible for sharing the details to confirm that it fit. The Black Rose. The places where the uprisings had started throughout the kingdom were the places her father had traveled to within the last year. "Everything fits. Including this." He pulled the marker out of his pocket and held it out.

Jamie came toward him, grabbing it.

"No," she whispered.

"I'm so sorry, Jamie. I wish it wasn't true. I wish it wasn't your father. But the Black Rose has caused terrible violence throughout the city. The king needed to have him stopped. It's the only way the city will be able to relax again."

"Not my father," she said.

Finn wanted to reach for her, to wrap her in a hug, but he didn't dare.

"I'm so sorry," he said again.

She stared at the marker. "This doesn't mean he's the one responsible." She looked up at Finn, and he recognized the desperation in her gaze. It was the same desperation he saw in so many other criminals he questioned— only this time, it was a desperation in the eyes of somebody he cared about.

"No, it doesn't," Finn said. "But that's not the part that matters. It's everything else." If it were only the marker, Finn could have believed that Master James had been hired to create them, but it was the other pieces that fit too.

What didn't make sense was why the Alainsith structures had been targeted within the city—*and* outside the city. When he questioned her father, he hoped to have answers for that. Once he learned, then he could go to Esmerelda, and perhaps the two of them could figure out how to protect the remaining Alainsith structures from crumbling into the strange dark decay.

"You can prove this?" she asked him.

"I can prove most of it," Finn said. "The rest... My job is to uncover the truth, Jamie. I serve the king."

"You serve the king."

Finn looked up, taking a deep breath and nodding. It was the first time that Finn wished he hadn't worked with Master Meyer. It was painful in a way that it had never been before. It was a burden in a way that it had never been before.

"I'm sorry."

He started toward the door, then froze.

His mind was working differently now than it should have been. Normally, he would have processed things much more rapidly, especially considering the circumstance, but he hadn't reacted quite the way he thought he should have when it came to the comment Jamie had made when he'd first come across her.

"What did you mean earlier when you said, 'after what I went through the last time I left the city'?" he asked, turning toward her.

He'd never told her what happened to him.

The Black Rose.

They'd been after the sword—something that could disrupt witchcraft.

Jamie was only a few steps away from him, and she had her arm behind her back. "I really wish you wouldn't have come here," she said.

"I never told you I was attacked." He hadn't told anyone besides Esmerelda, Lena, and Meyer.

The attacker had the mark of the Black Rose on them.

Either her father had told her what happened—and given her reaction, that seemed unlikely—or he had the wrong person.

"You told me you traveled with your father when he went out of the city. You traveled with him."

Jamie looked at Finn and took a deep breath, bringing her arm around. She held a long, slender wand in one hand. A witchcraft wand.

"I really wish you wouldn't have come here," she said again.

"Your father isn't the Black Rose, is he? It's you."

She darted toward him, though the movement was clumsy, not from somebody used to attacking. He caught her hand, twisting her wrist, and forcing the witchcraft wand out of her hand so it dropped to the ground.

"I never figured out how you were even still alive. They wanted you dead. That was part of the agreement. Part of why they'd fund Verendal."

His mind spun as Finn tried piecing it all together.

Fund.

The money paid to the protesters.

The Black Rose was a part of it, but not directly.

And Esmerelda's warning that there was someone else out there, someone powerful, came back to him. More than that, he thought he understood why she hadn't wanted him looking into the damage to the Alainsith structures.

She'd wanted to protect him.

"Unfortunately, whoever is paying you overlooked many things," Finn said, flicking his gaze to the wand lying on the ground before looking up at her. "You and I are going to talk about why the Black Rose is supporting witchcraft."

CHAPTER THIRTY

Finn had returned to the debtors' prison, curiosity getting the best of him—and he no longer felt guilty about having that curiosity. Perhaps he shouldn't have felt that way in the first place. He stood in front of Reginald's cell, studying its bars.

The thud of boots echoing along the stone caught his attention, and he looked up to see Warden Arlington coming toward him.

"Can I help you with anything, Mr. Jagger?"

"I was just completing my investigation."

"In this cell?" Arlington didn't bother to hide his irritation with Finn.

"I'm not completely convinced that Reginald killed himself."

The warden stopped a few paces away. "I assure you that the guards had nothing to do with his death."

"I didn't say that they did."

"You didn't need to say it. You implied it by your presence here." Finn looked over to Arlington. There was no point in arguing with him about that. "Does Master Meyer know that you have persisted in this investigation?"

Finn smiled tightly. "I'm sure he doesn't care."

"Which means he doesn't know."

Finn ignored Arlington as he looked into the cell. There had to be something more here. He just hadn't found it yet. He could look in the cell, he could go to Reginald's home, and he could question the iron masters, continuing to dig, but he wasn't sure there was anything to those threads that he would uncover.

And maybe it didn't matter.

He had another place he needed to go. More questions to get answered.

"If you see anything unusual, please pass it on," Finn said.

Arlington regarded him for a moment. "That's it?"

"I am concerned about what happened here, but I don't have the answers. If you find anything, anything at all, let me know. It might be useful. It might not. But we won't know until we look into it."

He started off, and could practically feel Arlington's gaze on his back.

Finn headed across the city, eventually reaching the women's prison.

The inside of the women's prison was different than most of the other prisons. For one, there was more sunlight drifting through the large, curved windows, and there was also a different energy to the place. It was quiet, though the warden of the women's prison brought in an instrumentalist on many days, who played soothing tunes. Finn smiled to himself as he made his way through the halls. He rarely came here, mostly because the women's prison was not occupied at the same rate as the other prisons throughout the city.

He had ensured the iron masters at all prisons were trained the same though. In this case, given what had happened with other prisoners, he was determined to ensure Jamie lived. Partly that was selfish. He still couldn't believe she could be the Black Rose.

He reached the cell where Jamie sat, her back facing him. Chains linked her legs to the wall, keeping her from running or getting too close to the bars of the cell. Finn glanced to the iron master at the end of the hall before reaching for his keyring and unlocking the door, stepping inside.

"I have nothing to say to you," Jamie said.

"I think you owe me some answers."

She snorted. "Owe you?" She glanced over her shoulder, darkness in her blue eyes. "Why would I owe you anything? And here I thought you would understand, coming from the section that you did. A man who managed to get out, if only a little."

"That doesn't mean I would hurt others who came from my section."

"Not hurting them. Freeing them."

Finn took a seat. There wasn't a place like the chapel in the women's prison. In that way, it was more like the debtors' prison, more of a holding cell than anything else —primarily to ensure those who owed would be given the opportunity to pay their debt.

"You weren't freeing them," Finn said.

"And you know this?" she asked.

"Turn and look at me."

She grunted, but she didn't turn toward him.

"At least talk to me. Help me understand why you did what you did."

"You know why I did what I did," she said.

"I know what I read. I know what I've seen published. I know what others in the city have claimed. But I still don't really *know*," Finn said.

"Then you haven't been paying attention."

"Because you feel slighted in some way?"

"Is that what you really believe?"

"How should I not?" he asked. "Your father had gotten out of his section as well."

She snorted again. "He'd gotten out. Do you remember what happened when you first met me?"

"I remember I came looking for information about Reginald. But you were using him."

"He deserved what he got."

"And what was he guilty of?"

"He hadn't paid," she said. "Like so many others. They think themselves better than us. Than my father. All his work for nothing. He showed me how those who viewed themselves as above you would take advantage of you. There were far too many people in the city who were eager to hire a craftsman with my father's skill, but they knew his background. They knew he was from the wrong side of the river," she said, shaking her head. "And because of that, he was cheated."

"You could have reported it," Finn said.

"Do you think we didn't? We reported it time and time again and got the same response each time."

Finn studied her for a moment. "I reopened the investigation into Reginald. I looked into the others listed in ledger. You were moving money. Laundering it to the movement. What I still need to know is who is behind it all."

Jaime may have coordinated the movement, but it had become clear she wasn't behind the funding of it. That was probably tied to whoever had wanted them to use witchcraft on Alainsith structures.

Would she even know?

Jamie looked away from him.

It had taken Finn the better part of a morning to investigate, but after the first five shops that he had visited, the truth had come out. None of the entries in the journal had known what they were doing. They were passing money through, getting a cut, and moving it out and to Reginald to fund the Black Rose movement.

"You don't even want to acknowledge it? Why did Reginald have to die?"

Finn had never been convinced that it was suicide.

"Once he was jailed, I needed him out of the way."

Finn was shocked by her coldness. It left him wondering how he had sold misread her. He had never misread somebody so poorly before.

Jamie looked up at him, and for a moment, there was a flickering in her eyes, the woman that he thought he knew her to be. Then it was gone.

"Who funded you?" Finn asked.

She stared at him, then smiled defiantly. "I don't even know. And I don't care."

He had failed reading her once before, but he believed this.

"When you first came to us, I thought maybe you understood," she said, her voice still hard. "I thought you knew what it was like to have no real standing in the city. To have those with power trample on you. But you didn't. You outgrew who you were." She looked up at him. How could he have thought her innocent before? "I never did."

"So you started a rebellion."

"I didn't start it. And I'm not the only one responsible for it—perhaps I am in Verendal, but not elsewhere."

That was more than what he'd learned so far. "You only continued what had already been started in other cities," Finn said.

She laughed bitterly. "The Black Rose is in more places than just Verendal."

There was a threat underneath the comment, and she offered him a knowing look. Would he be able to question her the way he questioned others? In order to find the truth, he would have to.

That was his path. That was his responsibility.

"You're saying you're not the leader of the rebellion."

"Oh, no." She said, a dark smile coming to her face. Finn had always thought her beautiful, and she was, but her current expression made her seem terrifying, and it disturbed him. "You aren't going to like what's coming."

"And what *is* coming?"

She turned away from him.

"Why did you have them attack the Alainsith structures?" he asked, and she stiffened. "You didn't know I made that connection."

"You really are the Hunter, aren't you?"

"There are several outside of the city that have been attacked, including outside of Weverth. And several within the city as well. Why?"

"You wouldn't understand."

"I think I would," Finn said. "They were attacked for the same reason your attackers wanted my sword. Tell me why."

"All we had to do was use the wands on certain buildings. They wouldn't fund the revolution otherwise. And they knew your sword would counter them." She shrugged. "They wanted to destroy it."

Finn frowned. He'd thought this was all some conspiracy, all tied together, but what if she *had* been used? There were certainly those who knew about the power of the sword, but *his* blade didn't have nearly the power that Justice had. That would have been the sword to claim.

"You didn't even know what you were doing."

"Did it matter? We saw what those wands were capable of doing. If it destroyed something within the city—"

"It destroyed the history of this city," Finn said.

"A history of oppression," she said.

"The Alainsith never suppressed our people. We pushed them out."

She turned away. "It doesn't matter. It's done. And I wouldn't have changed anything."

"You wouldn't have changed allowing witchcraft to be used within the city?"

"No," she said.

"I'm sorry you feel that way," Finn said.

This time, she turned to him, meeting his gaze. "You should pick your side carefully, Finn. When the darkness comes, will your king see you through it? Or will you be just another tool he uses?" She shook her head. "I don't intend to be a tool."

She turned away from him again, and Finn doubted he would get any more answers from her. Not this way. In time, as he questioned her, he thought he would find out more, even though he didn't like what it would involve.

He got to his feet. "Your father has been released." She tensed. "I questioned him. You are responsible for that, unfortunately, and he denied everything."

"You believed him?"

"Should I not have?"

She shuddered. "He didn't know anything."

"But you still let him take the blame."

"I didn't intend for him to," she said, her voice soft.

"But you still *let* him. He will be given an opportunity to prove himself, though because of what you have done, he will be watched."

"We are all watched. Even you, Finn."

Finn waited for her to say something more, and

thought about all of the things he wished he could say to her, the ways he might be able to get through to her, but she had betrayed him—she had betrayed so much—and there wasn't anything he could do at this point.

He stepped out of the cell, locking it again. As he stared through the bars, he knew the circumstances would be even worse than they were now when he next saw her. He would be tasked with questioning her, trying to understand what she had done and the reason behind it, and Finn doubted that he would get much in the way of answers.

When he reached the end of the hall, he found Master Meyer standing there, watching him. "You don't have to do this," Meyer said.

He was dressed in his gray jacket and pants, with a satchel hung over one shoulder and dark lines in the corners of his eyes.

"Why shouldn't I?"

Meyer flicked his gaze along the hall. "It can be hard when you have to question someone you care about."

Finn squeezed his eyes shut for a moment before opening them and looking at Meyer. "I always thought it would be Oscar."

"So did I."

"She's not the only one involved." He turned so he could look down the hall, though he wasn't able to see anything. "There was witchcraft involved in the destruction of the Alainsith buildings. I don't know what it means, but I can suspect."

"That's what the king feared," Meyer said, his mouth tightening.

"What do you mean?"

"I've been wondering why the king had us get involved in this. Something like this should have been handled by the Realmsguard, or even the palace Archers, but he didn't use them in this case. I wasn't sure why. And perhaps even now, I'm not sure. But if it did involve witchcraft, then perhaps the king knew, and he wanted to ensure it was stopped before it had a chance to take hold."

"I'm concerned that witchcraft has started to spread throughout the kingdom." Finn thought about the last attack, when Holden had targeted the city. He had intended to use the Alainsith in order to power something greater. Finn might even have unwittingly played a part in that.

He looked over to Meyer, and found him still frowning.

"If it's witchcraft, then we should—"

"We can't leave it," Finn said.

That was what the king wanted of him.

He was the Hunter.

"You've done well." Finn regarded Meyer for a moment. It was high praise from him. "You've done what the king wanted of you, as well," Meyer stated.

"And what is that?" Finn asked.

"You're serving in your way, not mine." Meyer shrugged. "That is what he asks. That is also what the court would ask of you. So long as you serve justice, you will find that there is not one single way it must be done. What would you have us do now?" Meyer asked.

Finn didn't really know, but an answer came to him nonetheless.

"I'm going to be gone for a while," Finn said to Meyer.

"For what?"

"Trying to ensure we stay ahead of whatever attack is coming for us."

"How?"

When he learned that Jamie had betrayed him, it felt like she was one more person who had let him down. Throughout the time he had served as an executioner, it felt as if so many people had. Even Oscar had not wanted to be a part of what Finn did. Not that Finn could blame him.

There was only one person who had helped him through all of it. One person who had shown a willingness to offer their assistance, knowing who and what he was.

It was this person he had to go to now.

"It's time for me to involve the hegen. It's time for me to ask Esmerelda for a favor."

Meyer's eyes darkened for a moment, and Finn understood.

Both were worried—not about the hegen, but about why witchcraft was spreading throughout the kingdom.

———

The epic conclusion of The Executioner's Song series: The Master Executioner!

SERIES BY D.K. HOLMBERG

The Chain Breaker Series

The Chain Breaker

The Dark Sorcerer

The Dragonwalkers Series

The Dragonwalker

The Dragon Misfits

The Dragon Thief

Elemental Warrior Series:

The Endless War

The Cloud Warrior Saga

Elemental Academy

The Elemental Warrior

The Dark Ability Series

The Shadow Accords

The Collector Chronicles

The Dark Ability

The Sighted Assassin

The Elder Stones Saga

The Lost Prophecy Series

The Teralin Sword

The Lost Prophecy

The Volatar Saga Series

The Volatar Saga

The Book of Maladies Series

The Book of Maladies

The Lost Garden Series

The Lost Garden

Made in United States
North Haven, CT
27 May 2022